The Novak Legacy

by

John Douglas-Gray

A Bright Pen Book

British Library Cataloguing Publication Data.
A catalogue record for this book is available from the British Library

ISBN 978-0-7552-1321-4

Authors OnLine Ltd
19 The Cinques
Gamlingay, Sandy
Bedfordshire SG19 3NU
England

This book is also available in ebook format, details of which are available at www.authorsonline.co.uk

Deception is a state of mind and the mind of the state.

James Jesus Angleton.
Director of Counter Intelligence.
CIA 1954-1974

Prologue

August 10th 1987. Spandau Prison. Berlin.

A sonorous metallic clang broke the silence as the bolt on the cell door was drawn open.

'Good morning, Number Seven. How you doing today?' the American guard asked.

'Not well. No, not well.' The guttural German accent had not softened over the years. 'Have you come to kill me?' The old man didn't look round from his armchair as he spoke.

'Here, eat your breakfast,' the American said, setting a tray on the table.

The cell, which had been the old man's home for almost half his ninety-three years, was basic and sparsely furnished. An ammonia stench of stale urine wafted from the aged water closet, its plastic lid gaping open. A roll of toilet paper, several sheets dangling free, flapped limply on a wooden holder beneath the bars of an open prison window.

'It was a terrible.'

'What was terrible?' the younger man asked, with no real interest, as he looked out of the window, following a plane's contrail high in the clear blue sky above the city. He longed for this tour of duty to be over and to return to the fat, hard-fighting trout of his childhood home in Montana.

'I don't remember,' said the German, dabbing at his one good eye with a handkerchief.

The head rail of the iron bed was stained black where he had struggled to pull himself upright over the decades. The bedclothes, crumpled in a heap at the end of the mattress, exposed the incontinence sheet underneath, and a single pillow lay on the floor where it had fallen during the restless sleep of the hot summer's night.

'Eat your breakfast and don't get yourself so worked up.' The crew–cut guard was in his late thirties. His Marine fatigues, immaculately ironed, bore the two inverted chevrons of a corporal. Brushing crumbs from his sleeve, he picked up the soiled linen and opened another window to let in more fresh air. The clackety-clack rumble of a distant train was just audible above the birdsong in the gardens below.

'When will they come to end it?'

'Eat your food, for Chrissakes!' said the American, in exasperation.

Above a cracked hand basin, the door of a bathroom cabinet swung slowly open in the balmy draught, casting reflected light on institutional green walls, partially covered by maps and photographs of the moon.

An easy chair, the arms worn from the constant fretting of his frail hands was by the bed. A dining table in the middle of the room, its veneer ring-stained, had a single wooden bench as company.

'I told the young French boy what I remembered, and they murdered him.'

'He hanged himself with his rifle strap, up on the watchtower,' remonstrated the guard, impatiently.

'No, no. They killed him. Do you have a cigarette?' The old man held out his trembling hand.

'You know the rules, Number Seven.'

In the far corner, on a mahogany reading desk, a copy of 'Die Welt' lay neatly folded beside a pair of thick reading glasses, one of the lenses an opaque white. **Prisoner 7. R. Hess**, was written in heavy red felt pen across the top margin of the newspaper.

'Sometimes I remember. That's why they keep me here, but I don't tell the Russians. Pigs, all of them.'

'Drink your coffee before it gets cold. I'll take you for a bath after you've done eating,' said the American, swinging open the heavy steel door.

He left it slightly ajar, and made his way down the corridor to the laundry room, his boot steps echoing loudly in the central atrium of the prison building.

His chest wheezing, Rudolf Hess, former ReichsMinister of Germany and deputy to Adolf Hitler, sat down at the table, hunched over his tray of mixed sausage meats, cheese and buttered bread rolls. He ate the way the very old often do; a slow laboured chewing, mouth open, a fixed stare at the large map of the moon next to him. Then, with his one good eye, he studied the slices of wurst on the wooden platter, slowly poking at them with his plastic fork, inspecting them carefully, to see if they had tampered with his food.

He took another slow bite at his roll. Resuming his stare at the wall opposite, he raised the coffee to his nose and sniffed at the steaming cup several times before putting it to his lips. Suddenly he stopped chewing, his mouth dropped open and a mash of coffee, wurst, cheese and bread dribbled down his unshaven chin. He swallowed hard and sat upright, rocking backwards and forwards in his chair like a distressed animal. His skeletal face grimaced.

'Jetzt erinnere ich mich. Oh mein Gott! Jetzt erinnere ich mich. Dr. Kammler,' he shouted at the open door, food spraying from his mouth.

'Now I remember. Now I remember. Dr. Kammler. We must find it, before it destroys us all.'

12th August 1987. Whitehall, London.

The meeting suite lights flickered on. With a hiss of air, the heavy soundproofed door swung shut and locked behind the two men, as one of them turned on the red 'engaged' light at the wall. The whole department had recently been redecorated and a hint of fresh emulsion hung in the air.

The narrow room was a strange amalgam of the old and the new. The gilt-framed paintings around the walls, all oil portraits of former Kings, Queens and Ministers of State from the seventeenth to the end of the nineteenth century, were discreetly lit from above by small brass lights fitted to the frames. The carpet was a rich burgundy, matching the upholstery of the chunky beech chairs and the leather inlay of the long meeting table.

Traffic in Whitehall was a faint murmur through the triple-glazed windows of the fourth floor.

They sat opposite each other, both pouring a coffee from the flasks before them. The taller of the two men spoke first, in an educated Boston accent. His suit was expensive and hand made, as were his shoes. His features were sharp. His fingers those of a pianist or artist, long and thin but not lacking power. The top of his head was balding, but elsewhere his hair was a well-groomed white. He was in his late fifties.

'The President says that we're going to have to tell the Soviets soon.' He took a long draught of the coffee.

'The Prime Minister's of the same opinion. Have you read this article in Der Spiegel? Gorbachev intends to lift the veto on Hess's release as soon as possible. Von Weizsäcker has persuaded him to delay until the Soviet guard cycle in November.' The accent was public school with a hint of landed Scot.

He pushed the magazine across the table with his perfectly manicured hands. Younger than the American, he was in his early forties. His long grey hair was combed back from his forehead, and he regularly ran his hand through it to pin it down behind his ears. He was slightly overweight but his tailor was an expert.

'Gorbachev sees continued imprisonment as an obstacle to the reunification of Germany. We need to tell them and we need to do it soon,' the American emphasized.

'Agreed. We can't allow his release. We managed to make the French Guard's death look like suicide, but the Frogs still have their doubts.'

'He was shouting in his cell the day before yesterday that he remembers,' said the American, taking off his glasses to clean them.

'Did he talk to anybody?'

'No, but we have to stop it now.'
'We can send our team in again. Can you fix things your end?' the younger man asked, pouring a glass of water from the jug in front of him.
'We ***have*** to fix it.' The American shifted in his seat.
'Will that be an end to it?' the Englishman asked.
'Unless there were copy documents, yes. Kammler was convinced there were, maybe with the second device. If anything gets out in the press, there'll be panic throughout Europe. When are the original papers released?'
The Englishman smiled wryly. 'In 2017…er…some of them.'
'Well then, it's not a burning problem,' said the American.

17th August 1987. Spandau Prison. Berlin.

Two SAS men waited for the American guards' shift change at midnight, and slipped into the complex by a door in the prison wall that had been left unlocked for them. They made their way through the grounds to a small wooden summerhouse in the garden, still alive with the buzzing of flies and the heavy scent of roses. It was sparsely furnished with a dilapidated rattan table and four chairs on a worn rug.
Dressed in the uniform of American marines, they quickly and silently went about the business of getting readied and a small communications radio set up. One of the men held up a two-metre length of electrical cord attached to a small table lamp and showed it to his companion. The other nodded and gave a thumbs-up. The first man ripped it from the lamp and coiled the flex, hanging it on a nail in the windowsill.
He pressed a button on the radio equipment and seconds later it clicked twice, very quietly, in reply.
'Okay, Pete, Base know we are here. Just a matter of waiting for him to take his walk and for the Yanks to give the okay. I'll secure outside, and then let's get some kip.' Steve, the shorter

of the two, spoke with a Midlands accent.

He went out into the garden and placed a pencil-thin movement sensor by the path leading to the summerhouse. When he returned, both men lay in the dark, only the sweep of the searchlights on the watchtowers occasionally illuminating the room.

'All this shit for one man. A prison to hold six hundred, over thirty-five guards, four officers, cooks, a padre, an MO, and a laundry. Christ knows how much this bloody lot costs, and all for one old Nazi who nobody gives two fucks about anyway,' said Steve.

'How old is he?' asked Pete.

'Ninety-three. Let's hope he does come out for a walk and we don't have to go in and get him,' Steve answered.

'Why do you think they want him taken down?' Pete adjusted his weight on the hard wooden floor.

'Fucked if I know. Fucked if I care. Do you want to do first watch?'

Pete nodded. 'Two hour switch, all right?'

'Fine,' said Steve, wishing they hadn't chosen him for this gig.

They spent the rest of the next day waiting for a signal from HQ in Hereford. At 12.30, the radio clicked twice. Steve pressed the transmit button and back came the coded signal. 'Thank fuck for that.' He rubbed at his face. 'All go.'

Pete yawned and ran his hand over the stubble on his chin. Most of their lives in the SAS had been waiting and observing, very little of the time had been hard action.

He finished his watch at 16.00, and stretched, scratching at the American uniform and narrowing his eyes against the bright sunshine outside.

Steve opened his small pack and took some dark chocolate out of his rations. Breaking it in two, he went over to the window and gave one half to Pete.

The radio clicked into life.

'Here we go.' Pete pushed transmit. He watched as the LED flashed out its message. 'Right, he's on the way down.'

Steve retrieved the movement sensor from beside the pathway. Some ten minutes later, the door to the garden opened and Hess emerged with his guard. The latter remained behind, leaning against the wall, removing his cap and mopping his head with his handkerchief. The elderly German stopped at the base of one of the watchtowers leaning on his walking sticks.

'What's he doing?' Pete took the lamp flex from the nail where it was coiled.

'He's just staring up at the guard in the watchtower, just standing stock still and staring up.'

'Well we can't go and get him. Both the guards will see us.'

'We'll have to, if he looks like going back to his cell.' Steve shifted position, so that he could get a better angle of view to the tower.

Hess stood looking up for a good quarter-of-an-hour before slowly turning and making his way back along the path past his guard and on towards the two waiting SAS men.

'Here he comes. No fucking about Pete, get it done and then we're out of here.'

Steve stood to the left behind the entrance, Pete, with the flex, to the right. They could hear the sound of boots dragging along the gravel and the grunt of exertion as Hess lifted himself up onto the veranda of the summerhouse.

As the first walking stick appeared over the threshold, Steve jumped out and grabbed the old man by the coarse lapel of his prison jacket, pulling him into the room. Pete had the cord around Hess's neck, but even at ninety-three the old man still had strength left in him. He dropped both sticks, his legs flailing and kicking as he tried to gouge at Steve's eyes. Steve was careful not to damage Hess's face in any way.

'Hilfe! Hilfe! Secret…I remember…I…'

His larynx collapsed with a sickening crunch, followed by a

foul stench as his bowels emptied. Pete kept on the pressure for a few seconds more, until he was sure the man was dead. 'Ok Pete, he's down. Let's get out of here.' Steve lay Hess on the ground.

Pete quickly fashioned a noose from the flex and tightened it around the dead man's neck. Steve pressed the transmit on the radio, then two short and two long. Back came a single long flash. Pete dragged Hess to the window and attached the other end of the wire to the latch. He then leant the body forward, so that it took the dead man's weight.

'Gimme the suicide letter, mate.'

Steve pulled out a small sheet of paper, wrapped in cotton, from his wallet. Pete took it, shoving it roughly into the German's trouser pocket. He then removed the strip of material, leaving no fingerprints.

'Job done. Let's fuck off. Have we made contact?' Pete picked up his pack.

'Transport's waiting,' said Steve, stowing the radio.

They swung around the blind side of the summerhouse to the sound of boots running up the gravel path, and made for the prison wall on the other side of the grounds. Frantic shouts and the barking of orders broke the late summer afternoon tranquillity of the garden behind them, as they slipped through the door, and crossed the road to an American military vehicle waiting on the other side.

April 1988, CIA headquarters, Langley, Virginia.

'Take a seat, Sir William. Help yourself to anything you want,' said the American, pointing to the assorted drinks and snacks on a side table in the windowless room.

'No thanks, not for now. I'm trying to lose weight.'

Benjamin Tromans laughed, running his long fingers through the thinning white hair at the side of his head. 'Tell me about it.'

Sir William Rush found the drone from the fluorescent tubes irritating, the unnatural light making the deep-pile carpet a more garish blue than it really was.

'Well, Mr Secretary. I hear we have a problem,' he said, trying to figure out who was the ex-president in the painting opposite.

Tromans nodded. 'Since our last meeting in August and our subsequent meetings with the Soviets, they have, of course, been told about our friend Hess. They were a little pissed at not knowing a lot earlier, but have been reasonably understanding about why not. We also informed the French about our plans to stop him leaving Spandau. Gave them a whole load of bull about secrets involving the British Royal family, as we agreed. I'm sorry about the delay, but they didn't give us the go-ahead until the 17th August. I thought that'd be the end of it. However, the Soviets contacted me last week. They're convinced that copies exist and that someone within your department knows the whereabouts of the second device.'

Both men fell silent. Suddenly the hum of the air conditioning seemed unbearably loud to Rush.

'Playing games do you think?' Sir William shifted in his brown leather seat, trying to conceal the shock in his voice.

'No. No I don't think so. They say they have intelligence that Bormann escaped from Berlin and primed the weapon to activate in the summer of 1945.

'Do they know about the Olof Palme killing in Stockholm?'

'Yes. We needed them to believe us. We told them everything,' said the American.

'I see. You said that you had invited Petrakov. Is he coming?' The Englishman suddenly found his mouth very dry and got up to get a drink of water.

'Yes, he should have been here by now. They are smuggling him through the back door, we don't want to cause too many raised eyebrows.'

The phone rang. 'Tromans…Yes, thank you.' He turned to Sir William. 'He's here. Can I suggest that we put him at the top of the table; they like that kind of thing.' He smiled and went to open the door.

'Come in, Gregor.' They gave each other a bear hug. 'You know Sir William, of course.'

'Yes, hello Sir William, how are you?' Petrakov shook his hand. He was a man in his mid-fifties with rounded face and bull neck. He was not overly fat, but squat, and had the look of a weightlifter, his arms pushed out to the side by his lateral muscles. His face broke into a smile.

'Still on the diet brother Rush?' he asked, his breath laced with vodka.

The Englishman patted his stomach and smiled. 'Under the wife's orders, Gregor.'

'Ha! In Russia we get another wife.' He roared with laughter, patting his own bulging midriff.

'Where do you want me to sit, Benjamin?' Taking off his coat he laid it over the back of one of the chairs.

'I think you should sit at the head of the table, Gregor. You have some important stuff to tell us, I think.' The American pulled the seat out for Petrakov.

'Thank you,' he said, looking pleased.

'Fire away, Gregor.' Tromans leant forward in his seat as did Rush.

'So, we were shocked to hear about the Hess affair. To our scientists, the fact that this thing was primed and didn't go off doesn't mean that it never will. We understand that to have known was neither here nor there, but okay, now we know. There is a problem gentlemen, actually two problems. And they are big, and I mean big. We haven't been entirely honest with you either.'

After three long hours, a plan had been born. Three agents' names had been put forward, one American, one Slovak and one British.

Chapter 1

The Lake District.England. Fifteen years later.

The bedroom was rank with the odour of stale whisky, vomit and sour sweat. Consciousness had arrived like an unwelcome guest.
'Christ.'

The light had been on all night, forgotten in his drunken stagger for the bed. The single uncovered bulb hanging limply from its Victorian rose. On the table beside his bed, stood a picture of a beautiful young blonde, in an art nouveau silver frame. He picked it up and stared at it, as he had done a thousand times before. Christina Karranova was a Slovak and a senior KGB officer. The cause of most of his misery and fall from grace.
Lying beside the picture, the official acceptance of his resignation, worn from constant folding and unfolding. A letter read again and again, yet always carrying the same message.

David John Lennox was educated at St. Dunstan's College and Caius college Cambridge where he was recruited to MI6 in one of their so called 'milk runs'. After several posts abroad, he returned to Hereford as liaison officer to the SAS. Then came Slovakia and dishonour.

His apartment was on the top two floors and the main peel tower of a Norman Castle in the Lake District. The 'penthouse suite', as the estate agents liked to call it.

Most of the other residents avoided him now because of his recent drinking, but he gave them the occasional cheery wave, muttering a 'fuck you' through the smile. Most of them were nervous around him, and he enjoyed it.

The estate management gatherings reminded him of Joint Intelligence Committee meetings: all 'talk talk' and not much action, but at the last encounter the Directors had demanded that he repair and redecorate his apartment.

He heaved himself up and staggered to the toilet, prising loose his dental bridge - a result of none too gentle Bolivian interview techniques - before emptying the contents of his stomach into the stained bowl.

On his way back, a wayward foot caught the telephone cord, dislodging the handset which dropped with a dull plastic clunk onto the bare parquet floor, shedding its innards. A minor cruelty, as it had been disconnected for months.

'Bollocks.'

He took a long gulp from a bottle of Bells which was on the floor beside the unkempt bed, and gradually began to feel the numbness recede. He was scared by this recovery every time it happened, and it had happened a lot over the last few months. His drinking was getting out of control. He had continually put off visiting his doctor, but now he felt so bad, it could wait no longer.

Some hours later he got up, holding his head in his hands to try and stop the throbbing that threatened to split his skull, and went into the kitchen to fill the grimy kettle. The raucous cries from the rookery, twenty metres away, making him feel nauseous again.

He dug amongst the piles of unwashed crockery, cutlery, and plates of half-eaten meals, searching for a reasonably clean cup.

Through the open door to the hallway, he saw the newspaper had been delivered, and sitting on it were a couple of bills and two letters. He returned to the kitchen supporting himself on the door jamb as he went in. Black coffee, two sugars.

He opened the mail, trying to control the shake in his hands which had started some weeks ago.

One of the letters was from Cornwall. He didn't recognise the writing, but turning the envelope over he saw that it was from Victoria Mason, the daughter of a good friend of his, Griff Mason. He opened it, releasing a subtle hint of perfume.

“Dear David,
Long time no hear and no see. Dad is not doing so well chest-wise at the moment, so I would love you to come down and visit us soon. Please don’t tell him that I have written to you, he gets angry when I go on about his smoking and his health. It would be great to see you. I tried to ring, but I think there is something wrong with your phone. I am quite a good cook now, so you won’t starve to death. Please, please David, say YES, and come down.
Look forward to hearing from you.
All my love, Victoria. xxx.”

It was the second letter that jolted him fully awake. Postmarked 28th October, Berwang , Austria, it contained a single sheet of blue conqueror, and said simply in large bold type.
“OS OL6 Grid reference. 323038 494457. December 12th, 12.00 local time.
Be there, alone. Phone no-one. Any irregularity will mean immediate end to contact.”

Today was the 2nd November, so just over six weeks.

Could it be the press? It could be a set up. There were so many official inquests and inquiries going on. Had somebody dropped him in it?

He knew the map reference without looking, it was the Trig point at the top of Caw, six miles to the north of his home.

Middle of nowhere and you could see for miles. No chance of directional listening devices. Clever.

****

The letter from Berwang had spurred him on to make an appointment with the village surgery, to see his doctor.
John Gillan, had the ruddy complexion of a drinker, but only saw excessive alcohol intake as a problem that his patients had.

‘Wish I could retire at forty-five,’ he said, removing the sphygmomanometer cuff from David’s arm.

'They retired me actually.'
'Your blood pressure, David. It's not good.'
'Wonderful.'
'You are putting on a lot of weight, and your liver function tests are bad. How much are you drinking?
'Too much.'
'Do you want to talk about it?'
'Not really.'
'Well, you know where to find me. I'll give you some blood pressure pills for now, and talk to you again in a few months. '
'Fine.'
'Leave the new receptionist alone on the way out.'
'What's her name?'
'You just leave Rebecca alone.'

****

David didn't see Gillan again for many weeks, but the liver function results had scared him. So he religiously took the tablets, which he collected monthly, direct from the surgery, and gradually began addressing his health.

Exercising regularly, his weight began to come down. He had lost almost a stone and had about another to lose to reach his target of thirteen. He went out walking; short, two-hour walks at first, and then longer, up to seven or eight hours. The drinking had been harder to control, but limited visits to the pub and fewer calls to his vintner's had cut it down a lot.

He had had the telephone and broadband reconnected and finally he had moved into a hotel for two weeks and had the apartment cleaned, renovated and redecorated. He was almost back in the land of the living.

The next time he saw the Doctor was at the apartment. Gillan came in, his faced flushed from the cold northerly that had been blowing all day.

He explained that there had been a break-in at the practice

surgery the night before.

'The police said it was very likely to have been kids looking for drugs, but we don't keep any listed drugs on the premises. David.'

After the police had left Gillan had asked Rebecca, the receptionist, to unlock the filing cabinets containing patients' records.

'Then I noticed a piece of paper and some packets on the floor. I picked them up and saw they were your repeat prescription, so I looked for the file to replace them. Your records were all mixed up, as though they'd been dropped and hurriedly been put back. It'd been tampered with, David, and as you've been very cagey about your former civil service employment, I thought...'

'Have you mentioned this to the police?' David asked.

'No, I wanted to ask you first. Why would anybody want to look in your file?'

'I really don't know, John.'

'Well, I felt I should tell you.'

'Absolutely,' said David.

'So, how are you feeling?'

'Much better, thanks.'

'Good to hear. Well, must be off .' He got to his feet digging into his coat pocket.

'Thought I'd save you the walk. Here are your pills for next month.'

After Gillan had left, David stood at an arched window in the peel tower, looking at the rugged peak of Caw in the distance and thinking about the letter from Berwang and the break-in at the surgery .

He ran a bath, adding some aged lavender salts that he had been meaning to use for the past three years, and lay in the aromatic warmth like a big old bull hippo. His mind was racing. He desperately wanted to phone a few former contacts to see if he could get any small buzz, any nuance of tone in their voices that would reveal that they knew something. 'Phone no one,' it had said.

He had changed in the last few weeks. He had a challenge and a mystery to solve, and he wanted it. They must have known that he would rise to the bait and not just throw the letter into the fire.

Was he so bloody predictable?

After shaving for the first time in some days, he made a decision, got his coat on, and went down the long drive to the village to get a haircut.

Twenty minutes later he was running his hands over his now stubbly head as he headed across the square and back up the drive to his apartment.

The entry phone rang just after he had arrived. It was a DHL delivery of a small parcel. The docket said 'London', and the contents listed as 'mobile telephone'. He took it into the apartment, dropped it onto the kitchen table and brewed a pot of tea.

David had always been very careful with parcels, ever since his time in Beirut when Tim Adams had lost both hands and an eye, and had been 'lucky to live' they had all said. David had met him three years ago, and he hadn't seemed very lucky at all.

He looked in a drawer for a piece of kit that he should have given back when he resigned. It was black and the size of a packet of cigarettes. Finding some batteries, he turned it on and passed it slowly over the package. The LED display flickered. It registered a small current, which meant a charged battery. He felt very carefully around the edges of the plastic, the content was loose and it had travelled from London, so if it were a bomb it couldn't be a mercury movement. He could feel no wiring around the sides, so he found a Stanley knife and held an old wooden ruler hard on the edge of the package, carefully cutting all the way down. He then very slowly inserted the tip of the blade and lifted one surface so that he could see inside.

It was, as stated, a mobile telephone, swathed in protective bubble wrap. He slowly removed it, slid the battery from the

back and inspected the interior as best he could.
It was a satellite phone. The weight felt right, but so do the ones Mossad manufacture to blow your head off. Casting caution, and hopefully not his fingers, to the wind, he turned it on. It asked for the pin code. It wouldn't be complicated.

He entered 0000. 'Code accepted'. Beep Beep, Beep Beep. A message had been received.

"Contact will be made on this phone on the 12th December. Do not attempt to trace sender number or all communication will be terminated."

He scrolled through. It was sent the previous night at 23.30.

Chapter 2

Just before midnight on the night of the eleventh of December, he started getting his stuff together and then dialled for an alarm call. He was too keyed up for sleep and dozed fitfully, thinking that it was strange, but he didn't want a drink.

Leaving the castle at 02.30, he set off across the grounds and up through the woods at the top of the hill. The cloud cover was light and the moon cast a dull yellow glow on the fields and trees. He was beginning to pant and sweat a bit, so he took the opportunity to rest and look south, back down the kilometre of open land behind him. A dull electronic whine was barely audible as he switched on the night vision goggles. Another piece of kit he should have returned when he left the service. Nothing moved.

As he turned, he thought he glimpsed something enter the trees a hundred metres in front of him. He swept the area with the goggles but couldn't see anything out of the ordinary. The woods were full of deer and he had probably disturbed one as it made its way down to the river to drink.

He exited the woods and then cut down to a disused railway line which he followed north up an uphill track which narrowed and led him across the main Coniston road. After a mile of open fields, he reached another road which could eventually take him to where he was going at the foot of Caw. At Jackson Ground he looked at his watch. 04.00, he had made good time. Another three-quarters-of-an-hour or so, and he would be there.

He pushed on over Long Mire Beck, releasing the sour tang of rotting vegetation from the bog at every squelching step, and climbed up the side of Broadslack Crag. Exhausted from trying to keep his footing in the dark, he arrived at the top, blowing and puffing. From here, he could cover all the possible routes to the top of Caw, except from the north and some of the north-west. Finding a sheltered spot among a circle of rocks which he would make his home for the next seven hours or so, he started collecting dead bracken for bedding.

As he was finishing, something disturbed the rocks someway behind him. He switched on the goggles again and slowly panned three hundred and sixty degrees. Nothing.
Sheep, he reasoned, as he carried on with his preparations.

Soon he had his sleeping bag down and covered with a matt-green foil blanket. With his head inside he was almost invisible to infra-red detection as it would mask any ambient heat. He had switched the phone he had been sent to vibration only, and as the day broke, he had a good sweep of the surrounding country with binoculars. He concentrated on the view to the south-west of Caw because at the bottom of nearby Stickle Pike there was a place to park popular with walkers on the Broughton Mills road to Seathwaite.

Soon after 08.30 the rain started, light at first and then torrential. Thick cloud came in thirty minutes later, shrouding the area in an impenetrable mist. Cold and miserable, he wished that he was at home in the warmth of his bed.

The wind picked up from the west and gradually the cloud cover lifted. He scanned the ground to the south and worked clockwise through the surroundings. It was then he thought he saw something in his peripheral vision glint twice, very briefly, among the rocks on the side of White Pike, above and beyond Caw to his north-east. He tracked back, but nothing moved.

He was cheering up, now that the rain had eased, so he pulled the blanket over his head to mask the heat and poured a cup of tea from his flask, the sweet smell of sugar filling his nostrils. After a small block of chocolate and an energy bar he drew back the foil and had a look around.

There it was again. Something was catching the light up on the fell below White Pike. He looked through the binoculars, safe in the knowledge that the lens coating would not give his position away. Nothing moved.

It was 11.30 when the telephone started to vibrate.

'Yes,' said David

'Good morning, Mr Lennox,' said a deep voiced man with a heavy German accent. 'You must be very cold and bored by now, as is my colleague who followed you here early this morning. Please raise your left hand above your head, Mr Lennox.'

Damn. That wouldn't have happened ten years ago. The rocks falling as he arrived. How could he have been so stupid?

He obediently took his arm out of the sleeping bag and held it in the air.

'Now look at the back of your hand, please.'

David looked up and saw the sniper's red laser dot smack in the middle, just below the knuckles. 'At least we know that you're alone. Do as I say and you will not be harmed. I'll be coming into your field of view from the west in two minutes, and will continue to the top of Caw where we can talk.'

He saw the lone figure coming along Park Head Road; a footpath four hundred metres away to the west. The man was walking at some pace, cutting up north east towards the summit. David shouldered his day bag and set off to the north and his meeting.

He arrived on the peak four minutes after the German. The chill factor was high; the wind had picked up even more from the south-west, bringing with it the smack of the Irish Sea.

'My name's Fischer. Good morning, Mr Lennox.' The man took off his right glove and held out his hand. His grip was firm and dry, his eyes piercing and azure blue, like alpine lakes in his sun-bed tanned face. He was, David guessed, in his late forties and looked as though he worked out in the gym on a regular basis.

'Thank you for accepting our invitation. So sorry about the need for my colleague with the sniper rifle, but you know how it is.'

'No, actually I don't.'

'Can I suggest we move to the north, and get out of this wind?'

They found a sheltered spot and sat on a piece of relatively dry rock just below the summit. 'I won't waste any time, it's freezing and both of us would like to be somewhere warm.

There's a good reason to meet here, because there's some danger. At the moment to me, but after this meeting to you too.'
'Great,' said David.
'The risk will be worth it, Mr Lennox.'
'I'd rather make that decision myself,' said David, starting to cool to the man.

Fischer explained that he had been an officer in the Stasi, stationed in Meiningen in the former East Germany. He was now, he grinned, self employed.
'Why did you break in to the surgery and tamper with my medical files?'
Fischer looked puzzled and, David thought, a little frightened.
'When was this?'
'You mean it wasn't you?'
Fischer looked worried. 'Only your files?' he asked.
'As far as I know, yes,' said David.
The German was looking agitated now. 'All right, Mr Lennox, you know a little about me, and I know a lot about you. Our former link to the Intelligence Services is just one of life's strange coincidences. Your father was John Clifton Lennox, Lance-corporal Royal West Kent Regiment, captured at Dunkirk in 1940 and a prisoner at Stalag XXB in Marienburg in East Prussia. Now Malbork, Poland…'
'For God's sake. We've established who I am.' David said.
'It's because of your father that I'm here to speak to you today.'
'My father?' asked David, incredulously.
'He died in 1995 I believe.'
'Yes…and?'
'In the late winter of 1944, he got something from a German guard at the camp who wanted to avoid being taken prisoner by the Soviets. In exchange your father smuggled him a British Army uniform. When the prisoners moved out, the guard

slipped away unnoticed. They never met again, because the Wall went up. The guard was in the East and your father in the West.'

'My father was on the death march south, in the winter of 1945. He survived, thousands didn't. What happened to the guard?' David asked.

'He was badly injured by a piece of shrapnel to the brain during the last days of the war, and lived, severely handicapped, with relatives in Berkach, East Germany, until his death in 1988. A letter was found among his papers. It mentioned your father's prisoner number at Marienburg, 4283, and that he had something vitally important. I'm willing to pay you one million US Dollars for it.'

'***How much***? This sounds like bullshit to me.'

'I assure you that what I've told you is true,' said the German.

'What the hell is ***it***, that it's so important?'

'I can't be sure.'

'Yet you want to offer me one million US dollars? My father never spoke about this. Well not to me anyway.'

'Do you have any POW papers or letters from your father to his family or to your mother?'

'She died last year and many of her possessions are in a bank vault waiting for sorting out. I haven't had the time,' David said.

'You mean, for a few months you haven't been sober enough.'

David was about to tell the German to 'fuck off', when he saw the red laser dot in the middle of Fischer's forehead. A split second later, there was a sound that he knew well, like a coconut shell being broken open with a machete. A high-velocity round hitting flesh and bone. The German's skull exploded covering David's clothes and face in a fine red mist of Fischer's last thoughts.

Chapter 3

What was left of Fischer's head dropped forward into David's lap.

He fell back, waiting for the next round, but it didn't come. He pushed the body to one side and lay on the ground, gagging at the metallic smell of blood and brain tissue.

'Keep cool, keep cool,' he admonished himself.

The shot had come came from the north east. He scrambled for the binoculars and trained them on the fell below White Pike where he had seen something glinting earlier. There, running east down to the valley below the pine plantation at Natty Bridge was a camouflaged figure with a rifle. David kept the sniper in sight, and spotted a Land Rover driving out of the trees and down the forestry road to pick up the runner.

'What the hell's going on?' he gasped.

He raced round to the south side of the summit and saw a second person in a green hiking jacket, with a rifle, four hundred metres away, scurrying down from Broadslack Crag.

He raised the glasses.

The second figure crouched and aimed at the Land Rover, six hundred metres to his east. David saw the recoil, but heard no sound.

Both fitted with silencers. These people were not amateurs.

The Land Rover disappeared back among the trees, making for the main road to Coniston at the end of the forestry tracks. The other figure looked back at David for a moment and then bagging his rifle, ran over the ridge down towards the beck, and was lost to view.

He'd been set up. What an arrogant idiot he was. Now think. THINK.

He rolled Fischer's body over. There was a sickening slopping sound as the remains of the man's brains fell out of what had been the back of his cranium. David expertly and thoroughly searched the pockets and clothing for any contents. A small packet of tissues and the mobile telephone he had used some short time ago. That was it.

'Shit!'

Fischer's phone vibrated. David ignored it. Then the phone in his pocket received a message. 'I PRESUME MY COLLEAGUE IS DEAD. YOU HAVE MADE A BIG MISTAKE.'

He scrolled to "use number" his hands numb with cold. His fingers were beginning to lose sensation in the tips as he attempted to punch in "call" with great difficulty. The number rang several times before a breathless German voice answered.

'Ja?'

'Just listen,' said David, thinking fast, 'your friend's dead, most of his head blown off. I didn't have anything to do with what just happened. Why in Christ's name would I kill a man who'd just offered me a million dollars? You…'

The phone cut off, either deliberately, or the signal had gone as the other German had reached the valley, and presumably his waiting car. David took a decision. Firstly, he had to buy time and then he had to get home and destroy the clothing he was in, boots and all.

Had the Land Rover occupants phoned the police? Most certainly, if it was a set-up.

He got hold of Fischer's feet and dragged him down into the dead bracken, three hundred metres below the summit. It was off all the walkers' paths, and the body could lie there for a couple of months, if the smell didn't get too bad. Hopefully, foxes and badgers would help by stripping the flesh. He took Fischer's phone and pocketed it, doing a very quick check of labels on the jacket. Nothing German. They would take a hell of a long time to identify his body, if nobody had tipped off the police.

Making sure no-one else was about on the fells, he went back to the summit where he found two largish skull fragments, the thick matted hair still attached, and threw them as far as he could. He then tramped all other brain material and blood into the ground, hoping that the rain would wash it away.

'So much blood. Please God, let it rain for a week.'

As if in answer, the heavens opened and rain began to fall, sporadic at first, then heavily. For the first time in the Lakes, he was ecstatic about the bad weather. He made off at a jog down the mountain to the south, returning along the route he had taken earlier in the day.

When he got back to Long Mire Beck, he washed himself in the icy water. He scrubbed his boots with his hands, wiping his jacket and trousers clean as best he could. He was now seriously cold and started to tab along the track to Jackson Ground to get his body heat up. The worsening weather had meant that, happily, he didn't meet anybody on the trek home.

Safely into the gardening shed in the grounds of the castle, he removed the contents of his pockets from his jacket, took off his boots and socks and stuffed all his outer wear into a bin liner. He couldn't see anything on his clothing, but he knew in a forensics investigation he would be in deep trouble.

Barefoot, he went along a small side path and lifted the hatch to the old underground water tank used as a standby supply for fire engines. Knotting the bin liner shut, he tied it to an iron lug just above the water line.

The tremor in his arm was bad as he climbed the stairs to his apartment, praying that none of his neighbours would see him.

Inside, he poured himself a couple of fingers of whisky and tried to think, all the time expecting the door phone to ring, but it never did.

The hot water of a bath was bliss after the biting chill of the fells, and he lay with his head resting on the end of the tub trying to figure out what the hell was going on.

Chapter 4

He had lied to Fischer about the bank vault. All his father's papers were in an escritoire in the apartment. He had never looked through them in detail, but there were several letters from the POW camp at Marienburg and several pictures.

Gathering them up, he took them over to his work table on the other side of the room. Three hours later he hadn't found anything significant. There were four photographs of prisoner groups in the camp; his father was in three of them. Of twenty letters, only five were relevant to the period Fischer had referred to. He ran his hand over the stubble of his newly cut hair, trying to think.

Among a few bits and pieces his father had had in the camp and had brought home with him, were two pipes - his favourite old one, which reminded David of the smell of his father's clothes, and another, a small meerschaum with floral carvings that he remembered seeing as a child, but did not recall his father ever smoking. The bowl was clean and didn't look used. The maker's name was engraved in very fine carving on the base, 'Burgmühle 1944'. Above that, was what looked like the Star of David.

Was the carver Jewish? It certainly looked like that. So, where did his father get it from? Was it a gift, or did he find it in the camp, or on the death march.

David carefully unscrewed the stem and looked down the pipe tube to the bowl. Nothing. He went back to look at the letters again and again. Nothing. The photographs…nothing, except the one his father wasn't in had the names of a few fellow inmates who had been circled. Sgt. 'Batty' Newal, Pte.L.Dumas, N.Breem and RSM.Ted Hill who had a scrawny looking cat sitting on his lap. A circle above it labelled, helpfully, 'Cat'. As far as he could remember, his father had not talked about any individuals in the camp of any nationality, let alone the guards.

His head started nodding with the uncontrollable urge to close his eyes, so he put everything back in the escritoire and went to bed. Sleep was fitful, full of vivid dreams of pipes, photographs and letters. A dead German with half his head missing was pointing to them and mouthing something David couldn't hear because of the noise of breaking glass.

He awoke with a start, and saw, down the hallway, the dim light from a hand held torch coming from under the kitchen door. Feeling under the bed for the hardwood truncheon that had belonged to his long dead grandfather, he eased himself to his feet.

In his early training, David had learnt that attack really was the best form of defence. It threw the aggressor. He rushed into the kitchen, the pungent smell of nervous male sweat from the intruder filling the room. Truncheon above his head, he brought it down with all his might on the dark figure in front of him, but as he swung, the person ducked to the left and David heard the crack of what was probably the man's collarbone breaking.

Something heavy fell to the kitchen floor, and at that moment David was punched in the crutch with sickening force. He felt the nausea at once. As he reeled back, he saw a silhouette going through the open window and falling with a clattering of broken tiles on to the first floor parapet roof under the kitchen. The intruder made one more jump then rolled on the grass below, before disappearing into the trees at the side of the lawns.

His throat burned as he vomited yellow bile into the sink. The throbbing pain in his testicles was agonizing.

Turning on the light, he found the object that had dropped to the floor. It was a double action 9mm Gurza pistol capable of penetrating at least thirty layers of Kevlar and 2.8mm of titanium plate at a hundred metres. A favoured weapon of the old KGB.

David released the magazine. It was full.

The nausea and the cramp in his stomach were lessening as he pushed the sash window shut. The area above the latch had been very professionally cut, so the 'broken glass' he had heard must have been a slate slipping on to the flat roof below.

These people wanted something very, very badly, and they thought that he had it. Or did they know that he had it?

He spent the rest of the night sitting up in an armchair, the Gurza placed very gingerly in his aching lap. In the morning he would accept the invitation from Vicky Mason and travel down to Cornwall.

Waking at around six o'clock, and after an agonizing pee, he went back to his father's letters. After an hour, he still had nothing - just a young POW's correspondence to his mother, father and fiancée. He would have been twenty-three when captured and twenty-eight when liberated.

'Nothing. Damn!'

He took the photographs again, looking carefully at the one with the names. He turned it over and scribbled on the back was 'A Tale of Two Cities' in his father's handwriting, and the figure 1850 in the same hand as the circled figures in the photograph.

Was it one of his father's books? Was that it? Was there something in the text or something physically hidden in the binding?

Most of his parents' books were in the living room and it took four or five minutes before he found it on the fourth shelf. The tremor in his hand was there again, it always was when he was tired, but it seemed to be getting worse. Opening the hardback, he shook the pages. Nothing. However, between the spine and the book was a thin roll of paper.

'Yes!'

It looked as though it had never been moved since being inserted. Easing it out with a pencil, he carefully unrolled it.

Dated 6th May 1990, it was a letter addressed to David in his accountant father's minuscule handwriting.

'Dear son,

I never asked you about your work in the civil service and you never asked about mine. I was only a controller of cash, but, as you may probably have known, cash for various projects which were highly secret at the time and some still are at the time of writing. Most of the secret underground telephone exchanges that I costed, will, by now, all be obsolete, but the locations are probably still in use, with new technology.

Recently I have had some very odd enquiries from several sources, as have some of my old wartime colleagues. These are the reasons for my rather cloak and dagger approach to what I am about to tell you and the concealment of this letter. The fact that you have found it, means that you have seen the photograph and must have looked at it for a specific reason. Presumably, as I will be dead, someone has approached you in the same way that I and my colleagues have been. The story is this:

In late 1944 I was working on a farm near Stalag XXB with several fellow prisoners. Early one freezing Baltic morning, an SS officer drove up with a passenger who was wearing what looked like striped pyjamas, (an outfit that we had never seen before), and stopped at the farm to pick up eggs. Food at this time in the war was scarce, even for the German troops and guards. The German officer went into the farmhouse and, because the farmer had two very pretty young daughters, stayed there for some time. The passenger, who was obviously a prisoner too, got out of the car to urinate and to plead for food. I asked him what the uniform was and gave him some cigarettes, chocolate and a tin of corned beef.

He told us that he was a Slovak Jew who had been a mining engineer before the war, that he was wearing the uniform of a Jewish prisoner and had been in the Concentration camps of Buchenwald, Nordhausen, Bergen Belsen and Sachsenhausen. He was scheduled to go to Stutthof near Danzig the next morning after having spent two weeks in solitary at XXB. At that time, I had no idea of the enormity of the horror he had lived through.

He said that he had survived only because he had skills the Nazis needed. Now the War was in its final months, and his work was finished, they had no use for him and he would certainly die in Stutthof for what he had done for them, and what he knew. The officer Von den Bergen was to drive him there that day. He gave me his name as Joseph Novak, and said he wanted to give me something, something that would make his life and his final days worthwhile. He had wanted to give it to other prisoners at XXB but hadn't had the opportunity.

He asked me where I came from, and I told him London. He asked me where specifically, and I said Eltham in south London. Would you believe that he had married a Blackheath girl and had lived in Plumstead in the early thirties! He had worked in Woolwich Arsenal as an explosives expert, the expertise stemming from his mining work.

He gave me a meerschaum pipe that he had made, and took from the lining of his jacket a photograph that he had been given by an Englishman who had been sent to Buchenwald for continuous escape attempts and had died at the hands of the SS Officer who was in the farmhouse.

As he was about to tell me more about the pipe and photograph, the German officer came out of the farm and shouted at us. 'Get away from the Jew!' Novak was bundled into the back of the staff car then the officer returned to us.

'What did you talk about?' Nobody said a thing. 'I want all your names.'

The names were duly given and the staff car with the officer and Novak drove off in the direction of Danzig. I never saw him again.

Very recently, I have had contact with several of the surviving POWs who were in Stalag XXB with me. They had all been approached about photographs or letters, or anything that they may have been given in the camp. These approaches were made by people purporting to be collectors and dealers in Nazi memorabilia. Some of the POWs sold things that they still had, and were paid large sums of money. But, here is the strange thing. Only those who had been present at the farm, on the day that Novak came, were approached. Twelve people in all.

I did some research through the Jewish organisations after

the War, and found out that a Joseph Ibrahim Novak died in Stutthof in March 1945. A Slovak from Poprad, he was beaten to death by a guard called Voss who was cited for War crimes, but disappeared in the chaos that was Europe in 1945. That is all I know.

The house was broken into late last year and I am convinced that it was something to do with the stuff that Novak gave me. Good luck son, do with this as you see fit.

All my love,

Dad.

PS. Your mother and I are very proud of you.'

Why had he not talked about the War with his father? The story from Fischer about the guard was rubbish.

Was that guard, Voss? Had he beaten Novak to death in an attempt to get information from him? Was he ordered to do so by Von den Bergen? Was Voss given the names and numbers of the POWs present on the farm that morning by Von den Bergen? Is that what Fischer knew? He knew there was something, but he didn't know who had got it. That must be it, otherwise why would they have bothered to trace all the others? That is why it had taken them so long to narrow down the list of those present on the farm that day. It had to be worth an awful lot for all the work they had put in. It must have cost a fortune in time and expenses. Who was paying them? Who shot Fischer? His head was spinning.

He repaired the broken window and, finding his fishing gaff, went out into the grounds and gathered a pile of wood and branches that had been stacked ready for burning. It was a bit wet, but it would do. Having made quite a pile in a sheltered spot behind the trees, he doused it in petrol and set it alight, feeling the hot blast, a little too near for comfort, as the fuel ignited.

He opened the inspection hatch and gaffed out the bin liner containing his clothes, putting it on the now blazing fire. He placed more branches and logs on top, and stood for a while, mesmerised by the flames and heat and the sweet fragrance of burning pine cones. It was then he realised how tired he was.

Back in his apartment he packed a sports bag with clothes to last a few days and included the two mobile phones he had got from Fischer and the 'Gurza'. He put the pipe in his pocket and put the photograph and the letter from his father in an A4 envelope.

He hid his father's letter, the photograph and the Gurza, in the false bottom of a fire extinguisher which he kept in the boot of his Land Rover Discovery. He had brought this piece of kit back from Germany. No one knew about it except the man that had made it, and he was dead. He would phone the Masons from a motorway service station, in case his phone was being tapped.

As he drove down the drive he checked the bonfire. The clothes were almost completely destroyed and the boots were well on the way. He dragged several more hefty boughs out of a pile nearby and loaded them all on to the burning heap. Resisting the temptation to stand in the warmth of the blaze he went back to the car, not looking forward to the long drive ahead.

On the hill to the north of him, a camouflaged figure lowered high resolution binoculars and spoke quietly into a mobile telephone.

Chapter 5

Griff Mason was an old friend who had taken early retirement, some years ago, from teaching art at a Technical college. He knew his doctor very well, and had managed to swing it on the grounds of nervous exhaustion. He had lived in St Ives when David had first met him, and was a talented artist who had studied at the Slade in the early sixties. His work was sought after and too expensive for David nowadays, although he was pleased that he had three in the apartment; two had been gifts, and one had been bought, but many years ago when Griff was relatively unknown.

He lived in a big old house down by the sea, on the outskirts of Marazion, with the daughter from his second marriage. His wife had died three years ago, and he now spent his time immersed in his painting.

David stopped at the first services station on the motorway to use the phone. He had kept a close watch on following traffic, and hadn't turned on his SatNav system.

Griff's raucous coughing made conversation difficult, but he was delighted that his old friend was coming down to visit for a few days.

He bought a Times and, whilst standing in the queue, had a long look outside. It wasn't too busy, and he couldn't see anybody watching him, so he made his way back to the car, drove to the petrol area, and filled the tank.

After paying, he saw a black BMW slowly pull away from the main car park. It was moving too stealthily for David's sensitive antennae, like a big cat stalking through savannah grass.

He pulled out slowly onto the slipway to the motorway, until he saw in his rear mirror that he was in a blind spot for the BMW, and slammed on the brakes. As the car came into view, there was a flicker of hesitation before it drove on past him. He didn't get a good clear look, but a man was driving and a woman in the passenger seat had long blonde hair covering her face. That moment of uncertainty had been enough for David's rusty but trained eye.

He waited until the car was out of sight, and slowly pulled into the flow of traffic. They would be waiting at the next exit. Well, he would surprise them.

'Still crazy, after all these years,' he sang, to himself.

Fifteen miles later, he took the exit slip road, and there, on the other side of the roundabout, was the BMW. He drove around and pulled up twenty metres in front of it, immediately reversing, flooring the accelerator and hitting the other car at twenty miles-an-hour. He heard and saw the hood buckle and the airbags explode. He then slammed the Discovery into gear, and drove back down onto the motorway. In his mirror he could see two distant figures on the bridge, looking down at the mangled front end of their car.

He pulled in to the next services at Lancaster, going round the back of the Land Rover to check for damage. The towing hook was bent, but there were no other problems. Opening the big swing back door, he got the sports bag and the little gem of equipment that he had used on the mobile telephone package from Fischer. He walked nonchalantly round the car stretching his legs.

At the rear offside wheel, the display cranked up a little. He leant against the boot, curving his fingers under and along the arch.

Prying loose the magnetized tracker, he took a slow stroll through the parked vehicles in his row. After a few minutes, he found a Vauxhall Corsa with a Manchester United sticker in the window.

'Enjoy Manchester,' he grinned, sticking the tracker under the chassis, near the exhaust.

The rest of his trip was uneventful, he had been extra careful in checking following traffic, pulling in twice more to service stations to see if anybody obvious was tailing him.

As he drove into Marazion, the tide was in, and the sea, dark and foreboding, was crashing against the foot of St Michael's Mount, whipped up by a wind, which although cold, was many degrees warmer than that at the top of Caw.

He manoeuvred through the narrow streets of the town, trying to keep his eyes off the view and on the traffic, before turning off down the cliff road to Griff's home.

The imposing stone house followed the angle of the slope, having two storeys above ground at the front and three at the rear. Griff had converted the basement into a self-contained flat, which led onto a football-pitch-sized garden stretching down to the pebbled beach. The palm trees and ferns bent and waved vigorously in the strengthening southerly; only the ivy, covering the leeward front wall, remained unmoved. The tang of seaweed and saltwater seasoned the ozone released by the surf.

He parked, and was going round to the boot when a voice hailed him.

'Hello stranger.' He turned, and there was the most stunning girl he had seen in a long, long time. She had been a leggy teenager and still had the same lithe adolescent figure. Her long auburn hair blew across her face in the sea breeze, and she brushed it away between her index and ring finger, which David found strangely exciting.

A sexually precocious youngster, with a string of admirers in constant tow, her obvious flirtations with David had been a source of mild discomfort at the time. Now, at twenty-seven, her face had become sharper in some way, and her eyes were a deeper green than he remembered.

'Victoria?' he said, unsurely.

'Were you expecting someone else?'

'I was expecting a fifteen-year-old I knew a long time ago.'

'Disappointed?' she asked.

'Only that I'm not a few years younger.'

'Oh, I like older men, I think they're more interesting.' She came over and kissed him on the cheek, as she did so her hair blew across his face. The smell and the warmth of her made him aware of things that been long dormant. Maybe it was just the lack of alcohol in his system. 'Thanks for coming. How are you, it's been too long,' she said, linking arms and leading him into the covered and glazed porch.

'Oh, not great, but it's getting better. By the minute,' he smiled.

She laughed a deep, throaty laugh that made David think that the next few days would be more difficult for him than he had imagined.

Griff came to the inner door, a tall, thin, almost gaunt, grey-haired man in his mid-sixties, a roll-up between his nicotine stained fingers. David was shocked by how frail and bony his friend had become and how he had aged since the death of Victoria's mother.

'Griff. How the hell are you my friend?' The two men bear-hugged each other, releasing the odour of stale cigarette smoke from Griff's clothing.

'Fine. Come in and have a shot of something.'

Griff took David through into the lounge with its wall to wall bay window and stunning view over the beach and the Mount beyond. The floorboards were stripped pine, covered with designer rugs. Everything here was the kind of thing you saw in up-market interiors magazines. Where David's apartment was elegant old school country pile, this was elegant chic and joss-stick.

David declined a whiskey, and they sat catching up on old times and new gossip. David couldn't keep his eyes off Victoria, and hoped to God that it wasn't too obvious to Griff. He also noticed that she was holding eye contact, and it was more than just the returned gaze of an old friend. Her legs went on forever, and her breasts, even under the jersey top, were full, and since the last long-held gaze with him, her nipples were visible.

Not to your friend, thought David, not to your friend.

He suggested booking a table for dinner, and Victoria recommended a new trendy restaurant down in Penzance.

'Okay, let's fix a taxi so that we can all drink,' said David.

When the cab arrived she was in the hall, wearing a low cut, short black dress, and looking spectacular.
'Wow!' choked David.
'Do you approve?' She gave a twirl.
'That's a really silly question,' he retorted.
She laughed that throaty laugh again as Griff opened the door to the car. 'I'm paying. No arguments please,' he said, getting into the front passenger seat. David slid in beside Vicky on the back seat, soon aware that she was pressing her hip against his. They drove back through Marazion, and as they turned onto the main road to Penzance they passed a long-haired blonde girl walking along the pavement.
'Hey, it's Joanna my friend,' said Vicky and turned to wave through the back window of the taxi.
As she did so, she put her hand on the inside of David's thigh as if to steady herself.
He felt a surge of excitement wash over him, and as she turned back she gave him a look that said ***yes***. It definitely said, one hundred per cent ***yes***.

During the meal she talked about her work as a freelance investigative journalist in London and her time up at Oxford, which seemed to revolve more around men than study for her 2:1 in politics. She had a flat in Blackheath, the last boyfriend having been booted out three months ago, and was now living the life of a Carmelite nun. This last statement was delivered with a very large wink to David. She was intending to stay with Griff for three days, and then back to the grind in London.
Griff related that he was resisting Vicky's attempts to team him up with a woman who was visiting him more often than he felt comfortable with. His painting was going well, and he was desperately trying to give up smoking as he had a wracking, chesty cough, that rattled his body every time he had an attack.
Both Griff and Vicky had pressed David on his news, but he was rather evasive and said that he wanted to talk to them when they were alone.

As they left, Vicky put her arm in David's and gave it a squeeze.

'Thank you, for a lovely meal. It's so nice to have you here. Dad's going out tomorrow morning, so we can have a long chat then.' She held his gaze again.

Griff poured three Armagnacs whilst David started to give them some outline of his last ten years, and a hint of the events of the last few days, with the proviso to Vicky that this was strictly not for publication and was a talk among close friends. He also left out Fischer's death on Caw.

'Christ,' Griff said, shocked.

'That's incredible,' gasped an excited Victoria.

'So you think that there's something in this photograph that's worth a lot of money to these people.' Griff was looking tired.

'I guess so,' said David.

'Well David,' yawned Griff, ' I have to go out early tomorrow morning, so I'm off to bed.'

'Me too.' Vicky stretched in a way calculated to raise David's testosterone levels. She hugged her father, blew a kiss to David, and left.

In bed, David took the photograph out and studied it. Still not a clue. Turning off the light, he soon fell into a deep, sea-air sleep.

He woke the next morning with a hand softly stroking his face. 'Come on Lennox, I have a cup of tea for you.' Vicky was sitting on the side of the bed. Her white dressing gown hung loosely at the front and David could see her firm right breast and erect nipple.

'Sorry what time is it?' he said, sleepily.

'Nine-thirty, here's your tea. Shift over.' With that, she shed the gown and slid into the bed. He felt her warm beside him, the smell of her perfume was pure aphrodisiac.

'Drink your tea, before it gets cold,' she said, in a matronly way.

'Yes ma'am, anything you say.'

She laughed her throaty laugh and hugged him. He felt her breasts against his chest, and as she wrapped her right leg around him he felt the smooth shaved skin of her crotch on his thigh.

'Am I allowed to talk?'

'Drink your tea.'

He managed a couple of gulps of the tea before Vicky slid her hand slowly down his stomach.

'My God! What is this?' she gasped.

The sex was raw and animal, and afterwards they lay in each other's arms for some time before she broke the silence.

'I've always liked you, you know that don't you?' she whispered in his ear.

'Your father's going to bloody kill me.' He lent on one elbow.

'You are such a romantic.' Again the laugh which David found so exciting. 'Well he won't find out will he?'

'No, he certainly bloody won't.'

'Will you take me back up to London and stay with me for a while? I'd really like to help you with this German riddle.'

'I'll think about it. There is some stuff I haven't told you about, it's dangerous.'

'How dangerous?'

'Fischer is dead.' He told her about the shooting on Caw.

'Shit! Now I'm scared for you.'

'I'm scared for me.' said David.

Vicky did the throaty laugh again. 'I'd better look after you then.' She nuzzled up to him, 'We've just got time for one more…'

They showered together, and were sitting drinking tea when Griff got back. David immediately felt a wave of guilt and noticed that Vicky's cheeks had flushed when greeting her father.

'Well have you intrepid researchers solved the picture problem yet?' he enquired.

They both shook their heads.

'Not yet,' said David.

'Come on then, let's have a look at everything.'

Griff studied the pipe. 'Burgmühle? Is that the name of the

maker?' he asked.

'No his name was Novak, according to my father.'

'Vicky, could you get the large magnifying glass from my office please,' Griff requested.

He went to the window and, painfully slowly, inspected it through the lens.

David saw Griff's face tighten slightly. 'Ah now. What have we here?'

'What've you found, you clever sod?' demanded David.

'There's something very tiny on the Star of David. I can't quite make it out, it's too small…old bugger like me. Vicky, you look.'

She held the pipe up to the light. 'There's a…small circle with the letters BK in it on the top of the upright triangle…a B on the left and a GK on the right. It's is so tiny, the engraving is so fine. Wait, there's something else, a small figure six on each side of that triangle…nothing on the lower triangle at all. Here, have a look David.'

He took the glass and looked. There it was. It was so fine it must have taken extreme engraving skill and a very large magnifying glass.

Vicky was looking at the photograph, very intently. 'Your father said that this picture was given to Novak?'

David nodded.

'Did Novak add the writing?' she asked.

'God knows,' said David.

She got up and went out, returning some minutes later.

'The figures circled on the photographs form a tilted and upside down triangle, exactly thirteen centimetres on the base and 7.2 centimetres on the other two sides. Is that important?'

'Very,' said Griff and David in unison.

David scribbled some notes. The top triangle of the Star of David on the pipe had a six on each side, a circled BK at the top, a B bottom left, and a GK bottom right. The photograph, thirteen centimetres base line between Dumas, Breem and Newal and seven point two centimetres between Dumas and

Hill, and Newal and Hill. Was one of the Bs on the pipe Breem? The figure 1850 on the reverse. Did that refer to the pipe in any way?

Vicky chewed at the ends of her hair, staring at the photograph. 'I'm going to get on the Internet and see if I can do a little research on the guys in the photograph.'

For the next two hours Griff and David talked about the old days in St Ives, the lovers, the drugs and the personalities, the good times and the bad.

Vicky shouted from the office. 'The connection here's so slow. It's driving me mad. I'd love to work on this in London, if that's okay with you, David? Why don't you drive me up, and stay? Dad was going to run me back as I came down on the train. My car's in for a service, and I didn't fancy the drive in a courtesy car or a hire car.'

'I…I…' spluttered David.

'Yes, why don't you?' Griff said.

Victoria had a mischievous smile on her face when she came back, and David felt the thrill of expectancy.

'So it's all set then. David and I can set off in the morning for London.' She brushed her hands together in a 'that's that' gesture.

'Women.' grimaced Griff.

'Women.' smiled David.

Later when Victoria was preparing dinner they sat talking in the lounge. Griff handed him a small whiskey.

'Cheers.' David raised his glass. 'Here's to old times.'

'Yes, to old times.' Suddenly Griff looked old and drawn. 'David,' he said, 'Vicky doesn't know, and I don't want her to know yet. They've found cancer in both my lungs, and it has probably spread. I'm still waiting for the results, but it's possibly only a matter of months, if that.'

'Oh Christ. You...'

'Nothing I can do about it. I'm not scared by the thought of dying, and I'm telling you, because you're a good friend. Victoria will be devastated when she eventually finds out. She has no really close friends, and I know how much she likes you. I'd just like you to be around for her, when the time comes.'

'Of course, Griff. When will you get the results?'

'Sometime this week I hope. Not a word to Vicky. Not yet, okay?'

The meal was superb, and after coffee, David said that he wanted to get a good night's sleep before the long drive to London in the morning. He thanked them both, kissed Vicky on the cheek and went to bed.

He thought it important to leave the two alone together, as he had felt like an intruder on a private grief that was surely to come. As soon as his head hit the pillow he was asleep.

The dream was vivid. Fischer with his head blown off, David's father in army uniform, Novak smoking his pipe and tapping his head with it. Voss beating him with a bullwhip, and the four men in the photograph standing in the background pointing at Novak and then at themselves. Then Novak taking a cat out of his pocket and an alarm bell going off…

A phone was ringing downstairs.

It was early morning and he heard Vicky bounding down the stairs to answer it. After he had showered he went down. He called out to Victoria but realised that she was still on the telephone.

'Do I tell him? I'm not happy with this at all...yes, this morning…well yes all right …all right yes…goodbye.'

She came into the kitchen and jumped with fright when she saw him. 'Oh, Christ, don't do that. I thought you were still in bed.'

'The telephone woke me up. Sorry,' he apologised.

Griff came down the stairs, hawking and coughing. 'Who the hell was that on the telephone at this time in the morning?' Griff checked his watch 'A quarter to eight?'

'Something to do with work, Daddy. They wanted to know when I was coming back to London'.

'Don't newspaper people ever sleep? Put the kettle on, David.' He sat down at the kitchen table, his body racked by a coughing fit.

After breakfast, David packed the car, and they both bid their respective farewells to Griff.

'I'll be down again very soon,' said David.

Griff smiled and gave him a tight bear hug, as he did so, David whispered in his ear.

'Good luck with the results, my friend.'

'Don't worry. Look after her and drive safely. Give me a call when you arrive, Victoria.'

Chapter 6

As they neared Exeter, he asked her about her journalism, and she told him about assignments in Afghanistan, Beirut, Israel, Bosnia, and more recently in Russia. She had written many articles for 'The Guardian' on the emergence of militant Islam, and was considering writing a book on the subject, as she felt so strongly about the maltreatment of the Palestinians.

She was more worried about Griff. His cough was getting very bad, and she had begged him to go to the doctor's, but he just told her to stop nagging.

'Has he said anything to you?' she asked.

'No,' lied David, 'all he said was that he was trying to give up the cigarettes, because the cough was pissing him off.'

'Well I think he's really ill with it. Will you have a word with him please, David?' She stroked his thigh and put her hand between his legs.

David was now intent on watching two cars, some distance behind him, a dark green Volkswagen Passat and a black Peugeot 306. There were other vehicles in between them, but it was sometimes the green car, and occasionally the black car leading. He carried on talking to Victoria but slowly decreased his speed from 80mph to 70mph. The gap remained the same. After some minutes he upped it to 85mph. Still they held station.

Back in the leading car, which was now the Peugeot, the driver rang the Passat.

'He's made us. Pull off at the next junction. We'll carry on to Exeter, but will stay a long way back.'

He keyed in another number.

'Martin, he's made us, pick him up on the M5 at Exeter. I'll contact you when we're nearly there, he'll be about two miles in front of us.'

The Peugeot pulled off at the next junction and the VW lagged further and further back, until it was no longer visible in the rear view mirror. David's gut feeling told him he had been right.

They knew that he had seen them. Now he must watch for where the other guys picked him up. How the hell did they find him? Was there another tracker on the car?

He didn't want to say anything to Victoria. It would only worry her, and there was no reason for that yet.

They joined the M5, and after two miles he started checking his mirrors. Nothing out of the ordinary, but he knew they were there. This was a professional operation; one he couldn't handle on his own.

He would have to contact his former employees at the ministry.

As they pulled around to the back of the Georgian house on Montpelier Row, where she had her apartment in Blackheath, she took a key fob from her bag and aimed it at the garage block. The large door swung open, and he just managed to squeeze the Discovery in with about five centimetres height to spare.

'I'll get the bags,' he said.

'Ground floor number 3. That door over there to get in, 7865 is the code. I need the loo.' She ran for the door.

Number 3 was a spacious two-bedroom flat with a small patio looking onto a well tended, and surprisingly large, garden. The décor was what he would have expected from Griff's daughter. Simple and understated, but slightly St Ives arty. Troika and Leach pottery was strategically placed around the flat, as were the paintings which David recognised as mainly Griff's. A small Ben Nicholson hung beside a larger Roger Hilton. Over the mantelpiece a Patrick Heron, with swathes of deep red, would have dominated the room, if it hadn't been perfectly placed.

They decided on a fish-and-chips supper, and went out to get them, just some four hundred metres away in the village. Vicky had her arm in his and he felt more alive than at any time in the last ten years.

Back at the flat, he told her in more detail about the break-in at the castle and the car that had been following him on the way down to Cornwall.

'Jesus.' She now looked worried. 'Did you notice anything on the way up here?'

'No,' he lied again.

Later she rang Griff and got no answer. 'I bet he's gone up to the pub,' she said, smiling. 'Let's go to bed now.' She kissed his neck.

'It's only eight o'clock. I'll never get off to sleep,' he protested.

'Who wants to sleep?' She laughed the laugh. 'Come on, we can make a start tomorrow on the German stuff.'

It was the first time he had spent the night with anybody for a long time, and it was nice to be wanted and to feel a sense of belonging. He drifted in and out of sleep, waking with every movement of her warm body beside him.

The dreams came again. The SS officer, Von den Bergen, with a magnifying glass looking at the cat. Novak, pointing to the four men in the picture, who said nothing, but pointed back at him. Voss with David's father, beating him with a large ruler. Fischer, whose head was back together, was paying large bundles of cash to a line of prisoners.

She woke him at nine o'clock with a cup of coffee, and he put his arm out to pull her to him. The flinch away was momentary, but David didn't miss it, wondering if he'd committed a faux-pas by sleeping in.

'Sorry, have you been up long?' he asked.

'No. Just came out of the shower and made the coffee. Now come on, drink up, we have work to do.' There was now a distinct distance and purpose in her voice. Something had changed.

David showered and dressed and could smell warm toast and fresh coffee. Hearing the plastic tapping of a keyboard, he wandered into the living room. Vicky was at her computer in

a little alcove office off to the left, and had obviously started looking for information on the Net.
'Help yourself to breakfast, and then come and help me.'

They found a number of contact addresses for Jewish organizations to try and trace Novak, but the photograph was less clear. His father's letter said that Novak was given the original picture by a prisoner, who he presumably had befriended, in Buchenwald.

That prisoner was a British POW who died in the camp after having been taken there for continuous escape attempts. He must be easy to identify and hopefully so were the other people circled in the photograph. There were numerous web sites and contact numbers for POW groups so they should be able to trace them.

They split the tasks as there were several telephone numbers to ring, and several sites to visit and to send emails to. David located Oberführer Matthias Reiner Von den Bergen, whose last boss was a Dr Hans Kammler, head of the underground rocket facilities at the end of the war and the driving force behind the building of Auschwitz and other camps. Kammler and Von den Bergen had both disappeared without trace in April 1945.

Oberführer was a very senior SS officer. What the hell was he doing with a Jewish prisoner like Novak? Novak must have been a seriously important guy to them.

At lunchtime, David suggested taking a break and going down to the village for a drink and a bite to eat.
'I'll just try Griff's phone again,' she said.
After a few minutes, she pulled a face.
'He's still out. I'll ring later.'

She got her coat, whilst David went out to the car, and replaced the papers in the fire extinguisher. On the way across the road, with Vicky hanging on his arm, he saw the two tails immediately.

One was a shortish guy in his mid forties, with a moustache, bomber jacket and trainers, outside an estate agents. Ex SAS.

Regiment written all over him, thought David.

As they turned left down the hill, he vaguely recognized a face from a past liaison meeting at 14 Intelligence Company. It had been about fifteen years ago, and the man had been waiting in an anteroom, but David remembered the face. He was slowly walking up the hill on the other side.

These guys were home team. What the hell was going on?

Sitting and chatting over a pint and a sandwich, David wondered how much of this to reveal to Vicky. He decided for the time being to say nothing. There was no obvious danger, and he began to think that these people were a part of the team following them on the motorway yesterday. But what was the ministry's interest here? This was all getting a bit too crowded.

He looked around the busy pub: nobody special sticking out. The other two wouldn't come in, they knew where he was, and they would quietly wait, or two other tails would be out there taking over now.

'Do you want another drink?' asked David.

'No, let's get back and crack on.' Again, he was aware of a hint of urgency in her voice he couldn't quite work out.

They walked the other way around the block and back up the hill to the flat. David didn't need to look this time. The tails were there and he knew it.

Back at the computer, they were soon surrounded by a heap of papers with scribbled notes and dates.

Robert Jan Voss had been an SS Hauptscharführer. 36th Waffen-Grenadier-Division, born. Trnava, Czechoslovakia, December 18th 1910. Trnava, was now in Slovakia. Both Novak and Voss were Slovaks. Voss was wanted for war crimes, and disappeared from Stutthof early 1945. He had earlier been transferred to the control of SS Totenkopf Standarte 3, Thuringen, at Buchenwald, the same as Von den Bergen, and was murdered in Berkach, Thuringen, March 1988, under a false identity - Artur Lutz Leimbach.

Hauptscharführer, Senior Sergeant or that kind of level, that tied in with what Fischer had said, that the guard had died in Berkach East Germany, just south of Meiningen in Thuringia.'

'Fischer was stationed in Meiningen with the Stasi,' said David. 'I'm sure I have a pre-unification map of Germany in the car. Give me a minute.'

He found the old Arals map and they looked at it together. Berkach was right on the old border, on the East German side, with Meiningen a few kilometres to the North.

'Who murdered Voss and why was he, a Slovak, living in a tiny village right on the East German border? He would've had to have had a special permit to live there, and his papers would surely have been scrutinised very carefully. Did he get help, to get away with his false identity?' he pondered, leaning back in the chair.

'Can we find out what the local paper was in 1988?' He went into the kitchen and made some coffee.

'Coffee is served.' He put his arm around her neck and pulled her to him. There was a stiffness, almost a shrinking away.

He was about to ask her what was wrong, when there was a 'ding' on the computer. 'You have mail,' it said on the screen. Vicky opened her mailbox.

'It's a reply to a request you made to the POW association. Do you want to sit here?'

'No, just read it out will you.' He relaxed with his coffee.

'Dear Mr Lennox, further to your enquiry of today. We cannot trace an RSM.Ted Hill, 23 Edward Hill's but no Regimental Sergeant-Major. They list them. We have 4 matches for L.Dumas, they list them, and 2 for N.Breem, again listed. We have no match for a Sgt. Newal. But 8 matches for Newal, again a list. Furthermore, none of the matches we have found were in the same regiment, or the same POW camp together. Apart from two inmates at Stalag 12B Frankenthal Pfalz, from 1943 to 1945. We have also listed the British servicemen who we know died in Buchenwald, but they have no known connection to the names above. They list them.

There is a Raymond Jules Langard SOE, Codename Jules Dumas, service number 282875, executed 03.02.45 aged 29 in Buchenwald. He again, has no match to any other listed man above. If we can be of further assistance...blah…blah and so on.'

'Was this Dumas the man who gave Novak the picture? It can't be Dumas in the picture, if he has no connection to the other three. Twenty-nine years old, they were all so bloody young,' he sighed.

He sat and sketched the pipe diagram. What did it mean? It had to be linked to the photograph. The upside down triangle of the ringed figures. But WHAT?

Tracing the photograph he added the measurements that Victoria had found plus the 1850 from the reverse. He then joined the ringed figures together to form the three sides of the triangle.

Her telephone rang.

'Victoria Mason...hello…yes...well it's a little difficult… okay…in about an hour…I think I should be able to make it. Where? Yes I know it…yes…bye.' She hung up.

'David, it's work. I have to go and meet somebody I've been trying to interview for some time. Do you mind? I'll make it up to you when I get back.' She laughed the laugh again, and kissed David on the cheek.

'I'm going up to Charing Cross by train, should be back well in time for dinner. I'll put the phone on answer machine, so you won't be disturbed.' She got a few things together and put her coat on. 'Shall we go out for dinner?' she asked.

'That'd be nice,' said David.

She kissed him again, this time on the lips, and he felt desire welling in him.

'Later.' She patted his inner thigh playfully.

David watched, well back from the window, as she went down the hill to the station. He saw a figure who had been looking in the estate agent's window, glance at his watch and move off down the road after her.

Why the hell were they following her? He puzzled.

The next few hours went uneventfully. He had put the two diagrams away and had spent a lot of time on the Internet, using several search engines to find anything relevant. He found the Thuringisches Staatsarchiv in Meiningen, and was delighted to discover that they kept full newspaper copies on microfiche, and since 1990 on disc, of at least four titles in the area going back to 1951. So they should be able to trace the murder of Voss. It was then that he heard a mobile telephone ringing.

It was coming from his sports bag and from the phone the Germans had given him. He hesitated for a second, and then answered.

'Yes.'

'Herr Lennox, we have spoken before. Since then, I know that you were not responsible for what happened on the mountain.'

'I tried to tell you that,' he said, wondering if this man's collar-bone was broken and his arm in a sling. Maybe he wanted his Gurza back.

'Please listen, Herr Lennox, I want to talk to you, but you have seen that I must be careful for my life. I will send you a text message tomorrow. Please follow those instructions and I will make you a very rich man.'

The call cut off.

Time to call the old firm, David decided.

He rang the contact number.

'The number you are ringing has not been recognised. The numb…'

'Damn!'

Well it had been a long time. He was just about to hang up when he heard the faintest of electronic clicks. He replaced the phone and immediately picked it up again, and this time heard the sound more clearly.

In the bedroom he took the current and signal detector from his bag, and then disconnected the phone. He passed the gadget over the handset. Nothing. In the kitchen was a cordless extension. Same procedure. Nothing. Bedroom the same. Tracing the telephone wire into the building, and then to the junction box in the hall, he took a small multi-tool from his pocket, and quickly unscrewed the box. No additions as far as he could tell, but technology had come a long way in ten years. He screwed the lid shut and returned to the flat.

This must be an official tap. MI5, or his former lot, or maybe the Police? Had they found Fischer's body? There had been nothing in the papers; he had checked them.

He scanned from room to room with the detector. Light fittings, electric sockets, paintings, toaster, kettle, and microwave. All innocent. Computer, television and hi-fi stack. Nothing.

The flat, as far as his 1990s technology was concerned, was clean.

So what the hell was their interest in this phone number, if they hadn't found Fischer and hadn't linked the death to him?

He returned to studying the diagrams again, but soon fell into that kind of drowsiness which is desperately difficult to stave off when you are trying to concentrate.

The sound of a key in the door woke him from a dreamless slumber. Victoria looked tired and a little drawn.

'Oh dear. Sleeping on the job.' She kissed him gently on the top of his head. 'You have that just woken up smell.' The hint of coldness she had shown in the morning had gone.

'Sorry, should I take a shower?' said David, in mock hurt.

'No, no I love it.' She ruffled his hair. 'I've been trying to ring Dad all day. No answer, he must be out on the razz. Shall we go to bed, and then go out for something to eat?'

'Sounds good to me,' he smiled. 'Did the meeting go well?'

He saw a momentary flicker of her eyes down and to the left, and he knew she was going to lie. He had been renowned, among his colleagues, for catching the slightest nuance of voice inflection, gesture or posture, whether at international meetings or sitting with fourteen year old, rat-arsed, AK47 wielding, crack-heads in the jungles of Africa. He saw eagerness to accept when a rebuff was offered, he saw fear in a face when everyone else was terrified by it, he saw potential movement where others saw intransigence and he saw bullshit, when it was being peddled as truth.

'Yes,' she said, 'very.'

He decided against telling her about the phone tap and the tail, and the phone call from the German. Something was beginning to nag at him, and he didn't like it.

Later they decided to walk down through the park to a restaurant in Greenwich. A chill wind was blowing and there was a hint of snow as they strolled arm in arm across the heath.

He couldn't quite put his finger on it, but there was something tense about her. Several times she turned to look behind them.

'Anything wrong?' he asked.

'Not really, It's just that one night I had a guy following me,' she said.

He didn't look back, but guessed they were being tailed again. Did she know?

They had an excellent Italian meal washed down with a bottle of Piedmonte red wine. David realised that, not so long ago, he had been very close to being alcohol dependent. Now he could drink it or leave it, and it was a pleasurable experience, not a means to deaden and dull, to wipe out or forget.

They walked back up Croom's Hill to the west side of the park, as the main gates were now closed, and on to the heath and home.

Just before they reached the village, she said 'I might have to go away for a few days for work. I'm sorry, it's something that came up today.'

'No problem, I must get back up to The Lakes anyway,' he said.

'I thought maybe you could stay here. I don't want you to go.' She squeezed his hand and David caught a hint of fear in her eyes.

That night the dreams came again. Novak pointing at him then throwing the pipe into the sea. The four guys in the photograph were standing against a wall, and Von den Bergen was shooting them in the back of the neck. Voss was in a watchtower, looking out over the East German border with a pair of binoculars, whilst a Land Rover, full of men in pinstripe suits and bowler hats, was chasing Fischer, who was carrying a cat.

He heard her showering at eight o'clock, and dozed off again until she came in with a cup of coffee a half-an-hour later.

'I'll be back in three days or maybe four. I'll leave the answer machine on, but I'll give two rings and then call again so you know it's me, and pick up. I do wish you would get a mobile phone.' She kissed his hands.

'I'll fix one today,' he promised.

'Make sure you do. Here are the keys.' She swept the hair from her very green eyes, and blowing him a kiss from the door, she left.

After breakfast he found the home number of Tim Adams, the ex-colleague who had lost both hands and an eye to a letter bomb in Beirut. A woman's voice answered.

'Is that Marion?'

'Who is this?' she asked.

'Marion it's David, David Lennox. I hope I haven't woken you. Is Tim there?'

'Hi David, long time no see.'

'I'm sorry. Been a bit down, and to be frank, a bit too fond of the hooch these past few years.'

'You're not alone there,' she groaned. 'I'll see if he's awake. He's rather too fond of the drink himself nowadays. You must come and visit again, David. Tim and I'd love to see you.'

'I promise a visit soon,' he lied.

'Just putting this on the loudspeaker,' she said.

'David, Hi, it's Tim, how are you?'

'Old, fat and poor. How about you, Tim?'

'Not so bad. Are you coming to visit us? I've some very fine bottles of Single Malt from the Scottish Malt Whisky Society.

Very fine.'
'I will do, my friend, but...I'm ringing for a bit of information, actually.'
'Oh I see.' He sounded disappointed.
'I don't want to bore you with the fine detail, but I need to contact the office rather urgently, and the number I have has been discontinued.'
'Well I have a number, old son, but frankly...'
'Yes, yes. I fully understand. Just wondered if you could give them a call and tell them I've been in touch with you, and get a number for me to ring. It's important, Tim.'
After quite a few seconds thought, Tim said, very slowly. 'Okay as long as you promise me that it's not going to drop me in the shit. I've enough problems to deal with here.'
'No I promise you it won't,' he said, not really knowing whether it would drop Adams in the shit, or not.
'What's your number?' Adams asked.
'Well, it's better if I ring you back later, if you don't mind. I'm at a friend's place, and their answer machine is on.'
'Young and pretty is she? You never learn, do you?' he scolded.
'Well actually she is, and no, I never seem to.'
'Ring me back after lunch, all right?'
'Yes, thank you Tim, I appreciate it.'
He went back to thinking about the pipe and the photograph, and was getting nowhere, so he went to the computer and turned it on. After some seconds, it asked for a password.
'Shit. Shit, shit and double shit.' He tried a few guesses without success.
'Damn!' Well, he would have to wait until she rang.

It was eleven o'clock when the mobile given to him by the Germans beep-beeped a message signal. 'Newfield Inn, Seathwaite. 18.00 tonight. I will approach you.'
The German didn't know where he was. That was interesting. The man must have gone to ground after Fischer's shooting.

He texted back. 'Sorry, can't do that, am not in The Lakes. Suggest we meet Cutty Sark, Greenwich, London. Tomorrow.13.30.'

There was a long pause. 'Agree, 13.30, tomorrow.'

He decided to get some exercise. It was a cold day, but there was a bright blue sky, reminding him of a typical spring morning in Scandinavia. He hadn't been to Lewisham for years, apart from driving through it on the way to Victoria's flat, so he decided to walk the mile or so down the hill and buy a mobile phone. Before he left, he checked his answer machine in his apartment. There were no new messages.

He left the flat and crossed the road to walk along the north side of the Village. He took a nonchalant look around. Nobody was watching him. He almost felt aggrieved. Where had they gone? Why were they not following him?

Taking a roundabout route down some of the side roads, he was now sure that he wasn't being followed.

It took him half-an-hour of easy walking to reach Lewisham High Street from Blackheath, and it was like going from one universe to another, from urban gentility to city jungle, from fresh air to exhaust fumes. A cold wind was blowing in his face and snow was not far away.

He walked along the High Street until he found a mobile phone shop. It took ten minutes to get the paper work sorted before he was handed everything in a plastic carrier bag, and told to ring the number given in the box as soon as he wanted. Within twenty-four hours everything should be operating.

He thought about taking a walk along to Catford and his old school, but decided that there was no nostalgia left in him for the day, so turned up the hill and back to Blackheath.

Maybe he would have a pint. But only the one.

As he sat drinking, he knew that something was not quite right, it just didn't add up.

Chapter 7

He got back to Victoria's flat at two o'clock, and was about to ring Tim Adams when the doorbell rang. He picked up the entry phone.

'Yes, hello.'

'Police sir. Can we come in?'

Shit. What now? It couldn't be anything to do with Fischer, couldn't be. The tremor in his hand had started up again.

'Yes…er…just push.' He opened the outer door.

Two men entered, both dressed in tired and creased suits. One, in his early forties, was short and stocky, the other a little younger, lanky and moustached. The short one flashed his warrant card.

'Detective Inspector Walsh, and this is Detective Sergeant Simons, sir. Is Miss Victoria Mason in?'

'Er…no. She's gone away for a few days,' David answered.

'When's she due back, sir?' Walsh probed.

'I don't know. Two or three days, she said.'

'Is there a mobile contact number we can reach her on, sir?' asked Simons.

'I don't have it. She said she'd contact me.'

'And you are, sir?' enquired Walsh, looking past David into the bedroom.

'My name's Lennox, David Lennox. I'm a family friend. Could you please tell me what this is about?'

'When did you last see Miss Mason, sir?' he asked, still looking into the bedroom.

'This morning when she left. Has something happened?'

'Have you been at the flat for some time, sir?' Simons asked.

'No we both drove up from Cornwall, two days ago.'

'Had you been staying with the family in Marazion, sir?' asked Walsh.

'Yes for a couple of nights. Look chaps, I don't want to be difficult, but please now cut the crap. What's all this about. Has something happened to Griff?'

'Would that be Mr Gregory Frederick Mason, sir?' Walsh read the name from his notebook.

David felt his mouth and throat go very dry. A wave of nausea swept over him. Oh God. He shouldn't have visited them.

'Yes. Now please, what the hell's this about? Has anything happened to him?'

'He's dead, sir,' Walsh said, matter-of-factly.

The blood drained from David's face, and he had to sit down before he fell.

'Oh Jesus. How?'

'Can I ask you again, when you last saw Miss Mason?' Walsh asked. No 'sir' this time, and a hint of rudeness. He walked to the bedroom door in a waft of cheap aftershave and stood with his back to David, whilst slowly surveying the room.

'How did he die?' asked David, still in shock. The tremor in his hand now very visible.

'Something making you nervous, sir?' asked, a now much cockier Simons.

David exploded. 'My best friend's just died, and you're asking me why I'm shaking. I know you ignorant sods don't have to have much of a fucking brain, but Christ Almighty, even your limited imagination should be able to work that out. Now, my best friend is dead , could you please stop buggering me about, and tell me what's happened.'

Walsh whirled round from the door his face flushed. 'What's happened is that Mr Mason's been murdered, and that you were one of the last people to see him alive, sir. What's happened is that Miss Victoria Mason's disappeared god knows where, and you're in her flat. That's what's happened. Even Neanderthals, like myself and Sergeant Simons here, would have to have a frontal fucking lobotomy to miss those facts, sir.' He whirled back round, looking into the bedroom again.

There was a long period of silence as David cupped his head in his hands, and Simons looked out of the window with a smile on his lips.

'Okay,' said David. 'I'm putting the kettle on. Coffee…tea?'

'Not at the moment thank you, sir,' said a visibly angry Walsh. Simons shook his head.
'All right, what do you want to know?' asked David.
'We'd like you to accompany us to the station, sir…please.'
David thought for a moment. 'Well, I know I could say no, but I'll do all I can, to help. I have to make a quick phone call first.'
'Do you mind if we have a look around here, Mr Lennox?' asked Walsh, who had now regained most of his composure.
'No. No, please do,' David acquiesced.
'Do you have a car here, sir?' Simons was looking at the Land Rover keys on the table.
'Yes. It's in the garage at the back.'
'Is it a double garage?' Walsh turned and looked directly at him.
'No, Vicky's…Miss Mason's car's in for a service.'
'Do we know where, sir?' He looked at his shoes.
'No idea, I'm afraid.' David was praying that Victoria would ring, and on the other hand, he was praying she wouldn't. This would devastate her.
'Do you mind if Sergeant Simons takes a look at your car, sir?'
'No…no.' David handed Simons the keys. 'The side door to the first garage is open,' he explained.
'If you want to make that phone call, I'll just have a little look around here. Okay sir?' Walsh asked.
'Yes, no problem.' He rang Tim Adam's number on Victoria's phone. Engaged.
'Don't you have a mobile, Mr Lennox?' Walsh asked.
'Funnily enough, I bought one today.' David said.
'What's funny about it?' asked Walsh, looking at a pile of Victoria's clothes lying on the bedside chair.
'Well then, 'coincidentally' is a better word, if we must be pedantic.'
'Pedantic, sir? I wouldn't know what that means, you don't have to have much of a brain to do my job.'

'O fucking K!' said David, 'I apologise. But for Christ's sake, my best friend's been murdered. How did it happen? Where did it happen?'

'I'm not at liberty to divulge that at the moment, we're still waiting for the autopsy results and the forensic evidence.'

Simons came back from the car and shook his head fleetingly to Walsh. Walsh signalled the office with his head, and both policemen had a cursory look around the flat.

'Well, do you want to get a coat, Mr Lennox?' Walsh opened the door to the hall.

'Yes,' said David, 'I guess I do.'

The interview room was small and claustrophobic. Three bare walls were a dull yellowing cream, a large mirror opposite David, covered the fourth. The stink of stale tobacco smoke and sweat was rank, and the floor was sticky to David's leather soles, as though coffee had been spilt and left to dry.

The one cracked window looked out over the yard and the parked police vehicles below. The blind, filthy and broken, hung limply down at one end. Countless cups of coffee and tea had ring-stained the table, where innumerable denials and confessions had been dished out across the dirty and unemptied ashtrays.

He cracked his fingers and stretched his feet, looking at the wide mirror on the wall. He could see that it was one-way.

Memories flooded back of the stinking room in Bolivia. One electrode attached to his tongue and the other to a soaking wet sponge underneath his testicles. The Glaswegian branch of the Hereford cavalry had come in to save his neck, shooting every man in the room before they even knew what was happening to them. All except the ugly bastard with the pliers who had, moments before, been very slowly removing David's front teeth and toenails. And then Ginge, smiling at David and coming out with the best rescue line he had ever heard, and was ever likely to hear:

'Will yeh look at the cock on yeh Lennox. Yer hung like a

fahcking Donkey, man.'

He remembered the madness that overwhelmed him, and how he had enjoyed beating the torturer to death, by smashing a rifle-butt into his face and head as he pleaded for mercy.

'Seńor…Seńor,'…thud…'por favor,'…thud, thud, thud… 'Seńor,'…thud, thud…'los mios,'…thud, thud, thud, thud… 'nińo,'…thud, thud, thud, thud, thud, thud, thud.

The bastard had still been grasping the pliers as his brain pulp oozed out of his nose onto the floor. That was the lasting image David had. Then Ginge pulling him off.

'Put some clothes on man, let's awah from this shitehouse, and back to a pint in Hereford.'

Walsh came into the room with Simons. They both sat down, and Walsh turned on the tape recorder on the end of the table.

'Interview room three, 15.30, Wednesday 17th December. Present, D.I. Walsh, D.S. Simons and Mr David Lennox who is helping us, voluntarily, with our inquiries into the death of Gregory Frederick Mason, of Chy Vean, Marazion, Cornwall. This initial questioning's on behalf of the Cornish Police. They'll want to talk to you later Mr Lennox. Do you understand?'

David nodded. 'Yes I understand.'

'Could you please run us through the last few days again, Mr Lennox.' Walsh leaned back in his chair.

'I drove down to Cornwall on a surprise visit, on Saturday…'

'Saturday the 13th December,' prompted Walsh.

'Yes, the 13th. I phoned Griff on the way down, to make sure they were in, and arrived there about 18.30. Later we went out for a meal in Penzance. I stayed another day and night, and left at about 10.00 on the Monday morning. Victoria Mason came with me and…'

'Why was that sir?' enquired Simons.

'Her car was in for a service, and she'd travelled down to Cornwall by train. She thought it'd be a great idea for me to give her a lift.'

'Are you and Miss Mason lovers, Mr Lennox?' Walsh looked

at him without losing eye contact.

'I don't think that's relevant, Inspector Walsh.' David returned the stare.

'Her father's been murdered and Miss Mason has, for all intents and purposes, disappeared, and you were in her flat, Mr Lennox. Two people had slept in the bed. Seems pretty relevant to me.' Walsh looked at the ceiling.

'We're very close,' David said, inwardly grimacing at this platitude. 'How was he murdered?'

'Could you please explain what you mean by very close, Mr Lennox. You don't know where she is, and you don't have her mobile number. Is that what you call close?' Walsh was leaning back in the chair with his hands behind his head.

'I hadn't seen her for over ten years, we were attracted, she likes older men. I drove her up to London; I didn't ask her where she was going, it wasn't my business. She said she'd phone me at the flat, she's probably already tried.'

'Did her father know about your…er…closeness, Mr Lennox?' Simons asked.

'He knew she was very fond of me.'

'Not so normal a relationship though, is it?' Simons said, looking out of the window.

'What's normal?' asked David starting to count the rings on the table.

'Did you sleep with Miss Mason at Chy Vean, sir?' Walsh leaned forward.

'Why's that important?' David was getting bored.

'Well, I think it's significant, if Mr Mason found you, 'in flagrente' with his twenty-seven year old daughter, Mr Lennox.' Walsh leaned back again.

'Griff and I are…were very, very close friends,' retorted David.

'Would be pushing the friendship though, wouldn't it, sir. Eh?' Walsh was looking at the ceiling again.

'Nothing like that happened.' David was thinking about Novak and how two people had died already. All these years after his

death and the end of the War.
What the hell was this all about?
'So when you left with Miss Mason, Mr Mason was still alive.' Simons shifted in his chair.
'Yes,' said David.
'Can anybody else verify that, sir?' Simons leant back, subconsciously mimicking the body language of his colleague.
'Not unless any of the neighbours saw us leaving,' answered David factually.
'Has anybody seen you and Miss Mason together in Blackheath?' Walsh said, getting up and going to the window. He parted the blinds with his thumb and forefinger, then seeing how dirty they were, rubbed his hand on his trousers.
'Maybe the Italian restaurant we visited last night would remember us. The waitress seemed pleased with the tip.'
Simons took the name of the restaurant from David and left the room, presumably to ring and check.
'15.52 D.S.Simons has left the interview room.' Walsh sat down again, tapping a pencil on the table and sucking his teeth.
There was a long period of silence, which David broke.
'I'm trying to help you here, but you seem determined to go up the wrong path. How did he die? I really want to help. He was a good friend, and we're wasting time here.'
David shifted on the chair, which was now becoming hard and uncomfortable to sit on.
Walsh tapped the table some more. Simons came back in and passed Walsh a note.
'15.56, D.S. Simons has come back into the interview room.' Walsh was still tapping and looking at the table.
'He was shot, Mr Lennox. Not in panic, not by an amateur. Once behind the left ear and once in the centre of the neck, both at close range. He had been tied to a chair. There was no sign of a break-in.'
David felt a numbness in the pit of his stomach and the tremor started again in his arm. He found it difficult to speak. 'Did you

know that he had cancer?'

'Yes we did.' Walsh was looking at him now. 'Can you think of any explanation for the manner in which Mr Mason died, Mr Lennox?'

'None at all,' David lied, his thoughts racing. What would Vicky think? She would blame him for the death of her father. She would of course tell the police about Fischer, Novak, his father, the whole bloody thing.

Walsh was looking him straight in the eye.

'Are you quite sure, sir?'

'Quite sure.' David held his gaze.

There was a knock at the door and Simons went out.

'16.04, D.S. Simons has left the interview room.'

David could hear what sounded like a heated, but muted, exchange just outside the door.

Simons put his head around the door looking very pissed off, thought David. He nodded to Walsh.

'Can I have a quick word, Walshy?'

'16.06, terminating the interview.' Walsh switched off the recorder and left the room.

This time, the exchange was not so muted, and David heard scraps of an argument between Walsh and another deep voiced man. Walsh was shouting. The other man's words were just a low rumble.

'Do what? You must be joking, on whose authority? Christ almighty!...okay...all right!'

Walsh came back into the room, visibly shaking with anger.

'You're free to go, Mr Lennox. I'll fix a lift back for you.'

'What? Just like that?' asked David incredulously.

'Yes, just like that, Mr Lennox.'

'Can I ask why?'

'It seems that the Cornish police have the case in hand, and you are not a suspect. They've apparently corroborated the story with Miss Mason.' Walsh could hardly contain his frustration.

'Where's Miss Mason? Is she back here? She must be desperate.'

'I really can't tell you, sir. I'm sure she'll ring, you being so close. BOB!' he bellowed.

Simons came into the room.

'Get Mr Lennox a squad car to take him back to Blackheath, will you please. Well goodbye, Mr Lennox.' He didn't proffer his hand.

'It's been a pleasure,' David said dryly.

The squad car dropped him off back at the flat. The place was in darkness, so Victoria hadn't returned.

Once inside the warmth of the flat, he sat in the gloom for a while, trying to come to terms with Griff's death and the fact that he had involved his friend and his daughter in something horrendously big....but ***what***? Victoria must be beside herself and hating him for what had befallen her father. He should have bloody well known, after what happened up on Caw.

Who had Walsh spoken to outside the interview room door, and what had been said to let him go like that? He tried ringing Griff's number in Marazion, and got the line unavailable tone. Had they cut the wire?

Something really didn't add up here, and he was in the middle of it. He rang 1471 to see if there had been any calls - only the call to Vicky from yesterday. The number had been withheld. He telephoned Tim Adams again.

'Hi Tim, it's David.'

David caught the nervousness in Tim's voice immediately. It wasn't obvious, but it was there, like a mosquito in the night.

'Yes. Hi David...look, they weren't very happy. I ...er...'

'Did they give you a number, Tim?' David tried to keep the exasperation from his voice.

'Yes...yes, old man, but please don't let me down here will you?'

Fuck you.

'No I won't let you down, Tim.'

'Got a pen?'

'Yes, fire away,' said David.

'08866 43445223, wait for the prompt then 556478...all right?'

'Yes. Thank you, Tim.'
'Good luck, David.'
'Yes. Thanks. I'll come and visit you and Marion soon.' David felt lousy for lying.
'Yes sure. Cheers, David,' Adams said.
'Cheers.' David hung up.

He rang the number. It rang ten or eleven times, then a recorded female voice answered. 'Wait! Press star button, wait, enter code.'

He entered 556478.

'Yes, Lennox. What can we do for you?' a young male voice asked.

'I'd like a meet please. It's important.'

'We'll establish what's important, Lennox.' The condescension in the voice angered David.

'Look, you patronising bastard, whoever you are, I'm telling you that this is important. I want a meet. You people've been following me and the girl and tapping the damn telephone, so I want a meet NOW!'

'Hold on please...tomorrow 18.30. Severndroog Castle, Eltham.' The line went dead.

David decided to stay in and wait for Victoria to call. A moment that he was dreading. He went back to thinking about the picture and the pipe. When he did crosswords, he very often found that sometimes you could look at 'The Times' cryptic and it wouldn't mean a damn thing. Put it down for a morning, and start again, and you would finish it within half-an-hour. He was trying the same technique with the photograph, and it still didn't reveal anything, so he turned the television on to watch the seven o'clock news. Nothing very interesting was happening and he soon fell asleep in the armchair.

The dreams came again.

This time the cat was sitting on Hill's head and Griff was looking at a map and pointing to his watch. A man with no face was embracing Novak who was standing within a large Star of David. Von den Bergen and Voss were looking at the pipe.

He woke with a start, at the sound of a police siren on the television.

Still no telephone call. She must really hate him for what had happened. He cleaned his teeth, and looked at himself in the mirror. What had he done to his best friend?

He went to bed and lay in the dark unable to sleep properly. After an hour or two he eventually dozed off.

Griff came again, looking at his watch and waving to the four guys in the photograph.

Chapter 8

He woke early and decided that he would walk over the heath and through the park, for his meeting with the German.

Not wanting to use the phone in the flat, in case Victoria rang, he called the number he had been given in the mobile phone shop. After all the information had been exchanged, he was told that the phone would be operative sometime within the next two hours.

Half-an-hour later, his new mobile phone bleep-bleeped and he had a welcome message from his provider. He got in touch with a few regimental and POW contact numbers he had found on the net, but drew a blank. None of the names in the photograph could be placed together in any regiment, or in any camp.

Looking in the Yellow Pages he found a photographic studio down in Greenwich and called them to see if they could digitally remove the names and markings from the photograph. They said if he brought it in now, they would have it done by mid-afternoon.

Something was bothering him about the dream and Griff looking at his watch; but he didn't know what, and he couldn't do anything else constructive without the computer password, and access to the Internet.

Retrieving the photograph from its hiding place in the car, he set out across the heath at a brisk pace. He had a careful and practised look around. Nothing today, not yet. So why the hell were they so interested before?

The wind was bitter, stinging his cheeks, but it was a beautiful, clear sunny day. He made good time and entered Greenwich park by the main gates on Charlton Way. It was quiet, just a few people out walking dogs.

As he got near to the top of the hill above the Observatory, he noticed a man in a woollen hat taking photographs by the Bandstand, two hundred metres down to his right. David sat down on a nearby bench seat, facing the man, who now turned away and started to walk east, towards Maze Hill.

Was it the German, or home team?

David got up, and hurried down to the Maritime Museum at the bottom of the park. He then turned left to the main village and the photographic studio. Waiting a few minutes near the address, he looked around for any tails before he went up the stairs to the second floor reception.

Nobody was there, so he rang the bell, as invited. A bespectacled man in his mid-thirties, with a long baggy pullover and out of control curly hair, came out of the room marked 'studio'.

'Good morning,' said Curly.

'Hi,' said David. I rang earlier about the old black-and-white photograph with the markings I want to remove.'

'Oh Yeh. Let's have a look then,' asked Curly, enthusiastically. He lifted his glasses on to his forehead and studied it.

'No problem. Come back about four o'clock. It'll be roughly forty quid.'

Back on to the street, David turned right into King William Walk. As he turned the corner, he almost bumped into the man who had been taking photographs in the park. He had obviously lost David, and had been walking around the block waiting to pick him up again. He was the same build as the man David had seen running and firing at the Land Rover on Caw.

He was convinced that this was the other German, making sure, well in advance, that this time they were alone. The streets and walkways along the riverside were very narrow, so it would be easy for David to check whether he had any other company. He turned left, then left again down to the river.

The footpath was deserted. As the wash of waterborne traffic lapped at the embankment, the unique aroma of the place, a damp blend of diesel fuel, mud and sewage, conjured adolescent memories.

He could almost recall the stench of the Thames on a hot summer's day in the fifties. God alone knows what it must have been like to live in Woolwich or Charlton. He remembered the trips on bicycles down to the Free Ferry, and then sailing for hours back and forth, the smell of oil and steam from the great brass pistons in the engine room diluting the stench from the river.

The vista from the path, opposite the Isle of Dogs, was always magic to a south Londoner, north to Blackwall on the right, and Tower Hamlets on the left.

He stood looking at the barges for some time and then glanced back the way he had come. Nobody was following, so he decided to lean against the railings, and watch the river activity until it was time to keep his rendezvous.

He should have asked for help, as soon as Fischer had been shot up on Caw. Victoria hadn't contacted him, and probably didn't want to. He ought to drive down to Cornwall and be there for her. He had promised Griff.

He turned around and started to walk back towards the Cutty Sark. As he got to the boat, it was nearly exactly 1.30. He slowly circled the clipper and saw, at the bow, the man in the woollen hat. He had been right.

He remembered the thrill of coming here as a boy, the tang of aged wood under deck, the cramped berths, the feel of what it must have been like on the high seas, thousands of miles from home and loved ones, and, below, thousands of fathoms of icy grave.

Stopping just to the right of, and a few feet behind the man, he took a long careful look around. Nothing obvious.

What he couldn't see was the remote camera, filming him from a window in the building behind them. The directional laser microphone, able to pick up every word.

The man did not look round.

'Good morning Mr Lennox, I'll have to be quick as I'm in great danger. As you saw, my colleague paid with his life. I'm sorry what happened to your friend Mr Mason. That had absolutely nothing to do with us. We want to offer you two million dollars for what you may have. No questions asked; you give me the information when I've transferred this sum into a bank account that you wish.' He remained staring at the boat.

David walked on a few paces as the man took photographs of the rigging. He was about David's build, maybe in his early fifties, his woollen hat covering a shaved or balding head.

'How do you know about Griff Mason's death?' David walked on a few paces.

'Because I know, Mr Lennox. Now, this information?' He started to take pictures again.

'I don't have any idea what this information, as you call it, is,' said David. 'All I know, is that two people are dead, one of whom is…was…my best friend, and it's clearly to do with you, and what you are after. What the hell am I looking for here?'

David walked on another metre or so, noticing as he did so that the other man appeared very nervous.

'You are looking for anything that was given to your father in Marienburg. Just that. When you hand this over, you'll receive the money.' He changed the lens on his camera.

'Supposing what I find turns out to be useless to you. What then?' David asked.

The hairs on David's neck were beginning to rise. It was an old feeling, almost psychic, but he knew that somebody was watching him. He casually looked round at the stern of the clipper, and saw the open window on the second floor of the building by the entrance to the dry dock.

'That's our problem, Mr Lennox.' He started walking back to the stern.

'My best friend's dead. That's ***my*** fucking problem.' David stayed where he was, but glanced occasionally at the open window.

'I said before. That was nothing to do with us. My friend's also dead, Mr Lennox.' Click…wind, went his camera.

'Who was it to do with then?' He strolled back towards the man, still keeping some distance behind him.

'The same people who killed my colleague. They want this information too.' The German looked at his watch.

'Why aren't they offering me any money?'

'I can't answer that. I repeat that I'm authorised to offer you two million dollars for any documents, or anything else, that your father was given in the camp.'

He looked at his watch again. 'I have to leave here in a few minutes, I have a train to catch. It's thirteen forty, no sorry, you say in English twenty before two.'

'Twenty ***to*** two,' David corrected him.

'Yes, of course twenty to two. So Mr Lennox when you have found this information, please contact me on the mobile we sent you. I'll keep in touch. My contact name will be Busch.' He walked off towards the village, as the window on the second floor slowly closed.

David strolled back to Greenwich Village. He chose to wander around for a while to see if anybody was watching him, but after ten minutes it was clear that nobody was.

They were following Victoria and now they were following Busch, but they weren't following him. Yet he had the information that most of them seem to be interested in.

He decided to take a walk up Creek Road, down Deptford High Street and back to Greenwich. He was losing weight daily, and could feel it in his legs. He was almost fit again.

There were forty minutes or so to wait before he picked up the photograph, so he bought a 'Times', and found a little café where he could tackle the crossword

As he was ordering a coffee, a silver Mercedes drove slowly around the corner. David immediately lifted the newspaper to cover his face, the woman passenger had been in the BMW he had reversed into on the way down to Cornwall, but this time he got a good look at her face.

Christina Karranova!

The car drove slowly on around the block and did not reappear. No wonder she had hidden her face on the motorway.

It had been more than ten years, but David still hurt. He had been stupid, and been ruled by his cock, as he had been now with Victoria. He had had to resign, but he had briefed them, ad nauseam, that she had got no information from him at all. His cover was that he was an English teacher, and he had no reason at all to think that she wasn't the engineer she had said she was.

It had been lonely there in Bratislava and she had been fun, warm, blonde and available. She had also been KGB, and a high ranking officer. A classic and easy-peasy set-up, and she had plucked him like a ripe plum.

He hadn't seen her since he had left Slovakia for the meeting at the British Embassy in Vienna, where they told him to take the next flight home to London. They would collect his clothes and belongings and send them on.

Here she was, in Greenwich. She had been on the motorway following him to Cornwall. Had she and the driver been up on the fells the day that Fischer was killed? She was a markswoman, he had learnt later, and fit as a butcher's dog.

The photograph or the pipe, or both, must contain something important, but for the life of him, he could not figure out what. He really needed to meet his ex-employers tonight, to find out what the hell this was all about

Leaving the café in a state of shock at this latest twist in events he walked back to the studio. When he got there, Curly was at the reception.

'Hi. I'm really pleased with this.' He gave David the doctored image and a CD.

David was truly impressed. You couldn't tell that it had been manipulated and he could now safely send the photograph from the CD to some POW sites.

'Perfect,' said David 'How much do I owe you?'

'Call it forty quid,' said Curly, in a way which seemed to convey that it should be fifty but as you are a nice bloke, etcetera.

'Call it fifty,' smiled David, 'but one favour: could you wipe the original image and the final version from the computer.'

'Yeh, sure.' Curly looked a little puzzled.

'It's my real father,' said David, thinking on the spot, 'not the one married to my mother, if you follow me…er…trying to trace him, and it's a little sensitive. Hope you understand?'

'Oh right.' Curly smiled again, but a little wider. 'No probs. Here, come and watch.'

He took David into the studio, rich with the odour of developing fluid, and showed him the files being deleted.

'Don't ask me for another copy now,' laughed Curly, 'it'll cost you another fifty quid.'

David took the original, the CD and three copies of the photograph in an envelope and stuffed them under his coat.

It started snowing as he set out back towards Blackheath, lightly at first, but then heavier and starting to settle. By the time he had walked up the hill and over the heath, it was like a Christmas card scene.

He got back to the flat at five o'clock, chilled to the bone, made a cup of coffee and sat taking in the warmth from the radiators and the hot drink.

The telephone rang twice, and then stopped. He had been dreading this, what the hell could he say that didn't sound trite and worthless. It rang again, and he picked it up before the answering machine cut in.

'Hello Vicky' He heard the choke in his own voice. There was silence for a minute and then she spoke.

'Oh, David,' she was sobbing. 'Oh, David.'

'Vicky…I'm so very sorry.' Jesus, this was awful. 'Are you in Marazion?'

'Yes…please come down. Please come down now…please.' She could hardly speak.

He had brought this upon them, and he should have known better. He should have called for help as soon as he had received the letter, but his bloody ego had ruled his head again. His cock and his ego, those two had been his downfall, throughout his life.

'Yes, of course.' He remembered the meeting at six thirty. 'I'll be down at around midnight. I'm so desperately sorry.' He was floundering. It was his fault and he knew it.

'Please hurry…please. I'm on my own here.' She sounded like

a fifteen year old, and David's stomach churned as he heard her anguish and desperation.

'Can I bring anything down with me? Do you need anything?' He had never felt so worthless and guilty in all his life. He really was a selfish egotistical bastard.

'Could you bring the computer tower?' The sudden flash of hardness made David's sensitive antennae twitch.

This didn't seem at all right. No, it wasn't right somehow.

Chapter 9

The drive across the heath to Severndroog castle, a belvedere tower near the top of Shooters Hill in Castlewood, was a short one.

It was a quarter past six when he parked near the steps leading up to the woods. Large flakes of wet snow were spiralling slowly down, covering the pavement and road in a deepening blanket of white.

He sat in the car, checking the dimly lit street. All the parked vehicles were empty, nobody to be seen, except for a woman walking a black Labrador, who crossed the road and entered the park.

The path was steep, and by the time he had reached the rose gardens below the belvedere, his breathing was laboured.

Two figures were sitting on a bench at the top of the steps overlooking the gardens and what would have been a fantastic daylight view to the south. As he drew closer, he saw three minders behind them in the darkness near the triangular tower with its white framed windows. David recognised one of the seated men as an ex-colleague, Peter French. The other person he didn't know.

French was a civil servant through and through, an ex-career diplomat who had been working for MI6 and the department, on and off, for more than twenty years. He was in his mid-fifties, just over six foot, and a little overweight. He always had a penchant for chalk stripe suits, and David could see, even in the darkness, that this had not changed. He hadn't disliked French, but he had a reputation in the department as a career man, and God help anybody who got in his way.

'Not as in good shape as you used to be, Lennox,' French said, in a seemingly friendly way.

'No, but it's getting better,' he puffed, as he sat on the bench beside them.

'This is my boss, Sir William Rush,' said French, introducing the distinguished looking man on his right. David leant across

French and shook hands with Rush.
The head of department was here? David's thoughts raced. He was now more convinced than ever, that whatever this was all about, it was more in their interests to meet him than it was for him to meet them.
'What can we do for you, Lennox?' French asked, nonchalantly.
'Gentlemen, your people were outside the flat in Blackheath, you're tapping the phone, you followed us all the way from Marazion to London, you filmed me meeting a German at the Cutty Sark. My best friend's dead. I think this is more a case of what can I do for you. Please cut the bullshit, then I'll tell you if I'm willing to get involved or not.'
'You are involved, Lennox, whether you like it or not.' Rush spoke in a very educated and considered RP accent that would have made him an instant star in any film of the forties or fifties.
'What the hell's this all about?' David turned and looked at both men.
'They told me you were good. A rogue element, not always a team player, but one of the best, and I see from your assessment of the situation that you're still an astute observer. Our car team on the motorway were some of our finest. The department had to let you go after the Karranova incident, and you accepted that at the time,' Rush said.
'I wasn't exactly overjoyed.'
'No, and understandably so. Times have changed, and I'd like you to come back, belatedly, into the fold.' Rush's voice betrayed no emotion, and David could not see his face clearly in the darkness.
The snow continued its slow and silent dance, and all three men sat with a light covering on their shoulders.
Like the three wise bloody men. David thought
'Why?' he said, employing the 'Keep it short and simple' philosophy.
'Because it is vitally important to the peace and security of

the world,' said Rush, very slowly and without a flicker of histrionics.

'How?' David was now hoping that he wasn't beginning to sound unhelpful. Christ almighty! The peace and security of the world. Please!

'I can't tell you that now, but I can assure you that your part in this is vital.' Rush brushed the sprinkling of snow off his arms and shoulders.

'What ***can*** you tell me...and who killed Griff Mason?'

'You have information in your possession that is of interest to many people. It's in our interest to find those people, and what they represent. We aren't sure yet, who killed Mr Mason, but we do know that your life's important to them, until they have the information that they want. We'd like you to carry on, as though this conversation never took place. We'll continue to observe. Any intervention from us now will completely destroy years - and I mean years - of work.'

'Do you know about the shooting in the Lakes?'

'Yes, we do now. We put two and two together and...'

'Why are you following Vicky Mason, and not me?' David asked.

Rush flashed a momentary look at French, and David knew that this was what didn't feel right. Something here didn't add up.

'Have you told Miss Mason that she's being followed?'

'Would it matter?' asked David, a strange knot forming in his stomach.

'Yes, it very much would,' said French turning to him. 'It very much would.'

'Do you know that Karranova's following me?'

'Yes,' said Rush, again with no emotion. 'Are you willing to work for us again, Lennox?'

'Is Karranova involved in this?' David was looking at the ground, which now had a good covering of snow.

'It seems they've an interest,' said Rush.

'What gun killed Griff Mason?' David's sense of something

rotten in the state of Denmark, was now almost overpowering.

French answered ' Glock 10mm.' He avoided David's gaze.

'Glock 10mm,' echoed David. His mind was reeling. "A professional job," Detective Inspector Walsh had said, "one behind the ear and one to the back of the neck." That was a bloody assassination. Glock 10mm...The Mossad.

'I didn't get Griff Mason killed, did I?' he asked, a light beginning to dawn.

'No, I don't think you did.' Rush got up and brushed himself free of snow. 'Are you with us?'

David really didn't know, but he felt more alive than he had done for years.

'Yes.' It was as though someone else had answered for him. He stood up, and the three men shook hands.

'We'll transfer sufficient funds to your bank account. Good luck,' said Rush.

'Nice to have you back, Lennox,' said French. 'We'll contact you, if we think it necessary.'

'You mean I'm on my own.' David pulled a wry grin.

'Yes, you're on your own.' French and Rush were heading back to their minders as French spoke. They disappeared into the darkness beyond the tower, and a car engine purred into life.

He started back down the steps to the terrace, and wished that he had brought the night vision goggles, or at least a torch. Thankfully the snow was now falling heavily, creating some reflected light to help him find his way.

As he turned right at the bottom, onto the path that would eventually take him down to the car, the barely audible sound of a twig snapping underfoot to his left stopped him in his tracks. He sensed a presence a few metres away in the trees. The Gurza was nestling in his coat pocket and he slipped the safety catch off as he struggled to see something in his peripheral vision.

'Mr Lennox, I have a gun pointed at your chest and I will not hesitate to use it. I'd like a few words with you, then I'll leave.' The accent was not easy to identify, it was dark and heavy with a hint of Slav.

David's grip was getting tighter around the butt of the Gurza. 'Carry on,' he said, 'you have my full attention.'

'I'm sure your meeting with French and Sir William was very enlightening. However, I don't think they'll have been very open with you. I represent a country that is, for the most part, friendly to yours, I know both men well...'

'Mossad generally looks after its own,' interrupted David, guessing, but not wildly. 'Why did you kill Griff Mason?'

'Because...because it was necessary. Your friend was a pawn who didn't realise the gravity of the game in which he was a player. He donated large amounts of money to causes that were fronts for serious terrorist groups. He thought he was helping the Palestinians, who he believed were oppressed. He was being used, and in the end, when he knew he was dying, his political naïveté became dangerous to the security of our State. Mason was funding terrorism, Mr Lennox, and MI6 knew that. Your arrival on the scene complicated matters a great deal. At first we didn't know how you were implicated, but now you are. So, we would like to offer you a deal to give us the papers that you have, and for you to quietly disappear from the scene. Doesn't that sound like a wise man's way out? You are fifty-one next birthday, time to call it a day with a fine nest-egg. Two million pounds sterling, Mr Lennox. Two million cash, to an offshore bank account that nobody will ever trace.'

'I happen to think that the Palestinians are oppressed too, actually.' David was angry and dismayed at what he was being told about Griff. 'And until you guys wake up to the fact that some of you are acting exactly the same way the Nazis acted towards the Jews of Europe, there'll always be a problem in Israel and Palestine.'

'I am but a humble servant of the State, Mr Lennox. Two million pounds.'

Obviously Griff hadn't told them anything, otherwise they wouldn't be offering him so much money. What the hell was in the photograph and the pipe? What was Victoria's role in all this?

Was she also connected to her father's funding activities?

It was just like Griff. A dyed-in-the-wool socialist from the sixties. But to get himself killed. For what? What had he been funding? He probably had no idea about the extent governments would now go to fight terrorism. One life eliminated, to protect the hundreds of innocents who would otherwise have limbs blown off, be blinded, or die in agony from their burns, was more than worth it.

'I'll think about it,' said David, wondering if they had broken into the car. He hadn't heard the alarm, but these guys had some sophisticated bits of kit. It would be child's play to this outfit.

'Don't think too long, Mr Lennox. This is very important to us. If you consider giving it to other parties, we'll be forced to act. I hope you understand.'

'I get the general drift,' said David.

'I'll be in touch again, Mr Lennox. Goodnight.'

The man turned away in the darkness and walked off down the path beside the green to the south.

It was snowing steadily, and there was a good coating on the car when David got back.

Seven vehicles back, on the same side of the road, was a Volvo with two men sitting in it. It was the SAS type and the 14 Int. man, the two tails he had seen on the first day in Blackheath opposite Victoria's flat. This time, they wanted him to know that they were there. That's why the Israelis hadn't touched the car.

David felt a knot of fear forming in his stomach and the cold hand of death tapping on his shoulder. He shivered, banged his shoes against the tyres and climbed in, glad to get out of the snow.

Chapter 10

It would take him five to six hours to make it to Marazion, if the snow didn't get any worse. The two department men didn't follow him, and on the way he paid very little attention to following vehicles.

As he joined the M4, the weather worsened slightly. The snow was wet, and dirt and grime sprayed up from the other traffic, making driving difficult.

He tried to make sense of the last week's events. So many people wanted the photograph, or was it the pipe? Or both? What secrets did they hold that was worth so much to them?

The road conditions began to improve, so he made good time down to Exeter. He called Victoria as he pulled off onto the A30. The phone rang for a long time before she answered.

'Hello…hello.' She was slurring and obviously blind drunk.

'It's David. I'm just past Exeter, should be there in two hours, between 12.30 and 1.00am.'

'Okay…um …I'm off to bed…wake me when you…you know.' The phone went dead.

David was glad that she had been so drunk, and hadn't said more on the phone. They would certainly be tapping the line, by now. He would check the house for electronics in the morning, when Vicky was sleeping it off.

The problem was how much to tell her. Victoria knew far more than she was letting on. Was this why she had wanted him to come down to Cornwall and visit them? It had seemed so innocent then, and so suspect now.

He arrived at the house at just past one o'clock, and prayed that she had put the key in the place that they always left it. The door was locked, so he put his hand up to the top of the door sill by the fanlight, and there it was.

Letting himself in, he took all his stuff, including Victoria's hard drive, from the car. The lights were on in the kitchen and the lounge, but no sign of Victoria, so he put the computer in the office, and took his bag up to the guest bedroom.

Quietly, he opened the door to Vicky's room. She was fast asleep and snoring gently. A bowl was beside the bed, and the sour smell of vomit hung in the air.

He checked that there was some mineral water on her bedside table, shut the door, and went to bed. He found it difficult to sleep after the concentration of the long drive, and it seemed like hours before he drifted off.

The dreams came again. Novak, Griff, Von den Bergen, Voss, Rush, French, the guys in the photograph. Busch was on a beach, the same one where Novak had thrown the pipe into the sea in a former dream. He was looking at his watch. 'It's ten before two,' he said. Griff was looking at his watch too and pointing again at the men in the photograph. Novak was playing with the Cat, and smoking the pipe. Voss was looking over the Wall and shouting something at Novak. Rush, French, Christina Karranova, Victoria and the Mossad man were on a spectators' stand, watching without reaction or comment. Fischer carried his own brains in a plastic bag, which he gave to Victoria in the stands.

He woke early, found some liver salts in a cupboard for Victoria and went up to see what state she was in.

As he reached the top of the stairs and knocked gently on the door, he could hear vomiting.

'Please don't come in now. I feel like shit, and I look like shit…sorry.' She retched again.

'I'll leave a cup of tea by the door, and there's a medicinal drink here too. Drink them both and you'll feel better. I'm going out to get a paper. If you want anything just bang on the floor.' He heard her 'thanks', followed by more gagging.

The sun was peering out from behind the clouds as he made his way down the hill to the village. He walked to the sound of the seagulls' shrill cries and the shingle being drawn along by the waves. It didn't matter where in the world he was, if he heard a seagull, he thought of Cornwall.

The paper had an article on Griff's murder, and there was a

half-page obituary. No mention of a shooting, just that he had disturbed burglars and had received a blow to the head. He had died from a brain haemorrhage, several hours later, whilst lying untended on his studio floor. The local police had conjectured that it was a case of professional art thieves, and Griff had disturbed them in the act.

David bet that the local police were fuming at being told what to conjecture. French and Rush must have moved very fast to suppress this one.

He lit the fire in the lounge. When it had started to crackle and spit, he cleared up the empty bottles, the debris of Victoria's binge last night.

Two glasses. One had a trace of lip gloss the other did not.

Inside the dishwasher, two plates and two sets of cutlery. The rubbish bin contained two pizza boxes, and under the salt cellar on the table, a bill for them.

The pipes rattled as she ran a bath, and there were sounds of movement from upstairs, so he climbed the stairs and called through the bathroom door.

'Are you feeling better now?' he asked.

'I feel terrible, but the liver salts have helped, thank you. I'll be with you in a little while.'

He took the detector from his bag and went downstairs to check the rooms. Nothing anywhere. It was a fast sweep, but this little bit of kit was good and would have registered anything untoward. He decided to quickly scan the bedrooms.

His bedroom drew a blank, the same with Griff's bedroom. In Vicky's bedroom, the LED display lit up like Oxford Street at Christmas, one in a socket by the bed, one in the alarm clock cum radio, one in the light fitting above the bed, and one behind the bedside cabinet.

This was professional, but who? David put his money on Mossad, after what he had heard last night in Castlewood. Interestingly, they were all around the bed.

They wanted her pillow talk. Was that why she had come to his bed, to avoid being listened to? Did she know her bedroom was bugged? Who shared the meal and wine with her last night?

She was sleeping with somebody whose pillow talk was of interest to an intelligence service. Whoever it was, the conversations had to be of some significance.

He put the monitor back in his sports bag and went downstairs. Ten minutes later Vicky appeared, looking totally drained and hung-over. She had a vulnerability about her, which seemed to David to make her even more stunning and desirable than before. She immediately burst into tears, and threw herself into his arms on the sofa, sobbing and shaking uncontrollably for what seemed an eternity to David.

'It'll be okay.' He stroked her hair, pathetically repeating the phrase.

Suddenly she leapt to her feet and started to rant at him.

'It's that fucking photograph and all that shit with your father. I wish we'd never got involved. Why did you come down here? Your best fucking friend. Why did you do this? Why didn't you tell me sooner that there'd been one death up in the Lakes already? You know a whole fucking lot more than you're telling me, and my Dad's dead. ***Dead!*** What about me? Am I next? You told Dad and me that you'd retired years ago from that shady, seedy, little job that you did. When I was a teenager I was really impressed by all that James Bond crap. You couldn't talk about this, and you couldn't talk about that...Bollocks! My father's dead and there's a massive cover-up going on. This isn't a fucking game. Griff's lying in the mortuary with two bloody great holes in his head, and they won't release his body to me because of the post mortem and forensics. Come on, Big man. Pull some strings, play the mystery man and get my father's body back, so I can bury the poor bastard.'

She ran out of the room sobbing, and slammed the door so hard that little grains of plaster and dust fell from the ceiling. A Troika vase fell off a shelf, smashing onto the floor below.

The pottery breaking, somehow summed the whole mess up for David, but he knew that he hadn't been responsible for

Griff's death. Griff had been responsible for his own death, according to the Israelis.

Why hadn't she asked him who could have killed Griff and why? Was he murdered because they thought that David had passed on the information that they all wanted, and were so keen to spend a fortune on? Was his visit the catalyst in all this? They couldn't wait any longer, fearing that Griff was in possession of something vital.

If that had been an act by Victoria just now, then it had been worthy of a BAFTA award, it had been genuine hurt and anger, but was it really directed at him?

He didn't know what to do: to stay or to go. Several hotels overlooked the bay, and perhaps he should book into one, just for the night. Or was that the easy option? He could hardly leave her alone in this state.

Well okay, he could do something positive. He got the phone directory and rang the local police to find out who was in charge of the investigation into Griff's murder. He was given a number in Truro and the name of a superintendent Marshall. He rang and was put through.

'Superintendent Marshall.'

'Good morning Superintendent. My name's David Lennox, you don't know me…'

'On the contrary Mr Lennox, your name's been bandied about more than most today.'

'Ah, I see,' said David, not seeing at all. 'Look, it's on behalf of Miss Mason, she's very distressed about not having her father's body. I know the coroner's rules about forensics and…'

'The rules seem to have been rewritten, Mr Lennox. I'm not a happy man about any of this, but I've had my orders and that, as they say, is that. I'll arrange to have Mr Mason's body available today. If you'd please instruct undertakers to collect, then we'll all be happy. I hear you have upset my colleagues in London as well, Mr Lennox.'

'I seem to have upset everybody,' said David, 'but thank you for your help.'

'Don't thank me, Mr Lennox. Thank whoever's pulling the strings here.' He hung up.

David looked in the Yellow Pages and found what looked to be the funeral parlour with the most age and gravitas. A Mr Sims said he would pop round to the house after lunch.

He sat trying to read the paper, but couldn't concentrate on anything but the photograph and pipe.

Novak had been a mining engineer and an explosives expert. So that must mean that the Nazis had used him in that capacity. So there had to be a tunnel or a mine system or systems that he'd been involved in. Something they wanted or didn't want to get discovered was in there somewhere.

The photograph and the pipe were clues of some sort, but what? The triangle between the four guys must be important, but he couldn't trace them, or their camp. He must get the digitally revised image published on some POW Internet sites to see what turned up.

Victoria came back down the stairs an hour later, looking as though she hadn't stopped crying since she had stormed out.

'I'm sorry David, I don't think it's good for you to be here just now, I've a lot of stuff to do and…you know.'

'Yeh, sure…er…I got Griff's body released and, I hope you don't mind, I fixed for an undertaker to call. He should be here sometime soon. I'd, of course, like to come to the funeral, Vicky.'

'Yes of course…I didn't mean…you know.'

'I know,' said David. 'Vicky, I have to talk to you about your Dad, there are things that you should know, but now doesn't seem right, okay?'

'Yes, okay.' She wasn't interested in anything but him going, David could see that.

'I'll just get my things.' He went up the stairs to pack his bag, and could hear Vicky's sobbing from the room below.

The telephone rang as he was zipping up his bag. Victoria was raising her voice in anger, so he went to the top of the stairs, where he could listen to her half of the conversation. The volume was suddenly muted as the door to the lounge was slowly pushed to.

'Of course I haven't asked him. No, well live with it. He's going now…I don't know, do I? Yes it's here. No I don't know where they are…look I'll ring you later…yes…YES! I have to bury my father, you insensitive bastard. Yes, I will…tschüs.'

TSCHÜS? 'Jesus Christ!' he gasped.

The German 'tschüs' or 'goodbye' had been involuntary and automatic. He crept back to his bedroom and waited, pretending to be packing. He heard the lounge door open, and could almost feel Victoria listening there, wondering if he had heard anything. He waited for a few minutes and then went down.

She was at the bay window, looking out to sea and the Mount.

'I'll be off then. If there's anything I can do, let me know. I'm sorry you feel the way that you …'

'I don't know what I feel, David...sorry. Drive carefully and I'll phone in a couple of days about the funeral and everything. I'm sorry I dragged you all the way down. I just don't know…I just…' She started sobbing again.

David leant forward and kissed her on the cheek.

'See you,' he said, 'I'll let myself out.' He picked up his sports bag and opened the inner door to the hallway. Through the outer door glass he could see somebody about to ring the doorbell. David opened it, and a short, sombrely dressed man, in his early fifties, was standing looking at a clip-board.

'Mr Sims?' enquired David.

'Yes that's right, you must be Mr Lennox.'

'Good afternoon,' said David 'I'll just get Miss Mason. Please come in. Vicky, the undertaker's here.'

'Coming.' He heard her blow her nose.

As David was getting into the car, Sims was going into professional mode.

'Terrible business, Miss Mason. Terrible shock, must be. Leave everything to me.'

He turned the ignition key and drove up the slope to the road. Griff's murder was on the national and local news. Nothing new. French and Rush had done a good job.

All he could think about was Victoria's use of German.

Had she been talking to Busch on the phone? Had he pretended not to know that David wasn't in The Lakes, and had known very well that he was in Vicky's flat in Blackheath?

It was around Exeter that David pulled in for some petrol. When he went in to pay, he bought a sandwich to curb his hunger, eating it as he walked back to the car, and thinking of the long drive ahead of him.

Christina Karranova was sitting in the front passenger seat of his Land Rover.

Chapter 11

She was one of the most beautiful women he had ever known, turning heads wherever she went, and keeping them turned. An honours engineering graduate from Charles University in Prague and a star pupil of the KGB training institute in Moscow. Best shot of her year on both indoor and outdoor ranges. She had been born and raised in the high rise flats of Petrazalka, the Slovak version of the Bronx, on the other side of the Danube from Bratislava city centre.

Her engineer father had given most of his free time at home to the extra-mural tuition of his son and daughter. She, fluent in German, French, Russian and English, had risen quickly through the ranks of the KGB. Her younger brother, struck by a Soviet military vehicle, at the age of twenty-three, whilst crossing the road three hundred metres from their home, never awoke from a two-year coma.

After all these years there she was, sitting in the front passenger seat of his car. He opened the door and got into the driver's seat.

'Hello, David Lennox.' She didn't look up, her eyes hidden by her long blonde hair.

The Slavic drawl was pure sex. He had forgotten the thrill of her voice and the smell of her. It was raw aphrodisiac; that was the only way to describe it.

Damn! He thought he had got over this. He fumbled with the keys.

'Hello, Christina Karranova.' He avoided looking at her; because he knew that then he would be finished. 'Any particular reason I shouldn't throw you out, right now?'

'I could be saving your life,' She raised her head.

'Well that's an interesting start. Where are we going?'

'I'm coming to stay with you, if that's all right?' By her tone, she knew that it would be all right.

He drove off, onto the motorway. 'Is your friend following us?' He looked in the rear-view mirror.

‘No…and he’s not my friend’ He could hear the smile in her voice. ‘He’s very angry about your stunt on the motorway, and I’ve still got a stiff neck.’
‘Sorry, but I didn’t know who the hell was in the car, and I wasn’t going to get out and ask. Did you enjoy Blackheath?’ he asked, still not wanting eye contact.
‘So, you saw us. No, not very much, I got a little jealous, when I saw you with the girl. I didn’t expect that, and my new colleague doesn’t smell so good in the car…’
‘New?’ he asked.
‘Yes, the first one, who smells better, is at the embassy with a broken collar bone and torn neck and knee ligaments. You have his gun, I think.’ She laughed out loud. ‘He has a very battered ego and’s in big trouble for losing the gun.’ She laughed again.
‘Well, you can tell him that my crutch still aches, if that makes him feel any better.’ David said.
They both laughed and Christina leant across and gently kissed him on the cheek.
‘I’ve missed you, David Lennox, and I know I’ve a lot of explaining to do.’ She kissed him again, but David pulled away.’ He wasn’t going to be ruled by his cock again.
‘Why should I trust you?’ He still didn’t look at her.
‘You were sent home before I had a chance to explain. I promise to tell you tonight, when we can talk seriously. Now, I want to know everything that has happened to you since that little flat in Bratislava.’
‘Well…’

They spent the next few hours talking about old times and recent times, and it seemed very little of it had passed before David was pulling up the drive to the Tower.
‘It’s so beautiful here,’ she sighed.
‘Is this your second visit?’ he asked, innocently.
‘No, this is my first visit.’ She looked into his eyes. ‘No really, I haven’t been here before.’

He parked the car and went round to get his bag from the boot and found two of hers beside his.

'Hell, you're pretty sure of yourself, aren't you?' He tried to sound less aggrieved, but couldn't quite manage it.

'No, but I'm sure you'll want to listen to what I know,' she smiled.

'It's good to be so predictable.' He picked up the luggage, pretending to strain as he lifted them. 'What the hell have you got in the bags, are you staying for three months?' he said as he led the way up the stairs to his apartment.

'We have to travel, David,' she grinned.

'We? Take a seat.' He dropped the bags in the lounge.

'It's such a beautiful flat, David.' She went to the window to look at the view north, to Caw and to Harter Fell, just visible in the bright moonlight.

'Would you like a drink?' he asked.

'No thanks, not now, but a shower would be nice…that okay?' She put her arms around his neck.

'I'll get you a towel.' He prised himself loose and went upstairs to get one, then led her to the guest bathroom. 'Give you a guided tour when you come out,' he said.

Returning to the lounge, he tried desperately to think clearly. For some reason, he trusted her.

She came out of the shower wrapped in the towel, and picked up her bags.

'Where do I sleep? Can I sleep with you?' she asked.

God, she smelt good.

'Sorry. I need to know a lot more, about everything,' he said, 'put your stuff in the guest bedroom, there's plenty of room in the wardrobes.'

He was determined that he would not succumb to her charms, until he was sure of the full picture.

'Okay,' she answered, the disappointment obvious in her voice.

'I'm going to have some red wine?' he said, walking back to the lounge.

'That'd be nice, I'll be there in a minute,' she called, pulling a sweater over her head.

David opened a dusty bottle of Charmes-Chambertain, and left it to breath a little.

'Where's that wine?' She put her head around the corner, smiling.

'It's on the side there. Are you hungry?' he asked.

'No. It's too late for me, but you go ahead.'

'Too late or me too,' he smiled.

It was as though the years had been swept away. They were both back in the flat in Bratislava, laughing, happy in each other's company. Carefree, he had thought. Well here they were again.

She raised her glass.

'Cheers. It's so nice to be with you and to talk to you again. I feel at home. Mmmmm, you have expensive taste in wine, this is lovely.'

'Explain.' He tried not to sound and look too harsh, so grinned wryly. 'Now, please.' He stopped grinning. 'My life took a nose dive after meeting you. No job, and nearly drank myself to death. Explanation please.'

'All right. Seriously, I'm so sorry for that time. I had fallen in love with you and I missed you a lot, it was no act. In the spring of 1990, just after the wall came down, my bosses told me that you were staying at the Forum Hotel in Bratislava. Yes, I made eye contact in the bar, and yes, it was my job. I didn't know you were in British Intelligence and at first neither did my station boss in Bratislava. You must remember that then we were Czechoslovakia, and the old ways of the KGB and the GRU still ruled. The European Union and NATO were in the future, you understand…'

'You didn't know I was an Intelligence operative? Why did you pick me up then?' he said angrily.

'You were one of fourteen people named on a list given to a Stasi investigator in Meiningen, East Germany. The Soviets told us to contact you and find out anything to do with your father's time as a prisoner in Stalag XXB in Poland. Twelve on this list were past prisoners, and two were sons of prisoners. They got your details somewhere from West Germany, where you were posted, and then found that you were in Bratislava, supposedly as an English teacher. So you lied to me too, David.'

'We lied to each other.' he put down his glass.

'Yes we did, but I promise, at first, as far as I knew, you were just an English language teacher. I was told that it was absolutely vital to get any information I could from you, to visit you in Britain, and perhaps meet your father and mother. They told me repeatedly, that it was of the highest priority to get that information, whatever I had to do. That's why I slept with you at first. But it became a pleasure, and I grew very close to you.'

'Somebody approached my father some years ago, but why were they interested in me?' David asked.

'You were in Germany for some years, and they linked this in some way to your father's stay in Marienburg, in the camp,' she said.

'But why?'

'Maybe they thought you were looking for something. I'll tell you what I know about that later. So, I reported to my ministry that I had very close contact with you, that I'd asked you about your father's time in Poland…'

'I remember that now, it seemed so innocent, as though you just wanted to get closer to me and my family. I knew nothing about my father's time in the camp, actually very little about his war, he never spoke about it,' he interrupted.

' Yes...yes. I told them this, so they told me to drop it. That day, I came home to be with you, without any double dealing, and you were gone. No note…nothing. A man from the British embassy in Vienna came a few days later, to collect your things. He didn't speak much, only collected your things and left. I cried for days.' Her eyes were glistening now and David desperately wanted to go over and kiss her.

'Carry on,' he said, warmly.

'Some months later on, I learnt you were a senior operative with a very secret unit, linked to 22 SAS and 14 Intelligence unit, and I found out that you had to resign because of me. Your people know that I didn't ask for any information about your work.'

'How long have they known?' David was beginning to think that they had known from the beginning.

'They've known for a long time.'

'Why are you still involved, and who else is concerned?' David was wondering how much to tell her.

'Later, after you had left, I saw some papers relating to your father and the reasons they wanted some important information from him. It seems that your father, and it has to be your father because all other leads came to a dead end, met a Jewish prisoner who gave him a map or something similar, in Marienburg, in late 1944. A camp guard murdered this man shortly afterwards. The Jew was a Czech, Joseph Ibrahim Novak, born in Poprad, now Slovakia, in 1905. He died in Stutthof concentration camp in February 1945.'

David didn't betray any facial signs that he already knew this.

'I repeat, why are you involved now?' David poured her some wine.

'My mother's unmarried name was Novakova. Joseph Novak was her father, my grandfather.' A tear rolled down her face.

David sat riveted.

'You realise that other groups of people seem more than interested in this 'map'? How many are you aware of, and why are they interested?' David wanted to know a lot more before he discussed the photograph and the pipe.

'Your friend Griff was killed by the Mossad because of his donations to the Palestinians. It's clear that he didn't know that most of the money was going to fund terrorism, but I must show you something, and I want to play a video recording we took recently.' She stroked the top of his hand across the table.

'Do you want some cheese?' David moved his hand away.
'No thanks.' She went to her bags and came back with a pretty hefty pack of papers.

She handed David three photographs, one was outside the flat in Blackheath, the other outside a building somewhere in Israel to judge from the signs in the background. The third was somewhere in a war zone.

In the first photograph were two people. One was obviously Vicky. The other was an Arab-looking man in his mid-twenties to early thirties. They were leaving her flat in Blackheath. The date and time were on the bottom of the photograph. 23rd November 2001. 08.10. London.

The second photograph was Vicky with two men, one was the Arab in the first photograph and the other was the German who called himself Busch. 28th November 2001. 15.46. Beirut, Lebanon.

Victoria's 'Tschüs', thought David.

Christ! How many people were setting him up here?

The third showed Busch, the Arab and a man with a long beard, dressed in combat uniform. It was dated 18th June 2000. 14.54. Grozny. Chechnya.

'The Arab is a Saudi, Faisal al Masri, a very high-ranking Al Qaeda fund raiser and quartermaster. The second is Hans Jürgen Gehrling, former Stasi officer and KGB operative. He was based in Thuringia, East Germany, and is now a freelance seller of anything, from nuclear materials and technology to Heckler and Koch sub-machine guns. He's based in the old East Germany, in Eisenach. The third man, with the Kalashnikov, is Dzhokar Maskhadov, a Chechen warlord. The lady you know, I think.'

David's head was spinning, but he kept a poker face. What the hell was coming next? Christina handed him another photograph it was a copy of a German newspaper from Meiningen, and pictured two men, the two men who had been on Caw, Busch and Fischer. David read the German caption underneath. Berkach, 28th March 1988.

"The two officers investigating the brutal murder of Artur Leimbach have drawn a blank so far. Hans Gehrling and Johannes Zapf say that they have no leads at the moment and urge local people with any information to come forward."

She handed him another newspaper clipping, this time from June 1988, and from the same Meiningen newspaper.

"The murder victim Artur Leimbach, whose body was discovered in Berkach, in March of this year, was living under a false identity. His real name was Robert Jan Voss born in Trnava, Czechoslovakia in 1910. Anybody knowing more about this man should contact…"

'How was he murdered?' David asked.

'Tortured. It took maybe two or three days. He was gagged and drugged with sodium pentothal. The drug stopped his heart in the end; I saw the report in a Stasi file. We think it was Gehrling and Zapf, they knew about his false papers and went to question him about that. He was wanted for war crimes, so he panicked and started to offer them something to buy them off. It was Voss who clubbed and tortured my grandfather to death in Stutthof. He was a camp guard there in the Waffen SS. The orders to get closer to you had come from information first sent by Zapf, through his KGB controllers. Voss had something they wanted, but we think he only told them a little of what they needed before he died,'

'What is it that everybody wants? What does the "map" show? Something hidden, obviously.' David took a chance. 'A lot of the information about Voss, I knew, but you must understand, I want to be very careful here. I believe what you've told me, but I need more.'

'There's one more photograph you must see.' She pushed the photograph across the table. It could have been of the Mossad man he had met in Castlewood, but it had been dark. 'Aaron Har Shoshanim, a very senior operative in Mossad and a marksman. I believe you saw how good he is, up here on the mountain.' She looked for more papers.

'Ah, I thought that might've been you. I saw your file on my return to London, you have a reputation as a shooter too.' He was beginning to get a picture. 'So there's the Mossad, and your lot I presume, the SIS in Slovakia.'

'We're cooperating with the former KGB, now the FSB, the British and the Americans. We're cooperating as much as they are, which means, when it's in our interest,' she answered.

'I was supposing that this was to do with buried Nazi treasure, but it must be much, much more than just that, surely?' David poured more wine.

'There's a fortune buried somewhere, but you're right, there's much more to it than that,' she affirmed.

'Care to tell me, how much more? Because Zapf was offering me a million dollars just before he was shot, Gehrling bid two million, and the Mossad two million pounds sterling.'

'We knew about the German offer, but not the Israeli's. I can't tell you any more, because we don't know all the details and nor does anybody else, or so they say. Do you have this map David?'

'Not exactly, but I've a small problem here. Victoria Mason has all the details that I have, and she asked me to take the computer tower with me in the car to Cornwall, which I did.'

'That's not a problem.' She grinned from ear to ear, 'We wiped her hard drive when you were at the police station in Blackheath.

David shook his head and laughed.

'You Slovaks.'

'What else does she know?' Christina looked worried.

So, now it was crunch time, he thought.

'Are we going to work together?' He looked her straight in the eye.

'Yes, I'd like that.' She held his gaze.

'Are you going to let me down…?' He swallowed the 'again'.

'I didn't let you down last time, David. I was doing my job.' She half smiled.

'Thank God you didn't say, just following orders,' he said, with some feeling. 'Good, I'm going to get something for you to look at. Put the kettle on, and we will have a cup of coffee.'

He got up to go to the car, and the hidden cache.

'When you get back we must watch the video tape.' She went to the sink to fill the kettle.

'Is it pornography?' He grinned.

'I'm afraid it is a bit.' She didn't smile.

When he returned to the flat, which was now thick with the aroma of freshly made coffee, he handed her the letter from his father.

'Where did you find this?' she asked, sipping from her mug.

'In the spine of a book.' He sat opposite her, aching to make love to her but determined not to.

'How did you know where to look?' She was very thorough, very KGB.

'I'll come to that later.' Now he was in the driving seat.

'What of the man…er...Von den Bergen?' she asked, referring to the letter.

'He was a senior SS officer in the same unit as Voss.'

He showed her the original photograph.

'The measurements between the figures is odd, it's an upside down triangle at a slant. Thirteen centimetres along the base and seven point two along the sides.'

'Why did you measure it?' She really was thorough.

'I didn't, Vicky Mason did.'

She raised her eyebrows at that news.

'What does the 1850 mean, here on the back, and the Tale Of Two Cities? Was that the book where you found the letter?'

'Yes, as my father says, he was worried after the break-in, and hid the letter for me to find. The Tale of Two Cities is in his writing. The 1850, I've no idea.'

'Is that all?' She was studying the photograph intently.

'No, I tried to identify the people in the photograph with old war records and prisoner of war camp records. None of it fits.'

'Does the girl know all of this?' She looked worried.

'Yes, and this.' He passed her the pipe.' I'll get you a magnifying glass.' He went to the office to get one.

She took the glass and went to the stand under the kitchen spotlights. 'Star of David. Top triangle six,six,six. BK…B… GK, Burgmühle. Any ideas from clever Miss Mason?' She couldn't hide the contempt, and some jealousy, thought David.

'No, nobody had any idea on this one,' he admitted.

'Did Griff Mason know all this?' she asked.

'He saw the photograph and the pipe, not the research we did on the Internet. I've had the photograph digitally cleaned up, to remove the names, and will put it on-line tomorrow to see if anybody recognises a face.'

'I think we have to put our heads together, and quickly, David. The Mason girl's dealing with deadly people, and she knows as much as you and me.'

She went to her bags again and took out a video tape. 'It's important you see this, David.'

He took her upstairs to the television lounge and inserted the video. Nothing but darkness at first, and then a light going on. It was Victoria's bedroom.

'I missed the camera in my sweep of her room.' He shook his head.

'No, they took it out some time ago, the battery was flat and we had what we wanted.'

Some muffled voices from off screen, and then Victoria got on the bed naked. A man followed, his back to the camera, he too was naked. Victoria rolled the man over, and started fellating him. Now his face was visible. Faisal al Masri!

David wasn't saddened, but he was beginning to see the enormity of the situation that Griff had been in, and Victoria still was.

'I don't want to bore you with the sex scenes, David, but she's his lover and that's important for you to know. It was just coincidence that Zapf and Gehrling knew your name, that one of their clients was al Masri and that his mistress knew you.'

Victoria was on top of al Masri now, and as Christina fast-forwarded the film, the sexual antics took on a comic

Chaplinesque absurdity.

When the action was obviously over, she pushed the 'play' button. Vicky and al Masri lay in each other's arms. He spoke first, in a very educated English accent.

'Educated at Harrow school,' smiled Christina.

'Ungrateful bastard,' said David.

The sound wasn't great, but it was good enough. Al Masri spoke first:

'Zapf says that Lennox must have the map. All the other leads have drawn a blank. He and Gehrling are going up to Cumbria next week, to try to buy it from him. I have to be very careful, the Mossad know that I'm in Britain. I entered under a false passport from South America, but if I stay too long, they'll find me. If only a half of what the Germans say's true, it could be the most important thing that's ever happened to our organisation. We must get that map from Lennox, you must write to him again or go up there, whatever it takes, sleep with him, whatever. It's that important. After you have the map, I'll have him killed.'

She rolled on top of him. 'I only want you inside me. Supposing he hasn't got it, or his father hid it, or destroyed it. What then?'

Al Masri shifted her off him, sat up and lit a cigarette.

'He must have it, he must.' He laughed, 'and all this, thanks to a Jew.'

After he had finished half the cigarette, he stubbed it out and rolled on to her. Soon they were making love again.

Christina stopped the video.

'So, now you know that this little girl's in, very deep, with one of the world's most dangerous men. This is why I might be saving your life, David Lennox.'

'My local doctor's surgery was burgled. Someone looked at my medical records. Who and why? Did you know about that?' David asked.

She looked puzzled. 'Well, it wasn't my people. I wonder why they wanted to look at your medical files?'

‘I’d assumed that it was done to let me know that they were there. I presumed it’d been Zapf or Gehrling, but Zapf appeared genuinely worried when I told him about it.’ David looked at his watch. ‘Come on, time for bed.’

‘You know how to talk to a girl,’ she said, smiling.

It was a magical smile, which he had only seen on the lips of Czech and Slovak girls. It was both innocent and mischievous at the same time, and it never ceased to send a thrill through him.

‘After you.’ She swept her hand in a low arc. I remember that you told me you were a member of the Black Douglas clan, “jamais arrière”, is your motto, isn’t it?’ She was laughing now.

She linked her arm in his and lay her head on his shoulder and let him lead her to the bedrooms.

‘It feels so good to be with you again.’ She squeezed his neck. ‘Don’t let go of me this time, please.’

He kissed her forehead. ‘Don’t worry…I …don’t worry. I need time to think, okay.’

As he closed the door, he saw that she was still looking at him from outside her bedroom, as the opening to his, narrowed to a thin chink of light.

Chapter 12

The telephone woke him at eight-thirty. He struggled to get his arm out of the knot of sheet and duvet cover that had twisted around him during the night.

'Hello. David.' It was Victoria. 'I'm really sorry about yesterday. I was out of order, so upset, sorry.' She was crying. 'The funeral's the day after tomorrow, Monday, two-thirty. There's a short service in the church in Marazion, just to keep the family happy, then on to the crematorium in Truro. I'm not asking anybody to make a tribute or any crap like that, and I'm not inviting everybody back here. Couldn't face it.'

There was a tiredness and a hopelessness to her voice, but at the same time the hardness he had heard before.

'I'll be there at around lunchtime. Do you need help with anything?' he asked.

'No the undertaker, Sims, has been great.'

'Okay, as long as I can't do anything.'

He remembered the fast-forward sex scenes from the video. 'I'll see you Monday then.'

'David, I'd like to talk, but I'm so upset, you know.' She started sobbing again.

'No problem. Take care, we'll talk on Monday.' He hung up.

'Victoria Mason?' asked Christina, putting her head around his door,

'Yes,' said David. 'Griff Mason's funeral's on Monday afternoon. She didn't say anything about her computer, so she can't have tried to use it yet.'

'You're going to the funeral, of course?' she asked.

'He was one of my oldest friends.'

'I'll get up,' she said, 'we've a lot of work to do.'

After breakfast, David took the photograph and the pipe from the temporary hiding place, at the back of the pots and pans.

'Here you go,' he said handing them to her.

Christina studied the photograph intently.

'So, you put the photo on the World War Two prisoner sites. I'll concentrate on linking Von den Bergen with my grandfather.'

She took the pile of notes they had made and started to sift through them.

David found several sites he had visited before, and began contacting them. It was two hours later, when he was in the kitchen making a cup of coffee, that Christina shouted for him to come in. She was peering into the screen.

'I've got the war crimes charges for Von den Bergen and Voss. Both charges are for Nordhausen concentration camp and Buchenwald. They relate to the death of thousands of Jewish labourers who worked in the secret underground factories for V2 rockets and other secret weapons. There's a note that the East Germans reported Voss dead in 1988, it lists his alias and place of death, which we knew. They didn't find Von den Bergen. He disappeared from Stutthof at the end of the War. He was also in the SS Devisenschutz Kommando, which took all the currency and artwork from the occupied territories. At the end of the War he was involved in hiding gold, silver, platinum, paintings and weapons, at sites all over Germany. One strange thing. The man in charge, General Dr Hans Kammler, disappeared, and all mention of his name in the Nuremberg war trials was deleted. He wasn't even charged, even though he was responsible for the development of the concentration camps.'

David thought for a minute.

'So our mystery photograph man from Buchenwald could've been with your grandfather Joseph, both of them working in the underground tunnel systems. And all the top men have just vanished into thin air.'

Christina nodded and took her cup of coffee from David. 'Thanks.'

'It seems likely, that your grandfather was being used by Von den Bergen and Kammler for his mining and explosive skills. Could you have a look for all the buried treasure sites in Germany and a map of the concentration camps? I think there's going to be a strong link between Joseph Novak's movements between camps, and mine sites used for hiding the loot.' David sat and looked at the photograph again.

Something was bothering him, something tangible, it was like a name you had on the tip of your tongue. It was nearly there, but not yet. It was something to do with time, the dreams, Griff looking at his watch.

Half-an-hour later, Christina had two maps printed out, along with some other pages of information. The first was a map of German concentration camps. She circled those connected to her uncle; Buchenwald and Nordhausen, then north of Hannover to Bergen-Belsen, north of Berlin to Sachsenhausen and finally east to his meeting with David's father in Marienburg and his death in Stutthof. The second map was a map of Germany in April 1945. It showed Nazi treasure finds, ODESSA escape routes for gold and art treasures, and land in German and Allied hands.

'Jesus.' said Christina.

'Well…well,' David looked at the printouts.

Everywhere that Joseph Novak had been in the concentration camps was near a buried Nazi treasure site. One was the Merkers salt mine in Thüringen, near Buchenwald and Dora Nordhausen and very close to where Voss had died in Berkach. David read aloud from the printout.

'After the Reichsbank had been damaged in 1945, they moved one hundred tons of gold bars and millions in currency. They took forty-five cases of paintings to the Kaiseroda mine near Merkers and other treasures to Heiligenroda and Bad Salzungen close by. All of these are very close to Buchenwald and to Berkach,' he said, looking at the map. 'Göring had blown up his mansion after clearing it of his massive hoard of looted treasure, gold and paintings. The route that this treasure took, went south via Thüringia on its way to the intended destination in Berchtesgaden, but it didn't all get there.'

David thought aloud.

'Why did Voss stay in the vicinity of Merkers and Kaiseroda after the war? Why did he stay so close to the border, actually right on the border with West Germany? Did he know the location of a hidden mine complex somewhere close by, and one day found himself on the wrong side of the wall, and trapped, powerless to do anything about it?'

'What's the time David? My watch has stopped, must be the battery.'

'Er…five to one.'

'Can I have another coffee please?' she asked.

'I'll put the kettle on.'

As he made the coffee, he was again bothered by questions about time. He had been troubled when Gehrling had said 'ten before two' down at the Cutty Sark.

The computer announced 'You have mail.' David stood behind her as she sat at the keyboard.

'You take a break and I'll read it,' he said.

It was from a Charles Stoney:

"Dear Mr Lennox,

I happened, by chance, to log on to a site that I hadn't looked at for a long time. I was uploading some newly discovered POW letters from my father, and saw the photograph and message you had posted there.

I recognised my father in the photograph. He is Staff-Sergeant James 'Jimmy' Stoney, and is sitting with the cat on his lap, in the front row. The picture was taken, I believe, in early 1943 at Stalag X1 B, Fallingsbostel near Bremen. His regiment was the Grenadier guards.

My father passed away in 1997 and I had not seen this photograph before. I have attached some other pictures taken at the camp. I do know that the chap second from the left in the back row is Lance-corporal William Kenton. My father didn't talk much about the War, but I know that this chap volunteered for paid work. He went to a lead mine somewhere in the Harz Mountains along with a hundred and fifty other Airborne Division chaps from the camp. Some of them had been miners in the Midlands and North-East coalmines before the War. My father didn't go with them, but told me that this chap had been sent to Buchenwald for continued escape attempts, had been shot by the SS, and was buried somewhere in Germany.

He had been a friend of my father's, and my Dad had wanted to visit the grave, but we couldn't trace it. If you have any information on this man, I would appreciate it.

I hope this has been of help,

Yours sincerely,

Charles Stoney."

David stared at the screen, excited but confused. The man must know his own bloody father. So, who the hell was Ted Hill? Kenton must be the man who gave the picture to Joseph Novak in Buchenwald. Did he first meet Novak in the lead mine?

'What is it, David?' Christina read over his shoulder.

'This doesn't make sense.' David looked at the original photograph. 'It says Ted Hill. What are we missing here?' he asked.

'Look at a site about Stalag X1B, maybe there's a story or history of this lead mine. Dora concentration camp was near the Harz Mountains. Kenton may've worked with my grandfather.'

Christina took the photograph from David and started to study it. Minutes later David found something.

'I'm into a site about Stalag X1B…result! A hundred and fifty men from airborne divisions volunteered to work in the lead mines at Bad Grund, Harz. They were paid for their work, and after their keep was subtracted, they had a little spending money. There are some pictures from X1B here; let's have a look and enlarge them.' He clicked on a photograph.

'There's Newal.' Christina stabbed at the screen excitedly. She compared the two photographs 'Yeh, it's definitely him, look.'

David took the photograph back and held it up to the screen.
'Yes it's definitely him. Only one problem, it says here that his name's Private Bill Masterson.'
He clicked on another camp photograph.
'There's Stoney, and it says Stoney. There's Masterson again, and it says Masterson, Kenton, and it says Kenton. No sign of Breem or Dumas yet, but I've a feeling that they'll have other names as well.'
They looked at several other photographs before he found Breem and Dumas in separate groups. Breem was unnamed, but it was clearly him, and Dumas was identified as Lance-Corporal Geoff Underwood.
David logged off the site and turned to Christina.
'I'm going to make some more coffee.'
She was deep in thought.
'So, these names must to be a code for something, but what?' She wrote the names down on a writing block. Sgt. 'Batty' Newal, N.Breem, Pte.L.Dumas, RSM.Ted Hill.
'Here,' he said, handing her a mug. 'Let's have a look. Bad Grund's only fifty kilometres from Dora, and about a hundred and ten from Buchenwald. Kenton must've tried to escape from the lead mines, and was sent to Buchenwald. I wonder whether we can establish that he met your grandfather in the mines at Bad Grund, as well as in the concentration camp. Did Kenton and Joseph Novak know the location of a hidden shaft or mine complex, or something?'
'What's the time David?' She cuddled into the cushions, as he came and sat with her.
'Ten to two. Jesus Christ! It's 13.50. That's it…that's it!' He leapt off the sofa and grabbed the photograph.
'What's it?' Christina had spilt her coffee during David's explosive departure.
'The 1850 on the photograph, is the scale; it's ten to seven. Ten to the power of seven…ten million to one. Thirteen centimetres in the photograph, becomes one thousand three hundred kilometres. Seven point two centimetres becomes

seven hundred and twenty kilometres. That's a huge triangle. The names must represent places not people. Let's look at the names.'

He copied them from her pad, and they both buried their heads in concentration. After half-an-hour Christina broke the silence.

'I can't think of anything, except the letters N.Breem make Bremen.' She leant her head on his shoulder. 'I don't think that's it.'

'Let's have a look on the map. N.Breem on the photograph let's see. Six point eight centimetres from Newal and six point two from Dumas, all in a straight line angled down to the left.' He started up the Autoroute programme on the computer and selected the measuring tool.

'You clever sod. Six hundred and eighty to Malbork or Marienburg as it used to be and, the other way, six point two in a straight line, is London. Sgt. Batty Newal…Newal…Bugger! Of course. It's an anagram of Stalag Twenty B. Pte.L.Dumas, London. Pte.L.Dumas…PLUMSTEAD! My father's letter says that your grandfather lived in Plumstead when he worked at Woolwich Arsenal. How can I have been so stupid, and missed that?'

Christina was at his side, barely able to contain her excitement.

'Finish the triangle.' She jumped up and down on the sofa, on her knees.

'Right. Seven hundred and twenty kilometres from Malbork and Plumstead, it's going to be Berkach. No, it's a town next to it called Mellrichstadt. RSM Ted Hill, there's no A, no C or T.'

'There is when you add CAT,' she said. Her face broke into the widest smile he had ever seen.

'RSM Ted.Hill and Cat. MELLRICHSTADT, and it's just to the west of the old German border, only six kilometres from Berkach on the East German side. Voss must've been separated from Mellrichstadt by the Wall,' he said.

Christina was suddenly sombre.
'As I said before, we have a lot of travelling to do, David.'

Chapter 13

They spent the rest of the day planning the coming weeks. They would go down to Cornwall together, David going to the funeral and Christina doing the tourist thing in St Ives. They would then drive back to London and fly to Frankfurt, where they would hire a car for the journey on to Mellrichstadt. David deleted the email from Stoney, unplugged the computer tower and took it to his cleaner, Anne, for safekeeping, telling her he would be away for some time

The drive down to Cornwall was uneventful, and six-and-a-half-hours later they pulled off the main road at Hayle, on the road down to Carbis Bay and the long hill down into St Ives, where David knew there was a reasonable hotel on the hill just above the town.

He got the bags from the car and they went up to their adjoining rooms, which were a little too chintzy for Christina and stank of stale tobacco smoke, but had a fabulous view down to the sea and Godrevy lighthouse beyond. Christina took a shower while David ordered some coffee from room service and poured them both a drink from the mini-bar.

Some minutes later she appeared through the connecting door, wrapped in a towel. David fought the urge to go up to her and put his arms around her neck.

'Do you feel human now?' he asked.

'Yes, almost,' she smiled.

David looked out of the window at the now dimming light from the sea and the flashing beam of the lighthouse across the bay.

'You said before that we were looking for far more than just hidden Nazi treasure. What else could there be?' He remained at the window, not looking around.

'I'm not sure, David, but it's something that the Arabs are very interested in getting their hands on. Everybody else is trying to stop them.'

‘Weapons, chemicals, germ warfare?’ He turned to look at her.

‘I don’t know, but…’ She looked into her Gin-and-Tonic.

‘But?’ he asked.

‘I know there was a meeting between Al Qaeda people, other Islamic groups and German arms dealers, in Berwang, Austria, in September last year. I believe that Gehrling or Zapf, or both of them, were there.’

‘My first contact with them was by letter postmarked Berwang, at the end of October,’ said David, pacing the room.

‘I think we should visit there on our travels, David. It’s just across the border from Garmisch. Should be no more than six hours from Mellrichstadt.’

David went into his bathroom and ran a bath.

‘Are the German secret service in on this, Christina?’

‘No they aren’t.’ From the nervousness in her voice, David knew she was avoiding something.

‘Care to tell me, why not?’ He came and stood in the doorway.

‘You certainly know of the deals they did with the Palestinians after the Munich Games?’ She poured herself a coffee.

‘Yes, there hasn’t been a terrorist attack in Germany, or on a German plane since, apart from the disco full of G.I.s in Berlin, and that, allegedly, was the Libyans.’ David smiled wryly. ‘Won’t they be a tad pissed off when they find a major operation’s taking place on their territory?’ he added.

‘Our people don’t want to include them,’ she said.

‘Mine have said that I’m on my own on this one. Yours?’ David held her gaze.

‘I’m on my own, until we find something.’ She smiled weakly.

‘What then?’ David saw a look of fear cross her face. It was very fleeting, but it had been there.

‘I don’t know. Que sera, sera.’

Whilst Christina was drying her hair, he got into his bath. When she had finished, she came in and sat on the closed toilet seat.

'David, you know the danger. There are too many interested parties here, and the Mossad are very aggressive. If they thought that they could end this thing with your death, I'm sure they'd kill you now. As long as we're the only people with the map and pipe, we're in danger. Victoria Mason saw the photograph, but does she remember the details without her notes and the computer?' She rubbed her glass between her hands, and looked into the liquid as if expecting to find an answer there.

'She's a clever girl and a journalist, I'm sure she'll remember enough.' David turned on the hot tap to warm up the cooling water.

'Then we must make sure she doesn't pass the information on. Do you understand what I'm saying?' She looked up from the glass and held eye contact.

He stared back, silent for a moment.

'No, absolutely ***no.*** She won't have had the time, or the inclination, to think about it. We'll be ahead, until after the funeral. My best friend's dead for God's sake, and you're talking about killing his daughter. Are you sure that this business is that important? Christ!' he said finally, standing up to dry himself.

'They brought it upon themselves, David, they really did.' She went over and kissed him gently on the cheek. 'They really did.'

'I can't do that. Please don't ask me to do that.' He stepped out of the bath. 'Just ***don't*** ask me.' He put on a bathrobe and sat with his drink looking out at the lighthouse.

Before she went to her room, she kissed him on the mouth and said, 'Goodnight, David. I still love you very much.'

'Goodnight. Give me a little time, all right? All this has been very quick, I'm still confused.' He kissed her forehead. 'It'll be better soon I promise.'

In the morning, she left for the town at around ten o'clock, agreeing to meet him near the New Tate at five. David relaxed on a large leather chesterfield in the lounge, armed with a pot of coffee and the 'Times'.

On page six was a small paragraph about a body found in the South Lakes area, near a walking route. A walker's dog had found the body, which appeared to have been shot at long range with a high velocity rifle. It was the body of a male, in his mid - to late forties, who had been dead for some days and had been stripped of any identification. Police were asking for anybody who had any information to come forward. They said that the body did not match any missing persons on file, and suspected a gangland killing.

David was sure that Peter French would sit on this story, but he would check in with them, if things got out of hand. In the meantime, he must get rid of Zapf's mobile phone.

Dressed in a dark suit and black tie, he checked out of the hotel at around midday, deciding on the coastal route all the way round to Marazion. He took the narrow winding road out past Zennor, remembering many a pint and game of darts with Griff in the Tinner's Arms there.

As he drove, he passed abandoned tin mines along the cliffs; their crumbling stacks silhouetted against the dark-blue-grey of the ocean and the churning white of the breakers.

Pulling up in a lay-by near a disused mine, he took the dead German's phone out of his bag. He climbed the fence by the 'Keep Out. Danger' sign, and removed the SIM card, bending it until it broke. He wiped the phone carefully, and lobbed it down through the mesh at the top of the open shaft. There was a satisfying splash, as it hit water some eighty feet below.

Turning off the coast road, he cut across country to Penzance and Marazion, throwing the pieces of the SIM card out of the window on the way.

He arrived at the house just before one o'clock. Victoria opened the door, looking as though she had not slept for days, the pale white of her face a sharp contrast to the black of her dress.

'Hi,' he said.

'Hi. Thanks for coming.' She hugged him and kissed him on the cheek. 'I was out of order the other day. I'm sorry, it's all been such a horrid shock.'

'Of course.' He returned the kiss.

Several family members were sitting in the front room. One man, bearing a remarkable likeness to Griff, was surely a brother. David reflected that in all the years that he had known Griff he had never once met any of his close relatives.

Victoria introduced him to a sister of Griff's, two brothers and assorted cousins, and he took a seat in the corner. The atmosphere was difficult, and a paranoid David began to think that Victoria had warned them of his coming, and his role in her father's death. She hadn't, of course, but he didn't feel comfortable sitting here in this sombre group. His thoughts wandered, and he imagined Christina on the sea front at St Ives, the chill Atlantic wind blowing her hair into her eyes.

Victoria came back into the room and David went over to speak quietly to her. 'Shall I make my own way to the church?' He took her arm.

'No...no, there's plenty of room. Family in the first cars and then a car for close friends. Dad's coffin will be waiting at the church.' She pulled her arm away, not roughly but firmly.

'I forgot to thank you for bringing the computer down. You didn't drop it or anything, did you?'

Shit! 'No...why?' He tried to sound nonchalant.

'Everything seems to have been wiped. Everything.' There was the hardness he had seen before, and a trace of accusation.

'No really. I was very careful, and it was wrapped in a travelling rug in the back.' He kept eye contact.

'We'll have to load up all the Novak stuff again. I'd really like to work on it with you, if that's still acceptable after my outburst the other day.' She managed a strained smile.

'I have to go back up North straight away after the funeral, but I'll call you tomorrow first thing. All right?' he said.

She knew something. He could see it in her face.

'I heard that the police in London questioned you about Griff's death.' She was looking at her feet, lifting her toes and tapping them lightly on the floor.

'Yes, they did.' He felt how far apart they had become in the few days since her father's murder.

'Did you tell them about the photograph and the pipe, and everything else?' She suddenly looked up and straight into his eyes. The icy coldness in her stare shook him.

'I didn't think it would help,' he said.

'Help who?'

'Anybody.' He held her stare deliberately, and this time he saw fear. He turned away to look out of the window.

She stood behind him and took his arm in her hand. 'Of course you're right. I'm upset, we must talk later.' She went over to take care of her relatives.

Some minutes later there was a ring at the door, the cars arrived and everybody filed out.

It was a very short drive to the C of E church in Marazion; the service was brief, as the vicar had been politely asked not to talk about a man he had only met once at a gallery opening, some years ago. David recognised several faces from the past in the congregation, hoping that he had aged better than some of them.

The thirty-minute drive to Truro and the crematorium, a few miles outside the town, was mostly spent in silence, as nobody was in the mood for small talk. Victoria had asked for Griff's favourite piece of music to be played, and they entered to the strains of Vaughan Williams's 'Fantasia on a theme by Thomas Tallis.'

After a short and simple reading, the curtains closed, and Griff Mason was no more. David felt a numbness, which he could not explain, a major part of his early life was gone, and in such a base and degrading manner. He looked over at Victoria who was obviously inconsolable. What must be going through her head now?

Back at the house, Victoria had fixed some sandwiches, tea and coffee, for the family and close friends. David found her in the kitchen and took her aside.

'I'm sorry, but I have to get off now, is there anything I can do to help?'

'You will ring me tomorrow?' she asked, with a hint of desperation in her voice.

'Of course.' He kissed her forehead and was moving away, but she held his arm in a firm grip.

'Have you got the photograph with you, David? I could photocopy it now, if you like.'

'No, I hid it up at the Tower,' he lied.

'Ah... all right, it'll have to wait then.' She smiled, but it was an effort.

He picked Christina up at the arranged time outside the Tate. She climbed in, leant across and kissed him.

'Hi David Lennox. I've missed you.' Her hair was wild and the way she shook it free from her face sent a shiver through him.

'Have you had a good day?' He drove up the Stennack and the road out of the town.

'Yes, great. And you?' She kissed him again.

'Crap. I hate funerals, and especially with the circumstances of Griff's death, whether he brought it on himself or not. Victoria was really pressing me about the photograph, and she didn't hide her eagerness.' He remembered her grip on his arm.

'I booked a hotel at the airport, and I told them we would be there about ten o'clock...it's a double room,' she said, looking out of the window, grinning. She levered down the sun-visor and tidied her hair in the vanity mirror, before patting his leg affectionately.

The drive up-country was long and tedious, and the farther north they drove, the worse the rain became.

They pulled into the hotel car park at Heathrow at ten-thirty and checked in to a room like a million other rooms. It was clean and comfortable, but nondescript.

Christina swept the place with a device that looked a lot nattier and more effective than David's, pronouncing it free of intrusive ears or eyes.

Sometime around midnight, the call signal sounded on his mobile. The LED was flashing Anne's number, his cleaner at the Tower.

'Hello Anne. Something up?'

'Hi, David, I'm afraid there is. You've had a burglary. The police just called here. They were told at the Tower that I hold a key. I'll go up now, and see what's what, and give you a call from there.'

'You're a star, my dear. Are you sure?'

'No problem, I'll go straight away, don't worry. Talk to you soon.'

'What is it David?' Christina asked.

'The flat's been broken into again. Not your lot is it?'

'No, definitely not. As soon as we made contact, they briefed me that your place wouldn't be touched.' She filled the room kettle. 'Do you want a coffee?'

'Yes please. God it's hot in here.'

He went to the window to let in some fresh air, as he opened the curtains he had a good view of the car park.

Two figures crouched at the back of his Land Rover.

'Hoi!' David shouted instinctively. 'Hoi!'

He grabbed Christina's digital camera, which she had left on the windowsill, pointed it in roughly the right direction, and took a photograph.

FLASH.

Two men turned and ran quickly to another car. One jumped into the front passenger seat and the other into the back. With a squeal of tyres, they were gone.

FLASH.

He took another photograph of the receding car, as it braked at the exit.

'Bugger!' He threw the camera to Christina, grabbed the keys, and dashed down to the car park.

When he got to the Discovery, it was clear that they hadn't broken in.

'Thank Christ,' he said, shivering. He took the contents of the fire extinguisher from their hiding place. Nothing was missing.

'Everything okay?' Christina was stirring a cup of coffee for him when he got back.

'I think so. Let's have a look at the pictures I took.'

She took the camera and looked. 'The people's faces aren't so clear, but the car registration number is. Oh dear, 225 D 276,' she said.

'Official German diplomatic vehicle. According to you the Germans weren't in on this. Is there something you're not telling me? I've a feeling sometimes, that you have pieces of this jigsaw that I'm missing,' he said.

'David, I promise you that my people told me the German secret service did not know of this operation, but I've a hunch that whatever we're looking for's something so important, that our lives count for nothing. I'm not sure whether what I was told, or what you were told, is the truth. However, I think they know you'll find it for them, and after that, you or we are …' She drew her finger across her throat. 'Also, ex Stasi people work in the new security departments of the unified Germany, some of them at the embassy in London. This is certainly an unofficial visit from some of them, if they have contact with Gehrling.'

His mobile rang again. 'Yeh, hi Anne. Yes…I see. Okay, if you could clear up after the police have finished, it would be great. I'll give you a ring or a text before I come back. Could be a few weeks.'

Christina was getting into bed and looked as though she was thinking something through.

'Did you tell the Mason girl that everything was hidden at the Tower?' she asked.

'Yes, I did. My cleaner, says the whole flat has been turned over. Books and papers everywhere, but no sign of forced entry. It's no coincidence. We're going to have to change cars several times in Germany, if we're going to shake off all the people who now seem to be following us. Let's get some sleep.'

He climbed in beside her and felt the warmth of her body against him.

'No sleep just yet, Mr Lennox.'

They made love with a tenderness and passion he hadn't felt for years, it wasn't the raw sex of Victoria, it was a belonging, a giving; a complete surrender of self to the other.

It was home, but was it a safe home?

Chapter 14

They touched down at Frankfurt Main at around noon, and passed through passport control unchallenged.

Making their way to the car-hire desks, at the back of the arrival hall, David saw what he had been expecting. A tail, by the newsagent's shop, nonchalantly reading a newspaper. The man glanced, fleetingly, beyond David, and gave an almost imperceptible nod of his head.

Placing his documents on the car hire counter, David deliberately dropped his passport. Bending down to pick it up, he glimpsed a rather sternly dressed, middle-aged woman, roughly ten metres to his left, who was speaking into a mobile phone.

'Have you seen them?' Christina asked.

'Yep,' said David, producing his driving licence and passport for the assistant.

'Thank you very much, Mr Lennox. Please sign here and… here, thank you. It's a black BMW and it is on level 2, Row 227, number 58. If you walk through the door to your left, you'll see the lift to the floor you require. There's a map in the car.'

'Thank you,' he said.

As they started walking to the exit, he turned to Christina.

'When we get through the doors, we have to cross an exit road to the car park. Turn right, walk down a few metres, and then stop. Let's see if these guys know where we're going anyway.'

He pushed through the doors into the open air and a refreshing gust of icy wind hit them as he did so.

The woman followed first. She glanced briefly in their direction, and carried on to the lifts. The man passed a few seconds later, and did the same thing. The lift arrived after an eternity, and both tails got in.

'Now they're discussing what floor to get out at,' mused David. ' I think they'll split and it'll be 3 and 5.'

'No,' smiled Christina. 'If they're real Germans, they'll both get out at 2.' The lift stopped at 2 and remained there.

'Smartarse,' he said.

'Men are such bad losers.' She pecked him on the cheek.

They went to floor 2 and located the car. No sign of either the man or the woman.

'What now?' she asked.

'Hop in. I'm going to try something,' he said, with a wink.

He took the exit, drove around the block and back into another car park, but down to the basement level. Finding a reasonably crowded row, he pressed the button for a ticket, waited for the barrier to lift, and squeezed in between two four-wheel drive vehicles.

'I think I know what you're doing, Mr Lennox. Clever.'

'You wait here. I'll be about twenty-five minutes. They'll be waiting on the road out of the airport, before the motorway. It's the only exit, they have to hang around there.'

At the railway station, three floors above, he bought two tickets for Darmstadt with his American Express card, making a point of repeatedly asking for the platform number, until he had annoyed the clerk enough to be remembered.

Back to the Arrivals Hall, and the car hire office furthest away from the Hertz desk, where he had first hired the BMW. He was lucky to get a car, a Mercedes, on spec. The Germans would eventually trace it, but by that time he would have checked in for at least another two cars. Her Majesty would have to pick up the bill.

The new car was also on level 2. He stood in the shadows, behind a pillar, for some minutes, watching very carefully for any sign of the two tails. They must be, by now, shitting themselves that something had gone wrong. He paid for the parking on the original ticket and put it in his pocket.

Satisfied that all was clear, he went to the new vehicle and drove it around the block to the basement. He took another ticket, and parked near the BMW to transfer the luggage.

Christina got into the driver's seat, pulled a woollen hat over her head as far down as it would go without looking comical, and angled the sun visor down. David got into the back seat and onto the floor.

'Here's the exit ticket,' he said. 'Take the A3 to Würzburg and then turn right to Hanau. After that directly to Fulda and the A66.'

Four minutes later, he could see, looking up, that they were outside on the short exit road to the autobahn. Christina spoke, without turning around.

'There's a Mercedes parked fifty metres up ahead, with two people in it. Yes, we just passed them and I recognised the woman's coat.' She concentrated on the rear view mirror. They're not moving, well done, David.'

He shifted his weight in the cramped space at the back of the front seats.

'I'll stay here until you take the turn-off. We'll drive to Fulda, park the car, get a train to Schweinfurt, then hire another car to drive up to Mellrichstadt. That should buy us a lot of time. Do you have any false cards and passports, or is that a silly question?'

'I have some. You can choose which ones you want to use. What is the name of the hotel in Mellrichstadt?'

'Hotel Streublick. I've got the number in my wallet. I'll ring when we stop at a service station, should be in ten to fifteen minutes. By the way, it's bloody uncomfortable down here.'

A quarter-of-an-hour later, he heard the indicators clicking.

'Okay David, we are turning on to the A66. Do you want to stop, or are you going to climb over?' She pulled a mocking face.

'Pull over please, and not so much of your cheek.'

She stopped, and David quickly went around to the passenger door.

'Give me a name you want to use for the hotel,' he said.

Christina rummaged in her bag and handed over two passports. They were South African, for a Mr and Mrs Sheehan.

'Good God. When did you get these done?' David looked incredulously at the passport photograph that was an exact copy of the one in his own passport.

'I ordered them from the Lakes, as soon as I knew we were

going to travel together. My people gave them to me in St Ives, when you were at the funeral.' She smiled a little too patronisingly for David's liking.

'Where the hell did they get my passport photograph?' he demanded.

'I found them on the desk at your flat. I took two. One for me to look at,' she blew him a kiss, 'and one for my people. Hope you don't mind.' Her face took on a hurt puppy look.

He feigned indignation, but couldn't quite hide the smile.

When they reached the first service station, he rang the hotel and booked a room. Fifty minutes later they were passing to the west of the Rhön National Park in the north Bavarian area of Unterfranken. He had been watching the road behind them, and was relieved that he hadn't seen anything following them.

The mountains were coated in snow, and the farther they drove, the deeper the snow covering on the fields. David pointed out the Wassserkuppe; at nine hundred and fifty metres or so the highest peak in the area.

A few miles before Fulda, they passed the spoil mountain of the Kaliwerk mines, a huge mountain of waste, a hundred metres high, and topped by a cross.

'The same company owns the Merkers mine,' said David, peering up at the vast monolith of earth and rock.

'Merkers, yes,' said Christina 'where the Americans found Nazi cash, gold and art at the end of the war. I heard that all the money and everything else went to America.'

'Your Grandpa Joseph could've worked in the Merkers mine. It's not so far from Buchenwald and Bad Grund. Most of the slave labour to mine the salts came from Buchenwald or Dora Nordhausen. It's a vast complex, over four thousand, six hundred kilometres of tunnels. The whole area's a maze of workings running from the surface to depths of eight to nine hundred metres. They say that this mine here's linked to Merkers, and that's almost fifty kilometres away.'

'My people briefed me that the tunnels ran under the old border. There was a lot of tapping into NATO cables and very secret exchanges of prisoners underground. Do you think we're looking for something deep in the mines?'

'Mmmm.' David shrugged his shoulders. 'Merkers is a tourist attraction now, maybe we should take a look.'

They took the exit for Fulda Mitte, and parked in a multi-storey car park next to the Hauptbahnhof, the main railway station.'

Christina bought tickets in the name of Jirina Hinnerova and found that they could get an ICE to Schweinfurt at 14.55, a wait of twelve minutes. They found their seats in an almost empty carriage, and settled down to the hour-long journey.

'Do you mind if I sleep for a bit?' he asked, relaxing into the comfortable, soft leather seat.

'No. I think I will too.' She nestled into the upholstery with her arm firmly clasped around the computer bag holding the pipe.

'Are you hungry?' David turned to look at her, as she'd not responded, and realised that she was dead to the world. He studied her face for some time. She wasn't telling him everything, and he didn't like it.

The dreams came again. Voss was sitting on a wall watching al Masri giving Victoria a piggy-back ride, Von den Bergen, David's father, Gehrling and Zapf, were all outside a room padlocked and boarded up with 'Geheim' written on it. 'Secret'. What was the secret? Voss said he knew, Von den Bergen said he knew. 'Do you have a ticket for the secret room?' he asked, smoking the meerschaum pipe. Then he shook David's shoulder.

'Tickets…Tickets'. David awoke with a start, the Guard gently shaking him awake.

'Ihre Fahrkarten, Bitte.'

David sat up straight and stroked Christina's arm.

'Where have you put the tickets?' She looked around in a daze for a few moments and David was immediately in the flat in Bratislava, remembering that look as he woke her every morning.

'Schweinfurt in fünf minuten,' the Guard said as he inspected and franked the tickets

Schweinfurt was the centre of German ball- and taper-bearing manufacture during the war, and as such was a major target of allied bombing raids. In one day, there were seventeen separate raids and sixty allied planes lost. Over six hundred airmen lost their lives as did many civilians in the city. Very little production was affected, most bombs missing the factories and hitting the dwellings, thus some of the old town survives, but precious little.

Oddly, it was here that David's father had been released to the Americans after the death march from the camp in Poland, in the Spring of 1945. The Stalag XXB guards trying to avoid capture by the advancing Russians had marched south to meet the American Army who were approaching from the west.

It was late afternoon, snowing, cold and dark, and the grey industrial town did little for either of them.

'Let's get out of here, please,' said a tired and unimpressed Christina.

They left the station concourse and looked around for a car rental office, finding two in a row of shops nearby. There must have been a shift change at the factories at four o'clock, because the evening rush hour had just started. Traffic was beginning to build up at a bottleneck bend in the main road, where it curved round to the right as it ran parallel to the railway track. The cars were crawling past them, making a depressing slushy noise as they inched through the wet snow in the dull yellow glow of the sulphur-lit streets.

'If you fix the car booking, I'll call the hotel and tell them we'll be there around six o'clockish,' David said, carrying the bags into the rental office.

They loaded the luggage and set off for Mellrichstadt with David driving. Leaving the grim, redbrick factory buildings of Schweinfurt behind them, they headed north and up onto the Rhön plateau. Open fields stretched either side of the road, and beyond, just visible in the darkness, pine forests covered the hillsides.

The temperature was dropping fast as they gained height onto the Hochrhön, where the snow was lying deeper, but the sky was clearing.

'I think it's going to be a very cold night and a beautiful clear day tomorrow.' He patted her arm.

'Are you looking forward to starting our hunt?'

He glanced round at her and saw another flicker of fear. It was only there for a split second, but it threw him.

'I've a bad feeling about this, I don't know why, it's nothing concrete, just...you know.' She gazed out of the passenger window at the deepening piles of ploughed snow at the roadside. 'I'm just tired, David. Don't take any notice of me.' She put her hand on his knee. 'I'll be all right, when I've had some sleep.'

They drove through a succession of pretty little villages along the river Streu until they finally reached Mellrichstadt. On the outskirts of the town, just off the main road to their left, was a tall building with 'HOTEL' illuminated on the roof.

It was a tower block, built, David guessed, at the height of the Cold War. It was functional but certainly not beautiful. This had been, until 1989, the end of the road in West Germany. This is where tactical nuclear weapons would have been used first, as Soviet Bloc tanks rolled through the Fulda Gap on their way to the Rhine. It was the same route the American 3rd Army under Patton had used in the spring of 1945, on their way east to meet the advancing Soviets. It was the original 'Ground Zero'.

David turned at the 'Streublick' sign, and drove in to the hotel car park.

The interior was a pleasant surprise. Lots of carved wood panelling and antiques, quite different from the impression given by the stark exterior. They chose a luxury room in a villa at the other end of the car park. It had a patio, and looked out onto the gardens.

Over dinner, David poured over the map of the town he had

picked up from a display of tourist pamphlets in the main foyer.

'Oh yes!' He took a piece of paper from his pocket and excitedly started to look back and forth from the map to a sketch of the pipe. 'Oh yes!' He handed the map to Christina.

'What? Is it the markings on the pipe?' She started looking at the map and then at David. 'Come on. Don't be cruel.'

'Look at the old town wall.' He was smiling from ear to ear.

'Yes?' She looked up with some impatience 'Yes?'

'Look particularly at the north corner of the wall, marked Number 4 under 'historical sights.' The smile was becoming almost painful it was so broad.

'Oh my God! Burgmühle, built in 1303 and still a working wood mill. Is there a B, a GK and a BK?'

'600 metres to the south-east of the Burgmühle is the Grossenberg-Kappelle or GK, and 600 metres to the west of that and 600 metres to the south-west of the Mill is the town bridge, Brucke, the B. The BK is at the site of the mill. Whatever we're looking for is there.'

Chapter 15

After dinner they decided to walk down to the Burgmühle. The temperature had dropped to around minus ten, as there was no cloud cover in the clear, star-filled sky. A half moon cast an eerie yellowish light on the snow as they walked at a brisk pace, trying to create some body heat.

They passed several allotments, one with an extensive private aviary consisting of several cages full of exotic birds, all of which started screeching and squawking as they neared.

'Bloody birds,' David hissed.

He peered down to the end of the gravel track, where paths ran off to the left and right, fifty metres ahead. He consulted the town map.

'We want the left turn and then a right and we should come to a small bridge.'

Skirting some horses in a small paddock, they saw the mill and the bridge in the lights of the floodlit walk on top of the town wall just beyond. One hundred and fifty metres behind them the birds in the aviary suddenly started to chirp, cluck and crow in alarm again.

Christina caught his arm, hurrying him over the small bridge, down onto the riverbank, and pulled him under the wooden span. As he bent almost double in the small space under the walkway, David's right foot slipped, and he felt his shoe fill with ice cold water from the partially frozen river.

'Bugger,' he moaned

They heard footsteps coming closer and pause above them. A cigarette butt was cast onto the ice, where it glowed briefly before slipping into the freezing torrent. The sound of crunching snow then receded towards the mill and the short path up to the town centre.

'My foot's absolutely bloody soaking. That was probably an ordinary German doing what ordinary Germans do. Taking a fucking walk,' he whispered angrily, as he took off his shoe and poured out the excess water.

Christina couldn't control her giggling.
'I'm sorry David, I know it's not so funny, but you should see your face.' She hugged him.
He put the shoe back on, grumpily.
'Come on, let's find what we have here, and then get back to the hotel before I get frostbite and bloody pneumonia.' He gave her a forced smile.
They clambered back up the bank and looked at the mill, twenty metres to their left. The main building was on the riverbank, the mill-wheel hanging between that and another structure on a small island in the middle of the river. The river actually split before this, going either side of this island and another smaller island upstream. The bridge just covered the downstream tip, so you crossed both flows before they rejoined.
Between them and the main building was a partially covered yard with cutting belts and, attached precariously to the mill building, a large aged crane for lifting the timbers onto the belts. All the equipment was at least fifty years old if not pre-war.
Thirty to forty large tree trunks lay stacked in the open part of the yard awaiting cutting. The sweet smell of freshly sawn pine scented the night air.
Connected to the mill was a beautiful, old timber-frame dwelling house, lights on in several rooms. Above the doorframe, the marks left by the young visitors on Dreikonigstag. The day of the Three Kings, January the 6th. The Christmas trees coming down and being burnt, the children at last able to eat the chocolates that had been decorating them. C+M+B, written in chalk above the door; Caspar, Melchior and Ballsathar protect this house.
'Where the hell do we start looking?' she asked, nervously, keeping an eye on the path, in the direction the smoker on the bridge had taken.
'Let's walk to the other end and see what we can see. My foot's bloody freezing.'
He stamped it vigorously on the snow covered gravel, to

hammer some feeling into his numbed toes.

'Oh, you poor thing,' pouted Christina in mock pity. Seeing the hurt expression on David's face, she added, 'Come on. We'll have a quick look, and then back to the hotel.' She took his arm.

They walked slowly past the mill building, hugging the old town wall to their right. From here they could see the top end of the small, downstream island on which the mill-wheel rested. Upstream they could just make out the other island, which seemed, in the moonlight, to be about sixty metres long. It had a few trees, mostly silver birch, but had no visible means of access, without wading across the river from either bank.

'This is going to be difficult. It's obviously a working mill and the house is lived in. We can't just do it in broad daylight. We're going to have to be very sure of where the hell we're looking, and for what,' David said, troubled.

Christina pulled his arm. 'Come on. Back to the hotel.'

They turned away from the river, up a slope onto a small access road, through an arched gate in the mediaeval wall, and strolled along the cobbled streets through the old town centre.

Behind them, in the shadows, a cigarette glowed once, and then described a graceful arc in the dark, as the smoker flicked it away between thumb and forefinger.

At the other end of the town, a small bridge straddled the river Malbach and the main bridge the Streu. The mill was on the Streu, the two rivers joining near the hotel, a kilometre to the south.

'We're six hundred metres downstream now. This bridge doesn't look old enough for 1945, but the original bridge must've been here. It's the B on the pipe.'

The temperature had now dropped to around minus fifteen centigrade, and his foot was getting seriously numb, causing him difficulty in walking.

'What is the BK at the mill then?' she asked. She noticed him limping and pulled at his arm to hurry him along. 'Only another ten minutes to the hotel.'

'BK? God knows? Let's sleep on it.' He gritted his teeth as he tried to control his wayward foot.

Two hundred metres behind them, at the other end of the old town wall, another cigarette was discarded, as a car pulled in to pick up a hooded figure coming down from the wall.

Chapter 16

Von den Bergen was naked, and making love to Victoria as al Masri filmed them. Novak pointed to the four men in the picture, and Voss sat on the town wall smoking the pipe. Christina shot Voss several times, but he just kept relighting the pipe and laughing. Zapf and Gehrling were playing cards with Peter French and Sir William Rush, and David's father kept saying sorry to everybody.

Suddenly all the players were in a small amphitheatre. The audience were the Israelis, the Arabs, the Germans - all in full SS uniforms - Jewish camp inmates in their striped garb and Prime Ministers and Kings and Queens.

As one, they all looked at David. They said nothing; just looked. A fire alarm sounded in the theatre and David told the assembly not to panic.

'Stay in your seats. Don't move until we've found the problem. Don't move...don't....'

He awoke with a start.

Christina was replacing the phone from the wake-up call.

'That sure was one hell of a dream. You were shouting and tossing and turning, covered in sweat. I had to towel you down at one point. Do you feel all right? You are burning up.' She felt his forehead.

He sat up.

'Christ. I feel like I have a hangover...splitting headache. I need some water.'

He staggered to the toilet, knowing he was going to vomit. He closed the door behind him, so that Christina wouldn't see him removing his bridge, and was immediately hit by nausea and giddiness. His stomach convulsed.

A few minutes later, he felt good enough to swill his face with cold water, and rinse his mouth with mouthwash. He came back to lie on the bed, to escape the feeling of biliousness he had when he was upright.

'David, you don't look well at all. Should I ask the hotel to call for a doctor?'

'No, I'll be okay, just a bug, or something which has disagreed with me. I think I'll skip breakfast.'

He reached for the large bottle of mineral water by the bedside, gulping down the whole litre.

'Is there any more?'

Christina took another bottle, and again David downed the lot. 'I'll be fine when I've had a shower and brushed my teeth. Go on…go and have some breakfast.'

A little later, he began to feel better and opened the door on to the patio. It was a fabulous day, very cold, but the sky was a clear bright blue. The view to the surrounding hills and forests was stunning.

Today they would drive to Meiningen, Buchenwald and, if they had time, Nordhausen. A new autobahn was being built, but it wasn't open yet. Meiningen, in the old DDR, was twenty minutes drive to the north east. There they would look at any archive material they could, concerning Gehrling, Zapf and Voss.

Christina came back from breakfast, holding her stomach in mock pain.

'I've eaten too much. How do you feel David? You look much better.'

'Better, yes. Still feels like I have a massive hangover though.' He kissed her mouth. '***Now*** I feel much better.'

Christina waved a handful of leaflets.

'The receptionist was very helpful, she rang the Thüringisches Staatsarchiv in Meiningen to fix a little room for us to work in for some hours. She also called the archives department at Buchenwald, and they're expecting us too, at around one o'clock.

Five minutes' drive out of the town, after passing through the old border village of Eusenhausen, they started climbing a winding forest road. On the top of the hill, a great swathe of open land stretched right and left.

It was the old DDR border, and in front of them stood an abandoned watchtower. In fact it was a control building, much bigger than the normal towers. Underneath would run a network of tunnels to accommodation blocks and machine gun pillboxes scattered along the forest's edge, behind the minefields. It was pockmarked with what looked like bullet scars. Obviously after the fall of the wall it had become a favourite for target practice.

On the other side was a small Grenzmuseum - a border museum - and a derelict accommodation block, covered in graffiti.

In Meiningen they parked up and set off for the old town centre. They found the Staatsarchiv easily, introducing themselves to a short lady, in her late forties, with dyed red hair.

'Grüss Gott. Oh Ja, We are waiting you together. Sorry, my English is not good, I am Frau Wilk.'

They followed her up to the very large, open plan, first floor, full of shelves laden with years of records and files, and the smell of dusty documents. People broke briefly from their reading, to look inquisitively at the newly arrived pair.

Frau Wilk led them into a small room to the right of the main reading hall. Along the side wall was a large wooden table, upon which was an antiquated microfiche machine and an angle poise reading lamp. In the middle were two worktables with a computer on each.

'Ja...hier ist the room für Sie.' She went to a large book on another small table. 'Hier ist alles...the...,' she waved her hands at all the record shelves in the main hall, '...alles. Ein bisschen ist in the computer and ein bisschen ist hier in the Archiv.'

'This is the main...the Haupt... reference book?' asked Christina with a large, upward inflection at the end of the question.

'Ja genau. Sprechen sie Deutsch?' Wilk asked.

Christina shook her head. 'Nür ein bisschen. Sorry.'

'Oh sorry, alles hier is in Deutsch.'

'When we are home, we can translate everything. Heim…alles übersetzen. Verstehen sie?'

Christina was doing a miraculous job of disguising that her German was pretty nigh perfect.

'Alles okay. You want, you ask. Ja?' Wilk left, closing the door behind her.

Christina was already deep into the main reference book, and was looking at the notes they had made earlier in the Lakes vis-à-vis Zapf, Gehrling and Voss.

'All right, two local papers. We want 28th March 1988. One is the cutting we saw on the Internet the other's in row 32/shelf 6-32/17254/ 1988. How do you feel? Can you get it?'

'Yep, sure.' He wrote the number down, and made his way down the rows to 32. Shelf 6.

He took down the file. Jan…Feb…April… May.

'Shit!'

The microfiche and disc were missing for March. He went back to Christina.

'It's not there. Well, March isn't there.'

'What do you mean, not there?' She seemed almost irritated.

'I mean, my little Slovakian pearl, that it's NOT BLOODY THERE.' He exaggerated the last three words by speaking very slowly and loudly. Outside, several heads looked up from their studies in the reading hall, in indignation. David mouthed a silent 'Sorry,' raising his open hands and shoulders in abject apology.

'Right. Let's look at the cutting we saw. Row 32, shelf 6 again 32/17556/1988.'

'Okey dokey.'

David returned to the alleyways of shelves. Jan…Feb… April…May…June.

'Guess what, and don't bite my head off.' He came into the room and sat down.

'Do we ask the woman, Frau Wilk?' Christina had that worried look again, and David didn't like it.

'Not if we don't want to cause a stir.'

Christina didn't answer. She was clicking through some pages on the computer.

'The 28th March is deleted from both papers.' She typed in Voss. No files found. Leimbach, Gehrling, Zapf, the same.

'Well David, they have done a thorough job.'

'Try underground Nazi tunnels'. David started looking through the main reference book.

'Sure. There are four pages here, where do we start?'

'We can come back to that. Try Von den Bergen.'

Christina was muttering to herself as she keyed in the search.

'Yes. SS Oberführer Matthias Reiner Von den Bergen, SS Totenkopf Standarte 3, Thüringen. Here we are. Secret Nazi tunnels in Jonastal…er…27. 2. 27/14435.'

He ran his fingers down row 27, found the file, but the contents were missing. He stood for a while deep in thought, and looking out of the window at the traffic passing outside.

Fifty metres across the square, two men sat in a parked navy blue BMW, drinking from plastic cups. David pulled back a little from the window, but knew that with the bright light of this clear winter's day, they could not see him, through the reflection. He went back to Christina, who was making copious notes in Slovak.

'Sorry, David, but I write faster in my own language. I'm sure you're going to tell me that the microfiche isn't there.'

'Correct. What are you making notes about?'

'The Jonastal project, I'll tell you all about it in the car. I think we have to come back here, when we have more specific information. Somebody knew we would show up in this area, and they took out any relevant files, long before we got here.' She returned to her furious note taking.

'I fear that this somebody's here now. We have two tails sitting in a blue BMW across the square.'

That look of fear crossed her face again, but only fleetingly. Like a trout just below the surface on a flat calm lake, you know it's there, looking at the fly. There is just the gentlest of ripples on the water then it's gone.

'Are you sure, David?' The composure was back.
David raised his eyebrows, offended.
'Right, my dear. After thanking Mrs Wilk for her help, we'll split up. I'll go back to the car. You have a look at the shops in the square, maybe buying us a couple of nice cakes. Make sure you go right past our friends, and get a good look at them. We'll meet back in fifteen minutes,' he said.
They thanked Frau Wilk for her help, but didn't mention the missing files.
'Kommen Sie wieder, Kommen Sie wieder. Auf Wiedersehen,' she entreated, as she showed them out.
David kissed Christina on the cheek, and took a long detour to the car park. He stopped to browse in shop windows along the way, making sure he wasn't being followed. When he got to the car, he had a good look around the level he was on, and then took his little black box to do a sweep of the chassis.
Flash…flash…flash, by the rear bumper.
He checked there were no CCTV cameras, and got down on his knees. The tracker was dirty, so it must have travelled with them from the hotel. It was probably put there last night, while they slept.
David was certain that nobody had known the route that they had taken from Frankfurt to Mellrichstadt, with all the changes of cars and the train. These people, whoever they were, had been expecting them in this area, had expected them to visit the Staatsarchiv.
He waited twenty-five minutes for Christina before he began to feel a tug of worry in his diaphragm.

A cigarette arched through the air, and landed onto the floor on the other side of the car park in a mini shower of embers.
'Hello David.'

Chapter 17

The rich baritone voice was from the American deep-south. The drawl was unmistakeable.

'Hello Jimmy.' David tried to keep the shock out of his voice.

A man in his late fifties came out of the shadows, from behind a van parked opposite. He was six foot two, had an all-American crew cut and a tanned face, lined from years of weathering in exotic locations.

Jimmy Nolan, a senior operative on every dirty little game that the CIA had played over the last few decades. He was still a big man, and looked pretty lean and fit to David.

'How you doin' boy? Thought they'd put you in dry dock?'Nolan said.

'Well Jimmy, they scraped the barnacles off, wiped my arse, and sent me out to sea again.'

Nolan was a tricky bastard. David remembered the times they had worked 'together' in South America. While the bastard with the pliers had been removing David's front teeth, Jimmy had been sitting on a plane back to Washington. He hadn't exactly dropped David in the shit, but he certainly hadn't helped.

'So. Are we all at sea, David?'

'I don't know Jimmy. I really don't know. You now complete the…er…wolf pack, as it were. What's going on Jimmy?'

'I'm wondering how straight to be with you, I really am.' The American held out his hand. 'Good to see you are well, my friend.'

David shook his hand and saw the spark of truth in Nolan's eyes.

'Why Meiningen, Jimmy?'

Nolan paced a few steps from David, and stood rocking on his feet, looking at the floor.

'All righty.' He turned suddenly, as though he had made a decision. 'My department has been keeping a watch on Miss Vicky Mason. You know her.'

David nodded.

'Until recently, we'd done this with no consultation, if you follow what I mean.'

'I get your drift.' David held Nolan's gaze.

'Then we realized that the world and its fucking mother were all watching Miss Mason, and then… Holy crap! Your face pops into the frame. That was a shock boy, I can tell you. We've intercepted every email, every phone call and every letter from that young lady, for months. So we just waited for you to turn up here in Meiningen. Two South Africans, man and wife, contacting the Staatsarchiv in Meiningen in December. Too easy, my Boy.'

'Can you listen into bloody everything?' David asked.

'Mostly, yeh.'

'And my emails and phone calls, Jimmy? Is this the Echelon programme?'

'Yep. Your people very kindly let us park up our little huts on Menwith Hill, to listen in to everybody. The Echelon operation's our ears to the world. We can listen to electronic traffic in Afghanistan, Turkmenistan, Pakistan, anywhere on the planet. We can hear an MP scratch his nuts in the British House of Commons. So…We usually get co-operation from GCHQ on Echelon, but recently they've been less than helpful, vis-à-vis you and Miss Mason. Any particular reason for that?' He stopped pacing, but continued to rock backwards and forwards, looking at his feet.

Behind them, two women were returning with shopping, to their cars.

'Can we sit, old friend?' Nolan nodded towards David's car.

'Sure, it's just that I'm waiting...'

'She ain't joining you for a while. She's a guest of the good old U S of A for a few days, as a kind of insurance policy, you understand.'

'Your people outside the Staatsarchiv?'

'Yep. She'll be okay, I promise you.'

David looked him in the eye, and again saw what was, for Jimmy Nolan, the nearest thing to sincerity. 'She sure is a looker, you lucky bastard. Cause of your fall from grace, wasn't she? And yet here she is working with you.'

'Why the hell do you want her as insurance? For what?'

Nolan nodded once again to the car and they got in.

'The fact is, I know what they want me to know, but I have my ways and sources. There's a map or a code of sorts, which you may or may not have. From our intercepts of the Mason girl, I assume that you have. But here's the cruncher. Whatever it is, everybody wants it, or is trying to stop it getting to the wrong hands. So I ask myself, why don't they just bang you on the head, and steal it?'

'When can Christina walk?' David looked out of the window at the sky and the clouds that were beginning to form, dark black, snow-filled and heavy.

'I don't know. My people don't trust the Soviets or the Central Europeans, and vice versa. Let's cut to the pay dirt. I've been told to give you a name. But take this first.'

He reached into his pocket and took out something in a cloth. He carefully unwrapped it, looking out of the car window to check for any passers-by. It was a Glock 21 automatic .45 magnum, fitted with a silencer. From his other pocket, Nolan took a box of ammunition.

David could tell by the weight of the Glock that the magazine was already full.

'Do I need it, Jimmy?'

'Yep, you certainly do.' He took out a folded piece of paper from an inside pocket. 'Here is a name, in Sweden. It was extracted from an Al Qaeda operative that we entertained for a while. Unfortunately, we entertained him a little too well, and he's now in the company of all those virgins in paradise. This name's in some way connected to what's happening here. The powers that be have told me to give you this. It was an intercept of a cell phone in Sweden that was used only once, triggered by a word, name or phrase, that has something to do with whatever the fuck all this is about.' He held his hands up. 'Don't ask, I just don't know.'

David took the sheet of paper and read.

"Matti Fjällman, Sweden. Mobile intercept, Gothenburg 10.06 local time, 3rd October 2001. Call made to male with Arab accent, at telephone kiosk in Eisenach Hauptbahnhof, Germany. Intelligence report adds that 3rd October is Reunification day in Germany."

'Who's giving me the gun and this name, Jimmy?'

'There was a high level meeting at the last G8 summit between the Russkies, the Brits and the US. When I say high level, I mean the highest. After that meeting I was briefed, somewhat, and told to give you the name. The gun, was my little contribution.' He smiled wryly.

'Why'? David didn't return the smile.

'I always liked you, and I…well…felt a little guilty over Bolivia all those years ago. I was ordered back, David. Really.'

'Forgive me for sounding a little naïve here, Jimmy, but the Yanks and the Russians talking about this together I can believe, but why the hell should the UK be the only other party present?'

David looked at the name again, with a gut reaction that it meant something to him. The feeling he often had with crosswords.

'Well, with respect to you Brits, I've pondered that one too. Only thing I can see is that they were the three Allied powers at Yalta. Maybe this thing goes way back. Our intercepts of the Mason girl keep pointing that way. All righty, let's be as straight as we can be. I know that you have a photograph, which we guess is a map, and a pipe with something written on it. Those have led you here to Meiningen with the former KGB star Karranova, now working with the Slovaks, who are supposedly on our side. You know she's Jewish, I guess?'

David nodded, slowly. Something was bubbling to the surface and he knew he wouldn't like it.

'Thirteen trips to Tel Aviv in the last four years under different names. Did the tourist bit, but hours of time when she slipped surveillance. Who's she really working for, David? Eh…eh?'

The same nausea he had experienced in the morning, hit him

without warning. Perspiration was running down his face, and the odour from his armpits was sour and pungent.

'There was a German diplomatic car in the hotel car park before we left. They were trying to break into my car, and there were two tails waiting at the airport. Your people, or the Germans?' David asked.

'The Germans know something's going on, but they don't know what. Your visitors, and I'm guessing here, are ex-Stasi people linked to Victoria Mason. Maybe doing a bit of moonlighting.'

'Where's Vicky Mason now, Jimmy?'

'At six o'clock this morning, she was in bed in Blackheath. At seven she was on to American Express asking for flights to Frankfurt on the twenty-first. This Friday. You have two days, my friend.'

So she had figured the photograph out. Or had she?

'Last question, Jimmy. Who authorised taking your insurance packet?'

'I did. I think you, me and Karranova, are being set up. I'm looking after all three of us, I really believe that, David.'

'I'll do a deal, I'm going to drive to Buchenwald and Dora Nordhausen now, and on Friday morning I'll fly to Sweden, but with Christina. I'll keep you informed every night, but on Friday she walks. Yes?'

'All right, I feel a little better about this now. We'll meet on the town wall in Mellrichstadt tonight at 20.00. What's the significance of the mill building?'

'Was that you on the bridge?'

'Yeh, those birds scared the shit out of me, you must've heard me coming a mile off. I nearly froze to fucking death watching you.'

'Well you're good. I'll give you that. For a big man, you're good.'

A broad smile widened on Nolan's face as he got out of the car.

'I need more info than just Gothenburg, Sweden, Jimmy.' David called after him.

As Nolan walked across the car park, David put on his seat belt and looked once again at the name on the paper. Matti Fjällman. Matti Fjällman. There was something, damn it.

The drive to Buchenwald took roughly an hour and a half. David varied his speed from the downright dangerous to a fifty mph dawdle, to make sure he wasn't being followed.

Up the hill from Weimar, he turned into 'Blutstrasse', the 'Street of Blood', which lead to the camp.

He felt the need to slow down, as if speeding along this almost empty road would be disrespectful to the thousands who had perished and suffered the most appalling degradation here. The monument to the dead stood high on the hill overlooking the town of Weimar.

They hadn't known what had gone on here? Christ! They must've been able to smell it.

He drove into the main parking area, making his way to the reception building through several coach parties of schoolchildren, noisily disembarking from tour buses.

David introduced himself in German, and was told he had been expected. He explained that he would like to look around for a bit, and to visit the museum at the far end of the camp first. He left the reception area and its crowds of young visitors, and turned towards the main gates.

The huts had long been demolished, but the electric fences, their ceramic insulators still attached, bore testament to the evil of the place. Only the walkways and streets remained.

He passed the site of hut 17, where Canadian and British prisoners had lived and died. Jo Novak and William Kenton had walked these streets, and Novak had carved the pipe, which David now carried in his pocket.

Taking it out, he held it in front of the remains of the buildings.

'Welcome home.'

The beauty of this place moved him. High on a forested hill, the paradox of the natural setting, and the horror camp that they had built here, was unreal. He laid a hand on the stump of an oak, which in its prime the prisoners had named the Goethe tree, used by the guards to hang inmates.

The museum was at the bottom of the camp, and he walked past the buildings where Uncle Jo Stalin had incarcerated the Nazi SS after the War. Thousands of them had died from typhoid and diphtheria - and so the wheel turned.

Back at the reception area, he was shown to a large room, where several modern microfiche machines sat in a row. Outside, the sounds of the school children in the car park were now somewhat muted, as they boarded their buses for their homeward journey.

He looked for William Kenton first, and after some time, found what he was looking for.

"William George Kenton. Number 44368.
DOB: 3rd July 1908. Gateshead. GB.
Arrival. February 1943.
Hut 17. February 1943 to March 1944.
Seconded, March 1943, for mining labour: Charge of SS. Ofü. Matthias Reiner Von den Bergen. Jonastal project.
DOD: Allegedly executed by Von den Bergen in Mellrichstadt. Kreis Bad Neustadt. March 1944.
This forms part of War Crimes Indictment against Von den Bergen. (See separate entry)."

David gasped.

'Jesus Christ! Mellrichstadt.'

Excited, he looked for Joseph Novak.

"Joseph Ibrahim Novak. Number 43728
DOB: 3rd July 1905. Poprad. Slovakia.
Arrival: November 1942.
Hut 43. November 1942 to March 1944. Permanently seconded to charge of SS. Ofü. Matthias Reiner Von den Bergen. Jonastal

project.
DOD: Allegedly beaten to death by Waffen SS. Hauptscharf. Robert Jan Voss. March 1945. Stutthof KonzentrationsLager Poland.
This forms part of War Crimes Indictment against Voss. (See separate entry.)"

They shared the same birthday. Maybe that was the basis for the start of their friendship?

"Robert Jan Voss. Camp Guard. Waffen-Grenadier Division.
SS.Hauptscharf. Later, SS Totenkopf Standarte 3. Jonastal Project.
DOB. 18th December 1910 . Trnava. Slovakia.
Arrival: November 1942.
Departure: March 1944.
Indicted by International War crimes Tribunal on various charges at several camps. Disappeared from Stutthof KZ Poland, in Spring of 1945. Lived until his death, under assumed name Artur Lutz Leimbach, in Berkach Thuringen. Murdered. Berkach, Thuringen, 28th March 1988 by person or persons unknown."

"Matthias Reiner Von den Bergen.
SS. Ofü. Totenkopf Standarte 3.Thuringen. Jonastal project.
DOB: 4th April 1912. Bamberg. Franconia.
Arrival: November 1942.
Departure: March 1944.
Indicted by International War Crimes Tribunal on several charges at several locations. Disappeared from Stutthof KZ Poland in Spring 1945. Has never been traced, although some evidence that he escaped to South America and later to Sweden. Not traced in Sweden. Presumed dead."

David swore out loud.
'Shit!' He took out the piece of paper that Nolan had given him.

Sweden. Sweden. Matti Fjällman. The Swedish call their mountain region the Fjällområdet. Matti Fjällman, Matti man of the mountains, Matthias Von den Bergen. That can't be a coincidence, can't be. He would be nearly ninety. Could it be him?

Chapter 18

He looked at his watch, it was half-past three, and it would take another hour-and-a-half to get to Dora Nordhausen. Dusk was already drawing in, so he decided to drive back to Mellrichstadt, to have another look at the mill. He could see Dora and Merkers tomorrow.

Half way down Blutstrasse, on the exit from Buchenwald, the nausea hit him again. He stopped the car and retched out of the open door, the sweat soon dripping off the end of his nose.

Falling back into his seat, he waited for the giddiness to stop and his vision to return to normal. His body was drenched. He could feel the sweat running down his legs, as he fought an urge to get out and take his trousers and jacket off, just to cool down. He was burning up.

After five or six minutes, he felt well enough to continue, and drove, with some discomfort, back to Mellrichstadt.

Back at the hotel, he explained that Christina was staying in Weimar for a couple of days, to do some research.

He realised that he must look awful, when the receptionist asked if he was feeling okay.

A look in the mirror, shocked him. His features were drawn and gaunt, the dark bags under his eyes were the colour of storm clouds, in his ashen face.

He had no real appetite, so after a long refreshing shower he decided to go down to the Burgmühle and see if he could find anything. Once again taking the back streets, he was soon passing the aviary, with its cacophonous chorus, and on his way down to the river.

Jet black clouds covered the moon, and big flakes of snow spiralled silently down to the water. The mill house was in darkness, and the floodlights on the town wall were switched off. David wondered why, and stamped about, pretending to put life back into his frozen feet.

No dogs barked, only the sounds of the mill race rushing under the ice broke the silence. He took out Christina's mini torch and made for the back of the wood yard and the two islands beyond.

The first island was reachable, via the mill wheel housing, by crouching down along the side of it, where there was an access platform. The water around the wheel was unfrozen and the strong flow roared past to disappear below the sheet ice beyond.

David got on to the island and found the ground firm, his shoes scrunching on the crisp frosty grass beneath the snow. He started looking around, searching for anything on the trees or boulder outcrops. Nothing.

BK. What the hell was BK?

There was a thick wooden plank, stretching across to the smaller island. He walked gingerly over the small stretch of frozen river that forked here, as it parted to form the mill race. The trees were mostly silver birch, and in the light of the torch he looked to see if anything was carved in the bark or attached to a tree in some way.

Nothing.

BK…B bloody K?

Near the northern tip of the island, was a large rock outcrop, and he crouched down to have a closer look. Nothing, not a bloody thing. He went round to the upstream side.

Something was carved on the surface. It was weathered with age, but there was something definitely there. He plucked some grass and moss, and went to the river's edge, to soak the handful in the freezing water. Returning, he wiped the area clean.

It was a crude, and obviously hurried, carving of a pipe.

There was something else, but it was not clear. David went back to the river, scooped a handful of water and threw it over the carving.

'2W.BK'.

2 metres west, or what? BK…BK?

It was seven forty-five. His meeting with Nolan was at eight o'clock, and although the town wall was only a hundred metres away, he didn't want to rush this search. He would have to get off the islands now, come back later, and hope to God the mill house would still be empty. He covered the torch with his hand to diffuse the light, and made his way back the way he had come. When he was sure of his footing, he turned it off, and stood acclimatising his eyes to the darkness, listening for any sound of movement.

His vision was still trying to adjust, when he heard a sound up on the wall. Somebody was running away south, in the direction of the main town bridge.

He waited for a few more minutes. Something, or someone else, was moving on the wall above him.

'David…David!' It was Nolan, and he was in trouble.

He ran past the mill building, up the slope towards the town, and on to the wall. Fifty metres in front of him he could see Nolan, slumped over the iron railings. He grabbed the American, to pull him upright.

As he did so, Nolan grunted with pain. He was haemorrhaging badly, the blood spilling copiously over David's hands. There is no mistaking the feel and smell of warm blood, David had experienced it many times, and still couldn't stomach it.

A large hunting knife was lodged in Nolan's chest, just below the sternum.

'Come on, Jimmy. Lie here. I'll call an ambulance.'

He lowered Nolan onto the frozen path, the blood forming a growing pool of dark black against the snow, like a thick glutinous gravy.

'Doctor, David.' The words were gargled and blood was gushing out of his mouth.

David knew that the main aorta had been severed. There was nothing he could do. Nolan would be dead within seconds.

'Yes, Jimmy, don't speak. I'll get a doctor.'

Nolan started shaking his head frantically, blood spraying out of his mouth. He grabbed David's sleeve with incredible strength for a dying man.

'No, David…doctor...dying. Doctor, please listen Prussian…'

'Prussian' was the last word that Jimmy Nolan ever uttered. Who was the Prussian?

He lay Nolan's head down on the path, and walked back off the wall to the river bank to clean up. For the second time in two short weeks, David was standing by an icy river, washing blood off his hands.

Four lives lost; Voss, Zapf, Griff and now Nolan. Novak's Legacy. How many more?

He heard the metallic clunk of a gun being cocked behind him, the sound of the rushing water having masked any sounds of movement nearby.

'Put your hands out to the side, you sonofabitch.' This was a New Yorker.

David did as he was told.

'He was dying when I got to him. Why the hell would I kill Jimmy, when you have Karranova as insurance. Why the hell would I? He said he was looking after me?'

'Get up very slowly, my friend, and turn around even slower. Any funny shit, and I'll blow your brains all over the fucking river.'

He turned to face another tanned, crew-cut American in his late thirties, built like the proverbial brick shit-house; one of the pair who had been waiting in the car outside the Staatsarchiv.

The icy water trickled down his arms as he held them aloft.

'Somebody ran off along the wall, as I was walking up to meet Jimmy. He called out to me, and I ran up to help him. He was obviously in trouble, haemorrhaging like a stuck pig, there was nothing I could do.'

A screech of car tyres sounded on the access road beyond the town wall, and another man, in his thirties, came running down the slope towards them. He was not as big as his colleague, but looked just as fit. These were obviously Jimmy's minders.

'I lost him, Bob. He was picked up at the other end of the wall by a car with Erfurt plates. The control box for the wall lights has been forced open, and the wires cut.' He paused to catch his breath. 'Shit…that guy could run,' he gasped.

David thought of the figure who had shot Zapf up on Caw, and the speed at which they had run down the mountain. Could it have been the same person? Could it have been Shoshanim?

Bob put down the gun, and motioned for David to drop his hands.

'Okay fella, Jimmy told us we were looking after you. Fuck alone knows why, but here we are. Did you see the guy running?'

David shook his head.

'No, no I didn't. It was too dark up on the wall.'

'Right, this is what we're gonna do. J.B…' He nodded in the direction of his partner. '...and me, we're going to clean up here, as fast as we can, and get Jimmy into the car. Then we're going to drive you back to the hotel for a change of clothes, and to get rid of what you're wearing now.'

'Have you got a small shovel in the car?' David asked.

J.B.'s jaw physically dropped. 'What, in the name of fuck, do you wanna shovel for? Jesus Christ!'

'Have you got a shovel, please?' David looked towards their vehicle.

'Just give him a fucking shovel, J.B. Let's for chrissakes get Jimmy into the trunk, and clean up before anybody comes down here. Thank the Lord it's a dark night.'

Bob took a body bag from the car, up on to the wall, whilst J.B. ran back down to David, with a small, collapsible US army trench shovel.

He left them to it, and went back, through the millwheel building, on to the islands. Pacing out two metres to the west of the rock, he began digging through the frozen topsoil. A half a metre down, the right hand edge of the shovel hit something odd.

David shone the torch into the hole, and cleared away some earth with his hands.

'YES.'

He lifted out a ceramic container, about twenty-five centimetres deep and twenty centimetres wide. Wiping the soil off, he could see, scratched clearly on the side, the letters BK. All those days pondering the picture and the pipe, and here it was. Whatever the hell ***it*** was.

Taking the box to the river, he carefully washed off the residual mud, wiping it dry with his handkerchief. He then placed it in the poacher's pocket in his overcoat, and after filling-in the hole and covering it with fresh snow, went back to the wall.

The two Americans were brushing up the blood-soaked snow, covering it with fresh handfuls from the slopes above. David helped them, using the torch to look for any areas they had missed. When they were satisfied that they had covered most obvious signs of gore, they went back to their car.

'When you've cleaned up, we need to talk, my friend,' Bob said, looking at the muddied blade of the shovel. 'What've you been digging for?' he asked.

'I thought I might find something. Just a hunch, but didn't find anything. Jimmy knew about it,' David said, hoping the bulge in his coat wasn't obvious.

Bob kept his gaze on the shovel, and then at David and his coat.

'Well, he sure as shit didn't tell us about it. Maybe if he'd shared a little bit of information, he might be alive now. Get in the car, we'll go back to your hotel.'

Once underway, Bob craned his neck to talk to David who was sitting in the back seat.

'Jimmy told us Jack Shit about what he was doing, and before we call in with the news, we need some answers, or my arse and J.B's will be pâté.'

'I'm not sure I know any answers, but I'll really try to make sure your arses stay intact.'

'Don't fuck with me, you shithead. Our man's lying in a body bag in the trunk,' Bob snarled.

'I've known...I knew Jimmy for many years. He was a professional. I'm certainly not happy he's in the boot. It could well've been me. I'm trying to tell you that I'm pretty much in the dark myself. Did you take Jimmy to the meet tonight?' David questioned.

J.B., who was driving, looked briefly at his colleague. Bob spoke without looking round.

'We didn't know there was a meet. We'd just had a meal in the town, and he said he wanted to walk a bit on the wall, to have a cigarette. Then we got a panic signal from his bleeper, which has a GPS positioning system. We're gonna be arse fucked for this.'

David avoided commenting further on Bob's anal fixation. He thought it best not to, in the circumstances.

When they got back to the hotel, the two Americans had a drink from the mini-bar, whilst David went into the bathroom to take a shower. He put his blood-stained clothing into a bin liner, which J.B. took out to the car and threw in the boot alongside Jimmy.

David quietly opened the bathroom window, and placed the ceramic pot on the grass under the sill. He then shut it, and went back to the bedroom to get some clothes. He dressed in the bathroom, returning to find both Bob and J.B. looking agitated.

None of them saw the small laser dot appear in the bottom corner of the window overlooking the car park.

'Okay, guys, fire away,' David said, taking a seat.

Bob spoke first. 'What the hell's going on? Why did Jimmy meet you in Meiningen?'

'He had orders to contact me,' answered David, truthfully.

J.B. sat forward in his seat.

'Why?'

'I don't really know.'

'Bullshit, man. Jesus Christ!'

'He said he was looking after me, and that he was taking Karranova as insurance, to cover his …er…' David couldn't resist it, '…arse.'

Bob glanced at him angrily, not sure if he was taking the piss, but decided to let it drop.

'Yeh….and?' he said, not hiding his dislike of David.

'I said I was going to go to Sweden on Friday, and Jimmy said the girl could walk then, to go with me.'

J.B. studied his drink.

'So my friend, you'd be amazed, no doubt, to learn that one of our female operatives has just regained consciousness after being belted on the head by Miss Karranova, and that Elvis left the building well in time to be able to stab the fuck out of our boss, on the town wall.'

David tried not to react, but could not disguise his sharp intake of breath.

'Yes, that does amaze me. Was the situation clearly explained to her?'

Bob banged his drink down on the table.

'She knew fucking well that she was only there for insurance, on a short stay, buddy. And by the by, she didn't just tap this lady on the head, she nearly broke her fucking skull. Now I ask you again, what the fuck's going down here?'

David was very quiet, and thought for a long time before replying.

'I really don't know. I really don't know, that's all I can tell you. What happens now?'

Bob was up, and pacing the room.

'I have to check in to base. Jimmy was playing this one way out on a wing.'

He nodded to J.B. and tilted his head to the door. J.B. nodded back, and left the room with his satellite phone in hand. David could see him in the car park, shuffling up and down, having an obviously heated discussion judging by the body language and hand gestures.

After a few minutes, he came back into the room and signalled for Bob to join him outside. They had their backs to the window and it was impossible to gauge what their mood was. When they returned, J.B. sat down and Bob looked out at the car park for some seconds before starting to speak, still not looking at David.

'What were you digging for?'

David felt uneasy that the obvious place to look would be the immediate area of the bathroom, as that was the only place he had been alone.

'I told you, it was a hunch. It proved to be wrong. I thought that maybe something was buried on the mill islands, but there wasn't.'

Bob turned and glowered at him for a full minute before speaking.

'You were digging, while we cleared up the mess, and got rid of your old chum Jimmy Nolan in a body bag? That's one helluva hunch, my friend, if not downright goddam disrespectful,' he barked.

'It was important that I looked tonight. Jimmy told me that I had very little time before other players arrived on the scene. I looked, and found nothing.'

'What were you looking for, exactly?' J.B. asked, staring unblinkingly.

'At the risk of upsetting you guys, I have to say that I don't know. Really, I don't know.'

Bob fingered his crotch. 'I have to go piss, can I use your john?'

David nodded assent.

'Sure.'

J.B. kept staring at David, whilst Bob was in the bathroom. David knew he would look in the cupboards, but would he look outside the window under the sill? He heard one of the cupboard doors slam shut. They were on powerful return springs and snapped back, if you didn't get a good grip on them.

Bob came out a few minutes later, and only then did J.B. stop his intense staring. Bob looked at him and then at David.

'OK this is how it is. My people are not at all happy. In fact they're very, very pissed. Now J.B. and me, we're going to leave you. We have to talk to our bosses in Schweinfurt, but we'll meet you, without fail, at the mill at...it's 22.00 now, at 04.00. We want to see where you were digging. Be there or we'll come and get you, and next time we won't be so pleasant. Capish?' he sneered.

He hadn't opened the window, he couldn't have done.

'I think I get the gist of it.' David smiled a sickly grin at him. 'Only one thing, guys, I haven't got another coat. You don't want me to freeze my…er…arse off, do you?'

Bob gave him a look that definitely conveyed to David that he really didn't like him, one little bit.

'J.B. give him a coat. Mine will probably fit better. I'll pick up another in Schweinfurt.'

The laser dot disappeared from the window.

After J.B. had fetched a coat, they took their leave. David waited a good ten minutes before opening the bathroom window and retrieving the ceramic container.

The lid was sealed with something, and it took David some minutes to loosen it. A musty, rancid smell emanated from within.

His heart sank. It was full of ash.

Had there been something in there before, which had just rotted with age? He took a towel from the bathroom and emptied the contents of the container onto it. Just ash and small bits of bone.

'Christ almighty! It's a funeral casket.' This was somebody's ashes.

BK? Of ***course***, it was William Kenton's remains. BK - Bill Kenton. Jo Novak must have buried him there. Was all this just to find the remains of an English prisoner shot by an SS. Officer? So that Novak would finally have justice done? The photograph, the pipe, all this for Kenton's urn?

No. It couldn't be that. He inspected the casket again - nothing there. However, the inside depth wasn't as long as the outside, and tapping the end, it seemed to be hollow. He took a closer look inside, and could see that a crudely formed piece of fired clay had been forced down to the bottom.

He carried it out onto the patio and started to tap it hard against the side of the building. On the fourth blow it broke into three pieces. Out of the bottom of one dropped a piece of thick folded greaseproof-paper.

David unfolded it, noticing that his right arm was trembling again.

Inside was a coded Wehrmacht telegram from Martin Bormann to Heinrich Himmler, a map of an underground tunnel system with map reference numbers and a note in English and Slovak. All were faded but had survived the passage of nearly sixty years buried underground.

He read the note.

"Mellrichstadt. March 23rd.1944.

To be reading this, you must have in your possession a photograph and a pipe, both of which I used to fix the position of this casket. I would ask you to respect the ashes that are contained as they are the remains of my good English friend and very brave man, Bill Kenton, who survived with me the horrors of the camp at Buchenwald.

An SS officer, Ofü.Von den Bergen executed him yesterday, because he knew too much, and was expendable. I am still valuable to this monstrous animal, so I think I will survive a little longer.

The map is of the most top-secret tunnel system ever constructed by the Nazis. Bill and I were used in a special project to create a hidden chamber in the system, and find and map escape shafts. Nobody but Bill and I were left alive after the construction, the SS murdered all the slave labour from Buchenwald after completion, and even the German guards who were in charge of us were buried alive in a side shaft explosion set off by Von den Bergen.

Many of the systems were constructed for stolen treasures, and many others for weapon storage and production. There was also a living area with kitchens, bedrooms, living quarters, communications centre and cinema. The secret chamber (marked with a blue cross) held only five leather-bound books and a very large wooden crate four metres square by five metres high. As soon as these were in place, the chamber was sealed with three rows of brick faced with rock.

These five books, and whatever is in the crate, hold the key to some terrible secret.

Reichsleiter Martin Bormann organised their transport through the tunnel, and he waited until they were sealed in. He sent the encoded telegram before he left. Von den Bergen was instructed to burn it, but did not - I found it later on the floor of his staff car. What it says I have no idea.

We heard Bormann say to Von den Bergen, as he left. 'Die Hölle kehrt jetzt in die Tiefe zurück, wo sie hingehört.' 'Now Hell is back in the depths where it belongs.' Von den Bergen asked him what he meant, but Bormann just shook his head saying, 'Ask the mad dog Hess.'

Whoever you are, good luck. I have no idea when you will read this, if it is found at all. Maybe the tunnel system has collapsed, or maybe it has already revealed its secrets. If you could trace my relatives and tell them of this letter, I would be so grateful. I miss them and love them all very much.

My name is Joseph Ibrahim Novak. I was born in Poprad, Czechoslovakia, 3rd July 1905.

If you would also make sure that Bill's remains are returned to

his family in England, God will take you and keep you in the palm of his hand.
William George Kenton. Born 3rd July (Yes! The same as mine!) 1908. Gateshead, England. Murdered 22nd March 1944.Mellrichstadt.
Once again, good luck to you.
Joseph Novak."

'My God, they were only thirty-nine and thirty-six.'

A secret and sealed chamber with five leather bound books and a large crate. What the hell did they contain that Martin Bormann himself should oversee their safe entombment? What was so important, that every secret service and its mother wanted them? Did they know that they existed, and only the map of Joseph Novak would reveal their final hiding place?

It seemed an eternity since his meeting with Zapf up on the summit of Caw. In reality it was just twelve days. His life had changed beyond belief, and Christina was back in his life.
Or was she?

The map covered a huge area, stretching from Arnstadt in the old East, roughly fifty kilometres to the north-east of Mellrichstadt, and south to Fladungen, Völkershausen, and Ostheim, some few kilometres to the north of the town.

The latter three were over the old border, in the West. It charted a huge maze of main tunnels and side shafts over several layers, going down to eight hundred metres. Some were marked as old, interlinked mine systems, others were new.

A blue cross over a small side tunnel, must mark the secret chamber with the books and the crate, but it was well inside the old DDR.

Several entry points were in the East, but only three in the West. The tunnels around Arnstadt were marked 'Jonastal Projekt', and fanned out like bicycle spokes from a central hub. One of these spokes was a main tunnel system, leading to Meiningen and the three entry points around the Mellrichstadt area.

Why hadn't Voss been able to enter the system if he had got information from Novak? Why did he stay in Berkach?

He couldn't leave the map hidden in the room; any professional would find it within minutes. It had to be outside somewhere.

The coded message was impossible for David to understand. It would be Lorenz or Enigma coded, so he would need expert help.

It had started to snow heavily, as he stood on the patio, peering around the grounds of the hotel for a secure hiding place.

At the far boundary of the area was an old pitched-roof transformer building; the type found all over rural Europe. The map and the telegram went into a laundry bag, and he took a circuitous route around the back of the main building to the bottom of the hotel garden, and the transformer.

The door was locked as he had expected. However, several vents around the base of the building were accessible, and he stuffed the bag into one of these, making sure it wasn't visible from a squatting position. He then retraced his steps dragging a small pine branch, to harrow the snow behind him.

If the snow kept up they would be covered within the hour.

When he got back to the room, he looked around for something to contain the ashes. All he could find was one of his shoe bags, so he carefully transferred them into it, making an oath with himself that he would trace Kenton's living relatives, and return the remains.

Realising that he only had a few hours to go before he met the Americans, he went to bed, but slept fitfully, because the dreams had returned.

Christina was making love to al Masri and Victoria, Gehrling stood looking out to sea, as the rest of the players in the drama looked on. Tunnels stretched out in all directions. Hess came out of one of them rambling and incoherent, in his hand a leather bound book.

Chapter 19

The telephone alarm woke him at 03.15. As he got out of bed, nausea and giddiness flooded through him, he only just made it to the bathroom before vomiting.

Were all the years of drinking catching up with him? He promised himself a trip to a doctor, if it didn't clear up in a few days.

Outside, the snow was now lying ten centimetres thick. He got dressed, pulled up the collar on his newly acquired coat, and stretched his woollen hat down over his ears.

He walked at a brisk pace, this time deciding to go via the town centre, taking the wall route to the meet with the Americans. It was still in darkness, as he climbed the dozen or so steps up onto the walkway, but he immediately noticed that somebody had been there some minutes before him. The footprints were just beginning to fill with snow, and they led off towards the Burgmühle.

He slid the safety catch off on the Glock, following the trail along the path, until he saw the shape of the mill looming out of the darkness. A car was parked on the access road at the end of the slope down from the town, and its interior lights were on. He assumed it was the Americans', as it had Schweinfurt plates.

As he descended the steps at the end of the wall, he could see that there had been a lot of activity in the snow around the car. The footprints from the path led directly to it.

Squinting into the dark, he stayed close to the side of the ramparts. An owl hooted from the trees, then flew silently and low over the river.

The offside back door of the car was not shut properly, but the car appeared empty, there was nobody in the front seats. He used his peripheral vision to see if anything was moving, but all was still. With all the old senses coming back, the gun held out in front of him, he edged forward.

There was something in the back. Something that had legs and arms. J.B. and Bob were stuffed down behind the front seats and were patently dead.

He sensed the wire on the partly open back door, before he saw it. It was a crude and rushed job, but not amateur. It smacked of the Mossad, and he was sure it had been meant for him.

The charge was probably neatly packed under the Americans and would be both explosive and incendiary. By the time the fire brigade arrived there would be nothing but twisted metal and ash.

Why would they kill the Americans? What the hell was going on?

He couldn't leave the car like this. Children on holiday would be going out to play in just over four hours. Anybody could open the door, and get blown apart. He shone the torch into the back, took a multi-tool from his pocket and selected the pliers. He could see that the wire was around the lock button, so it was a purely mechanical device. When the door was opened it was pulled and…

Bob's leg shook and trembled.

'Shit!' He dropped the tool into the car.

It was only a death throe, the nervous system shutting down, but it had startled him.

'Shit…shit…shit…SHIT.'

He knelt down, pointing the torch into the bottom of the door well. He could see the pliers, and they were just reachable, if only he could do it without moving anything. As he groped inside, he could feel a trickle of sweat running down his neck, even in this freezing temperature.

'Come on . Come on… YES.'

He managed to get one finger around the gadget, and flip it out of the narrow gap between the door and the sill, onto the snow. With a great sigh of relief and a puff, he got up, but too fast, and felt another surge of nausea.

'Bugger.' He steadied himself against the rear of the car, until the feeling passed.

Gingerly, he reached round to the lock, and took hold of the wire with the pliers. It didn't feel right. There didn't seem to be any tension on it.

He withdrew his hand, and looked around. Using the torch had impaired his night vision, so he waited a few seconds, to get used to the darkness. He couldn't see anything, but he could taste danger. He slipped the automatic into the front of his trouser belt, and took the pliers again, slowly lifting the wire from the door lock.

It suddenly went limp. Automatically he dived to the ground, hands covering his head.

There was no explosion. Nothing. He got up, wiping snow from his trousers and coat and cursing the cold.

'Sorry to scare you, Mr Lennox. Please turn around, with your hands very clearly in sight. Sadly, on our second meeting, as in our first, I have a gun pointing at your heart.'

Damn! The wire was a dummy.

David recognized the deep, Slavic timbre from the meeting in Castlewoods in Eltham. The voice that had offered him two million pounds. He turned slowly, with his hands out to the side. He couldn't see the man's face clearly, as he was still struggling with his night vision.

'Before we go any further, Mr Lennox, I fixed the wire to the door to make sure you were occupied before I approached you. I didn't want you to shoot me, I hope you understand?'

He came closer and David recognized him from the picture that Christina had shown him in the Lakes. Aaron Har Shoshanim, Mossad.

'Why did you kill them?' David asked, screwing up his eyes to see Shoshanim's face better.

'We didn't, Mr Lennox, did you?'

'How come you're here, at the time I was supposed to meet them?'

'We knew you were to meet them at 04.00. We were here at 03.45. Both men were dying in the car. They'd been shot at close range.'

‘How did you know it was 04.00?’ He was sure the hotel room wasn’t bugged.

‘We have very good listening devices. There’ve been a lot of technical breakthroughs in the last ten years. You should get your people to bring you up to date.’

‘I’ll do that, Mr Shoshanim.’

The other man shifted his weight from one foot to the other. That shook him, the patronising bastard, thought David.

‘I’m impressed, Mr Lennox. And how pray, do you know my name?’

‘ESP, Mr Shoshanim. You should get your people to bring you up to date.’

David could see the man smile, even in the darkness.

‘Touché, my friend, touché. Mr Lennox, I want to have a talk with you and I’d like to get out of here now, before people are out walking their dogs. I’m going to put my gun away, and then I’d like to give you a lift back to your hotel to have a friendly chat. Is that possible?’ He put his gun into its holster, tilted his head slightly, and held out his arms in a gesture of rapprochement.

‘Okay,’ said David putting his arms down.

He followed Shoshanim past the mill and the slip road up to the town. They walked through the deepening snow alongside the river, for five hundred metres, coming eventually to a small chapel on the main road to Ostheim, where there was a car waiting.

Two people were in the vehicle. The driver, a young man of about twenty-eight, got out when he saw them approach and, with a nod to Shoshanim, opened the back nearside door. Shoshanim gestured for David to get in. A young brunette woman, a couple of years younger than the driver, was sitting in the front passenger seat

‘May I introduce Alexa and Isaac. Alexa and Isaac, this is Mr David Lennox, the British agent who has a predilection for beautiful young women, Alexa. Is that not right, Mr Lennox, or please may I call you David? My name as you probably know is Aaron, please let's use first names, all right?'

David nodded assent.

'No problem.'

Only Shoshanim came into the hotel room, and David offered him a drink.

'No thanks, David. I find it dulls the senses. What do you think?'

'I think it'd be a good idea, if we stopped playing mind games. You tell me what the hell you want, and I tell you whether I'm going to play ball. You killed my best friend.'

Shoshanim shrugged his shoulders, resignedly.

'All right, David, I'll tell you what we're about and why. May I take a water?' He nodded at the mini-bar.

'Sure. Help yourself.' David waved away an offered whisky, as Shoshanim drank from an opened bottle of Rhön Sprudel.

'Okay.' Shoshanim explained that for some months they had been aware that someone was trying to sell small nuclear weapons to various Arab groups. They knew from intelligence gathering that these were Soviet-made, the so-called missing suitcase bombs, over one hundred of them. The Soviet minister Lebed broke the news that the weapons were missing, some years ago, but everything was played down as bullshit at the time. The Soviets had labelled him a fantasist.

'Demolition weapons, as the Soviets called them.' David said, sitting forward in his seat.

'Yes. During the Cold War, the Soviets had them stored in tunnel systems, very near the border here, by the Fulda Gap. We believe that when the Wall went up, the Soviets and the East Germans blew a lot of the tunnel entrances and systems themselves, because they crossed under the border.'

He continued, that later, in the shafts in which the weapons were stored, there had been major tunnel collapses. The roof had caved in over several kilometres. This meant that, because they had earlier blown all the other entrances, the Russians and East Germans had no access to the bombs, and decided to leave them there.

It was only after it became clear that information existed from the time of the tunnel system's construction, in the form of a map or a code, they panicked. They had been denying the existence of these small nuclear weapons for many years. If the Arabs or any other terrorist group got hold of them…well!

'The people trying to sell the weapons have already contacted you because they know that the weapons are there, but they don't know how to get into the tunnels, and I believe you have the information to do that. At first, we didn't know what your role in this was, whether you were playing the field, or were being kept in the dark. The Brits, Americans and Russians have been very cagey, and we don't know why. Do you know why David?'

'Cagey about what?' David asked.

What the hell was in the secret chamber that could be bigger than one hundred nuclear weapons?

'There's something they're not telling us, David. Can you imagine what even one of these weapons would do to Tel Aviv, or any other major city?' the Israeli said, gravely.

'I can tell you that I'm not playing the field. If I'd been doing that, I would've accepted the biggest offer, and be swinging in a beach-hammock in Mauritius. I'll be honest with you, I'd of course figured out that this must've been linked to weapons of some sort, but I can assure you, I've been in the dark throughout all of these, ever more bizarre, series of events. Did you kill Zapf on Caw?' David asked.

'Yes we did.'

'We?'

'Yes I did,' Shoshanim admitted.

'Is Christina working for you?'

David saw Shoshanim's hand close fractionally. The Mossad man looked at the floor, moving his head from side to side. 'Yes and no…'

'What the fuck does yes and no mean?' asked David, angrily. You be straight with me, and I'll be straight with you, my friend.'

'Yes and no. Please let me finish. She works for the Slovaks, but she's a Jew. Worried about what she wasn't being told in all this, she came to us as a kind of insurance. We share some information that isn't forthcoming from our other, so-called partners. She's afraid for her life, and yours by the way. We have her safe with us now. She thinks...'

'Why did she belt the American woman hard enough to kill her?' David interrupted again.

Shoshanim was very careful to look David straight in the eye.

'Because David, the woman was going to kill her.'

'Did you break into my doctor's surgery, and look at my records?'

'No, we didn't. Is that relevant?' The Mossad man look puzzled.

'I really don't know, but it scared the shit out of Zapf, seconds before you blew his brains all over me.'

There was a knock on the window, and Shoshanim drew the curtain back. It was Alexa, breathing into her cupped hands, and stamping her feet in the falling snow. She motioned to the door of the villa, and Shoshanim went to let her in.They talked in the hall, before he put his head around the door.

'Alexa has been monitoring the German police radio frequencies, David. They've just been called to the mill, so we've only a little time. Victoria Mason's arriving in Frankfurt tomorrow at 13.15, so I guess she must've worked out where to start looking. Did you find anything around the mill area? We know from your conversation with the Americans that you'd been digging.'

David drew in his breath and made a decision.

'Yes I did. Yes.'

'Do you have a map?' Shoshanim glanced at Alexa, momentarily.

'Yes I do, but I have it well hidden.'

'David, I'm going to take a chance here. I don't want to threaten you again, but this is so important to my people. Do I have your

agreement that you'll keep us informed on this?'
'As far as these weapons go, if they're there, yes. You have my word.' David promised.
'All right. Will the Mason girl be looking around the mill area?' Shoshanim asked.
'Yes. It won't take them long to work it out.'
'Well, she won't have a hope for at least a week, it will be roped off as a major crime scene by the local Police,' said Shoshanim, smiling.
'I'm going to Sweden tonight. Where's Christina?'
'As I said, she's safe with us, but you're both in great danger. Gehrling wouldn't've killed the Americans at the mill, why would he? It has, per se, put the mill area out of bounds for at least a week.'
'Well who the hell killed them then?' David asked.
'I don't know. I just don't know. Is Sweden relevant to all this?'
Alexa pointed nervously to her watch, and Shoshanim nodded and rose from his chair.
'I've agreed to keep you informed. As of yet I don't know whether it's relevant or not,' said David, as he got up from his chair to see them out.
'Okay, David, we have to go now, to avoid any police road checks. I notice you haven't used my first name. Do you have a problem?'
'You killed my best friend. I'll get used to it, all right?'
'Okay David'
'I want Christina with me in Sweden,' David demanded.
Shoshanim took a pen from his pocket and scribbled a number down on the hotel map of Mellrichstadt.
'Call this number before you leave for the airport, and good luck to you.' He held out his hand.
David looked at it for a second, then shook it firmly. 'You too,' he said.
Alexa nodded goodbye, and they both got into the waiting car.

David decided to pack his bags and check out after a quick breakfast. Should he leave the map where it was or take it with him?

He decided to retrieve it, while it was still dark, and again took the circuitous route to the transformer, making sure, as far as he could, that nobody was watching him. He looked at his watch, it was a quarter past six, and another three-quarters-of-an-hour before they started serving breakfast.

As he was bending down to retrieve the laundry bag, and was just about to come out of the cover of the building, car lights swept the hotel grounds. A green and white police vehicle slowly drove the length of the car park, shining a spotlight on all the parked vehicles, its tyres crunching through the fresh snow.

They reached his rental car, stopped, and got out, shining a torch into the interior. David could see the condensation from their breath in the headlights, as they walked around the vehicle.

He prayed they wouldn't go round to the patio. The door to his room was ajar. He could plainly see it, even at this distance.

One of the policemen was on the radio, probably checking details with the hire company. The other walked back to the hotel, where David could see that the lights were on in the reception area. He ducked back into cover, and looked to see if he could make it to the back of the villas without being seen. The problem was that both had movement sensitive lights to the front door, and he was bound to trigger them. He decided to wait it out, and pray that they did not visit the room now.

He heard the scrunch of boots returning from the main building, and the two men stood together, one pointing to the villa and David's room. Bugger. They were going round to the room.

Both of them saw the light shining through the open door at the same time. The larger of the two stepped onto the patio, pushed the door, and stepped in.

A woman's scream rent the air, whereupon the man stumbled

back out of the doorway, tripped off the edge of the sill, and collided with his partner, both men tumbling into the snow.

Christina came out wrapped in a towel, shouting and cursing at them. They got to their feet, apologizing profusely in German. She was having none of the apologies, and went back to the room to get a paper and pen, noting the number of the police car and the numbers of the two police officers. The two men beat a retreat, getting back in their car and driving down to the hotel reception.

David sprinted back to the patio door and a hysterical Christina, who was laughing so much that tears were rolling down her cheeks.

'Where the hell did ***you*** come from?' David threw his arms around her and gave her a bear hug. 'Go in for Christ's sake, you'll get pneumonia.'

'You wouldn't believe how fast I got my clothes off when I saw them coming to the patio.' She was still wiping tears from her eyes. 'As they say, attack is the best form of defence.'

As soon as they got into the room, she pulled him to her and kissed him. David noticed an ugly looking weal on her neck.

'Where did you get that from?' he asked, running his finger along the mark.

'I'll tell you all about it, later.' She started to pull on her clothes.

'How on earth did you get back here?' David shut the patio door and immediately felt the warmth returning to his hands and face.

'I was at a hotel in Ostheim, under a Russian name. Shoshanim rang me as soon as he left here, and I took a taxi. The driver took a back road, because he told me the police had road-blocked the town, and it was crawling with police cars around the Burgmühle. Shoshanim said you'ld tell me what had happened. I asked the taxi driver to drop me around the back of the block, and I walked the last two hundred metres. The patio door was open, and you were nowhere to be found, only footprints down to the main building. Thank God, our two

Polizei friends covered your tracks when they drove in. Next, I saw them coming to the door and…clothes off. You should've seen his face, when I started screaming.' She began giggling hysterically again.

'Let's get packed and put the cases in the car, have some breakfast and then drive to the airport,' said David. 'We can talk about everything on the way.' He kissed her cheek and started getting the cases out.

'Okay. Where are we going?' she asked.

'Sweden,' he said, matter of factly.

'Sweden?

'Sweden,' he reaffirmed.

'Okay,' she said, smiling.

They packed everything, and went down to the restaurant in the main building at seven o'clock. The receptionist was at her desk, and as she saw them she came to the counter, hands in the air.

'Oh, Frau Sheehan, I'm so sorry about the Polizei. They saw the open door and, oh dear, I'm so sorry. There's been a terrible thing in the town, some people killed you know, by guns, it's horrible. This is a small place. We don't usually have such things. Oh dear, and you being Ausländer as well.'

'It's okay, it was just frightening for me, you know. Sorry about the screams, I probably woke all the hotel guests.' Christina placed her hand on her chest in a gesture of shock. 'I guess the police will want to speak to us?' She made the question understated and as if an afterthought.

'Oh no. I think no. I told them you were a very nice couple looking at historical things and such. I know both of them, they are good boys. They took copies of your passes, as they have to do this. They were so sorry to make a fright for you. Sorry.

'Oh that was kind. How awful, a shooting in the town, it seems such a sleepy kind of place,' said Christina

Don't push your luck, girl. He squeezed her hand firmly.

'We're going to check out after breakfast. Nothing to do with the Polizei in the room, really. So, could we get the bill when we come back, please?' he requested. We have to go to the airport.'

David wanted to have a spot of breakfast, and then get the hell out of Mellrichstadt, before the police really did want to talk to them. As they walked to the breakfast room, David took Christina's arm.

'How good are the passports?'

'One hundred per cent.' she assured.

They had breakfast, and then David went to the Internet access in the reception area to look for flight times to Sweden. He found a Lufthansa flight at 14.25 to Copenhagen and a connecting flight on to Gothenburg arriving at 19.30. Christina used the credit card in the name of Sheehan to book the flights, and then they checked out.

'Do you mind driving? I really haven't had much sleep.' David held out the keys to Christina.

'Yes, no problem. Can we check the car for trackers, before we start driving? You take underneath.' She smiled cheekily as David got onto his hands and knees in the snow, to look under the car with the torch.

'All clear up here, how are you doing down there?'

Her head appeared upside down on the other side of the car, pouting him a kiss.

'Nothing obvious down here. Open the bonnet, will you, and I'll give that a look.'

He rose to his feet, and staggered against the side of the car. He thought he was going to spew, but after a few seconds, the feeling passed.

'What is it, David?' Christina came round to take his arm.

'I got up too fast, I probably need some sleep.' He rubbed his face with his hands. 'Right. Let's have a look under the bonnet. Nope, everything's clear. Let's go.'

He tried to hide the fact that he felt awful, steadying himself for a few seconds before getting into the car.

They drove out of the car park, crossing the tyre tracks left by the police car, and turned down to the main road. It had been ploughed, and the morning traffic had already become quite busy. To meet the main highway to Fulda, they took a small country road, which had not yet been cleared.

Christina wanted to leave the exchange of information until they left the smaller roads, as driving in these conditions was difficult enough in the deep snow. No lights were obvious behind them, but they pulled off the road twice, to see whether they were being followed. After twenty minutes they reached the highway, relieved that it had already been ploughed and gritted. As Christina accelerated away, David turned in his seat.

'Okay, you first. Everything from the time we parted at the Staatsarchiv, and I mean everything,' he demanded.

Chapter 20

Christina related how she had crossed the street, and passed the two tails in the BMW. One of them had a camera with a telephoto lens, which he had put under the seat when she drew near. In the reflection of a shop window, she saw them getting out of the car, and coming across the square towards her. They approached, waving National Security Agency identity cards, and saying that their boss wanted a meet. She had told them that somebody was waiting for her, but they assured her that it had been taken care of.

They drove a few kilometres on the Suhl road, to a safe house, just off the main road, on a country track. There she was told to wait for their boss.

'Did they question you?' David glanced out of the window at a police car, parked in a lay-by. They didn't move, and were probably waiting for the end of a shift.

'No, nothing. After one hour, their chief arrived and introduced himself as Jimmy Nolan. He said he knew you. Is that true?' she asked.

'Yep.' David nodded, and remembered the feeling of hot wet blood pumping over his hands on the town wall above the mill.

Last night, she continued, he and the two younger guys had gone out, leaving her with an Afro-American woman of about forty, who didn't talk much, just sat with an automatic in her lap watching television and keeping an eye on the track down to the house.

Around six-thirty, as they were going to eat something, the telephone rang. The woman answered, but didn't say anything, and after about twenty seconds put the phone down. She had muttered something about making coffee, whilst Christina sat and watched the news.

The next thing Christina knew, the American had a wire around her neck and was strangling her.

'Look at the mark. She wasn't fooling, David, she wanted me

dead and quick. There was a glass bottle of mineral water on the table in front of me, so I picked it up and hit her on the head. She let go of the wire, and I really smashed her with her gun. Maybe I killed her.'

'No, actually you didn't. I'll tell you later.'

'So, I found keys in the kitchen for a car that was parked outside, and I got out of there, as fast as I could. I then phoned Shoshanim.'

She took his hand. 'I have to tell you now, David, I've been in contact with the Mossad for some years, and Shoshanim since Cornwall. My people aren't telling me everything and I wanted help. He was in a hotel in Ostheim with some colleagues and had followed the Americans to Mellrichstadt. He told me to stay put, and said they'd come and get me. Thirty minutes later, he and a colleague arrived and we went back to Ostheim. I checked-in posing as a Russian.'

'Did Shoshanim tell you what was going on?'

David was watching every facial expression, every eye movement, listening for every pause or tremor in speech. He had to be absolutely sure this time.

'No. All he did, repeatedly, was ask if he could trust you. Is this where I turn?' she asked.

'No, it's quite a way yet, keep straight on,' David said, pointing along the road.

'Well that's everything, up to the telephone call this morning.' She turned to David and raised her eyebrows, aware that he still didn't completely trust her.

'Have your own people been in touch, Russian or Slovak?' he asked, not accusingly, but pointedly.

'Not one word. So, now for your adventures,' she countered sharply.

'Well I've been a busy boy.'

He told her about his meeting with Nolan, his trip to Buchenwald and the information he had found there. He went on to relate his preliminary visit to the mill island and his find of the rock with BK written on it.

'What was the BK, did you find out?' she demanded, excitedly.
'Yes, it was William…Bill Kenton's grave.'
'Was that it?' She looked disappointed.
'Let me finish.'
He recounted Jimmy Nolan's killing, the first meeting with Bob and J.B, his return to dig on the island, the discovery of the casket and their later talk at the hotel.
'Was there anything in the casket?'
'Yes, Kenton's ashes, a letter from your grandfather in English and Slovak, a coded telegram from Bormann to Himmler and a map of a vast underground system of tunnels.'
'Oh my God! What's down there?'
'I'm coming to all that.'
She listened to him describe the planned meeting with the two Americans, finding their bodies in the car, and the trap that Shoshanim had set up with the wired door.
'What's happening here? Who killed them, was it Shoshanim?' she quizzed.
'He tells me no, and I believe him. Christina, we need to be very careful from now on. Somebody's on a killing spree, and you and I are on the list,' he warned.
'Yes I know that.' She fingered the ugly red mark on her neck.
'What do you know about Soviet nuclear demolition weapons. The so-called suitcase bombs?' he asked.
'Is that what this is all about?'
'Shoshanim thinks so, but there's something else. You can read your grandfather's letter at the airport. So what do you know about these weapons?'
'Well officially they don't exist, but the talk is that they were lost. Whatever "lost" means. The Soviet minister Lebed said so in public, he spoke of over a hundred bombs, but he was discredited to avoid causing panic. I believe there were a lot of tactical nuclear weapons stored all along the wall from the north of the DDR to Bulgaria. What happened to them, I don't

know. What does Shoshanim say?'

'He says that they're down there in the tunnel system, and that we have the only map to find the way in,' David said. He explained that other entrances had been blown or had caved in. 'Think what that would mean to a terrorist group, and how far they would go to get only one. Over a hundred, Jesus! Did you keep the American's gun?' he asked.

'Yes, it's in my bag here. Why?'

'I have one too, Jimmy Nolan gave it to me He also gave me a piece of paper with a Swedish name on it. He was told to give me the name by what he described as, "the highest level" after a G8 meeting'.

'What the hell does that mean? The President?' she wondered, mystified.

'God knows. Here, take a right here, and then after three kilometres take the A66 to Hanau and Frankfurt. The name he gave me is Matti Fjällman.'

'Does that mean anything to you?' She looked puzzled.

'It does when you know that the Swedish for mountain, as it is in the Lake District, is Fjäll or Fell.'

'Sorry, am I missing something?'

'Matti Fjällman. Matthias Von…?' he prompted.

'Von den Bergen? But he'd be over ninety surely. Do you think it's him?'

'Well it would be a massive coincidence with the name. He knew your grandfather and he knew the tunnel system.'

'Where do we start looking?' she asked.

'I have some old contacts in SÄPO, the Swedish secret police; we'll see how they can help.'

It was just starting to get light, as David drifted off to sleep. He woke as they were just joining the autobahn to Frankfurt.

'Good morning, Mr Sheehan.' She smiled, and leant over to kiss him on the cheek. 'By the way, I stopped at two service stations to check for any tails, and there weren't any.'

'Well done.' He stretched and yawned. 'My God, I have an awful taste in my mouth. Sorry, I just couldn't keep awake.'

Half-an-hour later, they were turning off to the airport. David thought about the possible danger to them in Sweden, now that the map had been found.

'We'll have to leave the automatics in the car. Can you arrange for Shoshanim's people to fix us with something, when we get there? I really think we ought to have some protection. It's just a gut feeling, but…,' he said

'Yes, okay I'll ring him from the airport. It shouldn't be a problem,' she replied.

There was plenty of time, so he suggested they went to the Eurolounge to relax. Christina decided to do a bit of shopping and as she left, patted him on the head.

'See you later.'

He arranged for some towels, and went into the men's room to take a shower and a shave. As he was dressing, he was hit by the tiredness of a broken night's sleep, and afterwards, whilst reading the newspapers in the lounge, he again fell into a deep slumber. The next thing that he felt was Christina shaking his shoulder.

'Come on now, Sleepy. We have to go.'

'Did you get any help from Shoshanim?' he asked, yawning and stretching. Immediately he felt the blood pulsing in his ears, and the nausea hit him again. He sat down quickly, and saw the look of worry in Christina's face, as she nodded.

'My God, David, this isn't tiredness, or a bug, we must get you checked up at a doctor.'

'Yes, all right, when we get back to Germany, I promise.' He stood up again, mopping the sweat on his brow with his handkerchief. 'Come on. Let's get going.'

After a tedious stopover in Copenhagen, they arrived at Landvetter airport in Gothenburg, on schedule at 19.30. As they wound the trolley around the waiting crowd in the main airport concourse, a short, middle-aged woman dropped a small bag on to their luggage as she walked by. She didn't look back, and kept on towards the side exit and the car park.

‘A Christmas present, from our Jewish Santa.’ Christina smiled, putting it into her shoulder bag as they crossed the airport exit road to the car-hire offices opposite. The traffic had compacted the snow to a sheet of ice, and a fresh fall squeaked underfoot in the minus eight degrees temperature.

The drive into Gothenburg took them down the long hill, past the Liseberg pleasure park and its huge Ferris wheel and roller coaster.The lights of the city below glittering through the falling snow.

David told Christina to take the turning for ‘Hamnar’, the ferry berths, and then west, parallel with Göteberg’s Älv, where the mighty Göta river flows out to join the Kattegat and Skagerrak after its short journey from the vast lake Vänern.

They passed the terminals for Denmark and Germany. The fish market, ablaze with floodlights, the workers in their orange waterproofs manhandling crates into small delivery vans, whilst forklift trucks serviced the larger lorries. Even with the windows closed the stench of fish and diesel fuel was overpowering.

Soon they were in the shadow of the bridge crossing the river, the Älvborgsbron, pulling in to a Novotel near its base.

Parking by the water’s edge, he went in to see if there was a room available. He came back smiling. ‘We have a suite with a sauna, overlooking the harbour, Mrs Sheehan.’ He leant into the car and kissed her.

‘How romantic, Mr Sheehan.’ She got out, shivering in the icy wind blowing in across the harbour from the north.

The suite was on the seventh floor and had a fabulous view over the whole length of the Göta Älv. Multi-storey ferries arrived and departed, lit portholes decorating their sides. A host of other small boats, water busses and cargo ships, ploughed through the icy cold waters like glow worms, navigation lights blinking and sparkling in the freezing air. It was a Nordic Venice: the Älvborgsbron the Rialto, the Älv the Grand Canal.

As soon as they had unpacked, David handed Christina the Slovak version of the letter from her grandfather. She read it in silence for some minutes before putting the letter down, tears in her eyes.

'Oh David, they were so young, and what horror they must've lived through. Here's a man I never met, but was my mother's father. He wrote nearly sixty years ago. A man who never ever saw his family or home again. A man with a secret that seems so important, all these long years later. He was beaten to death for this information. Christ! What must it've been like in those camps, in those tunnels?' she asked, her voice trembling. 'Let's study the map. It's the books and the crate in the secret chamber they want, yes? That's what all this is about. What can be there? All these deaths, all this time deep underground.'

David stood looking out at the boats, thinking to himself for a moment before he outlined his thoughts.

He felt sure feel sure that Zapf and Gehrling were dealing with the terrorists and Vicky Mason, and that their prime motive was the missing nuclear demolition bombs. He also assumed that there was a hoard of art and looted gold down there. Shoshanim and the Israelis were most concerned to stop access to the nuclear weapons. That's why they shot Zapf and Griff Mason. Zapf must've known that the bombs were there, but lost to tunnel collapse. Voss surely told him, under torture, about Joseph Novak, and that there were possibly other entrances to the system.

He guessed that the top brass of the Soviets also knew this, and hence the request for Christina to contact him. They didn't want it made public that there were over a hundred buried nuclear weapons very close to the East/West border. Somewhere along the line, Zapf and Gehrling went moonlighting and decided to sell these weapons to the highest bidder, but only if they could get into the system.

The big problem was the hidden chamber. In David's opinion it had been the cause of the Americans' deaths, and the attempt on Christina.

'I think they were going to kill you because you were no longer necessary to them, the same with Jimmy Nolan and his boys. I had the map, and therefore would've become the only player.'

He didn't think the Mossad or Zapf and Gehrling were even aware of the chamber's existence. What the hell would they want with books and whatever the crate contained?

'I think we're in very real danger. We have to go to ground tomorrow and stay that way, until we've thought this through. Why in God's name would they kill their own people? What's so important in the chamber, that Bormann had the contents sealed underground? Why did he mention Hess?' He looked into his drink. He had to trust her now. He had to.

'Christina, I'm going to tell you something from way back in the past, from my time in Germany. In 1987 in fact. I had to fix two missions at that time, and until now I've never questioned them. Both relate to Spandau Prison and ...'

'Hess?' She looked incredulously at David. 'Hess?'

'I didn't think about it then, but there were assassinations at Spandau that were carried out, on my orders, by the SAS. One was a young French guard who Hess had given secret information to and the other was Hess himself. The official line was that he'd been kept in solitary because, if he'd been released, he would've been able to talk about his trip to Scotland in 1941, and reveal information which would've seriously embarrassed the British monarchy.

We made both deaths look like suicide. Not everybody was convinced, but the hoo-hah died down after a few months. Now I'm wondering if there is a link here, a link between the need to silence Hess, and whatever's down there, underground.'

David carefully unfolded the map and the telegram and handed them to her. Christina spread the map out on the bed.

'Where do we start with this?' She ran her fingers through her hair and ruffled the back of her head in bewilderment.

'I think we start by finding Mr Matti Fjällman. I'll give my friend in SÄPO a ring, to see if he can help. Can you contact Shoshanim? Ask if he can find out which entrances were blown during the construction of the Wall, and which tunnel systems later collapsed?

We also need help to decode the telegram. I don't think we should try to contact our own people, until we're sure of our ground.

At half past eleven, and before getting ready for bed, Christina spread the map out again.

'Pass me my bag please, David, I have a green marker pen there. Could you draw a line where the old border was?'

'This is a rough guide, okay?' He drew a line along the boundary of the divided Germany. 'What we really need to know is, which of the tunnels are now impassable, and then we can try and locate the entrances which are still open. They must be well hidden, or they would've been found. The main shaft is thirty-five to forty kilometres long, at least, so we're going to have to get small scooters or motorbikes down there somehow. You made some notes about the Jonastal project at the archive in Meiningen. What was it exactly?'

She looked through her papers.

The work, she read, started officially in November 1944 and ended March 1945, but they knew that her grandfather and Bill Kenton were working there earlier.

The German line today was that the existence of a massive underground system, in which to build and store super weapons, was nonsense, and that only around twenty-five tunnels were excavated at the site. This was a total length of around 2.5 kilometres.

The number of workers needed for that would've been five hundred. In fact, they took twenty-five thousand from Buchenwald and other camps. Conspiracy theorists have always said that the site is huge, and that the number of slave labourers used, proves that. One American officer who arrived there at the end of the War, with Patton's troops, wrote of several layers of tunnel going out like spokes in a bicycle wheel, and that he saw several miles of tunnel. They could see on the map that this was also true.

The Soviets and the East Germans supposedly blew all the entrances to the system when they erected the Wall. It was a military zone until reunification and still was. Since then, many people and groups have illegally tried to find open entrances to the tunnels, but without success. So the conspiracy people still believe that there was something there.
'And we know, that there is,' she said.

He unzipped the bag dropped onto their luggage by the Mossad agent.
'Two Glock ten millimetres with silencers and sixty rounds. Very handy and I've a feeling, very necessary,' he sighed.

Chapter 21

They woke just before seven. David persuaded Christina to take a shower first, because he didn't want to let her know that he felt lousy and had thrown up again during the night. He sat on the edge of the bed holding his head in his hands, but regained his composure when he heard the flow of water in the shower turned off, smiling at the towel-wrapped figure, as she emerged from the bathroom.

'You look awful.' She sat beside him and ruffled his hair.

'Too much rich food and wine last night. I'll be okay after a shower.' He kissed her cheek and went into the bathroom.

Another bout of dizziness rocked him, and he steadied himself against the sink unit, looking at his face in the mirror.

'Jesus.'

It didn't look good. The bile rose in his throat, he knew he was going to vomit, and desperately tried to keep the spasms as quiet as possible so that Christina wouldn't hear him.

The shower freshened him up, and putting a towel around himself, he went back to the bedroom.

'Shall we go down for breakfast, David?' She was sitting in front of the vanity mirror and putting on her make-up. Never too much, he thought, just enough to highlight her beauty.

'I'll stick to the coffee I think. Well, maybe, I'll wait and see how hungry I get watching you eat. I'm going to ring my contact. They start work early in Sweden.'

After Christina had ordered some breakfast, David rang the Säpo headquarters in Uppsala.

'Ja, god morgon, jag söker Erland Lindén? Jag heter David Lennox.' While he was waiting to hear if Lindén was there, the breakfast arrived. He smiled at Christina and pointed at the coffee.

'Two sugars please.'

'It'll be one sugar.' She wagged her finger and pulled a face.

Lindén came to the line.

'Yes, Hi Erland, this is David Lennox.'

‘Good Lord. I thought you were dead. How long is it?’
‘Far too long. I took a few years out, but now I’m sort of back in circulation, and in Gothenburg.’
‘What brings you to Sweden after all these years?’ the Swede asked.
‘I’d like to give you a name, and to meet up with you, if that’s okay?’
‘ I’ll help if I can. Is this name in Sweden, David?’
‘In the Gothenburg area somewhere,’ David said.
‘Good, fire away. What have you got?’
‘Only a name. Matti Fjällman.’
Lindén was silent for some seconds.
‘No more on the telephone please. Where are you staying?’
‘Novotel, by the Göta Älv Bron, room phone number is 512 or 513,’ said David.
‘I’ll come down. 15.00, all right?’ The Swede hung up.
‘Yes, look forward to it,’ said David, to an empty line.
He put down the phone and looked at Christina who had put down her toast and was staring at him.
‘He knew the name, yes?’ she said.
‘It shook him. He’s coming down here from Stockholm as fast as he can. What the hell’s going on now?’
‘I’m going to talk to Shoshanim to see what he can find about the tunnel system. I think…’
David guessed at what was coming.
‘You ought to make the call from a public phone box, I’ve a feeling our friend Mr Lindén will have a tap on this hotel by now.’
‘Exactly.’ She smiled, and got up to put her coat on. It’s all right, I’ll go out in the freezing wind, you stay here in the warm, and put your feet up,’ she reproached, bending and kissing him on the head.
‘Take a gun, please.’ He got one of the Glocks out and loaded the magazine. He saw her slightly mocking smile. ‘Please, Christina.’
‘Yes, all right.’ She smiled and kissed his head again. ‘I won’t be long.’

'Don't talk to strange men.' He took her hand as she passed.

'I'll be careful, I promise. I am a professional, you know,' she chided.

'Yes, but you're a professional I really care for.'

When Christina had left, David sat thinking about the conversation with Lindén. The man had been thrown by the name Fjällman, really thrown.

After twenty minutes the room phone rang.

'Sheehan.'

'Hi.' It was Christina. 'My acquaintance told me your friend from Cornwall was meeting somebody in the Park Avenue Hotel. I'm walking with her now, and we met up with Mr Busch too. I have to run now because I'm at a taxi rank, and I don't want to lose them. Talk to you later.'

'Yes have a nice time, see you later. Take care.' He hung up.

He spent the next few hours pouring over Novak's sketch and a large road map of the area between Unterfranken and Thüringia. He drew rings around all of the marked entrances on the modern map of Germany, fifteen in all. They would have to narrow them down or they would be looking for years.

They were going to need transport underground, the distances were huge. What about an oxygen supply and gas detectors? Salt strata didn't have the same gas dangers as coal strata, but lack of oxygen could be a problem. That was if they could find a way in.

At lunch time he felt better, and ordered a snack from room service. Watching television as he ate, he glanced from time to time at the map, and hoped that Shoshanim came up with the information they needed.

He soon fell asleep and dreamt of his dead father. They were on holiday in Sandown on the Isle of Wight, where the beach turned into a muddy field. His father was sinking into a bog and David couldn't move, he was being sucked backwards into a huge cave which was the entrance to a long tunnel. He was shouting 'Sorry Dad, I'm so sorry.'

He was woken with a start, by the room telephone, and for

a brief moment didn't know whether it had been a dream or reality.

'Yes.' He coughed to clear his throat.

'It's Erland. Should I come up?' He still had that business tone in his voice.

'Yes, sure, we're on the fifth floor, 'Kung Gustav suite.'

'We?' the Swede asked, irritated.

'I'm here with somebody, but I'm alone in the room now, Erland.'

'Okay, I'll come up.'

David carefully folded the Novak map and cleared away any notes and maps that had been on the bed.

There was a knock at the door. David opened it, and Erland Lindén stepped into the room. He was in his mid-fifties and tall at six foot-four. His hair was white and clipped close to his tanned head. In the past, Erland had been an international cross-country skier for his country. When David had known him well, Lindén had skied, every March, in the Wasalopp in Dalarna, a race distance of eighty kilometres over rough terrain.

He had a large scar running from the corner of his mouth across his right cheek to the top of his right ear. The result of a high-speed traffic collision with an elk.

Lindén put out his hand and smiled.

'It's good to see you David. It's been a long time.'

'Much too long, Erland.' David shook his hand, paused, and then shook it again. 'Far too long. Would you like a drink?' he asked.

'Yes, whisky and ginger please, with ice.' He sat on the sofa and rubbed his eyes. 'It's a long journey from Stockholm down to Gothenburg by helicopter, and really noisy.'

He took the whisky, poured the whole of the ginger into it, and took a long draught.

'God, I needed that.'

'How's the family, Erland?' David poured himself a whisky.

'Marietta can't wait for me to retire. Lotta's married and has a little girl…Emma. I'm a grandfather now. I saw in the Swedish newspapers that you and your wife got divorced.'

'Oh, it's a long time ago now, Erland. Water under the bridge and all that.'

David saw that Lindén was beginning to look nervously around the suite, to the bedroom and the bathroom, and David guessed that niceties were now over. It was time to get down to business.

'Before we start discussing Matti Fjällman. Have a look around. There are no recording devices here, and we're alone,' he said.

'So sorry, David, but this is very sensitive and I have to be…'

'Careful. It's okay, Erland, have a look if you want to.' David waved his hand in the direction of the bathroom and the bedroom.

'No it's fine, David. So tell me, where did you get the name Matti Fjällman, and why?' He fingered the scar on his face.

'I was given the name by the Americans.'

'Who specifically, gave you the name?' Lindén asked, getting up and going to the mini-bar. 'May I?'

'Yeh, sure. Is it important?' David questioned.

'Was it Jimmy Nolan?' He stared hard at David.

Damn. David took another snap decision.

'Yes.'

Now it was Lindén's turn to decide how much to reveal. After a long pause, he sat down again.

'Where were you on the night of February 28th, 1986, David?' He took another long gulp of his whisky, put the glass down, and looked at David with eyebrows raised.

Oh Bugger. Thought David

'The night that Olof Palme was killed? I was in Stockholm, Erland. You must know that, otherwise you wouldn't've asked. What has that to do with Fjällman?' His arm was trembling, and the nausea returning.

'On that night, we have you on CCTV coming out of Stockholm Central station. One hour later we have Jimmy Nolan, not a coincidence I fear. We have CCTV of men with hand-held radios, we have cars with darkened windows and false number plates, and we have you and Jimmy Nolan. Before I talk about Matti Fjällman, what do you have to say about that, David? Please enlighten me.'

Shit. Did he have CCTV from anywhere else?

'Jimmy and I were going to work together in South America, to bust some of the drug gangs in Bolivia. Most of the trade was owned and run by government officials, and British and American Special Forces were asked to assist the DEA in covert operations. I met Jimmy in a Chinese restaurant on Sveavägen…'

Lindén interrupted.

'One hundred metres down the road, on the opposite side, to where Palme was shot down. Two leading Western intelligence officers are sitting in a Chinese restaurant, one hundred metres away, when the Prime Minister of my country's gunned down. And you were there to talk about South America?' His eyebrows arched even higher in incredulity.

'We left the restaurant at about midnight. We saw the police cars and a crowd, but we assumed that there'd been a road accident or a fight, or something of that kind. It wasn't until I got back to my hotel, that I saw the news. I thought that you had Mr Pettersson bang to rights for the shooting, whatever the appeal court ruled. Lisbet Palme identified him.'

'Did you ever meet Pettersson, David? If you bullshit me now, I'll walk.'

It had been in the middle of nowhere, in the north of Sweden. He had to be bluffing. David struggled to hold his composure.

'No I didn't, Erland. However unbelievable it seems, Jimmy and I were both in Sweden, and a meeting was fixed. There must've been thousands of people in Sveavägen that night, we just happened to be two of them. Why haven't you mentioned this before? Why didn't you contact me at the time? What the hell is it, that you feel you need to ask me now, after all these years?'

'You and Jimmy were booked in at the Birger Jarl Hotel, which is next to the police station responsible for the area where Palme was shot. You had meetings with members of the IPA, the International Police Association. A lot of them were right-wing activists.

After Palme's murder, my people cleared his office and desk. He'd had several threats to his life from various factions for his outspoken views on Vietnam, Franco, South Africa, the CIA and God knows who else. There was also a huge scandal, as you know, concerning arms sales from Sweden. He'd had specific intelligence warnings about the South African intelligence service, and a plot to assassinate him. On the outside of that file on his desk, there was a name written with large question marks beside it.

The name, David, was Matti Fjällman.'

Had Jimmy dropped him in the shit again, even beyond the grave?

David could not hide the shock of that revelation.

'My God,' he gasped.

'I see this was genuine news to you, David. Now you understand why I came down here immediately. The case has never been closed, although there's been incredible pressure from the Americans, to drop it and forget it. The gun was a magnum .357. We never found the weapon, but the bullets had been fashioned. Do you really think that Pettersson had the wherewithal to do all that? So, David, tell me more about Matti Fjällman.'

Lindén took another slug of the whisky, and settled back in his chair in anticipation.

'Well, I was hoping you could tell me. Jimmy gave the name to me shortly…er…the day before yesterday. We met in Germany. He gave no explanation, only that there was a telephone intercept between Fjällman, here in Gothenburg, and an Arab using a public phone, in Erfurt, Germany. They wanted me to trace Fjällman.'

David fingered the rim of his glass, as he desperately calculated how much he could say.

'Is Jimmy with you now?' Lindén was beginning to look nervously into the bedroom again.

In for a penny.

'He's dead, Erland, he died a few hours after he gave me the name.'

'How?' Lindén made to pick up his whisky glass, only realizing that it was empty as his hand was fully outstretched.

'He was knifed, just before he was to meet me again. He died in my arms. His abdominal aorta had been severed. Nothing I could do.'

Lindén walked over to the mini bar, and took out another small bottle.

'Why did he die, David?' He asked the question without looking round.

'I really don't know, Erland.'

The Swede turned and looked at David.

'Are you really asking me to believe that?'

'Yes I'm asking you to believe that, Erland. You're coming up for retirement soon and...and I'm asking you, very clearly, to listen to me, my friend. Two of Jimmy's minders died a few hours later, in the same spot. A lot of people are dead. I need your help, but I really don't want to involve you, I hope you understand what I'm saying.' He searched Lindén's face for any sign of resentment or anger.

After a few minutes Lindén answered.

'What does "Operation Tree" mean to you, David?' Lindén didn't look up from his glass.

Bloody hell. Did he know about Francovich?

'Should it?' David looked at the Swede but Lindén continued to inspect his whiskey.

'What about the name Allan Francovich?'

Holy Christ!

'I remember reading something in the newspapers, Erland, he was an American investigative journalist and film maker, wasn't he?' David got up and fetched a bottle of water from the minibar.

‘Yes, he died in 1997 at Houston airport, passing through the customs hall. He was about to publish a story about a secret organisation within NATO that was responsible for killing Palme in an operation called ‘Operation Tree’. Palme was shot thirty days before he was to have travelled to the Soviet Union. Francovich said that he had proof that Palme had to be stopped at all costs, because of something he was going to discuss with the Soviets. Francovich was about to name names, and he dropped dead of an alleged heart attack. Guess where your friend Jimmy was that day, David?’

‘It has to be Houston Airport, I guess.’

‘Ten points, my man. Another coincidence?’ Lindén asked.

‘I was out of action in 1997, Erland, so I don’t know, but it seems an interesting connection. Yes interesting.’

‘That brings a whole new meaning to the word “interesting”. If you’re looking for Matti Fjällman, David, I want…no, I need to be involved. I just need to be. Call it vanity or professional pride, or what you will, but I’m going to be there, okay?’

He downed the whisky, and put the glass down loudly on the table.

‘So what next. What’s the score? Who is Mrs Sheehan? I did check with the reception you know.’ He tapped the side of his head with his finger.

‘Christina Karranova.’

‘That’s the Slovak KGB agent who got you fired. What in God’s name are you playing at?’ He got up and started pacing the room, more, it seemed to David, in nervousness than in anger.

‘I am…how shall I put it, officially unofficial. Just help me trace Fjällman, that’s all I want.’ He pulled a ‘please’ expression and held out his hand.

After a brief moment, Lindén took his hand and shook it.

‘Erland, I have a name, an ex-Nazi SS officer wanted on war crime charges, his name is Matthias von den Bergen. Matti Fjällman, Matthias Von den Bergen...coincidence?’ David said, going into the bedroom to get some of his notes.

'Born Bamberg, Franconia 4th April 1912. Could he still be alive or is it a code name for somebody else?'

Lindén was making notes on the hotel pad.

'Yes, well he'd be what…eighty-nine. It's possible, yes. So, David, I'll stay here at the hotel and see what I can find in the records at Headquarters. Don't do anything without me, please. The Palme assassination is the biggest thing that's ever happened to our service, and we know the reason we haven't got to the bottom of it. We're playing against the CIA big boys, and, I suspect, people within our own team. We've been made to look incompetent and foolish. That pisses me off, David. He was a great statesman, whether you agreed with him or not, he was a great statesman.'

He's a dead statesman, Erland, thought David, and he's dead because Jimmy Nolan and I arranged it. Yes there were the men with radios, yes there were the vehicles with blacked-out windows and false number plates, yes we met Pettersson, and yes we gave him the Smith and Wesson magnum. I watched it crushed in a metal press a day later. I knew that Francovich had something on NATO before they fired me, and I guessed that his 'heart attack' was arranged.

Why had Palme had the name Matti Fjällman on the file? If Fjällman was Von den Bergen, then there was a concrete link.

He patted the Swede on the shoulder.

'I really appreciate the help, Erland. Give me a call to tell me your room number.'

After Lindén had left, David went to lie on the bed, breaking out in a cold sweat as the urge to vomit swept over him again. The room became blurred and waltzed and pirouetted around him. He soon fell into deep sleep, but with a gasp of apnoea was jolted awake by the telephone, a quarter-of-an-hour later.

'Sheehan.'

'Hi, it's me.' It was Christina again. He shook his head to clear the fuzziness, the nausea had passed, but he felt truly awful.

‘Hi. Where the hell are you? I’ve been worried.’ He reached down to open the mini-bar, cradling the phone between his shoulder and chin, and took out a mineral water.
‘I’m fine. I’ll be back in about twenty minutes. Did you meet your friend? Is he still there?’ David could hear the sounds of Muzak in the background, and guessed she was in a hotel reception area.
‘Yes, he was here, but he’s gone off to help us find our other friend. I’ve a lot to tell you. Where are you now?’
‘Tell you all about it, when I get back. Have you missed me?’
‘Haven’t had time. Yes of course, get back safely.’
He went into the bathroom and filled the hand basin with cold water, swilling his face with his cupped hands.
Twenty minutes later Christina rang the room doorbell and embraced him at the door.
‘You’re freezing, I’ll put the sauna on,’ he said, as he stroked her cheek with the back of his hand. ‘Come and tell me all about your day. I’ll make some coffee.’
‘Okay. I went downtown, and made a call to Shoshanim. I thanked him for the automatics, by the way. He told me that the Mason girl and Gehrling had driven north from Mellrichstadt, caught the ferry to Denmark from Puttgarden and then crossed from Helsingør to Helsinborg. Early this morning they checked in to the Elite Plaza Hotel. I saw the Mason girl there with a youngish Tunisian or Moroccan guy, in the bar. Gehrling joined them ten minutes later. Mason and Gehrling then took a taxi to an address outside the city centre at…’ she looked at her notes, …‘Redbergsplatsen. I checked the door-phone and there were six names, Wallin, Eriksson, Munkedahl, Eliasson, Henriksson and Björklund. Mean anything to you?’ she asked.
‘Nope. Nothing.’ David placed a coffee beside her.
‘Right. Twenty minutes later, they came out with another man who drove them to an area called Nolvik, on the coast. They went to a big villa, like a farm complex, but here’s the interesting thing. I asked the taxi to park, five hundred metres away, and I went through the forest to the edge of the place.

Three, maybe four people on guard, not too openly, but there. I thought it'd be better not to stay around, so came back here. I took some photographs.' She turned the camera on and showed him.

'They look very tired. After seeing all the police activity in Mellrichstadt, they probably left almost immediately, and must've driven through the night. But why Sweden? It must be linked to Fjällman. Do you know the other guy?' David asked.

'No. No idea.' She took the camera back and pressed the forward button. 'Here are some pictures of the villa, the driver of the car and the registration number, that'll help your Swedish friend.'

David looked at them. The building was a typical Swedish manor house or Herrgård, a main building with two wings, forming three sides of a square onto an entrance courtyard. At the back were various barns, animal sheds and stables.

David kissed her on the forehead.

'You're a wonder, Karranova, a bloody wonder.'

He dialled reception and got put through to Lindén's room. 'Erland, hej, we have something for you. Can you call in again? See you in ten minutes then.'

He sat down and turned to Christina. 'I need to fill you in on a few things, before Erland comes along, and I don't have time for explanations now, so just listen. The British Secret service and the CIA arranged the killing of Olof Palme. Jimmy Nolan and I were the executive officers. When Lindén and his colleagues cleared Palme's office after the shooting, there was a file on Palme's desk assessing a risk of his assassination by the South African security forces. Somebody had written a name on that file with a large question mark by it.'

'Matti Fjällman?' She sat up in her chair as David nodded. 'What the …?' She jumped visibly as the room door bell rang.

David went to the door. 'Come in Erland,' he said. 'This is Christina Karranova. Christina…Erland Lindén.'

The Swede shook her hand, making a three second assessment of whether he should trust her or not. Christina gave him her sweetest smile, taking his hand firmly. David saw the Swede's face relax and a grin spread across his face.

'They told me you were beautiful, and they were right, my dear.' He smiled broadly.

'Thank you, kind sir. Please, sit down,' she fawned.

'Well, what've you got for me?' He unscrewed the top of his pen, and took out a small notebook.

Christina spoke first.

'Today, I followed some people we think are linked to Matti Fjällman. I followed them to an address at Redbergsplatsen. Here are names from the entry-phone.'

She gave Lindén some minutes to absorb the list. If it meant anything to him, it didn't register in his face.

'Then they drove, with another man, to a place called Nolvik.'

David saw the Swede shift his weight in his chair, and knew that Christina had pushed a hot button.

'In Nolvik, they visited a large villa or farm, which had some security people guarding the place. Here's a shot of the villa, the car and the driver.'

She fiddled with the camera to get a close- up of the driver.

'It's not very good detail, but good enough for identification.'

The Swede sucked in air through his front teeth, and David knew that Lindén had recognised the man.

'Do you know him, Erland?' David asked, as he caught Christina's glance.

The Swede got up and went to the window, remaining silent for some minutes as his gaze followed the turbulent churning wake of a red and white ferry, making its way out to the open sea. He raised and lowered himself on his toes for some time. He spoke without turning around.

'Yes, yes I know him. He's a SÄPO man, one of mine, Tord Eliasson. One of the names on the door-phone at Redbergsplatsen. Within the IPA there is, as you know, a right-wing organisation and Eliasson is a leading member here in Sweden.'

He started moving around again, looking up and down the

estuary a few times before speaking, still seemingly fascinated by the harbour and its comings and goings.

'I have to think. Yes I have to think…this changes things. This changes everything, I'm sorry. I have to make some calls. This is one of my people, and I have to check. I had some information for you, but now things are different, sorry. I'll contact you in a while and see what we can come up with.' He turned suddenly, and without further eye contact made for the door and was gone.

'What was that all about?' Christina got up and went into the bathroom to check on the sauna. 'I'm getting in, are you coming?'

After a few minutes, David heard the slam of the sauna door and got undressed. As he joined her, he was immediately reminded of how perfect her naked body was, and felt desire stirring in him. He lay down on the lower bench, the warmth seeping into every pore and joint of his body.

'David, did you have any contact with this right-wing Swedish group within the IPA here in Sweden, before the Palme killing? She rolled over on to her back, exposing her firm pear-shaped breasts. He cupped one in his hand.

She slapped his stomach.

'Answer the question.'

'Yes, we did. Radios were turned off, calls unanswered and patrol routes were avoided, but I never met or heard of Eliasson. He looks too young to have been around at that time. What do you think?'

'Don't know, but the picture certainly shook Lindén.'

It was just after six o'clock when the telephone rang again. David answered.

'Yes, I see. When? All right, thank you, I'll come down and pick it up.' He replaced the handset and rolled over on the bed to face Christina.

'That was reception. Erland's left a message for us. I'll get dressed, and go down for it.'

'Okay,' mumbled Christina, struggling to open her eyes.

A few minutes later he came back to the room.

'This is a little strange. He wants us to meet him tonight at nine o'clock, out on the road to Nolvik. We should look out for a red Volvo parked along the way. He's written down the registration number.' He handed Christina the note.

'Is this his handwriting?' she asked, with raised eyebrows.

'No idea. Do you smell trouble?' He took the note back, and studied it again as he picked up the phone and rang reception.

'Could I speak to Mr Erland Lindén's room, please. I see... When? His office rang, I see. Thank you.'

'Somebody from his office checked him out. What do you want to do, should we go out there?' He stroked her hair.

'Yes. But we do this right, Mr Lennox. We do it right.'

Chapter 22

David had sealed the maps, telegram and notes in an envelope, and deposited them in the hotel's safe.

It was too cold to snow, and the road surfaces on the major roads were frozen and treacherous as they drove over the bridge to the other side of the river and the motorway to the north and Nolvik.

The forest on the minor road thinned a little, and Christina recognised that the villa was quite close. After another two kilometres, they saw a red Volvo in the headlights, parked on a forest track to the left.

'That's the car.' David slowed down and then backed up. The vehicle was empty. He reversed a little more, both of them looking around carefully on both sides of the road.

'David, go back three hundred metres, and park. Then we'll have a look.' She craned her neck around to check behind the car.

They got out, closing the doors as quietly as possible, putting the silencers on their Glocks and checking the magazines. They stood for some minutes listening and getting used to the dark. Everything seemed quiet, so they started to walk down the road to the Volvo.

Christina took one side, walking fifty metres behind him. The car was unlocked, and the contents of the glove compartment had been strewn about in the passenger floor-well and seat. He used the mini-torch to look around.

'These are papers for the car, registered here in Gothenburg to the police department,' he said, as she caught up with him.

'David, there are some tracks in the snow that lead away, and over those some tracks leading to and from the car. There's been a lot of activity here.'

'I don't like this, Christina. Thank God there's a fair bit of moonlight.' He peered into the darkness of the forest ahead. 'I can see some lights, is that the villa?' he asked, as he heard

Christina stumble and curse in the gloom behind him.

'Yes, straight ahead, three hundred metres. There's a field of four hectares, between the edge of the trees and the main building.'

David raised his hand in a stop gesture. He whispered, indicating direction with his head.

'I can hear something moving in front of us.' They both stood motionless, craning their heads to one side to catch any noise.

A warm animal scent drifted from the trees, and the soft whinny of a horse, close by, broke the silence as it sensed their presence. They waited a few more seconds before making towards the lights of the house, and on reaching the end of the trees they saw the villa, one hundred and fifty metres across the field.

Four horses, three of which were on the far side, were out in the snow covered paddock, which David found strange as it was so cold. The nearest horse saw them, shook its head, snorted, and ambled slowly over to the others.

He knew that anyone with a night-sight would pick them off easily.

'If I make it to the other side without incident, you follow me, okay? As you said, let's do this properly. I'll give you two short flashes of the torch when I'm there. Watch out for the electric fence, I just got a bloody shock,' he said, as he left.

Four minutes later, the lamp signalled once. But only once.

Eventually, the signal came. One, two. She ducked under the wire and struck out towards the house. He gave her another two flashes for direction, to where he was standing, behind a wall at the back of an outbuilding.

'Jesus, David. I'm frozen.' She took off her gloves and put her hands inside his coat.

'Sorry, I didn't like the feel of it,' he said. 'There are lights on in the main house downstairs, but nobody's moving. I've been around the outside of the whole building. If it's a trap, they must've seen us by now. Do you want to take the back or the front?'

'Let's both take the back, after we have a good look at all the other buildings and the windows on the ground floor,' she answered, peering into the darkness.

They released the safety catches on the Glocks, and David ran from the security of the shadows to the stable blocks. He saw the movement sensor far too late, as the whole area was immediately bathed in light, dazzling him after the darkness of the forest.

'Fuck it!'

He ducked into the stables, into the nearest empty stall, his gun held high in front of his face. Apart from some restlessness among the six or so thoroughbreds in the stable, there was nothing but the musty smell of manure and horse sweat. After some seconds came a very gentle double tap on the stable door, and Christina appeared holding her automatic low, but ready.

'Your speed when the lights came on was very impressive... for an old man.' She smiled as she took in every inch of the building. 'Look there, they must be racing horses.'

At the other end of the stables, several lightweight trotting sulkies were upright, leaning against the rear wall.

'Let's get on, the place seems deserted.' He peered outside. The whole area was still lit, as he carefully scanned the surroundings. Where the hell was everybody?

They looked at all the other outbuildings in turn, eventually realising that apart from tractors and farm machinery, there were no vehicles anywhere, so they made for the back of the main house.

David took the windows to the east and Christina those to the west. They met back after a few minutes. Christina was visibly agitated, holding her automatic high in front of her, keeping her attention on the outbuildings and grounds.

'Does Lindén have a tattoo on his leg?' she asked.

'Yes, why?' He remembered the first sauna with Erland, and the Swede's embarrassment at this student vanity. Her nervousness infected him, and he too raised his automatic, peering into the grounds, as the timer on the stable block suddenly shut off the

lights. 'Why, for Christ's sake?'
'An eagle?'
'Shit! Where is he?'
'He's in the kitchen, strapped to a chair. He looks dead. The lights are off , so I couldn't see very well with the torch.'
David thought for a minute.
'All right. We go in through the back door and sweep the top floor first. At least we can control the staircase from there. Let's move, I don't like standing out here like a clay pigeon.'
David covered them, as Christina tried the back door. It was locked, so she took a special tool from her pocket, inserted it, clicking the trigger five times and turning it to the right. With the door open, she entered the house, David warily backing in behind her.
They stood in the lit rear entrance lobby, looking into the main hallway. Its twin staircases joined in a small central landing, before rising again, and splitting to the right and the left at the rear wall.
As they climbed to the first floor, they saw patches of clean wallpaper on either side of the stairwell, where paintings had once hung, at least seventeen or eighteen. It was the same on the first landing and in some of the bedrooms.
'I'm guessing there's nobody here. Are you happy to stay up here on your own? I'll do the ground floor,' he said.
She nodded, and they parted at the top of the stairs. David checked the hallway, before going through the ground floor rooms, one by one. He finished the sweep, satisfied that they were alone in the house, and under no immediate threat.
Carefully opening the door to the kitchen, he saw a slumped figure bound to a wooden chair. He put his hand around the corner, and found the light switch.
'Oh Christ! No.'
The Swede was naked from the waist down. A blow lamp, that had been used to burn his genitalia into a charred mass, was lying on a small table next to him.
The bottom half of a fly-fishing rod, with a reel and a fly

line attached, lay beside it. It had been used to pull out both of Lindén's eyes by inserting a hook in the eyeball, then slowly reeling in the line. Both eyeballs lay on the kitchen floor, staring at the ceiling, one still attached by the hook to the fly line leader.

The coup de grâce had been a skewer through the eye socket to the brain. A pool of urine and excrement around his bare feet, and a trail of vomit down his shirtfront bore testament to his suffering.

Christina didn't see the body at first, because David was in her direct line of sight.

'Top floor's clean, most of the paintings have gone there too, and I guess other things with some of the empty…Oh my God!'

She sat down, as she saw Lindén's bloodied and mutilated corpse.

'This is Chechen work, David. I've seen this type of thing before, exactly this type of thing.'

David put his hand on the bloodied neck.

'He's still not cold, only been dead an hour or so I'd say.' David took the tablecloth and covered the body.

'Shit…sorry David.' She rushed to the sink and retched.

When Christina had cleaned herself up, David turned off the light.

'I don't think he talked. They would've waited for us if he had. I think they left in a hurry, I think there…'

There was a loud bang and two doors flew off a kitchen unit, David instinctively grabbed Christina and rushed to the door.

'Move!'

A secondary charge went off, with a burst of heat and flame, and David felt the hair on the back of his head burning. As they reached the back lobby door, a series of charges went off around the house, followed immediately by a massive sheet of flame from the dining room, adjacent to the kitchen.

At the end of the lobby, there was another blast, which

blew them out of the door, onto the snow. They both rolled instinctively, covering the outbuildings and grounds with their automatics. Behind them the wood crackled and spat as a fire took hold, as another couple of blasts came from the top floor. Then only the sound of the roaring fire, in the strengthening wind.

'Are you all right, David?' Christina got to her feet, still covering the outbuildings with her Glock.

'Yeh, I'm fine. How about you?'

'Okay,' she nodded, as he brushed snow from his coat.

The villa was now totally engulfed by fire, the heat forcing them to move away.

'Let's get the hell out of here. Come on,' he said,

Running through the paddock, they could hear the nervous neighing of the horses in the stables and the replies from those in the field. They had been spooked, and were trotting back and forth, the breath from their flared nostrils condensing in the freezing air.

Just as they were about to enter the edge of the forest, a Learjet passed low over the house. It banked its wings to port, levelled out, and flew west over the sea, its engines screaming as it rapidly gained height and sped away from the coast.

'That was definitely somebody linked to the house, there must be an airfield near here. It looked as if they were checking that the place was ablaze. Watch out, here is the electric fence,' David said, ducking under the wire and holding Christina's head low as she cleared it.

'Do you think we were meant to be caught in the fire?' She grabbed his hand as she tripped on a tree root.

'No. I think that they'd've waited, if they'd thought we were coming. Something panicked them, something Erland said to them. Poor bastard, he was about to retire. All those years of work, and then this mess.'

'Do you think our friend Matti Fjällman was on that plane?' She shivered, hugging herself as she walked.

'I'm bloody sure of it. I also wonder why they removed most of the paintings. They must've been worth it. I wonder if they came from a collection deep underneath Franconia, part of a list of looted art as long as your arm.'

They got back to Lindén's car, and looked for any sign of new footprints. David shone the torch on the snow around the Volvo,

'There's been nobody here since we left it, but there's sure to be a charge in the car too. Let's go,' he urged.

They checked to see if there had been any movement around their own vehicle since they had parked. Everything was clear, but as they opened the doors to get in, there was a muffled thud from down the road, and flames engulfed Lindén's car.

As David drove, the warmth returned to their extremities, and nerves began to settle after the horrors of the villa.

'I'm getting far too old for this nonsense,' he said, running his fingers through the stubble on his head. Feeling crisp ends at the back, he brushed them off, releasing the unmistakeably sweet odour of burnt keratin.

Two kilometres later, they saw a sign for an airport.

'That must be Gothenburg City Airport. The taxi driver pointed it out to me, on the way back today. That's certainly where they left from.' She rubbed her frozen hands together, groaning as she did so.

'Well, David, what do we do now? Where do we go next?'

'Don't know, but I'm sure Erland would've left us something, somewhere, he would've covered himself, he was too Swedish not to have done. He was a stickler for doing things right, that's why he went out there alone. He had to do it himself first, it was a pride thing.'

'His pride got him killed.' She turned in her seat to check some headlights that had drawn in behind them, but the other car turned off at the next side road.

Soon they were back among the city lights and heading for Hisingeleden and the Älvsborgsbron.

'I didn't have a chance to tell you what Shoshanim said. He's getting a list of all the tunnels that the Soviets blew up in the sixties, and the ones they know've collapsed. He must have access to records somewhere,' she said.

'Couldn't your people help?' David indicated to turn off, down the exit for Oscarsleden, and the hotel.

'I doubt it,' she said, 'to try to get any information from the East Germans in 1989 was a joke, and records in the old Soviet states are chaotic. God knows what's missing, stolen or destroyed every day. Shoshanim says that the Mossad had several double agents in the Soviet and Eastern Bloc intelligence services, from the 1950s up to the fall of the Wall. That information can be put together, to give us as complete a picture as possible. God, I'm hungry, aren't you?'

David hadn't been feeling at all well, since the rush across the paddock, and the very thought of food made him feel queasy.

'No, not at the moment, maybe later. You can order something from room service, it's too late to eat out.'

He turned off at Jaegerdorffsmötet, but too fast for the road conditions. The back of the car stepped out violently, and he just managed to correct the skid before they mounted the pavement, where they would have hit a couple of women waiting to cross.

'Whoa, we just survived being burnt to death, don't kill me outside the hotel.' She put her hand on his, on the steering wheel. 'You feel bad, don't you, David?' She stroked his fingers lovingly.

'I've felt better, yes.' He drove into the car park, and pulled up the handbrake with a long sigh. 'I'm going to have to sit here for a bit, sorry.' He leant back against the headrest and closed his eyes.

Christina leant across and felt his brow. 'You're burning up again, David. This isn't a virus or something you ate, this is serious, you have to see a doctor. You promised me.'

Chapter 23

It had been a night of fitful and feverish sleep. The bed linen was soaking wet, as was the pillow, and his throat was dry and raw from snoring. He reached out to touch Christina and realised that he was alone. Raising his head he peered into the gloom of the other room, able to make out the sleeping figure on the sofa, covered with a duvet and blanket which had been stored atop one of the cupboards.

Getting out of bed as quietly as he could, he went into the bathroom, to swill his teeth with mouthwash and try to rid himself of the acrid taste on his tongue. As he gargled, the green liquid burnt as it made contact with the soft tissue at the back of his throat, making him gag as he spat it out.

He was shocked as he urinated, both by the dark colour and the pungent smell of what he passed. It smelled metallic, like fingers do after cleaning a piece of brass or silver. Was this his liver or his kidneys packing up?

He got an orange juice from the mini-bar, gulping it down eagerly. Immediately, he took another bottle from its shelf.

'Thank God. You've stopped snoring.' Her tousled head appeared out of the mountain of bedclothes on the sofa. 'Seriously, how do you feel? You were turning all the time in the night, and you were soaking with sweat, so I slept on here. Sorry, but…'

'Did you get much sleep?' He sat on the sofa and brushed hair from her face.

'Not bad, but we must get you to a doctor. Agree?' She took his hand and held it to her cheek.

'Agreed,' he said.

'Okay, I'm going down for breakfast and some fresh air. I think we have to check out this morning. The villa at Nolvik will be full of police by now, and the car was one of theirs. They must know that Lindén took it.' She stretched, wrapping the duvet around her, and made for the bathroom. 'Do you want any breakfast David?'

The very thought made him feel unwell.

'No thanks. I'll take it easy and have a coffee. That'll do me.'

She came back out of the bathroom naked, and hugged him, burying her head in his neck.

'Please, David, fix a doctor while I'm having breakfast. Please.' As she pulled away, he could see the tears on her cheeks.

'Yes, I promise. Look, I think we have some time, the building was wooden, the roof and upper floors would've collapsed, covering Erland's remains. It'll take them some time to discover his body, or what's left of it. Let's both have a think about what to do next. After you come back, we'll make a decision.'

Christina wiped her eyes and went to the telephone, dialled reception, and gave David the phone.

'Here you are, no excuses.'

The concierge gave him the details for a doctor. Knowing the Swedes, they had already been at work for some time, so he rang the number. A female receptionist answered.

He explained that he was on holiday, and felt really unwell, describing some of the symptoms. The receptionist asked him to hold on, and some minutes later a man's voice came on the line.

'Doctor Hallberg speaking, how can I help you?' The voice was a cultured, rich baritone, the English excellent.

David repeated the situation and his symptoms, and the doctor asked him a few questions.

'Mr Sheehan, I think it'd be good, if you came in to see me, as soon as you can. We'll have a look at you, and take some blood samples. The results will take a couple of days. Is ten o'clock all right for you?'

'Perfect. Thanks for your help.'

Hallberg gave David instructions on how to get to the clinic, only a ten minute walk from the hotel.

The hair dryer stopped its whine in the bathroom, and Christina emerged and began dressing.

'Fixed up?' she asked.

'I have an appointment at ten o'clock. It's near the hotel. Okay?'

'Do you want me to come with you?' She brushed her hair and roughed it up with her hands.

He found himself gazing at her and realising that he was now under her spell again. She saw his reflection in the mirror and her image smiled back at him.

'That's a serious look.'

'I was thinking a serious thing. No I'll go on my own, it'll be boring for you.'

She kissed him on the cheek, and left to take her breakfast. Pausing at the door she came back, kissing him again. 'I love you David Lennox. See you in a bit.'

David sat for a long time, quietly thinking about the events of the last weeks. He took a long shower, and wondered what he and Christina should do next. He was towelling himself dry when he heard her coming back into the room. She poked her head around the corner of the bathroom door waving a letter.

'You were right. Your poor friend Mr Lindén, sent us a note yesterday, shall I read it out?'

David nodded.

Pulling out the letter, she read aloud.

"Dear David,

I have sent this as a kind of insurance, in case something happens to me tonight. I'm going out to the villa, to check it out. This is what I can tell you so far.

The place is registered in the name of a German national, Johannes Zapf, as a holiday home. He's listed as a security consultant, offices in Erfurt Germany and Berwang Austria." She paused and raised her eyebrows.

David's mouth dropped open. 'Alias Herr Fischer, whose brains are all over the top of Caw.'

'After a lot of digging, I found that Matti Fjällman came here via South America and South Africa. His original birth documents, as a Swedish national, are false. Somebody in my department deliberately sat on requests for information from the War Crimes Commission and the Jewish organisations. I think he's quite definitely your man Von den Bergen. He was registered first at an address in Stockholm, but after the requests from the WCC and the Jews, he disappeared. Somebody in the Swedish Civil Service must have tipped him off.

Locals in Nolvik say that they never meet people from the villa, but have seen an older man, a man in his late eighties, as a passenger in vehicles going to, and coming from, the property. They have also seen him walking in the grounds of the house. They assumed it was the father of the owner, but there's no paperwork linking the two.

His files were missing from the archives in Uppsala, but I have a very old friend in that office, he found me the original microfiche. Our man's thought, by our military intelligence, to have somehow given the South Africans the know-how and wherewithal to make, and successfully explode, a nuclear weapon in the Indian Ocean in the 1970s.

That's why his name was on the Palme file. I also discovered a file on a South African link to the death of Palme's colleague, Bernt Carlsson, on Pan Am flight 103 over Lockerbie in 1988.'

Christina stopped reading and looked at David.

'David, are you thinking what I'm thinking?'

David most certainly was.

'How powerful was the explosion in the Vela incident?' As he spoke he turned on the television and selected the Internet option.

'Here it is. "Vela satellite, 22nd of September 1979, Indian Ocean. Likely Vela detection of South African nuclear test classified as satellite error by the Carter administration. Yield circa three kilotons. Israel denies being involved with the South Africans." How powerful are the demolition weapons we suspect are underground in Thüringia?' he asked.

'One to five kilotons. Depends how you link them. Do you think Von den Bergen found them and passed them to the South Africans?'

'Absolutely. He knew how to get into a limited area of the tunnels, and no more. Maybe he found some of the weapons put there by the Soviets. Zapf and Gehrling must've known that there were a hell of a lot more down there after the tunnel collapses, but didn't know how to get at them, until they traced Von den Bergen as the source of the bomb or bombs to the South Africans. They must've struck some kind of deal, and Von den Bergen put them on to Voss. He knew that Voss must know something, as he'd stayed around the immediate area of the tunnels after the war. Zapf and Gehrling tortured Voss, and killed him too quickly in the process, but not before, I suspect, he gave them the list of the prisoners who'd met your grandfather, that cold winter's day in Poland, in 1944. They realised the significance of your grandfather's work on the tunnel system.'

Christina started reading again. 'There's a little more.'

"I've been contacted by Tord Eliasson. He has obviously installed an alarm system if certain subjects are entered on the department search engine. He wanted to know why I was interested in the names Von den Bergen and Matti Fjällman, and why this was linked to the villa in Nolvik. (The villa is called Franconia by the way.) He explained that he was working on infiltrating an arms ring, with the Danish secret service, and that the villa played a major part in the picture. He has arranged to meet me later and fill me in on the detail. I haven't mentioned you or your sources in any of this, and don't intend to."

Christina read the post mark on the envelope.

'Posted yesterday at 16.30.'

David was puzzled.

'He left the message to meet him at the villa much later. He must've learnt something new. Well, if they learnt that somebody had linked Von den Bergen to Fjällman, they would've thought it was time to move on. No wonder the haste in which they left. I don't think they got anything from Erland. They would've waited for us, no doubt about it. Poor bastard, I told him to keep out.'

'You ought to go, David, it's twenty-to-ten.'

He kissed her on the lips, and buried his head in her neck.

'I'm sorry that I feel so bloody awful.' He stroked her cheek and sniffed her hair. 'Back in a jiff, I hope.'

'Make sure you tell the doctor everything, I know what you're like.' She wagged her finger in admonishment.

'Yes, I promise.' He bowed his head in mock submission.

The walk to the clinic took a quarter-of-an-hour. The building was typical for a Swedish city centre, built in the late nineteenth, early twentieth century, with high ceilings, large entrance halls and antique open lifts, from which the staircase landings had at least four doors leading to private flats, small consulting companies, doctors, dentists and osteopaths of all description.

Some of these properties were starting to look a little shoddy and down at heel, but this building looked immaculate, and expensive.

He pressed the visitor button on the entry phone for Hallberg, and bent to the microphone.

'Mr Sheehan to see Doctor Hallberg.' The door lock buzzed, and he entered the elegant entrance hall. A wall plaque listed all the apartments and clinics.

Hallberg. Fourth floor.

Should he be lazy, and take the lift? No. He decided to take the stairs, wishing he hadn't by the time he arrived outside the clinic door. Leaning against the wrought iron, art nouveau banister rail, he got his breath back, before pressing yet another entry phone.

The door opened to reveal a very pretty blonde receptionist.

'Please take a seat in the waiting room, Mr Sheehan, I'll tell the doctor you are here.'

He sat down on a comfortable Swedish period chair, in the refined interior of the anteroom. Eighteenth and nineteenth century Scandinavian oil paintings covered the walls. One was an original work by the nineteenth-century artist, Zorn, worth a small fortune. David went over, to take a closer look at the picture.

'It's beautiful, isn't it, Mr Sheehan?'

David turned and greeted Hallberg, a tall man in his early forties, with cropped blond hair and the most piercing blue eyes David had ever seen in a man.

'Yes it certainly is.'

David wanted to tell the Swede that he had a similar painting, at home in the Lakes - his ex-wife had been related to Zorn - but as he was here as a South African, he had to be discreet.

'Do you know of our famous painter Zorn?' Hallberg came and admired the painting.

'Yes, I know of him of course, from visits to Dalarna where he was born and lived, but I don't know his work so well,' David lied.

They shook hands and Hallberg gestured to the corridor outside.

'Please take the second door to the left, Mr Sheehan, and let's have a look at you.'

In the consulting room David sat at a large mahogany writing desk opposite the doctor, who donned half-moon reading glasses and unscrewed a stylish gold fountain pen.

'So, Mr Sheehan I understand that you're feeling nauseous and giddy, and you have loss of appetite. You have a fever, and you're vomiting. Any rashes on the skin, any stomach cramps, weight loss?'

David had noticed a roughness on his hands of late.

'No rash, not really, but the skin on my hands is strangely rough. I put it down to the cold Scandinavian climate. Weight loss? I lost a lot on purpose, but now, I don't know. Stomach cramps? Not really.'

'Could I look at your hands, please?' Hallberg leant over the desk, and inspected David's hands. 'What's your date of birth?' he enquired.

'25th March 1957.'

'Any hair loss?'

David grimaced as he thought of the singeing he'd had last night, but he'd also realised that his scalp had become rather itchy. Some of his number two haircut, was becoming a number zero.

'Yes maybe.'

'Does the problem get worse after physical exertion?' Hallberg asked.

'It seems to,' David said, remembering the stairs.

'How's your urine. Coloured? Does it smell strange?'

'Yes to both. It's a dark brown and it smells, well, funny, almost metallic.'

'Do you work in the metal industry or with metals?' Hallberg enquired, looking up from his note writing.

'No. No I don't,' answered David, puzzled.

'All right, please remove your shoes, shirt and jacket, and lie down here, Mr Sheehan.'

David did as he was told, but as he bent down to unlace his brogues he experienced another feeling of nausea, and retched involuntarily. He steadied himself against the examination bed.

'Do you need some water, Mr Sheehan?' Hallberg studied David, with his remarkable eyes.

He shook his head.

'No, no thanks. That's been happening a lot, when I bend down or get up too quickly.'

He undressed and got on to the bed, feeling another wave of giddiness as his head hit the paper covered pillow.

'Are you taking any regular medication, Mr Sheehan?' As he spoke he wrapped the sphygmometer cuff around David's arm and started to pump it up.

'Yes, Lisinopril. 10 milligrammes daily, for my blood pressure.'

'Okay. Let's just check your reactions.' He took the cuff off and started to tap David's joints. 'Tongue out please. All right, well there's no evidence of stroke. I notice some muscle tremor in this arm. How long have you had that?' He shone an ophthalmoscope into David's eyes.

'Oh about two years now. I had a scan, it's the foramina in my neck apparently.' Hallberg put his light away and started to press on David's abdomen.

'Any pain here, or here?' He pressed just below the rib cage where David knew his liver was.'

Shit.

'Yes, that hurts a bit.' David winced as the doctor probed again in the same general area.

'Are you a big drinker, Mr Sheehan, or have you ever been?'

'Yes. Until recently, yes.'

'And now?' Hallberg lifted the earpieces of his stethoscope and listened to David's breathing and heart.

'Very little now. I have it under control, for several reasons.'

'Sounds like love to me,' the Doctor smiled. 'Could you undo the belt on your trousers, please?' He went over to a cabinet, and took out a packet of plastic gloves and some lubricating cream.

'Oh Christ, no.' David muttered under his breath.

'I'm going to have a look at your prostate and other organs, Mr Sheehan.' He saw the look of discomfort on David's face, and a broad grin grew into a spluttering guffaw. 'No, oh no. I'm going to use the ultrasound machine. Nothing intrusive, I promise you.'

With that he smothered the face of the apparatus with lubricating oil and turned on the monitor. He made several passes over David's liver and prostate.

'So. Your prostate's slightly enlarged, that's quite usual at your age. Your liver isn't looking so good, but that won't be the primary cause for your illness now, or at least I don't think so. Let's have a look at your heart and thyroid.' He applied more cream to the machine and scanned David's chest and throat.

'No problems there. All right, Mr Sheehan, please do up your belt. Sit up, and I'll take some blood. I'll also ask you to provide some urine, I'm a little concerned about the coarsening of the skin on your hands, but the blood and urine samples should provide some clues. How are you at giving blood? No problems with needles?'

David smiled and shook his head.

'Not so far.'

Hallberg took several samples of blood, and wrote details on the plastic phials. After he had put a plaster on David's arm, he handed him a small sample bottle.

'There's a toilet in the next room. I need you to take a sample mid-stream, if you can.

When David returned, Hallberg was consulting a large tome at his desk. David didn't know what to do with the urine, so he held it up meekly, like an awkward schoolboy.

Hallberg seemed lost in thought and note taking, seemingly oblivious to David's return. He eventually acknowledged the figure standing forlornly in the middle of the room, waving a bottle of dark liquid at him.

'Oh, so sorry, put it on the worktop there will you, and get dressed, then we'll have a chat.'

David did so, and sat opposite the doctor, who was still making copious notes. Finally he put down his pen and nodded.

'Well, I'll tell you what I'm going to do, Mr Sheehan. I'm a little surprised at some of the symptoms you're presenting, and I'm going to try and get these samples looked at this morning and ask you to come and see me some time this afternoon, when I should have the results back.'

He went over to David's urine sample, and after looking at it against the daylight of the window, wrote details on the container.

'Do you have any ideas?'

David was getting concerned at the seeming urgency with which Hallberg was processing his samples. Perhaps he just wanted to make sure he got his fee.

'I'd rather wait for the results, if you don't mind, and then we can look at it in a practical light. Is that all right?'

'Yes okay. Will you ring me at the hotel?' David got up to leave.

Hallberg covered his hands and nose with his hands in a gesture of prayer. He was going to ask something tricky. David knew the body language well.

‘Just one more question, Mr Sheehan. Do you have a regular partner?’

‘Well, I restarted an old relationship a week ago, yes. Is this sexual?’

‘No…no, but is he or she with you here in Sweden.’

He or she. Very Swedish.

‘Yes she is. Is that relevant?’ This line of questioning now alarmed David.

‘How long have you really been feeling unwell?’ Hallberg was now reading the large reference book again.

‘About four days I think. Yes, four or five days.’ Christ. Did Christina have some exotic disease?

‘Have I caught something? What do you suspect is wrong?’

‘No, nothing, really nothing. I just want as much information as possible, to tell the lab what to look out for. I’ll give you a call at the hotel.’

The doctor pressed a button on the desk, and the receptionist came in to show David out. He walked slowly down the stairs, preoccupied with trying to figure out where Hallberg had been going with his line of questioning.

He left the building, still lost in thought, only dimly aware of a vehicle approaching him from behind, its tyres cracking the frozen ice in the gutter.

As he turned to look, he was hit with violent force in the small of the back, by the onside rear door of a dark green Range Rover. He fell and rolled, having a momentary glimpse of blacked out windows, and a pair of jeaned legs beside him.

The blow behind his left ear was only painful for a brief millisecond, before the darkness of unconsciousness and the buzzing in his ears washed him onto a beach, where a smiling Joseph Novak was waiting for him, smoking the pipe and studying the map.

‘Hello, my friend. Come…come…we’re having a fish dinner.’

Farther up the beach, sitting around an open fire, were David’s parents, Bill Kenton and an old white-haired man, whose ghostlike hands were tearing off strips of flesh from a large fish cooking on hot rocks by the fire.

'This is Matti Fjällman, son.' David's father introduced the old man.

David sat and tore a succulent piece of fish off, exposing the spine, it tasted metallic, almost as though the hook was still in the flesh. He tried to get it out of his mouth, gagging as he did so.

At that moment Rudolph Hess came out of the trees at the high-tide line, dressed in full parade uniform, and holding the hand of a younger man who David vaguely recognised. This man was holding a bucket of water which he threw over the fire, soaking everybody in the process .

Somebody was forcing his fingers between David's teeth, trying to pull his tongue out.

Chapter 24

The headache as he came round was blinding. He was gagging and suffocating. The man he recognised as the driver of the car to Nolvik,Tord Eliasson, was forcing his mouth open, and attaching an electrode to his tongue. As he gathered his senses, he realised that he was naked, soaking wet, and had another electrode attached to his testicles.

Eliasson was a tall, well-built, man in his forties, who had cold grey eyes, with hooded eyelids that overlapped the eyelashes. David knew from his manner, that he didn't give a shit about human life, especially not David's.

The room was roughly six metres by eight, and was obviously in a basement, because although the beige blinds had been pulled down, they were small and high up on the wall. It was unfurnished, apart from the wooden chair that he was tied to and a small pine coffee table to his left where another, younger, thick-set man with long red hair was preparing a syringe.

David guessed that they were in a safe house, or a property that was on the market and empty, as there was an unlived-in odour to the place. There was no traffic noise at all, and it seemed probable that they were in a detached villa, somewhere on the outskirts of the city.

'Welcome back, Mr Lennox.'

Eliasson pressed a button on the charge unit, and David's spine arched as he let out an animal scream. He tried to eject his dental bridge from his mouth before he swallowed it and choked. He felt gum, and realised that they had already removed it, his mouth was full of bits of tooth and filling, which had split off as he had involuntarily bitten down.

Bastard.

'I want you to know, David - may I call you David? No matter. I want you to know, that that was the lowest setting, and in a little while, my colleague will inject you with a very modern hyperalgesic. I'm sure you are au fait with them. It'll intensify the pain from your nerve endings to unbelievable levels. Erland was very careless, all those phone calls from his mobile, so easy to triangulate the Novotel. He never stays there. Why was he there, I asked myself? He'd earlier left a letter for the Sheehans, the helpful receptionists informed us. Who were they? Mrs Sheehan wasn't at the hotel when we called, and the stuff they had deposited in the hotel safe was gone.'

Damn. Where was she now?

'When we looked at CCTV from the hotel. My Lord! David Lennox with a very beautiful blonde. When we ran a check on her photograph, we came up with Christina Karranova, ex KGB and we presume now working for the Slovak security services. What a catch. The concierge kindly gave us the address of the doctor's clinic he'd recommended to Mr Sheehan. So helpful. So, David - excuse me, Mr Sheehan - what did you tell Erland, and why? Why did he ask me about Matti Fjällman?' He warmed his hands on the radiator behind him.

Erland must have died without telling them anything.

Eliasson nonchalantly pressed the charge button again. The inside of David's head exploded in a light show of sparks and stars, his back muscles went into cramp, as did his right leg, which was firmly tied to the chair. The pain was so intense, his reaction so violent, that both he and the chair flew backwards. His tongue was now swelling badly, blood speckled froth dribbled out of the corner of his mouth. His legs were soaked with his urine.

The Swede's mobile phone rang, and he turned away from his work on David, to speak.

'Yes, Hi, Hans Jürgen. Yes…yes we have Lennox here…Yes he'll talk…No we don't have the woman yet. How's the old man? All right, I'll phone you later…no problem. We'll lose him from my boat. It's very deep off the main channel. Yes, bis später.'

He motioned for the other man to pick David up, which he did by grabbing the back of the chair with one hand whilst holding the hypodermic aloft in the other.

Eliasson nodded again and the man approached David with

an expectant grin, revealing very bad, nicotine-stained, teeth. The stench of his breath was overpowering, causing David to retch.

'Forgive me. How rude of me, I haven't introduced my Chechen friend, Ruslan. Say hello, Ruslan.' Eliasson put his hand on the younger man's shoulder.

David retched again, as the Chechen put his face as close as possible without their noses touching. He first plunged the needle into David's scrotum, and then, as Eliasson held David's head, into his swollen tongue. His grin widened, as he violently injected the remainder of the content of the hypodermic into the soft tissue at the base of the tongue.

'Hello, my friend. Welcome.' He twisted the needle, so that it broke off and remained sticking out of the flesh.

This had to be the bastard who worked on Erland.

'Now we must wait a few minutes, David, so that the nerve endings around your body are saturated. Then Ruslan can have some fun. He tells me that he can sometimes cum in his trousers, if people really scream for mercy. Personally, it does nothing for me, I just want to hear what you know.'

David looked at the Chechen who now had a visible erection, and was squeezing the end of his penis with the palm of his hand.

The dull noise of something falling in another part of the house alarmed Eliasson, and he opened the door, calling out to someone.

'Är det du, Johan?' There was no answer, so he motioned with his head for Ruslan to have a look.

As the Chechen got to the open door, a woman's voice shouted something in Russian. There was the metallic pop of a silenced round, and the back of Ruslan's neck exploded in a shower of bone, blood and gristle. He went down vertically, mid-stride, dead before he even started to drop. His head lay at an improbable angle to his torso, because he didn't have the middle two cervical vertebrae to hold his cranium on any more.

Suddenly, Christina was in the doorway. As Eliasson reached

for a weapon, she fired three more shots in rapid succession. Pop to the weapon arm. Pop to the right kneecap. Pop to the left.

The Swede lay writhing in agony on the floor. Christina took his automatic from its armpit holster, and stepped over him, deliberately treading on his mangled legs as she did so. Eliasson screamed and vomited, trying to hold his knees with his one good hand.

David managed a weak smile as she carefully removed both electrodes. The hyperalgesics had begun to take effect, and he stifled a cry as she accidentally touched the end of the hypodermic, still sticking out of the base of his tongue.

She undid the plastic ties securing his hands and feet, and stroked the top of his head, gently kissing it.

'Sorry I couldn't stop them sooner, but there was another guy in the kitchen. There's a shower across the hallway by the stairs, there must be hot water because the heating's on. I'll find a towel. Can you walk?' she asked.

He fumbled in his mouth for the end of the needle, and pulled it out, the pain like nothing he had ever experienced. He tried to soothe it by rubbing the underside of his tongue with his fingers, but his whole nervous system was a jangle of raw sensation. Even touching the floor with his bare feet was agony.

'How in Christ's name did you know where to find me?'

He got to his feet unsteadily, and made towards the door, past the now pitiful figure of Eliasson, who was groaning and whimpering on the floor, trying to feel his crippled legs, and staunch the gushing flow of blood from his severed popliteal artery.

'I got a warning call from Shoshanim. His people were following Eliasson, and listening to his mobile phone traffic. I checked out of the hotel before they arrived.'

He winced as he took another step.

'What do we do with him?' He nodded towards the inert Swede.

'I think we find out who is who and what is what. Yes?'

She stood over Eliasson, who was going through the first stages of neurogenic shock.

'I drove to the doctor's address, and when I arrived I saw them pushing you into a Range Rover, I followed them and…here I am.'

Bending down she felt Eliasson's pulse. 'He's dying. Go and have a shower, David. I'll try to talk to him.'

'Do you have all the papers and the map?' He steadied himself against the wall.

'Yes everything is safe with me.'

The pain of walking was getting more intense. He made it to the shower, letting the water flow until it ran hot, putting out his hand to check the temperature. He screamed in agony as the hot water made contact with his skin.

Christina rushed in.

'David, what's wrong?' She tried to hug him, but even that was painful, and he pulled away.

'They injected me with some kind of pain enhancer, and I can tell you it really bloody works. Even the hot water hurts.'

His swollen tongue was now making normal speech difficult, if not impossible. She turned down the thermostatic mixer on the shower, and tested the water.

'Try it now.'

He put out his hand and it was just bearable. He stood under the cascade for several minutes without moving, wondering if there was any ice in the kitchen to put in his mouth, to ease the swelling. He soaped his body gingerly, wracked with pain when he attempted to wash his genitalia. His scrotum had swollen to the size of an orange, and a throbbing ache had spread into his bladder. Christina had found him a towel, and put his clothes on a chair at the foot of the stairs. Sitting neatly on top of the pile was his dental bridge.

What the hell did she see in him?

It was now becoming almost intolerable to walk, the weight of his body pressing down on the nerve endings in his feet. He got dressed with great difficulty, as every touch of his skin now sent shocks through his entire body. He stumbled back into the hall as Christina was coming out of the dayroom.

'He's dead. I'll tell you about it in the car. Can you walk without help?'

'Yes, but it's getting worse. Where are we going?'

She helped him up the stairs, one riser at a time, into the ground floor reception hall. David looked around.

'Where's the kitchen?' he asked.

Christina opened a door to the right of the hallway, and nudged it ajar, helping David in, pushing it fully open with her shoulder. It was then that David understood the reason that she had needed so much force, a third man lay dead on the tiled floor behind it, one round to the head and one to the heart.

'You don't bugger about, do you?' he mumbled.

He went to the fridge, pulled out an ice tray, and crammed two cubes into his mouth, the rest he put in a plastic bag. The pain was so intense that he nearly spat them out again, but he knew he had to get the swelling in his tongue under control, if he was not to choke to death.

'We have to go, David. I'll phone Shoshanim later to see if his people can clean up in here.'

The villa stood on its own, two hundred metres off a quiet country track, so Christina had parked some distance away,

'David, you wait here, I'll get the car.'

The sky was cloudless, a typical freezing Swedish winter's day. As he waited, he took another couple of ice cubes and put them on his tongue.

A bull elk wandered out of the forest to his right, steam rising from its back. It stood looking at David for some minutes, before it turned and walked nonchalantly back into the trees at the sound of the car coming up to the house. As David pondered the silent beauty of this scene, he thought how macabre it was, compared to that inside the house.

He grunted in agony, as he manoeuvred himself into the back

seat, and fell rather than lay down. He stuffed some more ice cubes into his mouth, and mumbled to Christina that he couldn't speak.

'I'll talk, you can tell me about the doctor later,' she said.

Eliasson had said nothing before he died, but she had the last number dialled to his phone. The name was in the phone memory. Hans Jürgen Gehrling.

David inserted some more ice under his tongue. Sleep was overtaking him, but he realised it would be better to keep awake and rid his body of the chemicals that were tormenting his nerve endings. He held the remainder of the ice in the bag behind his swollen ear, generally feeling sorry for himself, as Christina drove as smoothly as the frozen road would permit.

After a few miles, they came to a small town with a street kiosk, where Christina bought some cold drinks and some newspapers.

'I think we'd better wait somewhere until you feel better. I think then it's the airport and the next flight to Frankfurt. I don't believe we can stay in Sweden any longer. At the next phone booth, I'll phone Shoshanim and tell him what's been happening, and what we're going to do next. By the way, he says he'll have the information on the tunnel system in a couple of days or so.'

'Does he know about the secret chamber?' David flinched as his tongue tried to work against his teeth and lips.

'Absolutely not, only that a map exists. He trusts us, David. Whatever's in that chamber is something we must deal with later, if we find it. Okay, here's a clearing in the trees, I'll stop here.' She pulled well off the road so passing vehicles wouldn't see them.

David attempted to sit up straight, but the pain in his testicles was too much, and he lay back down, letting the veil of deep, dreamless sleep descend.

It was nearly two o'clock when he woke. Christina had her seat reclined and was listening to the BBC World Service on

the car radio.
'Do you feel any better?'
'Yes. At least my tongue isn't so swollen. I still ache like hell everywhere else.'
'We should go soon, if you're okay, David,' she said
'I need to pee.' He got out of the car, with difficulty, to stretch his legs and to urinate.

The pain as he passed water was distressing but not excruciating, he could feel that walking was also becoming more bearable. He got back into the front passenger seat and breathed in deeply.
'Right the airport it is.'
'Now tell me, what did the doctor say? What does he think's wrong with you?' She asked, spinning the back wheels as they rejoined the metalled road.
'God knows.'

David told her about the really weird questions, the blood and urine samples and the fact that the Doctor seemed worried, wanting to send everything away for testing immediately.
'I was to meet him this afternoon to get the results. Damn. He was going to ring the hotel, I'll have to call him from the airport.' David checked in his pocket to see if he still had the number.
'What do you mean, weird questions?' She pulled a quizzical face as she manoeuvred the car around some deep snow.
'Wanted to know if I had a regular partner with me, male or female and…'
'Christ, David, does he think you have AIDS or something?' She took her eyes off the road and looked around at him, real worry in her eyes.
'No. Thank you for your vote of confidence, but I asked him if he thought it might be sexual, and he gave me a definite NO.' He raised his eyebrows and smiled at her. 'So relax Karranova, you're not going to die because you have slept with me. There was nothing wrong with my todger before our friends Eliasson

and Arslan or Ruslan, or whatever his bloody name was, attached it to large amounts of electrical current and stuck a very large hypodermic in my scrotum.' He smiled again, but this time with an expression of feigned hurt. 'Okay?'

'I'm sorry, but why was he asking about, well…me? Does he think I've got something?' She put her hand to her breasts in indignation.

'Christina, I just don't know what the hell he was driving at. I really don't. Let's wait until I've spoken to him. Now give me a kiss, to hell with the danger.'

He leant across and kissed her on the cheek, pleased to see a smile of pleasure on her face.

Christina rang Shoshanim from a telephone box in the next village.

Shoshanim wasn't there, but she had spoken to Isaac, she told David. They knew that the pair wanted to visit Berwang and were fixing to be in Garmisch-Partenkirchen, just over the border in Germany.

Berwang was a very small village with only one road running through the valley. It was very busy with tourists staying for Christmas, and it would be too easy to spot the Israelis or David and Christina. Isaac had given her some suggestions for hotels in Garmisch for the Christmas period. It should be possible to get a room, as there had been cancellations, because of poor snow conditions on the ski slopes round the town. He had added that someone would be picking up the automatics at the airport.'

'Christmas in Garmisch. That's very romantic actually.Can we both try not to get shot, or die in brutal circumstances for a few days?' He gave her a pleading look.

'It'll be tricky, but hell, let's try,' she said, stroking his cheek.

When they were unloading the luggage at the airport, David realised that natural sensation was returning to his nervous system and his walking was almost back to normal. The Glocks were back in the bag they were dropped off in, and on top of the trolley.

They entered the departure hall separately, in case the Swedish police had connected them in any way to the body they must have now found at Nolvik. As David approached the information desk, a young sharp-featured man in his late twenties approached him, deftly removing the Glocks in their bag, and walking on past to the exit.

They found a Lufthansa flight to Frankfurt via Copenhagen at 17.10, arriving Frankfurt Main at 21.10, and booked tickets, still using the name of Sheehan.

After checking in, they went to a private lounge, David going to contact Dr Hallberg whilst Christina got on the Internet to book a hotel for the night in Frankfurt and for the Christmas week in Garmisch.

'Hello, this is Mr Sheehan. I'm calling to speak to Doctor Hallberg about the results of my test.'

'Oh yes, Mr Sheehan, hold on please.' choral music was playing in the background.

Bach. Matthew Passion.

'Good afternoon, Mr Sheehan.' The music muted immediately. 'I tried to get you at the Hotel, but they said that you'd checked out.' A long pause signalled that Hallberg was looking to hear an apology.

'Yes, so sorry, bit of a drama at home with one of my children, I'm afraid. You know the kind of thing.' Shit. That was weak.

'Can you come in and see me this afternoon, it's…I don't want to worry you, but it's rather important?'

'I'm really sorry, but I'm leaving Sweden this afternoon.'

'Ah…Mr Sheehan, there's the delicate question of my fee, and I must tell you that you need urgent treatment.'

'Please give me your bank account details, Doctor Hallberg, I'll transfer the cash on the Internet straight away, you can rely on that. I know this is a little cheeky in the circumstances, but is it possible to give me some indication of what the urgent problem is?'

'I was going to tell you anyway. You need immediate medication. If you can give me an address, I can send you a report for your doctor, or the hospital.'

'Hospital?' Jesus it's cancer. 'Leukaemia?' David prayed that the answer would be no.

'You're being gradually poisoned by thallium, Mr Sheehan.'

Chapter 25

Hallberg explained that they knew that it was gradually, because the amount in David's blood, ingested at one time, would have resulted in paralysis of the lower limbs after a few days, and there were significant traces in the urine samples. It was normal to have minute amounts of thallium in the system, due to pollution, but nothing like the levels they had found, which meant that he must have been exposed to it today as well.

Somehow he had regularly, maybe daily, been ingesting small quantities of thallium, which is an extremely poisonous and dangerous metal. Put frankly, Hallberg said, if he did not get treatment very quickly, he would die.

Was that why Hallberg had asked him if he had a partner? The doctor thought someone was poisoning him.

'I want you to get this report, on thallium levels and your kidney and liver functions, to a doctor or a hospital as soon as possible. Give me a fax number and I'll send it to you.

The only known and only possible successful treatment is prussian blue and that is only available as a medication from a German manufacturer. I'll send all the details. You need a specialist now. Yesterday would've been better. Do you have any idea how this metal got into your system?'

'No idea at all. Really no idea.'

'Well please contact me, as soon as you have an address or a fax number. I must stress that your liver and kidney readings are reaching critical levels.'

'Yes. Yes, thank you, Doctor Hallberg. This has come as hell of a shock, as you can imagine. I'll call you tomorrow with the information. Thank you again.'

He took Hallberg's bank details, replaced the handset, and leant against the wall of the booth, his arms to both sides of the telephone and his head bowed against it.

Poison. What the hell was happening here? How was he ingesting thallium on a daily basis?

He felt Christina's hand on his shoulder. She slid it to the back of his neck, and gave it a gentle squeeze . Her voice was trembling.

'What is it, David. What now? What did he say?' She turned him round to face her, and kissed his face. 'What did the doctor say?' she demanded.

He returned the kiss and took her head in his hands, kissing her mouth softly and stroking her hair, brushing it off her forehead.

'I've been poisoned. The metal thallium, on a daily basis he says. I need treatment urgently, or I'm going to die. The test results say that my kidneys and liver are just about kaput.'

'Poisoned! How? I mean, how on a daily basis? That's why he asked if you had a partner. You don't think, David…?' She pushed away, holding him at arms length whilst she studied his face.

'No, of course I bloody don't. You've been on at me to see a doctor for days. No.' He pulled her back again and held his cheek to hers. 'No, okay?'

'Well, how then? How does he know it's on a regular basis,' she asked.

He told her what Hallberg had said.

'Well, what do you do daily? Clean your teeth. Is it your toothpaste or the mouthwash, the food, what?'

It hit him like a blow in the face.

'What did Jimmy Nolan say, just before he died?
"No,David…doctor…dying. Please listen …Prussian"
My God, Christina. "Prussian" was Jimmy Nolan's last word. It wasn't a person it was prussian blue. Jimmy knew I was being poisoned. He knew I was being poisoned with thallium, and he was telling me ***I*** needed a doctor, not him. That ***I*** was dying not him, and that I needed to take medication.'

Christina had her hands over her nose and mouth, in shock.

'David, I think I know what's poisoning you. You told me that your doctor's surgery was broken into, and your papers and your pills were lying on the…'

'My blood pressure pills. They've switched my bloody pills.

First thing I do after breakfast - take a pill every morning. Clever bastards. Who the hell's trying to kill us, Christina, and why are they trying to kill ***me*** slowly?'

He took his month's supply of pills from his pocket and studied the packet.

'Well if it is the pills, they've done a really good job. The packaging looks right. Wait a minute. Some of these pills are a little different in shape, every third one. One, two, and yes, today's would've been one of the different ones, that's why it showed up in my urine. I'm only taking thallium every third day, so the levels have built up slowly. They want me dead, but not straight away. What the hell is this all about?'

He handed the packet to Christina, who carefully scrutinised the half empty pack. She was staring at the floor, and spoke without looking up.

'It's been troubling me ever since we met, David. I think our people want us dead now. They tried to kill me, when they thought that you finally had the map, and I was of no more use. I always thought that, in the end, we were puppets in this business. Jimmy Nolan knew it too. I think his people killed him and his two colleagues, and then they tried to kill me. It always comes back to the Americans, the British and the Soviets, the three main allied powers. The three powers at the Yalta conference. I believe they want to find the secret chamber, but they know what's in there, and they don't want anyone to see it. You find it, and then…' She looked up with tears in her eyes, raising her eyebrows, looking for confirmation.

'I think you're right, which means we're really on our own, but what about the demolition weapons and anything else that's down there? How much do we tell Shoshanim?'

'We tell him about the weapons that could be used by enemies of Israel, and that's it, until we know what's in the chamber. Then we make another decision,' she said, wiping her eyes.

'That's if we're still alive.' David smiled sardonically. 'What if we just destroy the map now and go to ground?'

'We know too much, whatever it is. They have to kill us now.

If you're sure that this is linked to the murders of Palme and Hess, then they have to silence us. They'll find us in the end,' she said.

'So. It seems there are two agendas here. One is to find the so-called suitcase bombs, and that's what the Israelis and Gehrling's crew are after, but two - and it appears to be more important to our people - to find the chamber and whatever it contains. Moreover, they're going to eliminate anybody who gets too close to me.'

Christina handed back the pills, and looked up at the departures screen.

'We have an hour. I fixed a room at the Sheraton at Frankfurt Airport, and booked the hotel Bayerische Hof in Garmisch. Now I think we need to get you checked in to a clinic, as soon as possible. That's the number one priority. I'm going to phone Shoshanim, tell him about the thallium, and see if he can fix a good clinic in Munich or Garmisch. Whatever it takes, that's what we do first. By the way, the area code that Gehrling rang from was Berwang.'

She went back to the phone booth and rang the contact number for Shoshanim. David sat wondering why he was now entrusting his life to someone who had killed his friend Griff, and whose country seemed unable to get away from the 'eye for an eye' principle in their dealings with the Palestinians.

Because he was there. He was always bloody there, and he was good. Very good.

He pondered on the effect some of these suitcase weapons could have, in the hands of a suicide bomber, on the state of Israel, or any major city in Europe or the States. You could destroy the White House, the European Parliament, the Knesset or Downing Street from a mile away.

After some time, Christina returned, sat down beside him and put her arm in his.

'They're doing everything they can to help and said they'd contact us tonight at the Sheraton, although they're still not sure that we're sharing everything we know with them. God, I'm tired.' She nestled into his neck and he felt her warm forehead against his skin. 'How are you feeling? You have had a hell of a day.' She patted his leg and then tucked her hand under it.

'Well, since you removed the electrodes from my testicles there'd been a distinct improvement, bit of a bummer though, getting the news of my impending death so soon afterwards.'

They started laughing uncontrollably; it was both fatigue and release of tension. The more they laughed, the more raucous it became. David felt his stomach muscles cramping up, and realised that his body was not yet completely free of the hyperalgesic.

Christina took some tissues from her bag, and they dabbed at their eyes, still giggling quietly, occasionally breaking out in a mini fit of belly laughter again. It was a full five minutes before they regained some composure.

David rubbed his eyes and face and kissed the top of Christina's head.

'Oh Christ, that was good. I needed that.'

She squeezed his leg and then patted his thigh.

'Come on, let's go to the gate.'

The flight was delayed for some time, as the wings were de-iced, but soon they were on their way to Copenhagen. As they flew out over the Swedish west coast, David could briefly see the glittering lights of the city and the bridges below him before the clouds obscured them.

He thought about the four lives that had been so violently snuffed out during their brief stay. The Novak legacy was becoming a bit of a carnage.

How many more? Had his own father unwittingly condemned him and Christina to death by leaving the note and passing on the photograph and the pipe?

Fifty minutes later, he was woken by the jolt of the aircraft landing gear deploying as the plane banked sharply left around the back of the Danish airport and out over the sea, before turning again, levelling out for the landing at Kastrup.

Their gate to the onward flight to Frankfurt was in the same terminal arm where they had arrived, which was lucky for David as his legs were not yet fully back to normal, so he took a seat whilst Christina went off to have a look at the shops.

Having an hour to wait, he flipped through some of the magazines and newspapers available in the lounge. During a momentary glance up from his reading, he glimpsed somebody look away from him, as he caught their gaze.

A tall, wiry man of North African origin, in his late twenties or early thirties, was leaning against one of the support pillars in the adjoining lounge, watching CNN on the nearest overhead monitor. He was wearing a light blue suit with an open-necked white shirt, a sports bag over his shoulder.

Libyan? Moroccan? Tunisian? Maybe Egyptian? The face seemed familiar. Had he been the other man with Gehrling and Vicky Mason at the Elite Plaza?

David leant back in his chair, raising the newspaper in front of him so that he could read the top of the page, whilst keeping the man in his line of vision. He was definitely keeping an eye on David. From time to time he would walk slowly into the corridor to study the departure screens, before nonchalantly returning to the pillar and the television.

David got up and walked out into the passageway, making towards the nearest toilet. He passed a departures screen on the way and stopped, ostensibly to look at the information, but seeing the blue suit appear in his peripheral vision, he moved on.

He entered the toilet as an attendant had just finished mopping, and was placing a 'wet floor' warning cone in the small entrance lobby. David went into the second stall, locked the door and waited.

A few seconds later, he heard someone else enter, and use the hand basin. He closed the lid on the toilet and climbed on to it, as he did so he undid his trouser belt and pulled it free.

The lock flew off with a thunderous bang, as the door was

kicked open with tremendous force. The man in the blue suit stood temporarily frozen at the shock of David standing above him. In his outstretched hand, he held a large wad of cotton wool from which the heavy stench of chloroform was overpowering. David leapt forward and wound his trouser belt around the mans neck, pulling it tight with all the strength he could muster, whilst holding his breath.

The man struggled desperately, as David fought to retain his balance on the toilet seat. He still had the height advantage, and kept jerking the belt tight, finally feeling his assailant weaken. He jumped down, head-butting him twice, with a violence he had forgotten he possessed. He felt the man's nose break as his forehead made contact for the second time.

A dark stain spread across the attacker's trousers as his bladder evacuated, and David realised that he had added another soul to Jo Novak's inheritance.

His own breathing was now shallow and laboured, and his vision blurred, as a high-pitched whistling in his ears reached a crescendo. He retched and steadied himself against the wall.

As he replaced his trouser belt he saw a boarding pass and passport sticking out of the man's shirt pocket. The pass was for the same Frankfurt flight as theirs, so he ripped it up and flushed it down the toilet.

The passport was Moroccan, in the name of Khalid Ahmidam. It was stamped with multiple entries to Germany, Austria, the UK, Sweden and some to Iraq, Iran and Pakistan. David frisked his pockets, and finding a mobile phone, pocketed it with the passport.

Aware that somebody else could enter the toilet at any time, he dragged the body, with some effort, onto the toilet seat, propping it against the back wall before locking the door. All was quiet, so he climbed on to what little space was now left on the seat, and pulled himself over the dividing wall into the next stall.

He washed his hands and face, tidying himself up, and checking for any signs of struggle or blood. Satisfied that everything was all right, he made his way back to the gate lounge. It would be at least another hour before that toilet was checked again, by which time they would be off and away. However, if the Moroccan had checked in with a suitcase, the airline would have to unload the hold, as it would be unattended luggage, when he didn't show up for the flight.

David sat down where he had been before and resumed his perusal of the newspapers. He had a good look around to check whether Ahmidam had been accompanied, but could see no-one who was overly interested in him.

Christina returned some time later carrying several branded shopping bags from various outlets around the terminal. She held the bags up, smiling and pulling an 'I can't help it' face.

'Born to shop.' She put the bags down and looked at her watch. 'I'm not late, am I?' She leant across and kissed him on the nose.

David smiled and took the Moroccan's passport out of his pocket, and slipped it inside one of the airport's magazines.

'Have a careful look at this.'

She opened the magazine and studied the document.

'This is the guy that was at the hotel with Gehrling and the Mason girl. Where the hell did you get this?' she asked.

'He tried to chloroform me in the men's bog…'

'Bog?'

'Sorry, men's toilet. And I, not wishing to compromise the workings of my body any more today, strangled him with my trouser belt.' David raised his eyebrows in feigned innocence.

'Christ, David. Is he in there now?'

'Well, he hasn't come out yet.' He looked amazed at the daftness of the question. 'It's all right. They won't find his body for an hour or two. Could you kindly dump the passport on your way to the ladies' toilets? Have a look at his mobile phone memory while you are in there.' He passed her the Moroccan's phone and smiled a cheeky schoolboy grin.

'I can't leave you alone for more than half-an-hour before you are fighting for your life in the men's…what was it?'

'Bog,' he said.

As she got up she rubbed her thumb on his forehead. 'You have a bad little bump there.'

David felt the swelling gingerly.

'How much more can this aged frame stand?' He patted her hand affectionately. 'Go on, have a look at that phone memory.'

Christina had been gone for some time when boarding started.

'Interesting recent calls list and address memory. I'll tell you about it when we're on the way. I put the phone and the passport in a sanitary bag and in a big bin. Nobody will find them.'

When all the passengers had boarded, the captain came on the PA system, first in German and then in English.

'Good evening ladies and gentlemen, this is your Captain, Thomas Seitz speaking, we're waiting at the moment for one more passenger, however we don't want to lose our slot, so in five minutes we'll be taxiing for our Lufthansa flight to Frankfurt Main.'

At last the command was given to the cabin crew to set the doors to automatic, they were pushed back out of the gate , and started taxiing to the runway.

Ahmidam could only have had hand luggage. David wondered if they had found him yet?

Christina was copying something down from a scrap of paper she had taken from her bag. As she handed David a list of names in the memory and recent calls made and received, the plane's engines roared, as they started the race down the runway.

Most of the names were only letters, but David recognised the number after the letter V. Victoria Mason's. The most recent call, made ten minutes before the Moroccan's death, was to the number Gehrling had rung Eliasson from in Austria.

'They must've found Eliasson and his Chechen monkey, were monitoring the airport, and saw us checking in to the Frankfurt flight. They'll be expecting our late friend Mr Ahmidam to be on this flight, and of course he isn't. They'll be worried why they haven't heard from him, and will be waiting at the airport.'

David outlined a plan of action for when they got to Frankfurt.

If they assumed that Christina and David were on the flight, they'd be waiting for them to arrive together, and they weren't going to do that.

Christina would wait, for at least an hour, before going to the luggage hall and customs. He'd go and pick up the luggage and take it to the Schweinfurt car.

She'd go to the original car, the BMW.

'Here are the keys and the parking ticket. The floor and aisle number's on there,' he explained.

Christina would take that car around the block and return it to Hertz, then go to the hotel and check in. It was just across a walkway from the airport.

Some of them would follow him for sure, but when Christina and their late friend didn't turn up, he thought the others would leave. He knew the area around Frankfurt well, and would lose them sooner or later.

'In the morning we'll take the other car back to the airport and get the train up to Fulda and pick up the one we left there. That should confuse them.'

'Whatever you say, David Lennox.' She leant into him and put her hand over his, on his knee.

Soon they were descending through a snowstorm over the suburbs of Frankfurt, and the headlights of the traffic travelling east and west, on the A3 autobahn, between Frankfurt and Würzburg.

They landed in a strong side wind, and the plane bucked and slewed its way down on to the runway.

On the other side of the airfield, snow was being cleared from the military aircraft standing on the apron of the large American airbase.

David reflected that if they had been monitoring the Moroccan's mobile phone traffic, the Americans knew they were here too.

Chapter 26

They remained seated after the doors were opened, letting most of the other passengers disembark before they got up to collect their things, David needing several minutes to get the feeling back in his legs, which had begun to ache badly.

He kissed Christina on the cheek, and squeezed her hand.

'See you at the hotel later, give it a good hour,' he said.

'Take care, David, please.' She waited for several other passengers to go by, before following him out of the plane.

It was a long walk to passport control, and his legs were killing him. He used the South African name of Sheehan again, and after a peremptory glance and sweeping the passport bar code, the obviously bored official let him pass.

Once through immigration control at Frankfurt Main, there is another long stretch through to the main airport concourse before descending to the luggage reclaim area.

It was here that he saw the first of the tails. He was off to David's right, a man in his fifties with unkempt hair and a drinker's nose, wearing a grubby overcoat with an upturned collar. He was standing by the airport post office, and when he saw David he stiffened and moved away from the wall he had been leaning against.

As David got to the head of the escalator, he saw an attractive woman in her thirties, wearing a woollen hat pulled down over her ears, her long black hair falling from under it. She had been standing by the stationer's to his left and, like her male colleague, had reacted with her body language as she first caught sight of him. She passed in front of David and walked towards the escalators at the entrance to the main concourse, down to the arrivals hall, to where he would be exiting with the luggage.

When he walked out of Customs, the woman was by the car-hire desks. He couldn't see the man, but he didn't want to look too obviously, and let them know that he had seen them.

Taking the escalator down to the airport railway station, he walked through the ticket area, along the long corridor to the parking levels, to get an exit ticket.

He wheeled the squeaking trolley along to the correct lift for the car, knowing that the woman would be taking another, further down the corridor. Mobile phones operate in the underground area at Frankfurt, so she or her male colleague would be able to tell any tail what car to look out for. David wondered who was left waiting for Christina and the never-to-arrive, Mr Ahmidam.

At the car, he checked that the two automatics were still in the boot, and put one in his pocket. He then sat for a while, thinking what his strategy would be, to shake off the inevitable followers.

As he drove out into the night, up the ramp towards the autobahn, the snow was falling more heavily than ever, and he had to brake the car carefully, as he stopped for the traffic lights at the top of the incline.

A car behind him was holding back somewhat. The bonnet emblem of a Mercedes, just visible through the snowfall in the dimmed street lighting. He couldn't see the occupants, but guessed that it wouldn't be the two he'd seen waiting in the airport.

He decided to drive towards Würzburg, and pull in at the next petrol station about twenty-five kilometres to the east.

Driving steadily in the snow, which was now falling so heavily it was making visibility difficult, he kept an eye on the lights of the Mercedes two hundred metres back, tacking from lane to lane as it tried to keep its distance without losing him.

He gave the other car no reason to believe that he knew they were there, and was soon turning into the services slip road.

Whilst filling the car, he didn't look up as they drove slowly past him to the car park and the main services building. When he later pulled up in front of the restaurant, he saw the tails parked in the row behind him, ten cars down. He entered the toilets, dropping a coin in the dish outside, and freshened up.

He took his time, as he knew that while they had his car in sight, they wouldn't move, unless they thought there was a problem.

When he left, instead of turning back to the restaurant and the car park, he turned right and out to the rear of the building and the lorry pumps.

There was a hedge bordering this area and a small opening, which he went through. He walked fifty metres in the darkness, parallel to the main car park, until he found another hole in the hedge. Gagging at the acrid stench of urine, and wondering what the hell he was walking in, he pushed through, returning to the parking area.

The Mercedes was now to his left, four rows back. The two occupants were intent on watching the restaurant entrance, occasionally giving the windscreen a mechanical wipe so that they could see out.

Pulling up his coat collar, he walked between the cars to a bench at the back of the lot, clearing snow from it, and sitting down to wait.

It was a good fifteen minutes before one of the men left the car, to have a look at what was happening.

David ran along behind the back row, drawing the automatic from his pocket as he reached the Mercedes. Inserting his key ring in the palm of his hand, with a key sticking out between each of his fingers, he used the leather holding pouch as padding.

He checked the whereabouts of the other man, and seeing nothing to worry him, approached the car. The driver was focussed on the service buildings, glancing down occasionally at a photograph of David and Christina that he had on his lap.

David held the automatic by the barrel, in his left hand, swinging it as hard as he could against the driver's window. The glass shattered at once, and he leapt forward, smashing the keys into the man's eyes, and before the guy could react, smashed them into his face again.

As the driver screamed in pain, his left eyeball hanging from its socket, David removed the keys from the ignition.

‘That’s for Erland,’ he hissed.

He realised that the old aggression was back. He wasn’t sure that he liked it, but if it was keeping him and Christina alive, so be it.

He accelerated on to the motorway approach, seeing in the rear mirror the driver’s colleague running from the restaurant.

‘Too late my man.’

He may be full of poison, but he wasn’t done yet. Even as he thought it, he felt unwell and light-headed, and wondered if a visit to the doctor, might not now be pointless.

After a few hundred metres there was an exit, so he was able to get on to the other side of the A3, and make his way back to the airport. As he rejoined the carriageway westbound, he threw the Mercedes keys over the car roof, and into the trees.

Chapter 27

When he got back to the Sheraton, Christine was standing naked in front of the mirror with her head down, brushing her hair in the stream of hot air from the dryer. Turning it off, she put her arms around him, pressing her warm, showered and slightly damp body against his.

'Did anyone follow you?' she asked.

'Yes, but I lost them.' He didn't want to go into brutal detail. 'What about you?'

'No, nobody.'

He felt a surge of desire, and almost simultaneously a tidal race of biliousness, and knew he was going to vomit. He pushed her away and quickly made for the toilet.

'Christ. So sorry.'

He tried to remove his bridge surreptitiously, turning his body away from her and retching several times before throwing up.

It was mostly dark brown bile, which again left a strangely metallic taste in his mouth, but now there were flecks of dark blood which he knew were not from any rupture in his throat but from his stomach. He felt Christina's comforting hand on his back, before heaving again and trying to clear his throat of mucus.

'Shoshanim has fixed a doctor for tomorrow in Garmisch. They're flying in one of their experts from Tel Aviv. They'll sort it out David. They'll sort it out.'

He could hear the desperation in her voice as he heaved more dark blood and bile into the foul soup below him.

There were rats swimming in the bowl and scrabbling at the steep porcelain slopes, biting and scrambling over one another in their attempts to escape. They had human faces, Erland, Shoshanim, Vicky Mason and Griff, his father and mother, all writhing and struggling. A loud buzzing grew in volume until it blotted out all his senses, David was a kite above the clouds, someone had let go of the restraining string and he was free, soaring into the void.

The light returned as he floated down to land on a high mountain top, where he sat and rested his head in the freezing snow.

He came round, slowly able to focus on Christina, who was holding a wet towel to his head, which was cupped in her lap.

'Thank God. I was about to call an ambulance. You were talking nonsense before you collapsed. David, this isn't good.'

She took a tissue, wiping tears from her face and blowing her nose. 'Here, drink some water.' She handed him a bottle from the mini bar.

He gulped the cold liquid down and tried to get up. Immediately feeling the room spin, and having to put his head back down on the marble tiles. Raising himself on one arm for a few minutes, he could eventually, stand up. Steadying himself against the door, he waited for something like normality to return.

Christina passed another bottle through the open door, and he made his way into the bedroom to lie down.

'No you're right, that wasn't so bloody great. Christ. I hope this Israeli doctor's good. Could you ring Hallberg in Sweden and give him the fax number of the hotel, and when I feel better, I'll transfer cash to his account.'

He rubbed his eyes with his knuckles and took a long draught of the cold water, swilling it round his mouth. He gave Christina the doctor's number.

'You lie there, until you feel okay.' She picked up the handset and dialled Sweden. David could tell that she had at first got an answer machine, but suddenly it seemed that someone had picked up at the other end, as she was asking if the results could be sent that night. It appeared that they would be, because she thanked the speaker and hung up.

'He was working late. By the way, he says it was a pleasure to meet you, and please tell him how you get on. Oh, and good luck.'

David laughed. 'He doesn't sound too bloody optimistic, does he?'

He got off the bed slowly and went over to the Internet keyboard by the television, to access his bank account to pay

Hallberg.

Some time later there was a knock at the door and Christina took a brown A4 envelope from a young receptionist.

'There are pages and pages of it.' She threw them to David.

Christina ordered David some toast and something for herself from room service, and joined him to read the report.

It soon became clear that it was written to be read by a trained doctor, and not a layman. He couldn't tell whether his liver and kidney functions were bad or very bad. However, an exclamation mark beside his liver function readings, was presumably not a good sign.

Chapter 28

They were all ready to go before breakfast arrived at nine. David thought he was feeling better and could manage some food and coffee. Ten minutes later, he was regretting it and vomiting again. He was also experiencing a numbness in the legs and hands that seemed to be spreading upwards and inwards with alarming speed.

He heard the telephone ring in the bedroom and Christina talking to somebody and repeating an address.

'David, are you all right? That was Alexa, the Israeli,' she called.

He went out to the bedroom.

'David, you look awful.'

He shrugged, acknowledging the fact that he probably did. 'Shoshanim has booked us in to a private clinic near Garmisch. Their man, a poison specialist, arrives this morning in Munich. He's the best they have. You have a rest, and then we'll take a very slow walk over to the Railway station. Yes?' She brushed his chin with the back of her hand.

'Yes, that'd be good. I'm seizing up a bit at the moment, having some difficulty with my arms and legs, and I feel like shit,' he groaned.

He took the opportunity to stretch out and sleep, waking an hour later, with Christina gently shaking his arm, and kissing the end of his nose.

'Time to go. You were snoring like hell.' She bent down and hugged him. 'Come on,' she urged.

On the short walk to the airport complex and the lift down to the railway station. David was very careful to look for anybody who seemed to give them more than just passing interest, but all seemed innocent.

They had a fifteen minute wait, before the train departed on its two-and-a-quarter-hour journey to Fulda, so they talked about what they should do next.

'Assuming I survive,' he smiled.

'Presuming you survive, yes. That has to be number one priority. We'll talk about all the other things when you're better,' she said
'What do we do if Shoshanim wants to look at the map?'
'If he believes we'll find the weapons, and that the Russians, Americans, or your guys will then destroy them, he won't need to see it. But if something happens to us, he needs a guarantee. I think that we copy it, leaving out the secret chamber, and put it in a bank safe. We'll work out with him how he can get the map later, if we have a problem, okay?'
There was a slight jolt as the train pulled away and the platform started to slide by.
'Yes, that sounds all right. Do you mind if I sleep a bit?' he asked, snuggling down in the seat and putting his head on her shoulder.
'No, you rest. Try to sleep all the way.' She looked out of the window at the white landscape and the falling snow, and tried to hide the look of despair on her face.

David's breathing was laboured and noisy, a small trickle of yellowish spittle was dribbling out of the corner of his mouth, his rapid eye movement so intense that his lids were half open. Christina wasn't sure whether he was dreaming, or hallucinating. She stroked the top of his head and the growing areas of alopecia spreading like small pools across his scalp.

He woke when the intercom announced, 'Fulda station in five minutes', but found standing very difficult. It took several minutes before he regained full sensation in his hands and legs, and even then it was extremely painful to walk.

Christina went to fetch the car, whilst David waited outside the station with the luggage, feeling the worst he had ever done in his life. Certain that it was now too late for treatment.
Why did they want him dead before this thing was finished? It didn't make any bloody sense.

The journey to Garmisch took roughly five hours. Christina did all the driving, and they had, as usual, pulled off the autobahn from time to time to see whether they were being tailed. David had checked the car for trackers when they loaded the luggage, and all had been clear, so it looked as though they had lost everybody for the time being.

At an information point on the outskirts of the town, they pulled up to locate the address they were after. Two kilometres down the road they turned in to the exclusive looking entrance of the of the Heidelstein Clinic.

At the end of a five hundred metre wooded drive and perched atop a small hill, was an expansive modern building on one floor, bathed in light. Most of the exterior was glass and aluminium under an acutely angled roof, typical for areas of high snowfall. The ends of black metallic tiles were just visible at the boundary between the snow on the rooftop and the icicles hanging from the guttering.

They stopped in the small visitor's carpark, and Christina went in, coming out some minutes later with a short, rotund man in his mid-forties, holding in his hand the notes from Hallberg. The top of his head was bald, but at the sides his hair hung long to his shoulders, framing a small goatee beard.

David struggled to get out, so the man came to help him.

'Hi David. Steady there, my friend.' The accent was cultured mid-west American. As soon as David was out of the car, and had straightened, the man extended his hand.

'Hi, My name is Bill. Bill Timberlake.'

'David Lennox, nice to meet you.' They shook hands and David was pleasantly surprised at the firmness of Timberlake's grip.

'Let's get you inside, David. Showered and into bed, then we can start treating you immediately. Doctor Hallberg has done an excellent job. He might well've saved your life. You may want to thank him later.'

'Might've saved my life? Jesus!' David raised his eyebrows.

Timberlake chortled. 'Only a turn of phrase my friend, we'll sort you out.' He slapped David on the back. 'We'll sort you out.'

They climbed the ramp to the entrance, and were shown by a white-coated nurse, who did not introduce herself, to a suite on the ground floor. She was in her late thirties with a plain but kindly face, her brunette hair, conservatively combed back from her forehead, was tied in a bun at the back. She seemed shy, and David wondered if it was a problem for her to speak English or whether she had been instructed not to talk too much to them.

A sitting room had a dining table at one end and a sofa suite at the other. Floor to ceiling drapes covered sliding glass doors, which opened onto a patio overlooking the snow-covered grounds. Double doors separated two en-suite bedrooms. One of them, smelling pleasantly antiseptic, was really a hospital room with a treatment bed surrounded by monitoring equipment and medical drips. All the rooms had satellite television and CD players, and flowers and fresh fruit lay on the dining table.

A few moments later Timberlake came in, speaking to Christina first.

'You'll find a menu for you and David on the dining table. Everything will be served to you here - breakfast, lunch, etcetera. I doubt that David will want to eat. The treatment's essentially a process of purging the body of the thallium, and I see that it's already affecting his limbs. It isn't a very pleasant process I'm afraid. Can I suggest that for your privacy and your sleep, you close the double doors dividing the bedrooms, because we'll need to monitor and treat David both day and night.'

He smiled to Christina and then turned to David.

'All right, David, if you'd like to get into bed, we'll start straight away. Do you need any help or…?'

David shook his head and smiled. 'I could do with a large whisky.'

'That could possibly kill you at the moment, my friend.' David noticed that Timberlake was not smiling.

After a shower, he took a medical gown from the back of the door and put it on. As he got into bed, Christina was in the sitting room talking earnestly with Timberlake.

‘Okay, David. Let’s see what you’re made of. I’m going to make you feel like a bag of crap, in fact three bags of crap,’ Timberlake said.

‘Now that’s what I want a doctor to sound like. I’m definitely not going to die on you, Bill.’ David smiled and held up his arms. ‘Which one do you want first?’

‘Take this first please. It’ll taste dreadful, but just down it.’

He handed David a plastic cup with some deep blue liquid in it and David swallowed the lot in one go, immediately gagging and accepting the proffered glass of water with which to get rid of the taste.

‘You know, I guess, that was the prussian blue. We are, sadly, going to have to do that every hour for the foreseeable future. It’ll purge you of the thallium. I won’t lie to you; there’ll be some permanent damage to your nervous system and to some of your organs. We’ll know within fifteen to twenty days how serious, so that means you’ll be here for at least two weeks, over Christmas and New year.’

He slipped a thermometer under David’s tongue. ‘How much you’re going to feel like celebrating with us is debateable. All right, a little bit about me. Fifteen years at Oak Ridge in the States, in research and treatment of the ingestion of radioactive isotopes. So, the good news: I’m one of the best, and if you say you’re not going to die here, I’ll do my best to make sure you don’t. However, and it is a however, your readings are lousy. I’m going to get several drips into you, to make sure we keep your kidney and liver levels stable. Swallow these please.’

He gave David a tray with seven or eight pills on it, and left the room, returning some minutes later with the nurse. She inserted drip needles in both of David’s arms, and adjusted the height of the bags.

‘If we can’t stabilize you within two days, David, we’ll have to put you on a dialysis machine, to get some help cleaning your blood,’ Timberlake said.

David glanced into the other room, where Christina perched on the edge of the sofa, with a worried look on her face. He winked and smiled.

'Christina's given me one of the suspect pills. I'll have the results of analysis on those tomorrow morning, then we'll know what kind of levels you have been ingesting over the last few weeks.'

He took David's blood pressure and looked at the notes again.

'I'm going to give you something else for your hypertension over the next two weeks, and we're going to insert a needle into the back of your hand, so that we can monitor your blood readings continuously, without leaving your arms looking like a junkie's. Any questions?'

'How long before this prussian blue kicks in?'

'It's kicking in as we speak, David. You'll pee thallium, excrete thallium and, you'll vomit thallium. The more you do all three, the better chance we have of getting you out of this with your organs intact. Okay, the nurse will be back in forty minutes with the next dose. I'll be back in an hour. If you can't eat tonight, we'll fix up a drip to give you some nutrients and essentials. Please try to drink as much water as possible.'

As he left, he pointed to the bedside table, where there were three one-and-a-half-litre bottles of still water.

Christina came to sit on the side of his bed, and carefully took his hand, in order not to disturb the drip.

'Do you want anything to eat, David. The menu's very good.'

The tears were streaming down her face. He could feel them warm, as they dropped on to his hand cradled in hers.

'Please get well. I only just found you again. I lost my brother, and my mother's dying of cancer, I don't have anybody else. Please,' she pleaded.

She put her head against his, sobbing as he tried to hold her, without pulling out both tubes from his arms.

'Don't be so bloody silly, Karranova, how can I die now, when so many people are trying to kill me?'

He felt rather than heard the sobs turn to laughter. Suddenly her face was close to his, and she was laughing, sobbing and kissing him, all at the same time.

He took her face in his hands.

'Come on, old thing. I'm not going anywhere. Go and order something for dinner, I'll have a water. Go on. Have some wine with it. Christ, who's picking up the tab here? Me I guess.'

She dried her eyes, an occasional sob punctuating the laughter, and went back to the sitting room.

'I'll shut the doors, so you can't smell my food.'

Later, he could hear the sounds of a television, and decided to watch a little himself. As he was channel zapping, the nurse came in to give him his next dose of the prussian blue. She was very pleasant in manner and smiled sweetly, but didn't say a word apart from hello and goodbye in German, and that's how David guessed she wanted it.

The next two weeks passed by agonisingly slowly for David, and he slipped in and out of feverish consciousness, and nightmarish dreams.

Half dead, he knew that sometimes he was awake, but was only dimly aware of what was going on around him. He had a vague impression that both Alexa and Isaac had been at his bedside, but it was just that, an impression.

He had a sense of people wishing each other 'Merry Christmas', and a tree with lights. His one vivid memory was of painfully and regularly vomiting.

He was unaware that his heart had stopped, on three occasions.

Chapter 29

The sunlight made him blink for a few minutes. Involuntarily grunting as he fully opened his eyes, he tried to shield them with his hand, but something was restraining his movement. Confusion reigned as he struggled to fathom out where he was as the unfamiliar surroundings came into focus.

When he realised that it was a drip that made movement difficult, he finally remembered. He had a cracking headache, and his midriff was painful, but he was still alive. He looked at the wall clock.

Two o'clock. Two o'clock and all's well.

From the next room he could hear the television and the unmistakeable signature tune of CNN news.

'Hello. Hello. Christina?' He struggled to sit upright.

The double doors slid open, and there she was, looking gaunt and drained, but her smile was radiant, filling her face. She sat on the bed, hugging him so tight, he had difficulty getting his breath.

'Steady on girl, you'll finish me off.'

As she sat up, she brushed away tears with the palm of her hand.

'Timberlake says you're okay now. Your heart stopped, David, they had to defibrillate you three times,' she said.

'How many days have I been out of it?'

'Sixteen or seventeen, I've lost count. Lots to tell you, but that can wait. Bill took a lot of blood for tests yesterday, to see how your organs are. He says it's possible you can't drink alcohol anymore.'

'Christ. Is there any bad news?' He pulled a face and she giggled and leant against him.

'I'm so happy you're better, David. I was so scared that I'd lose you.' She hugged him tightly again.

The door to the room opened and the nurse came in. Seeing David upright and awake, she smiled and left again, leaving the door ajar. Some minutes later, Bill Timberlake put his head around the doorframe.

'Welcome back to the world, David. How are you feeling?' He nodded to Christina and winked. 'Could you give us five minutes alone, so I can have a look at him?'

He shook David's hand and then thumbed down the skin under his eyes to look at the colour of the tissue underneath.

'Yes of course,' she said, going into the sitting room and sliding the doors shut.

Timberlake felt the glands around David's neck and underarms, then in his groin. Bending the feet and arms, he asked if there was any pain, then gently pressed down on David's abdomen. The grunt that greeted every little pressure invoked a raised eyebrow from the doctor.

'All right, David. The good news first. As you so boldly told me, you're not going to die. In fact you've done remarkably well. You'd ingested almost four thousand milligrammes of thallium. There was a significant dosage in the six or seven pills that you had taken, roughly six hundred milligrammes in each. Four thousand milligrammes, is more than a lethal dose.

Now the bad news, you'll need to have some physiotherapy on your legs, and we need to get you in the gym every day to get you back in shape. That'll help some of your organ functions as well. Your kidneys have been damaged but not too badly, your liver, however, will heal itself somewhat, but you won't be able to drink any alcohol for the foreseeable future. Can you live with that?'

'I'm guessing that if I can't, I won't be living with anything?' David sighed, despondently.

'Correct.'

'In that case it's not a major problem. I've had my share of alcohol.'

'Good. Then I'd like you to take some solids now, and get some weight back on. I recommend the porridge. Later, we'll start with the physiotherapist and the treadmill in the gym. I'm happy that everything's turned out well, David.' Timberlake said, smiling.

David grinned. 'So am I Bill, so am I.'
'I'll order you a small portion of porridge then. Yes?'
'You're the doctor. I'll have a go.'
'The nurse will be along in a few minutes, to take you off the drips. There's some sports clothing and a pair of trainers for you, in the other bedroom. You can sleep in there now.' He winked, nodding his head in the direction of the sitting room.
'Now that ***is*** good news.' David took Timberlake's hand and shook it vigorously.

Timberlake left, and almost immediately the nurse entered. She smiled at David and, again without a word, removed the drips from his arms. She tidied some sample trays and catheters from the side table, smiled again, and bade him good-day.

David lifted the sheets, recognising that he would smell a little better if he took a shower, so he swung his legs off the bed and tried to stand, realizing at once that the two weeks had done nothing for his strength and coordination. He steadied himself on the metal frame, and when stable, hobbled off to the bathroom.

Drying himself in front of the mirror, he saw that he was now almost completely bald and had dark black bags under his eyes, almost as though he had been punched full in the face. The skin on his cheeks was drawn, and at a guess, he had lost around two stone. He put on a bathrobe, and joined Christina in the sitting room, where she was reading a copy of 'Newsweek'.

She held out her arm to grab him as he passed.
'What did the doctor say?'
'That I'm one hell of a specimen, perfect in every way. It's not too bad, no booze though. I'm just going to have some porridge, and later a session in the gym, are you coming?' He went into the bedroom to don the training clothes.
'Yes, okay.' She came in to watch him dress. 'Shoshanim came last week, and Alexa and Isaac were here twice. Shoshanim and I had a long talk about insurance for him, and the agreement was, that I travelled to Munich, and deposited one copy of the map with your name and one with my name, with the Commerzbank

there. In the event of both our deaths, the keys to the deposit boxes will be released to Shoshanim on the authority of a good Czech friend of mine. Hopefully, that won't be necessary. He also gave us a hundred extra rounds each, for the automatics. Now, after the gym, if you feel like it, we can look at the map, with the extra information he got from the Mossad intelligence archives.'

'Okey dokey, you're in charge, for now,' he smiled.

It took some effort to clothe himself, and he realised just how much condition he had lost, being bedridden for a fortnight.

The porridge was delivered by a pretty, teenage German girl, who spoke no English, or wasn't sufficiently confident enough to try. David ate slowly, feeling a hint of nausea as his stomach filled, but he finished the small plateful, then lay on the bed for a few minutes, until the sensation had passed.

An hour later, he was on the treadmill in the gym, under the watchful eye of a very fit, crew-cut, young German called Rüdiger. He was also very economical with his communication, and David now guessed that all the staff had been told to keep their own counsel.

After the fitness session, he was tired but feeling much better, and was able to eat some fruit, and drink a little green tea. Timberlake came in to check his blood pressure and give him a quick once over, telling David that he would take some more samples the next day, to see how everything was going.

They decided to update Novak's map. Christina got the original and Shoshanim's notes, suggesting that she would read the information, and David mark the map. They could work from the north down,

'First the ones that were blown by the Soviets and the East Germans. Holzhausen, Arnstadt, Stadtilm, Crawinkel, Plauen, Ilmenau, Geblar and. Sülzfeld,' she recited.

David marked these with a red marker pen.

'That leaves Ohrdruf, Mühlberg, Marlishausen and Meiningen as entry points in the old East Germany. If they were trying to stop people escaping through the system, how did they patrol these sites?' he asked, chewing the end of the marker.

'They were all military installations, and this is where they had access to the old border and could store the tactical weapons. I have my notes on the Jonastal project, and I found that some attempts to enter the system there, a few years back, failed because of rock falls. But, we have to look at those sites too. Although, Voss, Zapf and Gehrling were that side of the border, and must've checked,' she said.

'If they knew about the entrances.' David looked up at her.

'Yes sure, if they knew,' she shrugged.

'Does Shoshanim know about the other entrances, or the telegram?' he asked.

'He gave me what he knows, he didn't see the map, and I didn't ask him to look for special sites. I made a decision to give him the telegram to decipher, I didn't know if you'd get better…'

'…No problem, I understand. Have we got it back yet?'

'No, not yet.'

'It seems that we have seven sites to look at,' David said, ringing the sites on the map.

'Yes not so bad. We must think again about what we need underground. You made a list in Sweden but it was very long. Too long. I asked Shoshanim for a good gas detector for the tunnel system.' She started sorting the papers to try to find the notes David had made.

They spent some time prioritising the list of equipment, then decided to call it a day, as he was feeling very tired from the treatment and the day's activity in the gym.

Christina nodded towards the bed.

'Are you up to it, Mr Lennox?' She arched her eyebrows several times, in a mock suggestive fashion.

'I'm about up to a cuddle right now, he said, meekly.

He got into bed and felt the naked warmth of her as he drifted into deep, dreamless sleep.

The phone rang softly in the third floor office in Whitehall. Sir

William Rush took off his reading glasses, sleepily rubbing his left eye before answering.

'Yes...yes...Will he live? He took his time. Yes, keep me informed.'

Chapter 30

The last ten days had been a gruelling return to some degree of fitness, now it was finally time to check out. Rüdiger had been delighted with his progress, and Timberlake had been satisfied with the last lot of blood tests and the weight gain.

Christina was hugging Timberlake in the freezing early morning air, outside the clinic.

'I can't thank you enough, Bill, thank you so very much.'

'Yes, thank you for all you've done Bill.' David shook his hand. 'Without you I'd have died, that's for sure.'

'It's been a pleasure. I must say though, I'm looking forward to getting home and out of this snow. Take care you two, and try to stay out of trouble, wherever or whatever.' Timberlake turned, to stand in the warmth of the reception area.

Waving as they drove down the drive, David let out a long and weary sigh.

'Where now, boss?' He smiled, but he was still feeling exhausted from the events of the last weeks.

'We're meeting Alexa and Isaac at place called Griesen.'

She explained that it was fifteen minutes away on the Austrian-German border. The Mossad had a villa under observation in Berwang, and had seen al Masri and Dzhokar Maskhadov, the Chechen, in meetings with Mason and Gehrling at the Hotel Singer there.

No sign of Von den Bergen. The Israelis had tried to get a laser listening beam on them, but the village was in a small steep valley, and the hotel and the villa were difficult targets. The villa was on a hillside opposite the Singer and the front of the hotel was directly on the main village road. At the back was an open slope up to the mountains and skiing area.

Expertly correcting the car, as the rear twitched mischievously in the deep snow, she drove with difficulty up the private road. It threaded through a heavily wooded river gorge, to an imposing, three floor alpine villa where the Israelis were to meet them. The outer walls were decorated in paintings of cherubim and seraphim on one side, and the Virgin Mary and Christ respectively, on the other two visible walls.

Nestling in the cleft of the ravine, a beautifully crafted, covered wooden footbridge crossed the river from the house, to a pathway through the trees on the other side. A woodpecker was tap-tap tapping in its search for grubs, in their winter beds under the bark of a nearby tree.

The inside of the villa was expensively and tastefully furnished. It looked lived in, which suggested to David that it was a Mossad safe house. A grand open fireplace dominated the centre of the ground floor with a dog grate standing on a two-metre-square, white plastered plinth, open on all sides.

The smell of last night's wood fire still lingered, blending with the aroma of freshly ground coffee. A black, cast iron, square funnel over the fire rose past a mezzanine floor and through the ceiling of the level above. At the far end of the room a wide, wooden staircase led to the other floors.

Alexa was sitting at a low table with a coffee mug in front of her, and an assortment of photographs that she was marking and stacking. She got up and shook hands with David and embraced Christina.

'How are you guys doing? How are you, David?' she enquired, sitting down and gesturing for them to do the same.

'Much better, thanks,' said David, glad to get the weight off his feet.

Isaac came and sat down with them, he was older than he had seemed to David at their first meeting. Then, he had thought that Isaac was in his late twenties, but now revised that to middle to late thirties.

'Let's get to it. Christina has seen some of these,' Isaac said, handing him some of the surveillance shots to David.

David identified Vicky Mason and Gehrling, and recognised al Masri and Maskhadov, from the photographs Christina had shown him in the Lakes.

The sound of a car pulling up outside, prompted Alexa to go

to the door.
'That'll be Aaron. We can see what he has to say, then decide how to play this further.'
Shoshanim came into the room with his hand outstretched.
'Hi David. Good to see you up and about.' He shook hands firmly, holding David's arm with the other hand. 'Hi Christina.' He kissed her cheek.
'Aaron ...' David saw the saw the slight eye movement, as Shoshanim realised that David had used his first name. '… thanks for fixing the doctor, I owe you my life.'
'No problem, David. However, who was trying to kill you remains a mystery. Any ideas?' He sat down with them.
'Well it wasn't Gehrling's lot. I told you that Zapf was alarmed to hear somebody had messed about with my medical files. It wasn't you guys, so who the hell was it?'
Shoshanim pulled a picture from his inside jacket pocket.
'Do you recognise this person?'
It was a picture of an attractive brunette in her late twenties.
'Her face looks familiar, but I just can't place it,' David said, searching his memory.
He struggled with naming the woman, it was like someone you see often; the check out girl at the supermarket, who you then meet with her husband and kids on a beach in Thailand, and have no idea where you've seen her before.
'Her real name's Jenny Carter, but when you met her she was Rebecca Thomas.' Shoshanim volunteered.
The name rang big bells for David. 'I met her?'
'You did.'
'Oh my good God.' He looked at the photograph again. 'Yes it is. Jesus fucking Christ!' he groaned to Christina, 'It's the receptionist from Doc Gillan's surgery, in the Lakes.'
'***Was*** the receptionist. She handed in her notice and left the area six days after the supposed break-in,' Shoshanim said, raising his eyebrows.
'Supposed?' David waved the photograph and shook his head in incredulity.

'She's an expert at covert surveillance, the placing of monitoring equipment and burglary. She's one of the best of a new breed.' He nodded towards Alexa and Isaac.
'She's one of yours?' asked David.
'No my friend, she's one of yours. FRG in Ireland, then 14 Int., and lately, a highly secretive section of MI6.'
David threw the photograph on to the table.
'So she staged a break-in, and made it look like an amateur job. At first, I thought that Zapf and Gehrling wanted me to know that they'd looked at my file, just to let me know that they could. So, my guys are trying to kill me.' He stared at the floor.
'What the hell's going on here, David?'
Shoshanim fingered through the other photographs to see if there was anything new from Berwang.
'Why did your people ask you to help them, knowing they were poisoning you at the same time?'
David shook his head and shrugged his shoulders.
'Aaron, I just don't know. It doesn't make any sense.'
Shoshanim took some papers from a sideboard.
'Here's the telegram, as far as we were able to decode and translate it. It was in "Lorenz" code and extremely difficult, even with the computer power available today. There's a six-digit number at the end we cannot decode, it was unreadable on the original.'

Bormann to Himmler Stop
Further to your telegram yesterday Stop
Weapon 2 Chamber 2 armed as agreed Stop
If your negotiations with Allies fail Stop
Detonation 00.01. 1 August 1945 Stop Disarm code ?????? End

'Is there anything we haven't been told David? Does any of that mean anything to you?' Shoshanim asked, slowly and deliberately.
David was careful not to look at Christina.

'No, nothing,' he said.
Christina shook her head, also careful to keep eye contact with the Mossad man as she spoke.
'No. No,' she said.
Shoshanim looked worried, and didn't seem a hundred per cent sure that what he'd been told, added up.
'I'm sticking my neck right out here, right out. Is that crystal clear?' He was speaking directly to Christina.
'Aaron, I promise you, that if we learn anything, anything that's of direct interest to you, we'll tell you straight away.' She looked at David who nodded in agreement.
The Israeli clapped his hands.
'All right, let's discuss tactics regarding Berwang. We'd like to eliminate Mr al Masri and the Russians want Maskhadov. That leaves Gehrling and Mason and, of course, Von den Bergen. Von den Bergen's tricky, my people don't want him to be spirited to Israel for a show trial…'
'Can I ask why not?' David asked, a light dawning. Christina looked at him puzzled.
There was a fleeting glance between Shoshanim and Isaac.
'Don't know, David. As I said once before, I'm just a humble servant of the state.
You are lying my son, and I think I know why, David thought.
'So what happens to him?' David's mind was going into overdrive.
'If we find him, he has a heart attack.' Shoshanim said, coldly.
'I see.' David saw that Shoshanim was staring at him intently.
'Something troubling you, David?'
'No, not at all. What happens next?' David asked.
'Alexa and Isaac are going to book into the Hotel Singer as a honeymoon couple, and I have a meeting in Munich. You guys can use this place as a base. Make yourselves comfortable, there are plenty of bedrooms and all the sheets have been changed, so just sleep where you want. We'll be in contact here sometime

tomorrow, is that okay with you both?'

'Yep, no problems.' David smiled at Shoshanim.

'Here's the gas detector you asked for.' He handed a yellow box to Christina with a plastic bag containing a charging unit.

'Once again Aaron, thanks for everything,' David said.

As they stood on the veranda, watching the Israelis' cars disappearing down the long drive to the main road, David squeezed Christina's hand. Three short, three long, three short. Three short, three long, three short....S...O...S. She looked at him quizzically.

'Let's go for a short walk, I need to get some fresh air.' He kissed her, and as he pulled back his head he made an imperceptible 'shshsh!'

They got their coats, and began walking down the drive, treacherous with its compacted icy covering, both of them sliding and slipping, trying to keep their balance. Two hundred metres from the villa, David spoke, keeping his back to the house.

'Sorry about that, but the way they left us on our own like that, the villa's probably wired and CCTV'd up to the rafters. My own people were poisoning me, very cleverly, and Israel doesn't want to take Von den Bergen back to stand trial. Why not? I'll tell you why not, because they want to shut him up, and I think I know why. Shoshanim has always been around. He was up on Caw and in Castlewoods. He was in Mellrichstadt when the Americans were killed and he was there to pick you up, after you got strangled. He tipped you off about Eliasson coming to the hotel in Sweden. Mossad have known all along who Fjällman was. They let me get taken by Eliasson, and then tipped you off, knowing you'd get me out and probably kill him in the process. Who suggested the deal with the maps in the case of our deaths?'

'He did,' she said, her eyes widening.

'Then fixing Timberlake, the best in the business, and the clinic at such short notice. I think he's known since Caw that I was being poisoned. He was just waiting for us to ask for help.'

'I knew you meant something with that question about what they were going to do with Von den Bergen. So why?' she asked.

'Do you remember we looked up the Vela satellite incident, the Nuclear explosion in the Indian Ocean. Everybody denied it, including the Israelis who said that they weren't involved in cooperation with the South Africans. The hell they weren't. My bet's that they found out later they'd been dealing with a former Nazi wanted on war crimes charges, and they didn't want that to become public knowledge. Fjällman…Von den Bergen, lived a charmed life in Sweden, obviously being protected by one, or more than one, group of influential people. The Israelis want him dead now, because he's dealing with the Arabs. They want to permanently shut him up, for what he knows about the test in the Indian Ocean.

They must've known Lindén was at the villa in Nolvik and let him be killed, and then set you up to kill Eliasson. I think that if we go with the Israelis to Berwang, we'll die there, set up as Von den Bergen's killers.'

'How does this fit with your people trying to kill you? Why were they doing it slowly?' She shivered in the biting cold.

He put his arm around her.

'I really don't know, Christina, but I think we have to get away from everybody, let them sort it out. They've tried to kill us both, now it's time to get out. To hell with the bloody chamber and what ever's in there. The telegram talks of a weapon in chamber two. Is that the one on your grandfather's map? If so, it went off or didn't in 1945. Problem solved.'

'Come on. Let's go back inside, I'm freezing. Shoshanim's going to be very pissed off, but I agree, we should get out now, and find somewhere where they don't expect us to be. But first, I want Von den Bergen, before Mossad gets there. Can you understand that?' she said.

'All right, but then we get out for good. Agree?'

'Agree.'

'So where now?' He asked, pulling her to him.

'God knows. We are really on our own now, aren't we?' She kissed the end of his nose.

'Oh yes, oh yes.' He nodded.

They slithered and skated their way back up to the villa. Five minutes later they were preparing to leave.

Pretending to clear the car of snow, they checked for trackers. It wasn't long before Christina coughed, gave him a knowing look, and dropped something into the snow.

They drove slowly down to the main road, with David looking at the map, trying desperately to find a village near Berwang that was close enough to approach over the mountains on foot, and big enough to have a hotel or a guesthouse.

'Rieden,' he said. 'It's on the other side of the mountains from Berwang, to the west. There's bound to be a mountain path between them. It looks to be nine or ten kilometres. Let's drive down there, and see if we can get a room. If we can, we go back to Garmisch and buy some clothing and other equipment.'

They crossed the border into Austria, on the road to Lermoos, the magnificent Zugspitze to their left towering some ten thousand feet. Its peak invisible among the blue-grey, snow filled clouds. Ahead of them the Zwischentorn peaks of the Tyrolean Alps clawed at a darkening sky.

After the small village of Ehenbichel, they followed the Lech river valley for five kilometres, turning up a minor road to Rieden.

They pulled over at an attractive Gasthaus on the outskirts, and David went in to find if they had any rooms available. He wasn't too optimistic, as vehicles were parked everywhere. The road was busy with tourists driving to the nearby lifts and slopes of the Hahnenkamm, their car roofs laden with garishly-coloured skis.

They were very sorry, they were fully booked, but they rang another guest house which had a double room available for three days.

It was just up the road on the other side of the village, a smaller establishment, but the exterior walls were beautifully decorated in the manner typical for the Tyrol. From what they could see through the windows, it looked welcoming and comfortable.

The receptionist, it transpired, was the owner. A woman wearing traditional Tyrolean dress, in her late fifties, with mousy hair braided into a ponytail which she wore draped over one shoulder. She was holding her hands politely clasped behind her, as she greeted David when he entered the small lobby, only holding out her hand as David initiated the handshake. Behind her, he could see an old-fashioned bar and a small restaurant beyond. Everything looked charming and spotlessly clean.

She was delighted that David spoke German, but he struggled at first with her Austrian pronunciation and the speed of her delivery. She had introduced herself but he hadn't caught the name.

He beckoned Christina to come and have a look, and the owner took them to the first floor to show them the room, which was a little twee, but perfect for their needs.

A potpourri of dried lavender leaves delicately scented the spotlessly clean bathroom. The tiles were chintzy, but it had a bath and a separate shower cabinet.

'I think we have to change car again,' he said, as he returned with the suitcases, putting them on the double bed.

'Yes, I thought the same. What are we going to do with the papers and the map?' Christina asked.

David went into the bathroom and knelt by the side of the bath. He took his multi-tool and carefully prised off the chromed plugs on the white side panel, undid all the holding screws, and levered off the covering. Christina handed him the papers and the map, and he placed them under the tub.

When he had put the panel back, he was delighted that when he got up, he didn't feel any nausea or giddiness whatsoever.

'Right, let's go to Garmisch, and do the shops,' he said.

'Shopping, my favourite,' she cooed.

They parked in the centre of the tourist town, just off

Bahnhofstrasse. It was full of skiers and sightseers, so they had had to cruise around for a while until the sharp-eyed Christina saw an empty space.

They decided to skip lunch, and have a good dinner later. Pleased that he was getting his normal appetite back, David was looking forward to the meal.

Finding a sports shop which had all the necessary winter walking and skiing gear, they spent an hour kitting themselves out, buying a good quality SatNav and map with all the cross-country skiing and walking routes, and two digital compasses. They found some small backpacks, cooking equipment, quality sleeping bags and elasticated head torches with a battery life of one hundred and eighty hours. They had a look at the map in the shop, and found there were several trails from Rieden to Berwang, plus they could take a ski lift to the top from Heiterwang and Bichelbach to the north-east on one side, and another down the other slope to Berwang. Although if anyone was looking for them, it was an easy task to monitor the lifts into the town. Walking or cross-country skiing wouldn't be easy, but it was possible.

At a quality camera shop just along the street they got a night scope, a pair of binoculars and several spare batteries for the headtorches.

Next stop was an out-of-town shop for mountaineering gear where they purchased four, sixty-metre, lengths of rope, climbing ascenders, a full body harness, two helmets and a double micro hauler pulley for whatever they may encounter later, in the tunnel system under the Rhön.

Changing the car turned out to be a nightmare, with forms to be signed and extra charges for this and that, but eventually, and after making sure they had transferred everything, including the automatics, they drove away in an Audi estate.

It was dark by the time they set out back for Rieden, and they both wondered if the Mossad agents were, by now, looking for them, so they headed north from Garmisch and took the road to Linderhof to the north-west.

The route via Linderhof was a much longer journey. It was over an hour before they hit the main Lermoos to Reutte road, and turned up to Rieden.

They had a simple dinner in the guesthouse restaurant with some local red wine. David had mineral water, and was comforted that not having the wine didn't bother him at all.

'I think we should go tomorrow after breakfast, and have a look at the villa. With our hoods up and our sunglasses on, we should just blend in with all the other couples on the piste,' he said.

'How long will it take us, if we walk?' Christina stretched and David felt the old lust rising in him. The way she moved her body was so sensual.

'I'd guess three or four hours, if the snow isn't too bad. Are you ready for bed?' He arched his eyebrows.

'Are ***you***, David Lennox?'

Chapter 31

They breakfasted as the morning sun rose above the mountain peaks. On hearing of their plan to head south-east to Rinnen, the landlady, whose name they now knew was Frau Harting, made them a packed lunch with a large thermos of coffee, and assured them that the path to Berwang was 'immer zugänglich'...'always passable',

The sky was a cloudless azure blue, and the frozen moisture in the minus eight degree air sparkled and shimmered as they left the village. The climb, south of the Thaneller peak, which rose over two thousand metres on their left, followed the Rottlech valley upstream. The path through the forest of green alder and larch was crushed stone, but was packed solid with compressed snow, and comfortable to walk on. Although cumbersome, the thin cross-country 'langlauf' skis lashed to their backs, were manageable.

Steep in places, the track rose ever upwards as the temperature fell ever downwards. David was relieved that he had spent time in the gym at the clinic to put some strength back in his legs.

After two kilometres and climbing two hundred metres, the path levelled out somewhat at one thousand metres. Spectacular views greeted them as they walked out of the thick alpine forest of pine and spruce onto higher ground. The trail hugged the deep aquamarine of the river, the icy water roaring out its downward plummet to the valley below.

Donning their skis, their progress became much easier and they were able to glide effortlessly on the flat and downhill stretches.

At midday they came to the artificial reservoir which fed the power station at RotlechStausee. After clearing off the snow, they sat at a wooden picnic table overlooking the dam and the lake, having their lunch in the comparative warmth of the midday sun.

Forty minutes later, they were following the path up beside the river to Rinnen, and were soon emerging from the thick alpine larch forest into the next high valley.

David reckoned they were still half-an-hour from Berwang, and checked with the SatNav when they came to a fork in the path. They should go left, the device estimating that at their average speed they would be in Rinnen in fifteen minutes.

They entered the village at the side of a baroque chapel and a busy ski-lift, stopping to scan the mountainside to the east, to locate the villa.

'That's it.'

He handed the binoculars to Christina and pointed out the building he meant, just at the lower edge of the tree line, a kilometre away.

Berwang itself was the highest village in this part of the Tyrol, the peaks rose almost vertically from both sides of the valley, Thaneller to the north-west and Roter Stein to the south-east, both well over 2,300 metres.

She adjusted the focus on the right eyepiece.

'Yes, that's it. I recognise the painting on the side wall from the Israelis' photograph.'

'We have to get up in the trees behind the villa, and wait for darkness,' he said, looking at his watch. 'Only another two hours. It'll take us the best part of an hour over open ground to get up there. The ski lift should gain us some height and get us behind the house.'

She took the map from him, and together they located where they were. The lift climbed to two thousand metres, above the town to the south.

At the base station, and after having to queue for a few minutes, they were soon sharing a seat and pulling down the restraining bar to secure themselves from falling on to the icy slopes below.

The skis of brightly clad tourists dangled from the chairs of the lifts, and skiers and snowboarders on their way down to the bottom of the piste weaved gracefully between the support towers below. At the top, the pair followed a path along the ridge to the east, until David could see on the SatNav that they were in the forest somewhere above the villa. Here, they left the trail and hid the skis.

The light was fading as they reached the lower line of pines, and the deep snow had covered tree roots and fallen trees, making progress difficult on the steep slope. They found that they had gone two hundred metres past the back of the house, and had to double back west to get within a hundred metres of it. A recently fallen evergreen, which had pulled up its roots when it finally succumbed to the wind, provided good cover as the sun disappeared behind the mountains.

Christina trained the night scope on the white-walled property. It was bigger than it had looked from across the valley, surrounded by a stone wall roughly one and a half metres high. One corner of a large paved patio at the front was visible in the glow of the lights from inside the house, as was a separate double garage to the far side.

Built on the side of the mountain, the villa was two storey at the back and four on the downhill slope. From the other side of the valley they had seen the open verandas stretching across the two top floors overlooking the village, but they could only see one end from their position now.

Apart from the low bass throb of music drifting up from a car in the village below, all was quiet.

'Two guys. One patrolling the back, and one the front. There are four, no five, four-metre posts along the back, about fifteen metres from the house. Something on top of them. Could be movement sensors for lights, or an alarm system. Difficult to know,' she said, handing the night-scope to David.

He focussed on the back windows of the property, but at the angle they were at, it was impossible to see anything, so he turned his attention on the two men outside in the unlit perimeter. The one at the back was constantly in view, but David couldn't see if he was carrying a weapon. The guy to the front only appeared at their end of the house as he finished his patrol route, and was more difficult to see. However, after another ten minutes, he came to speak to his colleague and they lit cigarettes.

The image on the scope flared brilliant white as the flame from the match overloaded the intensifier. When the device settled down, David tried to establish whether the other man was armed, but it was impossible to tell, as they were both wearing heavy coats in the freezing mountain air.

'How do you want to do this?' Christina spoke without shifting her gaze from the house.

'The Mossad favour the early hours of the morning for a hit, so whatever we do, it has to be before then. That's if they're not here now,' he answered.

Remembering that he had stupidly and unknowingly let Gehrling follow him up onto Caw, he inspected the surrounding area very thoroughly with the night-sight.

'Well they're not here yet. So we have a window of opportunity, as the bureaucrats at NATO are so fond of saying,' he grumbled.

'All right, those two aren't going to move, so it looks like we have to move them, yes?' she said, looking at him and shrugging her shoulders. 'Yes?'

'Yes, I suppose so. If you see me getting ten skittles of shit beaten out of me, help, okay?'

'I wasn't thinking of fighting them, David,' she said, coldly.

'No, I didn't think you were,' he said, shaking his head.

Another two to add to the list. How many more had to die for this bloody map?

They fitted the silencers to their automatics, and crept out from behind the fallen tree, carefully trying to avoid dead branches nestling under the coating of snow.

'David you do this guy, I'm going to the front.' He gave her the diver's thumb-and-forefinger okay as she made her way around the north side of the building to the guard there.

David would have to pass one of the five posts to reach the back of the house. He could see them more clearly now, and they weren't lights, so they must be movement sensors. Sooner, rather than later, they would know he was there.

Suddenly, the goon at the back became agitated, stabbing

his finger into his left ear. Someone was talking to him on his earpiece, telling him David was there. The man pulled what looked like an Uzi from under his coat, donned night sight goggles, and peered into the forest, where David was now crouching.

It was now or never. David stood up, raising the Glock as the guard swung towards him. He pulled the trigger twice waiting for the 'pop…pop' of the silenced rounds leaving the barrel.

The gun jammed, and there was a split second of indecision or surprise from the other man, which gave David the opportunity to dive for cover behind the nearest tree.

He kept as cool as possible, remembering all his years of training. He was rusty, but it was coming back. Ejecting the magazine, he re-cocked the gun twice, and was reloading it when a silenced burst from the Uzi ripped into the bark above his head, piercing his face with wood splinters. He felt the warm blood running down his cheek, and rolled violently to the left, simultaneously raising the automatic. He saw the man silhouetted against the stars, and fired three times. This time the gun fired perfectly 'pop…pop…pop'.

He heard a grunt, followed by the Uzi being fired indiscriminately. Everything went quiet, until he heard a groan ten metres in front of him. There was another 'pop' and he knew that Christina had dealt with it.

'David…David. Are you all right?' she whispered.

He got to his feet, brushing the snow from his jacket.

'Fucking gun jammed. Sorry.'

'I'll take the front, you do the back, and let's be careful. The guy at the front was a German, let's see where this one's from.' She stooped and went through the pockets of the dead man at her feet. Holding up his wallet in the beam of her mini torch, she took out his international driving licence. 'He's a German too, both addresses in Dresden.'

'Ex Stasi?' asked David, keeping his eye on the villa.

'Almost certainly. Now we must get into the house before anybody else comes.' Christina threw the man's wallet back onto his body and scanned the villa with the night sight.

'The guard my side got a warning, as I came through the movement sensors, so I guess there's at least one more inside,' said David, holding a handkerchief to his bleeding cheek.

Christina saw the dark stain on the material.

'Are you hit, David?'

'Splinters, nothing really, we can pull them out later. Let's do the house and get out of here.'

As he spoke, all the lights in the villa went out. David bent down and removed the night-vision goggles from the dead guard, and feeling the stickiness of blood and brain tissue on the head-strap, wiped them clean in the snow.

Christina went around the front and came back wearing the other guard's set. They both stood at the back door, waiting a few seconds to get accustomed to the eerie light, then David tried the handle. As he had presumed, it was locked.

Christina used her burglary tool, but the door remained stubbornly shut, probably bolted. The windows were triple glazed and toughened glass, so breaking one would be difficult and extremely noisy. It was as they pondered the problem of how to get in, that an outside floodlight was turned on, and they were both blinded, as the night vision goggles flared brilliant white.

A rapid burst of fire came from an upstairs window, producing a cry of pain from Christina. David instinctively rolled to the left and flattened himself against the wall. Ripping off the goggles, he fired three rounds at the open window above, and another two as his normal vision returned.

Christina was tight against the building on the other side of the door, a trickle of blood from her left arm falling onto the snow at her feet. As the short barrel of an Uzi poked tentatively out of the window, David stepped back and fired three rounds. The figure behind the gun was caught off balance and staggered backwards. David fired two more rounds, this time sure that he was on target, and the Uzi clattered out of the window, falling at Christina's feet. Quickly picking the weapon up, she shot out the floodlight.

They stood in the darkness waiting, but no further sound came from the house. After two minutes, David donned the goggles, and leant out to look up at the open window, keeping his automatic at arm's length in front of him.

'Are you okay?' he asked.

Christina was taking her coat off and pulling up the sleeve of her thermal shirt.

'I'm trying to look. There's a lot of blood, but my arm, hand and fingers work. It hurts like hell. Do you have your torch? I can't get this hand into my pocket.'

David handed it to her, never lowering his gun, or taking his eyes off the upstairs window.

'Three or four rounds, just the flesh under my arm, it might need a few stitches. I have a small kit with me at the hotel, if you'll do it for me,' she said, stifling a grunt of pain, as she tried to pull her sleeve up.

'No problem. We'll find something to bind it with, when we are inside. It looks like we go in through that upstairs window. I'll see if there's a ladder anywhere.'

He went around the villa, to the side door of the large double garage. It was open. David felt for the light switch, turning off the night vision goggles as he did so. The neon tubes flickered and rattled into life, and two black Mercedes S class saloons gleamed in the blue-white light.

On the side wall, along with a neatly coiled garden hose and two mountain bikes hung on brackets, was an aluminium ladder, which would easily reach the open window.

David lifted the ladder from its retaining brackets, careful not to scratch the nearest car. They had tried to kill him for Christ's sake. Who cared about scratching their car? Even so, he lifted the ladder out, fastidiously avoiding the paintwork of the two cars. Bloody middle-class, public schoolboy education.

When he returned, Christina was nodding up at the window.

'No sound or movement. Nothing.'

He raised the ladder and started to climb, turning on the night vision goggles as he reached the bottom of the window. Peering over, he saw the slumped body of the man who had been firing at them. His right ear had been shot off, as had a portion of his skull on that side.

David gingerly lifted himself over the sill, keeping the rest of the room covered as he did so. It was a spare room with an unmade bed, and on the floor along one wall was a series of neatly stacked paintings and boxes of silverware and jewellery.

He found a pile of sheets and pillowcases on a chair by the bed, and ripped four pillowcases in two. He was just tearing the last as Christina's head appeared in the window frame.

'Can you help me in, David? My left arm's getting very stiff.'

He put his arms around her and lifted her into the room, as he did so he kissed her on the mouth.

'What was that for?' she smiled, taking her jacket off and pulling up her sleeve.

'I'm going to take a chance and put the light on, you cover the door, while I dress your arm,' he said.

Blood had started to congeal on her underarm, and there was extensive swelling around the trauma. The wounds themselves were not so bad, as the rounds had passed through the flesh, but would, as she had said, require stitching. He wound the linen around her arm, being careful not to wrap it too tight, in case of further swelling, and skilfully split the ends to tie the dressing neatly.

It was then they heard a noise from downstairs. David leapt to extinguish the light, as she quickly put her jacket back on. The tap, tap, tap, of a walking stick and the scuff of a dragged leg came from the floor below. There was the unmistakeable metallic clink of a gun being cocked and then silence. Minutes later the tap, tap, of the walking stick again, then nothing.

David nodded for Christina to check the rooms to the right, while he cleared those to the left. The risers on the wooden staircase were open, so that anybody below would be able to see them coming down. David took a chair from the landing, and threw it down to the ground floor, at the same time sweeping his hand down over a set of four switches on the wall which bathed the stairs and the room below in light. Nothing, only the dull tick-tock of a clock pendulum.

He took a few steps down the staircase, then knelt, looking through to the large open plan lounge below. The room was tastefully decorated, with various sofas and coffee tables set on quality Turkish rugs. Several doors led off the main area, with a dining room through an open archway, divided from the spacious kitchen by a waist-high serving worktop.

Wisps of steam rose from a recently boiled kettle and the silence was broken only by the sound of spitting and splintering logs, burning in an impressive open fire, set in the centre of the wall below the staircase.

As he carried on down, his non-slip soled boots making small squeaking noises on the pine steps, he beckoned Christina, and started checking room by room. He opened a door to his left, and entered an office with three work desks.

A small table in the corner had on it the movement sensor monitor that had detected him, on his way to the back of the villa. A mobile phone lying on it suddenly illuminated and vibrated. David picked it up and saw that the call was from Gehrling.

He heard Christina talking, then a man's voice calling his name. The accent was Germanic and the speaker's voice frail with age.

'Mr Lennox…Mr Lennox, please come and join us. Please slide your gun into the room, and enter with your hands above your head. Please do it now, or your pretty Slovak Jewess will die.'

He could see Christina's back, in a doorway opposite, and slid his gun past her into the room.

'Kick it to me please, Miss Karranova.' Christina did as she was asked. 'Thank you. Now, Mr Lennox, please come in, and do exactly as I say. I've killed many Jews and another won't make any difference to me.'

David entered the unlit room, which he could see in the gloom was a library, books lining all four walls from floor to ceiling behind wired shutters. The rich smell of cigar smoke hung in the air.

A hunched figure was sitting in an armchair, a walking stick in one hand and a very large Luger pistol in the other. He took his hand off the cane, switching on a lamp on the table beside him.

The face was gaunt, with sunken eyes and a hooked roman nose. His hair was snow white and wispy, the mouth thin, curled in a perpetual sneer, the jutting Teutonic jaw accentuating small patches of grey stubble where he hadn't shaved properly. His hands were like talons, mottled with age spots. There was a slight tremor in his gun hand, but only slight, David noted.

'Herr Von den Bergen, I presume, or is it Herr Fjällman?'

David glanced at Christina to check that she was all right, and she gave him a hint of a smile.

'You finished Mr Fjällman and his life in Sweden, Mr Lennox, for that you'll pay with your life, and so will your Jewess friend here.' He pointed the Luger at Christina.

'Did that gun kill William Kenton?' Christina couldn't suppress her anger and revulsion of the man.

'So, you know about Kenton. You must have found something in Mellrichstadt. That's a great shame, as my colleagues have gone there to look for themselves. I must telephone them with the news. So you do have what the little Jew Novak left,' the old man said smiling, a small drip forming on the end of his nose.

'Did you kill him too?' Christina was now quivering with rage and her whole frame was shaking.

'You know that I did not. Voss said he'd beaten him to death with a metal bar, in Stutthof. He lied. I was led to believe that the Jew never spoke again, but now I know that he did. He didn't die in the camp, he died in Jonastal, and he nearly killed Voss in the process.'

David put his hand out to calm Christina and immediately Von den Bergen raised the pistol.

'Your hands where I can see them please, Mr Lennox. My dear girl, why such emotion for Novak? Just because he was a fellow Jew, surely not?'

'He was my grandfather,' her voice quavered.

The old Nazi was briefly surprised and then a broad grin spread across his face.

'Well, well. History is in this room. Your father, Mr Lennox, and your grandfather my dear, and me, all together on that cold winter's day in Poland, at the end of the war. I was sure later that the Jew had passed something on, and now of course I know that he did, to your father, Mr Lennox. I should've had all the prisoners searched on the farm that day, but the Soviets were coming, there was no time.

To business. I'm an old man and will soon die, so please Mr Lennox, where can I find the map?' He turned the gun on Christina. 'I'll shoot her in the legs, again and again until you tell me, please believe me.'

David played for time.

'It's at a hotel we're staying at. It's a map of the tunnels, but surely you must know the system? You were in charge of the project,' he said.

'I was in charge of parts of the operation, Mr Lennox. The system was vast. The Jew must've got information from other prisoners working in the salt mines linked to the main network.'

He lowered the Luger and pointed it at Christina's knees.

'Where's the map?' he demanded.

'We've found a part of the map. We only have the section relating to the Jonastal project and the entrances around Arnstadt. I'm guessing that you have limited access already, and have found artwork and the Soviet nuclear demolition weapons which you sold to the South Africans and, unwittingly, the Israelis for the Indian Ocean test. I think you now wish to redress your mistake in supplying the Israelis, and want to find the remaining weapons, to sell to anti-Zionist terrorists.'

The German was visibly shaken.

'How was I to know the South Africans would deal with the Jews?' His gun hand was now shaking.
'The Swede, Lindén, knew your name, and the Mossad's here in Berwang now. They plan to take you early tomorrow morning, and get rid of their embarrassment. We're only interested in the secret chamber and what it contains.'
Von den Bergen was suddenly distracted.
'I won't let the Jews get me. You have, I presume, killed my bodyguards, and all this because of Hess and Kammler, all because of Hess and Kammler, the insanity of the Ahnenerbe, for God's sake why? The chamber was a secret, and I swore, on the honour of my Fatherland, that I'd never reveal its location. Gehrling doesn't know anything about it. He's only interested in his own greed and what he can sell from the art, gold and weapons stored underground. I pray to see the state of Israel destroyed, along with the vermin who live there,' he snarled.
'What has Hess to do with the secret chamber?' David asked, watching Von den Bergen's thin forefinger whiten, as it tightened against the trigger.
'Because, whatever's in there, is why he flew to Scotland, it's what drove him mad, it's what kept him a prisoner for all those long years. It's the reason he became a Judas, betraying the Führer. It's why Kammler was taken to the USA and given a new name. He was on the American plane from Prague to Spain with me, Eichmann and Gehlen. Franco was told by the Americans to deny the flight ever existed. Kammler and Gehlen did a deal for all of us and were flown to Washington. Eichmann and I flew on to South America, but the Jews came for us. When Kammler died, and they had Eichmann, they all started looking for me.'
'What the hell's in there?' David snarled.
The old man raised the gun again, this time with a rock steady grip.
'The Jews won't get me, and they won't get the map. You've reached the end of the road my friends. Blame your father,' he

nodded at David 'and your grandfather, my dear. And Hess.' He took aim at Christina.

All David saw, was her right hand come up through a ninety degree arc and a flash of metal. The glinting blade took the old man in the throat, and as he jerked back in shock, he involuntarily loosed off a round, which struck the books behind Christina's head.

David, deafened by the discharge of the unsilenced weapon, kicked out and knocked the gun from Von den Bergen's claw-like hand. As it fell to the floor, the aged Luger discharged again, the round embedding itself in the ceiling, causing a snowstorm of plasterwork to fall on the old man. He was now struggling to breathe, blood bubbling and frothing from his open mouth, his hand went to his throat as he tried to pull the blade out, but he only managed to cut his fingers to the bone on the razor sharp steel.

Christina leant over him and pulled it out, releasing a geyser of blood and a weak grunt of pain. She put her face nose to nose with the dying man.

'You see, old man. In the end the Jews did get you. Rot in hell.'

As she backed off, Von den Bergen spat in her face, a mix of blood and spittle slid down her cheek.

'Verpiss dich, Jüdische Drecksau.' He tried to stem the flow of blood with his hand, but it breached through his fingers and dribbled on to his shirt, which now had an Africa-like stain spreading on its tectonic plate across Von den Bergen's chest.

'Fuck you too.' She violently spat back, and he desperately tried to wipe away the saliva with his cut and bloodied hand.

'What the hell's in the chamber?' David shouted single-mindedly.

'Frage deinen Chef, Engländer, frage deinen chef nach… Gehlen.'

The last word was a rattle of blood and expelled air. Von den Bergen was dead.

'Ask my boss about Gehlen, what the hell did he mean?' puzzled David.

Christina was sobbing, her body shuddering, as she leant against the bookshelf shutters to steady herself.

'I'm so sorry, David, I just lost control. It isn't because I'm a Jew, I haven't been in a synagogue since I was a child, I don't feel Jewish. It was thinking of my grandfather and this, this animal, I'm sorry.'

She came to him and he held her, stroking the back of her neck.

'He wouldn't have told us anything of use,' he said. 'I'm not sure he knew anything, apart from the remarks about your grandfather and asking my boss about Gehlen. Perhaps they do know what's in the chamber, they just don't know where it is. We find it and goodnight,' he said.

'What did he mean about my grandfather dying in Jonastal? Did Voss take him back there at the end of the war?

'He must've done. He must've been trying to get into the system.'

'Who was Gehlen?' she asked, flexing her hand, trying to ease the pain in her arm.

Reinhard Gehlen was the Nazi's intelligence chief on the Eastern front during the war, he told her. After the German surrender, he had been recruited by the Americans, and sent back to Germany, to run an anti-communist spy organisation there, at the start of the Cold War. It was rumoured that he was the head of Odessa, the Nazi's escape organisation, and secretly recruited hundreds of German scientists and intelligence officers to the States via South America, all with the backing of the CIA. He ended up starting an organisation called Gladio in Europe, to fight communism, and later headed up the West German intelligence service, the BND. He died in the late seventies. All details of Kammler were erased from the Nuremberg trials. He was the Obergruppenführer in charge of the Ahnenerbe, the most secret arm of the SS, and later he was in charge of the Jonastal project.

'So Von den Bergen, Gehlen and Kammler escaped together at

the end of the war. I wonder if Kammler stayed in America too? How's your arm?' he asked.

'Aches like hell, but it's okay.' She patted her wound.

'Right, let's have a quick look around, and then back to Rieden. Can you manage the walk in the dark?' He cupped her chin in his palm.

'Yes, no problem. We'd better take the night-sight goggles with us.'

They took a quick look at all the other rooms, which were either empty or set up as bedrooms. In one David caught a hint of woman's perfume. Vicky Mason's.

They rifled through the drawers in the office, and Christina found a map of part of the tunnel system. It looked incomplete, but had extra information around the area of Meiningen. Under it was a file marked 'Voss' in bold red marker pen. She folded both and gave them to David who put them in his pocket. The mobile phone on the desk vibrated softly again, its LED display illuminating the name 'Hans Jürgen' in an eerie green glow.

Five minutes later, they were struggling through the broken branches and tree roots, on their way back to the trail at the top of the forest. The slope was steep, but the going was a little easier with the night-vision goggles. They located the hidden skis , and made their way south, along the steep ridge, back to the slopes.

It was half past seven when they got to the top of the chair lift. The runs were shut and the lifts had closed down, but the lower slopes were still illuminated around the base station. They descended carefully; slaloming down, and making wide shallow turns on the narrow cross-country skis.

Christina was finding the turns difficult with the ski sticks, her arm becoming increasingly painful as she made her triceps work against the incline. By the time they had reached the bottom, her hand was beginning to swell badly, so she knelt, holding it in the snow for some minutes.

'I have morphine and antibiotics in a pack at the hotel. That should fix it. Let's go before it gets worse,' she said, slinging the skis over her back and setting off on the road back to Rinnen.

'You okay?' He brushed her cheek with his gloved hand.

She smiled, then sunk her head, looking at the ground.

'I'm sorry, David, it's not my style to lose control, but I felt such hatred for that man. I wanted him to suffer. He died too easily, too quickly. I know that's a bad thing to say, but it's just how I feel right now. It finished too quickly.'

Reaching the trail for Rieden, they put their skis back on, feeling the bite of the evening air as they removed their gloves. Christina was struggling with her bindings, so David knelt in the crisp snow and fastened them for her.

They set off at a brisk pace, but soon Christina had to slow down, because she could only use her good arm to propel herself along the track. The wind had picked up by the time they reached the highest point of the trail, and David estimated that it was minus twenty or below.

'I need to stop for a rest David, just for a minute.' She leant in exhaustion against the ski sticks.

'We have to get out of this wind, Christina.'

He cradled her body, sheltering her from the icy blast. She was shivering badly, and he knew immediately that he had to get her moving, and back to a warm bath in the hotel.

'I just need to sit down, David. Please, just a few minutes.'

Her body shuddered and the staccato rattle of her teeth tapped out a Morse signal of distress.

He undid her bindings, throwing her skis into the deep snow at the side of the trail. He put his hand between her legs, carrying her in a classic fireman's lift, and set off for the forest below, to shelter from the freezing temperatures on the exposed heights. He had discarded his own ski sticks, and struggled to balance as he started to free glide down to the trees. As he picked up a little speed, stability became easier, and soon he felt the terrible chill of the wind drop as he reached the sanctuary of the forest.

The track down to Rieden was a series of small inclines and declines. He could feel the sweat running down his back under his thermal clothing, at every rise in the path. As he crossed his skis and waddled upward, the strength ebbed from his aching thigh and calf muscles, the lactic acid build-up becoming unbearable. His cheek was now throbbing from the embedded splinters.

It was midnight when he arrived at the outskirts of the town and set Christina down. She had stopped shaking, but he knew she was slipping into hypothermia.

He supported her under the arm, and walked to the hotel, praying that they wouldn't see Frau Harting the owner, on the way in.

Safely back in the room, he lay Christina on the bed and ran a bath, making sure it wasn't too hot. He carefully removed her clothes, cutting away the sleeve of her left arm where the blood had congealed to the fabric.

As he carried her to the tub, and lowered her gently into the water, it was obvious that her left forearm and hand were now badly swollen, so he went to her luggage for the medical kit.

Kneeling, he delicately pulled away the fabric from the wounds, and cleaned the dried blood away from the areas surrounding the lacerations, dabbing them dry with a sterile pad. He found some hypodermics, and shuddered at the vivid memory of the Chechen Ruslan and his foul breath. Some of the phials, neatly held by a leather loops in the pouch, were marked Novocain and others were an intravenous antibiotic.

He injected the area near the wounds with the Novocain, waiting a few minutes for the local anaesthetic to take hold. Taking a hooked stitching needle from the kit, and threading the synthetic gut, he gingerly started sewing the four separate flesh wounds. They were all very close together, needing ten stitches in total.

David had done this many times in the field, and had stitched himself on one occasion in Sierra Leone. The scar remaining, or the lack of it, was testament to his skill. The MO who had done his initial field medical training had said he was a natural.

Christina was coming round, as he neatly tied the end stitch, dabbing away the blood with a sterile wipe. He snapped the end of the antibiotic phial off, drawing the liquid into another hypodermic, and injecting a vein in the general area above the stitching. He gave the whole area another cleaning, then took a tube of antiseptic salve from his own toiletry bag. He didn't know if this was correct procedure or not, but he had nothing else, and presumed that it couldn't be that bad.

He covered the stitching in a gauze dressing and then bandaged the arm, finally ripping a hole in the bottom of a plastic bag, putting her arm through it, and tying it over her shoulder to keep it dry.

She shivered and opened her eyes, smiling weakly as David opened the hot water tap to warm up the water.

'Do you feel better? I've stitched and dressed your arm.' He pinched her nose between his thumb and forefinger. 'There's a course of some oral antibiotics here, er...Doxycycline. We'll give you another shot of the intravenous tomorrow, and then three a day of the tablets for a week. It should've settled down by then. It's going to hurt when the anaesthetic wears off, I'm afraid.'

He poured some more hot water into the tub.

'Stay in there 'til you look like a prune. I'm going to make you a cup of coffee.'

'What's a prune?' She looked puzzled.

'A dried plum.' he said, as he left the bathroom.

'Charming.' Her last comment pleased him, as he knew that she was recovering.

He returned with a cup of coffee as she was running more hot water into the tub.

'Thanks. Is there anything else in it?' She looked hopeful.

'Yes coffee.' He frowned. 'Do you know how many merchant seamen died, after they were taken from the waters of the Atlantic during the war, because they were given a tot of rum, supposedly to warm them up? Best way to lose body heat, is alcohol.' He wagged his finger admonishingly.

'Jesus. It was better when you drank.' She sank up to her chin in the water.

'Okay, drink your coffee hot, and raise that core temperature.'

He took some tweezers from his toiletry bag and sat in front of the bedroom mirror, pulling the tree splinters from his cheek, giving the whole area a good rubbing with the antiseptic salve afterwards. He sat on the bed, then lay down to think.

What the hell did they do next? Every bastard and his mother were after them now.

Chapter 32

The swelling on Christina's arm had gone down markedly. She still had some pain, but her hand was usable, and there was no purple discolouration to signal any blood poisoning.

David recovered the map and papers from under the bath tub before telling Frau Harting that they would be checking out, saying that friends had unexpectedly booked a villa in Garmisch. They had wanted to pay her for the three days they had booked in for, but she was adamant that they didn't have to, as there hadn't been any other enquiries for the room. He insisted that he pay for two at least, and grudgingly she accepted.

As David took the luggage to the car it was snowing heavily, that would obliterate any tracks that they'd left around the villa.

David drove, and they decided it would be safer to head west to Kempten, avoiding Garmisch.

'Do you think that Aaron has found the mess at the villa yet?' she asked.

'Did you take your antibiotic?'

She nodded with an exasperated expression.

'Yehhsss. Shoshanim?'

'Yes of course he has,' David answered, 'but I don't know what he'll do. He must be very pissed off. He might inform the Austrian police, tell them who to look out for, or he might not. My guess is that he won't. He won't, because he doesn't want the map to disappear, or to drop into the hands of the Austrians. However, he'll pull out all the stops to find us. Do we go south to Italy or east to Hungary or Slovenia, or can you fix cover for us in Slovakia, in the High Tatra?'

'I want to go on, David. With the tunnels, I mean,' she said.

'What the…! You told me that after Von den Bergen, that'd be it. Why the hell do you want to carry on now? Why've you changed your mind?' he said, banging the steering wheel with his palms in frustration.

'Because I read the 'Voss' file when you were packing the car,' she said, looking at the floor.

'And?'

'My grandfather's body's down there.' She looked up, tears in her eyes.

She told him what she had read. Voss had told Gehrling and Zapf, under torture, that he'd taken him back to Jonastal in the chaotic spring of 1945, with the promise that he'd go free if he could show Voss where the Nazi treasure was. He took Voss deep into the tunnel system, to an area where he knew the air was bad. Voss started to feel ill, her grandfather had tried to kill him, but wasn't strong enough, and Voss shot him. The spot was marked on their map, close to the hidden chamber.

'You don't need to come, David, no I don't want you to come. I want to get my mother's father so she can bury him before she dies. Her cancer's terminal. She hasn't got long to live, David.'

'Christina if you go, I go. Don't be crazy.'

'I don't want to put you in danger.'

He rubbed his palm down his face.

'Where to?' he sighed.

'No, I don't want you to come. It's my problem.'

'Where to?'

She kissed his cheek.

'Thank you. I appreciate it very much. I love you, David, but no.'

'There's no way you're going on your own, Christina. Now, where to?'

There was a long silence before she spoke.

'All right. The Mossad are certainly in Mellrichstadt, and so is everybody else. Victoria Mason, Gehrling, and God knows who else? Where do we stay?'

'We have one major advantage; we have the map.' David said.

'For now.' She looked worried. 'So, where the hell do we go?' She raised her eyebrows.

'Pass. I think the old East's out. Anywhere in Thuringia's going to be swarming with ex-Stasi people. If a foreign couple register at a hotel there in late January, they'll know about it within minutes.' He frowned in concentration.

'So it has to be in the Rhön somewhere.' She was studying the road map.

'They'll all be thinking the same as we're thinking, so we have to do something really unexpected. Let's bypass the area, and travel on the autobahn much further north. We can stay at a service station near a turn off for Merkers. Let's go down the mine there as tourists, to see what we can learn about the tunnel systems,' he said, indicating left to take the autobahn to Ulm.

'How long's the journey? I didn't sleep well last night, because of my arm.' She lifted the offending limb, and wagged it limply, smiling as she did so.

'Should be about four-and-a-half hours to somewhere to stay, reasonably near Merkers, maybe five. Anyway Merkers it is, yes?' he asked.

'Anything you say, Boss. Anything you say.' She curled up in her seat. 'Do you mind if I get some sleep?'

'No, you go ahead. I'll wake you, to take your next antibiotic.' He grinned sarcastically.

'Thank you.' She closed her eyes, but the smile lingered for some time.

On the way, he stopped for petrol and bought a map of the autobahn system and the hotels, booking a motel in Kirchheim, near Merkers, using their real names in case the name Sheehan was on the Police files from Mellrichstadt.'

As he drove, he was struck, yet again, how much his life had changed over the last six weeks or so, since he had first received the letter from Berwang.

He didn't push the car too hard on the journey, and they arrived at the motel an hour before sunset. They checked in, deciding to just relax for the rest of the day, and discuss their options for the next week.

Christina was pouring herself a vodka from the mini-bar, when she saw the look on his face.

'What's troubling you, David?'

He told her what he had been thinking. About why his people had been trying to poison him, and what Von den Bergen's comments about the chamber meant. The old man hadn't even seemed sure what information Voss had got out of her grandfather. He didn't think Von den Bergen knew what was in the chamber, but he'd come to the same conclusion that they had. Their bosses knew what was in there, or they were guessing what was in there.

What the hell could be that important, and what was the Hess connection? Von den Bergen had mentioned the Ahnenerbe, the section of the SS that sent expeditions to Tibet, searching for the true origins of the Aryan race, and to the Pole to search for entrances to the inner Earth that they believed existed. They carried out medical experiments on concentration camp inmates, and they believed in occult powers.

Kammler was in charge of the Jonastal Project, rocket research and God knew what else.

'Why would the Americans have given him another identity when he was one of the most wanted Nazis at the end of the War?' he asked, cupping his nose in his hands.

'You said that British and American intelligence were responsible for assassinating Hess. What do you remember about the briefings?' She started to make notes. 'Sorry, but I have to write things down, and look at them, to think clearly,' she said.

He gave her the story as he remembered it. Whatever secrets Hess had, they were briefed would seriously embarrass the British aristocracy and royalty. He had confided in a young French guard at Spandau, and they wanted to make his death look like suicide too.

Hess kept diaries, and they collected and burnt them every month. He wasn't allowed any contact with the International Red Cross or Amnesty, or to watch or listen to any news programmes, and his radio and television were controlled from outside his cell.

No physical contact with his family was permitted, and all his conversations were monitored, often interrupted, when the authorities wanted to shut him up.

'What the hell were they all afraid of? All this to avoid embarrassing the British monarchy? Bullshit!' he said.

'There was talk that the Soviets finally wanted to have him released during their guard assignment, which was scheduled directly after the American tour of duty, when he was killed. I thought it was all just a cruelty to an old Nazi, a sense of offended morality, a revenge, but now...'

'But now?' she asked, undoing the bandage on her arm, whilst David set her medical kit out on the bed.

She took another antibiotic, and removed the gauze so David could look at the wound. It was weeping a little from the stitching, and there was extensive blue and yellow bruising, but it looked clean and there was no sign of infection. David took a sterile wipe and carefully patted the area around the trauma.

'Let me look in the mirror at the stitches.' She stood and looked at the back of her arm. 'Very professional,' she said, delighted.

'I think you need another shot of antibiotic, just to make sure, all right?'

He broke the top off another phial, injected her upper arm and redressed the wound.

'Do you think that the German government know that this tunnel system exists?' she asked, flexing her hand as he tied the final knot on the bandaging.

'Yes, since reunification they must have intelligence that the system exists, but I'm damn sure they don't know about any weapons, and I'm absolutely certain they don't know anything about the chamber, or what it contains. Keep still now,' he demanded.

'You don't think they were told about it?' she wondered.

'No. The Hess assassination was top secret at the highest level, as was the Palme killing. The German government weren't told a damn thing about Hess.'

‘What do we do tomorrow?’ She spread-eagled on the bed.

‘First to Merkers, for a tour of the mine workings, then a look at the sites at, if I remember, Ohrdruf, Mühlberg, Marlishausen and, of course, Meiningen. We have the latitude and longitude coordinates and we have the SatNav. However, your grandfather drew this map in 1944, although they’re in degrees and minutes, they could be out by hundreds of metres.’ He finished bandaging her arm, and gently patted it.

‘So it’ll take a long time, you think?’ she questioned.

‘Yes, I’m guessing that Gehrling knows about most of the entrances in the old East Germany. They must’ve tried them and found them blocked, but can we take the chance, and leave them unexplored?’ he asked.

‘Do you think they know about the entrances across the border in Franconia?’

‘No I don’t think they do. No, I’m sure they don’t. We must have a think about what else we’re going to need in terms of equipment.’

He went to the mini-bar, and out of habit took a whiskey. As his brain caught up with his hands, he replaced it, and took out a mineral water. If Christina had noticed, she didn’t react.

‘I want you to know that I appreciate you coming with me, to look for my grandfather, David.’

‘Let’s hope we find him, before they find us,’ he said, seeing that glint of fear in her eyes again.

Chapter 33

In the Merkers mine car park, three coaches were disgorging German tourists from Cologne, as David and Christina changed into their boots.

The reception area in the main building was at the foot of the winding-gear tower. Unlike the exposed wheels of most British mines, this was enclosed in corrugated aluminium sheeting, from top to bottom.

A boutique at the back was selling crystals and semi-precious stones, and next to its entrance was a detailed map of the mine, showing over 4,600 kilometres of tunnel workings.

David despaired. It would need a lifetime to search through that lot.

The mine had employed over 3,000 at the height of potash and rock salt production in the DDR, the former for agriculture and the latter for road de-icing. Merkers continued to produce both, but it was now primarily a tourism business. The mine was linked to other complexes over vast distances, and interestingly, several of the tunnels ran under the old DDR/BRD border.

They were told, over the tannoy system, that they would be called by name and given overalls to wear over their street clothes. The trip would last for three hours, going down to a depth of eight hundred metres, travelling thirty-two kilometres into the system in open trucks.

Christina picked up a leaflet from the tourist information packs at the reception. It was for the Waldhotel Rennsteihöhe in Suhl, and tours to the former underground Stasi nuclear bunker and complex that was hidden beneath the grounds. It illustrated dining rooms, telephone exchanges, generators which still worked, briefing rooms, endless corridors and sleeping accommodation for one hundred and thirty.

Hundreds of these complexes were sited all over the old DDR, disguised as villas, holiday camps and hunting lodges. David realised that the hidden chamber and the body of Joseph Novak were somewhere beneath Suhl, but thousands of feet under the hotel bunker.

Three hours later, and back in the car park, they were both frighteningly aware of the enormity of such underground complexes and the huge problems they faced in their search.

On the drive back, Christina studied the original map against the map they had found in the villa in Berwang. In the top right hand corner was the logo of a roman sword.

'What's this sword here?' she asked.

David looked at it and shrugged.

'No idea. Rings a bell somewhere.'

There was some information about Jonastal. The area was now a training ground for the army, the Bundeswehr, and was a prohibited zone. In total there were twenty-three entrances. All but numbers thirteen to fifteen had been blasted, and thirteen and fifteen had been closed up with steel doors because of tunnel collapse. Fourteen was still open, but on the map marked, 'not passable'. Around Meiningen there was a red dot marking a point with a note underneath. They had found two suitcase nuclear bombs there. Both tunnels, east and west of the Meiningen entrance had collapsed.

Back at the hotel, they compared the maps, Novak's extensive one and Von den Bergen's more localised version. David took a red pen and the original map, as Christina studied the one from Berwang and called out information.

'Meiningen blocked in both directions from the entrance by a rock fall. Same with the entrances at Ohrdruf and Marlishausen.'

David marked Meiningen and Ohrdruf in red and drew a red square over the tunnels to signify that they were blocked, filling in the blown entrances blue.

'That leaves only one site to look at in the old East, at Mühlberg,' he said. 'That makes things easier. We can have a look tomorrow. Do you think Von den Bergen and Gehrling knew that this entrance was there?'

'Well it isn't on their map. Gehrling and Mason must know that we found something at the mill in Mellrichstadt, so if they know about the entrance, they'll be watching it.' She started undoing the dressing on her arm.

'We'll have to think about this carefully,' he said, swabbing her arm. 'Clean bill of health from Doctor Lennox.' He kissed her forehead.

'So what's our first stop? Mühlberg? How far's that?' She started scratching at her dressing.

'Leave it alone,' he chastised. 'An hour.'

'So, we should be there by nine,' she said.

A stocky man in his early forties dialled the direct line to Sir William Rush. He was in his room, in a small guesthouse, just off the Autobahn south of David and Christina.

'They're in a motel, sixteen kilometres north of here, sir.'

'Good man, Warren. Have you have received your revised instructions.

'Yes, sir…er about Mr French, sir.'

'You have your orders, Warren. Good day.

Chapter 34

They took the motorway to Mühlberg, stopping once to check the car for any trackers. Once they had pulled off onto country roads, Christina held the SatNav unit, telling David in which general direction to drive for the position reference on the map.

'Okay, south's nearly right, but we have to be much farther east.'

They avoided driving through the town, continuing along minor roads and through a heavily wooded area.

'Take a right here,' she said, pointing to the small road sixty metres ahead. 'We're exactly on 50° 52′ north and 10° 50′east, and what can we see? Nothing,' she snorted, scanning the immediate surroundings, but seeing only trees.

In the distance, on the top of a hill, were the ruins of a large castle, but around them the forest stretched right and left without end. They pulled off into a lay-by, where they had a good view along the road for a kilometre in both directions, and would be able to spot any unwelcome visitors.

Going deep into the woods, they tried to the right of the road first. Finding no evidence of any entrance or building camouflaging an access to the system below, they returned to the car, crossed over, and entered the forest on the other side.

Once through the deep snow piles which had been deposited by the snowploughs, they crossed a sparsely wooded area of silver birch, and after a two-hundred metre trudge they came across some ancient barbed wire and a **'Keep Out'** sign from the Bundeswehr, declaring it a military training area.

They pressed on, and came to a classic, two-storey, ex DDR military building, fifteen metres deep and twenty metres long. The front roof had collapsed under the weight of snow, and was lying, a mass of splintered wood and roofing tiles, on the first floor. This had partially collapsed at one end, pushing out the wall at an angle. One chimney had fallen, and stood upside down, its nose buried in the floorboards of the ground floor, like some strange modernist sculpture.

Broken windows and pockmarks on the wall were evidence of automatic fire, probably from Bundeswehr training exercises. To the side of the main building was a smaller structure with a large metal exhaust chimney protruding from the roof. The door was padlocked, but Christina soon had it open with her lock gun.

Inside was a diesel generator and a pump with an air intake. On the downstream side, a bank of filters, all now ageing and decaying, had left a rust stain on the concrete floor below. Against the side wall was an open chest of Russian gas masks which, apart from the covering of dust on the top layer, were perfectly usable.

Entering the main building, they found that at the rear the roof was sound, although the floor was covered in pigeon droppings and dead birds frosted with ice. The air was stale with the fug of damp rotting wood and putrid bird flesh; the wooden surfaces rough with blistering and peeling paint. Official notices adorned the walls, some in the Cyrillic script of Russian, and others in German.

Several spent cartridges lay on the floor and a clip of blanks, which looked reasonably new, had been left on a broken chair in the corner. At the back of the room was another padlocked door which at one time had been painted white, but was now a sickly dark yellow. A large sign was attached to the door.

"Achtung Lebensgefahr! Zutrittverboten!"

"Danger, life hazard. Keep out."

Underneath were a skull and crossbones and a radiation sign.

'Well, they don't want anybody to go in there,' David grimaced.

'Do we go in?' she asked, shrugging her shoulders.

As if in answer, there was a burst of light machine-gun fire from the forest, roughly three kilometres to the south, followed by a medley of thunderflashes and rifle fire.

'We'd better get a move on.' David grabbed her hand.

Christina swiftly made a mockery of the heavy padlock. As she opened the door, there was a rush of peculiarly scented warm air, which David vaguely recognised as a memory from childhood. As she shone her torch into the void, a flicker of reflected light from a small pool of water revealed a very steep stone staircase, which dropped twenty metres to another door.

They felt their way down in the erratic beam of the mini-torch; the handrails, pitted with rust, grating their palms. Beyond the door, was a small anteroom with a sliding iron hatch in the floor which had also once been white, the skull and crossbones still recognisable on its surface.

Against the far wall stood several canisters with Cyrillic script "Berech ot goryuchikh I vodi," which Christina translated as "Keep away from inflammable liquids and water."

'What the hell are those?' asked David, a little alarmed.

'I've seen them before, they're for the air conditioning system.' She undid the padlock on the hatch, and as she bent down she crinkled her nose. 'Can you smell that?' she asked.

'Yes, I remember it from somewhere. Haven't got it yet,' said David, sniffing the air like a Labrador.

As the padlock came off, David tried to slip open the hatch, having to heave on it with all his weight. It gave suddenly, and he fell as it slid open. There was a rush of air, followed by a waft of the aromatic odour again.

'I know what it is; it reminds me of when I was a kid with bronchitis, my mother used to have a lit camphor candle at the side of the bed.'

They both reacted at the same time.

'Oh Jesus! No!' She swung away from the hatch.

'Fuck!' he grabbed her hand, making for the door and the stairs and the fresh air of the forest.

They ran outside the building and sucked in air, as if they had just surfaced from five minutes under water.

'GD it must be. They must have stored Soman down there,' he gasped.

David remembered seeing Ministry of Defence footage of

Soman used on a group of chimpanzees at Porton Down. The vomiting and convulsions of the poor wretches before they finally died, something he found difficult to rid from his memory.

'Can those gas masks in the Generator room cope with it?' he asked, hoping the answer was no.

'If they're not damaged, they should be okay.'

'How strong a word's "should" in Slovak?' he demanded.

'Let's do it.' She made for the outhouse.

'Bugger.'

She threw him a mask, as the sound of more flashbangs and light machine-gun fire echoed from the trees. They were nearer, but still over two kilometres away.

Most secret sites in the DDR were connected directly to the national electricity grid, she told him. There would be a transformer, underground somewhere.

The diesel tank had fuel in it, so they should try starting it up and running the air-filter for a few minutes, to see how it was then. The equipment on the surface had been installed much later. The main fuel tank and generator would be deep underground, with an air conditioning and filter plant. Those places had been built to take nuclear attack.

'This building's reasonably new, everything should work.'

'There's that word again,' he said.

'What word?' she asked, confused.

'Should.'

On the wall behind the door was a circuit breaker . David heard a pleasing hum as he threw the lever, and lights started flashing on the control panel for the generator and the air conditioning unit.

'Unbelievable.' He shook his head, in disbelief.

'The wall only came down eleven years ago, David. This equipment was built to last,' she said, adjusting the strap on her gas mask.

He peered at the controls on the generator and pushed, what he guessed to be, the fire-up button. There was a wrenching sound as the shafts on the fuel pumps tried to move, suddenly freeing with a dull clank. The generator wheezed and coughed a little, then, surprisingly quietly, sprung into life. He pushed the green button on the air unit and heard pumps whirring reluctantly into action.

Christina pushed her finger on the plastic coating of the light switch, and for a brief millisecond the light came on, only to dim with an electric sizzle as the bulb gave up the ghost after years of inactivity. At least they had current, so they waited outside the generator room for five minutes, surprised that they couldn't hear the hum of the machinery with the door closed.

They donned the gas masks and entered the main building, going straight down the staircase, which was now lit by arc lights along the ceiling.

They could now see that the open iron hatchway led down to another level and another steel door, three metres below. The light switch was just inside, and David turned it on. Fluorescent tubes flickered into life, revealing a metal ladder.

David nodded to Christina to stand guard as he started descending, feeling the damp corroded metal of the handrails as he dropped. It was difficult to see in the gas mask, but he tried the handle of the door and it opened easily, a blast of warm air hitting him as he did so.

He put his gloves on, tucking his jacket sleeves into them to protect his skin from any contact with atomised GD, but praying that the air unit had cleared the problem.

On the wall by his head was another larger light switch, and as he activated it a long, narrow, downward sloping tunnel stretching out a hundred metres before him was revealed. Sealed heavy-duty lamps ran along overhead, two and a half metres above the floor. It reminded him of the foot tunnels under the Thames at Woolwich and Greenwich, such a source of adventure and excitement as a child.

Off the main corridor, through open arches, were several rooms. Here were desks with radio equipment, a small telephone exchange and beyond that a room with twenty or so bunk beds. Next were the toilets, an overpowering stench of ammonia and stale urine still noticeable through the gasmask. On the opposite side of the tunnel were the shower cubicles, now blackened by mould. In the final side room were the generator, fuel tank and the air filter system that Christina had known would be there.

He came to another metal door at the end of the corridor, and before this, on the wall, were three large brass manometers which David couldn't figure out, although, as he opened the door towards him, there was a massive blast of warm air and the readings on the dials shot up on all three.

David was now in a vast, bricked and cemented cavern. The arched roof, lit by sealed waterproof floodlights, most of which were still working, towered at least ten metres above him.

Abandoned Soviet trucks and motorcycles were neatly parked along one wall. He reckoned that there must be fifteen to sixteen large personnel carriers and over twenty motorbikes.

The cavern was roughly twenty-five metres across. The floor was smooth and flattened and three main square tunnels led off the chamber, all with electrical cables and air circulation tubes running along their concreted ceilings. All three exits were blocked by massive rock falls, and somewhere under the tons of rock, David surmised, were crushed canisters of Soman.

He walked to the entrances one by one, the odour of sour rubber from the mask making him long to tear it off. He looked for signs of gaps in the rock falls, but there were none. The problem could stretch for hundreds of metres or several kilometres for all he could tell.

Going back to the door he turned the handle down, and pushed against it.

It wouldn't move.

'Please don't do this to me.'

He pushed again, harder this time. The door was locked. It had to be linked to the manometers. The door locked if there was a negative pressure difference between the corridor and the chamber.

He looked around. To the right of the door, at its base, was a metal cabinet with a lid. Opening it, David saw a smaller manometer with a simple needle indicator within a green zone, a yellow zone, and a red zone. The indicator was showing a reading well into the red area, and this presumably had locked the door. At the side of the meter, under a thick transparent plastic cover, was a solitary button. David had no clear idea what would happen if he pushed it, and his finger hovered in indecision.

'What the hell.'

He pressed down and heard a pump somewhere drone into life. After a few minutes the gauge rose into the yellow area, as it reached the green, the pump cut out.

'If there's a God, the bloody door's now open.'

Depressing the handle, he pushed. It swung open. The feeling of relief was overwhelming.

'Thank Christ for that.'

Praying that the door at the other end would be no problem, he was heartily relieved when it opened easily and he saw Christina peering over the edge of the hatchway above him. She helped him straddle the lip as he clambered over the top of the ladder, and he heard a muffled voice from within the mouthpiece of her gas mask.

'Where the hell've you been? I was nearly coming to find you, I was thinking all kinds of terrible things.' She hugged him.

'Tell you all about it, in the car. Let's get outside and take these bloody masks off,' he said, the sweat running into his eyes. They shut the hatch, and Christina relocked both it and the door leading off the main building.

Standing outside, getting their breath back after the steep staircase, Christina removed her mask and shivered in the fresh winter air, David stood twenty metres away from her, keeping on his mask for some minutes, so that any traces of the Soman fumes in his clothes would be dissipated. She turned off the generator and the air circulation unit, threw the mains switch, then padlocked the door, making sure everything was secure.

As she finished, a flashbang went off no more than a hundred metres away, followed by a long burst from a light machine gun and the dumph…dumph... dumph…dumph of a heavier, vehicle-mounted weapon. The sound of platoon leaders barking orders was close enough to understand them.

They ran down to the birch trees, scrambling across the snow wall on the other side, and over the road to the car. The first figures, in winter combat fatigues, broke from the forest, taking cover in the derelict house, firing short bursts of automatic fire at unseen combatants deep in the trees.

Christina drove, the car wagging its tail in the snow as she accelerated away.

'Well, that was a bit too close,' she protested.

He told Christina all about the cavern and the vehicles stored there.

'So three exits, all of them blocked?' she said.

'Yes, and I had a close look too, there was no way you could get through that lot. One thing that occurs to me, with all those vehicles, it must've been a major transport site within the system. Gehrling and Zapf were local Stasi men; they must've known about it.

There had to have been a major vehicle access point to the tunnels, in the east. I'm guessing that was around Jonastal and that the access was closed by roof collapse.'

'Where now, David? One done, three to do,' she said, as they arrived at a fork in the road. She raised her eyebrows, swivelling her eyes from left to right.

'Left please,' he answered still studying the map. 'Trappstadt, it's a small village just across the old border, let's stay there for the night.'

The journey took them through Plaue and Ilmenau, both entrance sites on the Novak map, but dynamited by the Soviets and the East Germans when the Wall went up. As they crossed the old border, the sun was just setting, casting long, somehow ominous shadows across the road.

They found a small but comfortable guest house for the night, and discussed where they should go and what they should do next, over dinner.

'I think we should work west tomorrow. Agree?' David asked.

'Maybe there's still a way in near Mellrichstadt. Maybe Voss knew that.' She stabbed a forefinger at the map.

'Why didn't he go to any of the sites on his side of the border?' David watched out of the window as a steady stream of people made their way down to the Catholic church opposite for evening mass.

'I guess that the sites were DDR military, or Soviet, and he didn't dare to go there in case he was caught and his real past discovered,' she said.

'All right, if we have an early breakfast we should be able to cover at least two sites, unless we're very unlucky,' he suggested.

'Do you feel lucky?' She patted his hand.

'I feel a lot luckier than I did a week ago. Come on let's go to bed.'

As he slipped from consciousness, he realised that all the vivid dreams caused by the thallium poisoning had stopped, replaced by a dull gnawing fear.

Chapter 35

There had been a heavy snow fall during the night, but the roads were ploughed, even on the minor routes, as they drove towards Fladungen. The flat open fields on either side usually intensified snow drifts in high winds, but there was only a light breeze as they entered the town from the south-west.

The sky was slowly clearing, revealing patches of blue on the horizon to the west. An eerie blue-grey light tinged the reflected glare of the winter landscape.

Two roads led out of the town to the east, one to a small village called Brüchs and another to the hamlet of Sands. Christina wasn't sure which would take them nearest to the latitude and longitude they wanted.

'Take the Brüchs road first, and we'll see where we are,' she decided.

The two options ran parallel to each other for a hundred metres, then the Brüchs road turned sharply to the north. 'No, this is taking us too far north. Sorry, we have to take the other road,' she said.

They drove back down to take the left turn, up the steep hill, to Sands. 'This is right, we're almost due east, a bit too far north…another few hundred metres.'

After a sharp left-hand bend, they entered the forest, trees on both sides of them. David pulled over into a gravel lay-by and looked to his right.

'In there somewhere?' He nodded towards the trees, opening the driver's door. The rush of cold air was a refreshing change to the heated warmth of the interior.

'Yes, there was a path into the forest back down the road. Down there, where those two cars are.'

They walked to the vehicles, having to take the middle of the road as the snowplough had made only one early pass on this minor route. As they got close, David was relieved to see that the cars were locally registered. Both had stickers in their back windows.

Frankischer Höhlenforscherverein.
Franconian Potholers Club.

Shit, thought David.

'Shit,' said Christina.

'How is the SatNav position?' he asked, looking around the cars, studying the tracks going into the forest. 'Six, maybe seven people.'

'Little to the south and a bit to the east. Want to guess who we meet there?' She pointed at the back window sticker of the nearest car.

David laughed.

'The Franconian Pothole team. Maybe we can borrow a rope. Come on, we'll follow them.' He set off up the path.

The track rose steeply south, before turning to the south-east and climbing to over five hundred metres. Before them were the potholers' steady footprints in the deep snow.

'We've got about six hours of daylight left,' David said, looking at his watch and then at the clearing sky. 'Looks like we're going to get a bit of sun. That'll help.'

After thirty minutes, they heard voices coming from the trees. Forty metres to their right, down a smaller side path was a clearing in the forest where there was a modern, three-metre-high, barbed-wire fence, anchored to concrete posts. These were in a ring around a central circular concrete bunker rising a metre and a half from the ground, and measuring three metres in diameter. What looked like metal lids to this lay open like butterfly wings, hanging to either side of the structure. The top of the fence was angled back and topped with razor wire, and on the open entrance gate was a sign:

Eintritt streng verboten! Gefahrenzone! Strictly no admittance! Dangerous area!

A group of men and women were gathered around the bunker. One of the three female potholers waved a hello, so Christina took the initiative and went to speak to them. David followed behind, trying to look disinterested as Christina initiated the conversation. He waved acknowledgement to the men in the group, who all seemed more interested in talking to Christina, only half-heartedly acknowledging him

On the ground was a small canvas tarpaulin with several articles laid out on it. David asked if he could look at them, and one of the men nodded assent, briefly tearing his gaze away from the blonde Slovak to look at him.

An SS field flask, with its drinking cup still strapped in place, a small entrenching tool, a field cook pot, its lid held in place by a tattered leather strap, a group of three cartridge pouches and a belt buckle had been found. The latter was still covered in mud but looked to David like an SS officer's. Several unidentifiable clumps of camouflaged material that could have been SS smocks lay beside the remains of a Schmeisser MP28 submachine-gun, the wooden butt having long since rotted away.

David pointed the objects out to Christina, who was deep in conversation with the group. He walked nonchalantly over to the open bunker, and was amazed to find a vertical shaft dropping down as far as he could see. There had been an enclosed metal ladder inside the shaft, but this too had corroded to the point of being useless.

'Fünf und dreißig meter tiefe.' One of the men stabbed a forefinger at the ground, nodding at the shaft.

Thirty-five metres deep.

Christina came over to speak to him.

'They say it's an old World War Two secret site. The tunnel at the bottom of the shaft goes to the north-east for a kilometre before it's impossible to pass. There was a massive cave-in, and it's too dangerous to try to find a way through.

They come here once a month, only to collect what things they can find, and to do rope training in the shaft. Oh, and they're sure the tunnel goes on under the old DDR border.'

'Are you American?' a young brunette of thirty-something, asked.

Her face was smeared with mud. David reflected how difficult it was to read a person, when their features are camouflaged or covered in some way.

'No I'm English actually,' he smiled, as though she was forgiven for thinking he was American.

'You like it here, in the Rhön?' She swept an arc with her arm at the surroundings.

'Yes, beautiful, it's very beautiful,' said David, honestly.

Christina spoke. She caught David's eye and narrowed her own fleetingly.

'Please excuse us, we must get on now, good luck in your exploration.'

They turned and waved goodbye, as they rejoined the main path, and descended the hill back to the road.

One of the potholers, a thin, tall man in his late fifties, with a neatly trimmed beard and a thick East German Sachsen accent, excused himself from the group, saying he must take a pee.

After walking thirty metres from the clearing and making sure he couldn't be seen, the man punched in a number on his mobile phone.

'Sie sind jetzt hier in Sands. Ja beide,okay…tschüs.'

'They are both here in Sands. Yes both of them.'

Chapter 36

When they got back to the car, they decided to chance another hotel for the night, but one that was some distance from their last two hopes of entering the tunnel system.

Christina studied the map. 'We could go west to the autobahn and then south to Bad Brückenau. It's a spa town from the name, must be full of hotels.'

David nodded a 'why not' kind of nod, and drove up to the village of Sands to turn the car round, then set off back down the hill to Fladungen.

As they approached the lay-by where they had parked, they saw a red tractor with a snowplough attached, coming up the hill. David thought it strange that the plough blade was not deployed, and was twenty centimetres above the road surface as it sped towards them. He presumed it was easier to clear down the slope than up, and pulled in to let it go by.

It was then that they saw a black Mercedes stop fifty metres behind them. It waited in the middle of the road, even though there was room for several vehicles in the lay-by. Four people were in the car, but in the low light it was impossible to identify anybody. David drew his automatic at exactly the same time as Christina.

The snowplough didn't slow. As it got to the lay-by it swerved viciously and headed straight for them.

'Hang on,' he shouted.

David gunned the car in reverse, and even with the four-wheel drive, struggled to get a purchase on the deep snow. Suddenly the tyres found grip, and the Audi shot back onto the road, hitting the Mercedes in a shower of broken glass and plastic. The air bags exploded in the other vehicle.

He put the car into forward drive, slamming his foot down on the accelerator as the driver of the plough struggled to reverse out of the deep snow bank he had hit.

As the Audi was passing it, the tractor lurched backwards,

clipping the back wing and sending them into a spin on the icy surface. David dropped his gun into his lap as he fought with the steering to regain control. The back wheel hit the snow bank on the other side of the road, and they twitched and fishtailed down the hill.

He was twisting full lock to the right when the first rounds smashed through the offside back window, covering them in glass and insulation material. The car corrected violently, and David put on full left lock as another burst of automatic fire smacked and clattered into the bodywork of the boot. The Audi came straight, and he kicked down again on the power.

Tobogganing downwards, the car bounced off the snow banks as it slid from side to side. In the mirror he could see that the tractor was now blocking the path of the Mercedes.

As he braked sharply at the bottom of the hill, the Kevlar back bumper scraped noisily as it hung, flapping uselessly, in the snow. They crossed the main highway, heading west towards Fulda, and after five kilometres, as there was no sign of the other car behind them, David turned into the forest, making sure they couldn't be seen from the road.

He let go of the wheel and sagged back in his seat.

'Well. That was interesting,' he gasped.

'Good driving.' She leant over and kissed his cheek.

'We have to burn the car. If the police see us driving this, we'll be in big trouble.'

They got out to have a look at the damage to the rear. The boot was jammed and buckled and all the rear lights on the right hand side were broken and hanging out. A row of bullet impact holes was very visible at the base of the boot and had raked the rear offside passenger door.

Ripping off the damaged back bumper, he stowed it in the back seat, then knelt in the snow and dug down to the earth below. Taking a small branch from a nearby tree, he broke it at an oblique angle, so that he had a sharp tool, and began scraping at the soil until he had a small mound of wet clay. He kneaded it to the right consistency, then took the mix and smeared it across the back door and boot, covering and filling the bullet holes. He tidied up the rear light cluster as best he could, and washed his hands clean in the snow.

'Plan, I think…' he said, '…is to drive in to Fulda after we've found somewhere to burn the car. Drop you off to get a replacement, then you come back to pick me up.'

He washed his hands again, trying to remove the caked mud under his fingernails.

'How the hell did they find us? Was it the potholers?' he grumbled, as he wiped his hands on his jacket to dry them.

'Sure,' she said. 'We weren't followed, if they knew about the access to a tunnel system in Fladungen, they would certainly have had somebody there in that group. If they were tipped off, they had thirty-five to forty minutes before we got back to the car.' She took his hands in hers and rubbed some heat into them.

They drove over the county border into Hessen, and soon, on their left and to the south, the mighty Wasserkuppe rose nine hundred and fifty metres into the darkening afternoon sky, its white, snow-covered form, ghostly in the dimming light.

Deep within the Hessen Rhön Nature park, they found a minor forestry road and a navigable track coming off that. The perfect spot to get rid of the Audi, and hope that it wouldn't be discovered too soon.

He dropped Christina by a public telephone booth on the outskirts of Fulda, where she could phone for a taxi to take her to a car hire office, and an hour-and-a-half later, she drove up the forest track where David was waiting. The olive green Range Rover she had rented, making light work of the snow.

The boot of the Audi finally lifted open, with a groan of complaining metal after David had struggled with it for several minutes. They emptied the car, transferring all the contents to the new vehicle.

Christina had brought a full plastic petrol can with her from Fulda.

'Thought this might be useful.'

'You're the business, my dear.'

David took the can and doused the interior of the Audi and then the open boot. 'Time to move,' he said, opening the car's filler cap.

He took out the cigar lighter, giving it a good soaking in a pool of petrol in the foot-well. As Christina moved the Range Rover out of the way, David inserted the lighter and pushed it home to the ignite position. He ran to the cover of the other car and clambered aboard as Christina reversed back towards the road.

WOOMPH. The Audi lit up, bathing the trees in a flickering yellow light.

WAWOOMPH. The petrol tank blew, moving the car sideways with the force of the blast, and causing an avalanche of falling snow from the limbs of neighbouring trees.

Within minutes the whole body was ablaze and the tyres exploded, dropping the chassis on to the rims. They waited until they were sure the interior had been destroyed, then drove out on to the main road.

Bad Brückenau was busy. The hotels were full of convalescents, there as guests of the German National Health system, as well as others there to take the waters.

Christina pulled in to an information board just outside the town, to look for accommodation, pointing to a hotel name on the board.

'Village, five kilometres south of town. Oberleichtersbach. Hotel looks nice and secluded,' she said.

'Done,' said David.

On the outskirts of the small village, they arrived at a four storey, traditional Franconian style hotel with carved wooden balconies and dormer windows protruding from the roof, and checked in to a comfortable double room.

Later they both lay on the L-shaped top bench of the hotel sauna with their feet touching in the corner. There were repeated sighs of pleasure as they relaxed in the heat, inhaling the eucalyptus scented steam released from every ladle of water on the hot stones.

'Where next, David, Ostheim or Volkershausen?'

'Volkershausen, I think. It's a tiny village and well off the main road, it's literally bang on the old border.'

He poured on some more water and covered his face with his hands as the superheated air hit him.

'Oh God! That was hot.' She rolled onto the bench below. 'What do we do, if both sites are blocked?'

'I have no idea,' he admitted.

'Who do you think it was, in Fladungen today?' she asked, dabbing at the wound in her underarm with her towel. David took her arm and inspected the stitching. Everything was healing nicely.

'We can take out the stitches in a week, and we'll put some more antiseptic salve on it, before we go to dinner. Your question. Don't know, more likely to be Gehrling's lot, but who knows? Certainly wasn't the Mossad. We wouldn't have got away so easily.'

'Easily? I have to go out David, my arm's stinging like hell.'

She got up to shower, and he felt that old surge of excitement again. It was the way she moved, it never failed to get his blood circulating.

'How long will it take to get to Volkershausen?' she shouted from the changing room.

'An hour, or a little more on the minor roads and avoiding Ostheim.'

The stones hissed as he poured on more water. As the heat enveloped him, he wondered what in fact they would do, if both the Ostheim site and Volkershausen were blocked.

As he lay relaxing, two BMW X5s drove along the small road through the village, slowing at the traffic calming zone, as it narrowed to one lane outside the hotel.

The driver in the lead vehicle spoke, in a thick Glaswegian accent, to the other car on the radio.

‘Charlie 1 to Charlie 2. The Range Rover is there. We’ll pick them up when they move in the morning. Over.’

‘Charlie 2. Roger that. Out.’

Chapter 37

They decided to risk staying at the hotel for a couple of days as they were far enough away from the remaining entry sites, and still hadn't found access to the tunnel system. David spent half-an-hour in the morning, carefully moving a wardrobe and taping the tunnel maps on the wall behind it.

Völkershausen took fifty minutes to reach along minor roads, through the forests and open fields of the High Rhön, the last few kilometres running parallel to the old DDR boundary, five hundred metres to their left. They headed north up the hill to the village with Christina driving and David studying the SatNav. The road snaked right and then left, past the village church and on upwards to the old border.

They parked off the road, the paved East German patrol paths to their left and to their right, running along the cleared land that had been mine fields during the Cold War. They got out and studied the SatNav.

'We need to go along this track to the left. It looks driveable to me, and I don't like the car being here by the road Christina. The number plates are identifiable as a hire car, and they must be looking for us,' he explained.

'Look at this, David.' Christina was looking at a notice board beside the patrol path.

He came to look over her shoulder, and read that two young men from Meiningen had attempted to cross this minefield on an Easter Sunday morning in the sixties, and had both tripped mines. One had been injured in an eye, but had made it to Volkershausen, the other had had a foot blown off, and had lain injured in no man's land for some time before villagers, West German soldiers, police, and firemen rescued him.

Both survived after having been taken to hospital in Mellrichstadt. David wondered how the two men would feel, after so many years, knowing that now they would be able to walk here from west to east with no hindrance, hearing only the sound of wild birds and the wind stirring the branches of the trees in the forest. He thought back to Buchenwald, and its setting in the trees, high on the hill above Weimar. Here as there, nature had hidden the horrors of the past and reclaimed the future.

Driving along the patrol track north-west for two hundred metres, ignoring the 'No vehicles' sign, they took the Range Rover off-road and uphill, until they couldn't be seen from the track. David consulted the SatNav.

'South-west about one hundred metres.'

A forest path, to the left, went in that general direction, and they struggled through the snow, having to lift their legs high at every step up the hill. Something caught David's eye on the slope down to the south.

'There are some remains of buildings there, fifty metres down the hill.'

'Yes, I see them. How's the position?' She started down the slope.

'Well, it's around here somewhere,' he said, scanning the surroundings.

They entered an area which had, long ago, had several structures on it, spread over a square kilometre. An obvious entrance in a cliff face to their right looked promising, but a rock fall just inside looked permanent.

'This looks like an old mine works, David.' Christina went up to the mouth of what was left of it.

'Look here.' She was pointing to the rusted remains of an ancient ore wagon, three of its wheels completely oxidised and the fourth only just recognisable by its flanged rim.

David kicked at the snow, but couldn't find the remains of a metal track.

'This doesn't look interesting, I'm going to look over there,' she said, pointing to a pile of debris and bricks which had created a miniature Mount Fujiyama in the snow.

David walked forty metres past the entrance, and carried on in the general direction in which the tunnel disappeared.

'Christina, over here,' he called.

She struggled through the snow towards him, swearing under her breath in Slovak at every hidden obstacle which conspired to trip her.

'Look there.' David pointed to a metre-square patch of melted snow at his feet.

'There must be warm air under there.' She took a dead branch and started to dig at the soil. It broke several times as she hacked at the frozen surface, slowly uncovering the outline of a heavy concrete cover.

David knelt and looked at the ground.

'We need to come back with a shovel or a pick or something, and a rope. There's definitely a slab covering an access shaft under here, that's why the snow's cleared. It must link to the main tunnel system. Let's have a look around and see if we can find anything else.'

They covered the ground with some difficulty, as they stumbled on the old brickwork lying under the snow. The site had not been a working mine for many, many years. There were no signs that utilities had ever existed, and it looked as though all the labour here had been done by hand.

Nearby was another smaller patch of melted snow and David stuck a broken branch in the ground to mark the spot, so that they could investigate further in the morning.

'Come on. Let's have a look at Ostheim and come back to this place tomorrow.'

It started snowing again as they passed back through the village, on the way down to Ostheim three kilometres to the south. As David drove, Christina was checking the SatNav.

'We're too far south. It must be there, over to the west.'

On the top of the hill above Ostheim, the top of a medieval tower loomed out of the forest.

'It must be there somewhere.' She studied the map. 'Its called the Lichtenburg. If possible, turn right in two hundred metres?'

David turned at the next side road, and they drove through residential streets of expensive looking villas overlooking the town.

'I recognize this. Up there, on the right, is the hotel I stayed at with the Israelis.' She looked up the road nervously. 'They're really going to be pissed off with us, especially me.'

'Let's hope they don't find us, until we have something for them,' he said.

They drove for another block and then saw the sign pointing right for Lichtenburg. After another two hundred metres up the hill, heading north, Christina confirmed they were going in the right direction. The road snaked up the steep incline for a kilometre, and then the tower came into view above the trees.

Tarmac gave way to cobblestone, and the tyres drummed and rumbled as they passed between massive square-stone walls and under a long arch in a battlement wall. This led on to an outer courtyard with a half timbered building to the right and the entrance to the main building on the left.

A large parking area cut into the hill had a spectacular panorama to the east. Opposite, through another ancient archway, was an inner courtyard.

Several 13th century structures enclosed this, most derelict or empty apart from the main, ivy covered, three-storey building. The twenty metre high tower, which was separate to the castle, had no windows until the very top, and must have served as a look-out post for raiders.

'Look, there's a restaurant here, and it's open. Lunch.' She took David's arm and pulled him up the slope through the archway.

'Where the hell do you put all this food?' he marvelled.

A heavy oak door opened on to the dining area. Solid tables and built-in seventeenth century wooden upright benches made of the same dark wood, stood on a worn stone floor, painted with the names of town worthies and huntsman of yesteryear. The room had the redolent scent of blazing logs and ancient timber.

As they ate their wurst and sauerkraut in the warmth of the open fire, four men left a BMW X5 in the lower car park, two hundred metres down the hill, and entered the forest. They were all clad in white salopettes and wouldn't have been remarkable, apart from the high powered binoculars around their necks and the small transmitter-receiver carried by one of them.

Christina paid for the meal, and they made their way down to the car. David looked at the SatNav.

'North-north-west a kilometre,' he said, looking at the map. 'There should be a footpath if we head north for a bit.'

They left by a gate at the end of the castle wall, following a path down the steep slope that, after two hundred metres, joined the track that David had identified on the map.

'We're making for the top of the hill over there,' he pointed, 'at eleven o'clock.'

The narrow path started to rise through the tightly packed trees, and in front of them, in the snow, the unmistakable tracks of a hare crossed this way and that, two-one-one, two-one-one, two-one-one. A buzzard circled overhead, its cry breaking the perfect silence of the forest.

'Somebody's watching us,' he said. He didn't break stride or turn around.

'Where?' She took his hand.

'Don't know yet, it's something I sense. Better since I stopped drinking. Usually accurate. There's a path coming up on the left. Wrong direction, but takes us up into the trees, where we can find somewhere to wait.'

The buzzard was circling two hundred metres behind them, but it had become silent. Something big was moving below it, and like a hawk hovering at the side of the motorway, waiting for prey to be frightened into movement by the traffic, it was hoping an animal would betray its presence.

David watched the bird as it spiralled slowly down to just above the trees.

'Behind us, seven o'clock, and if it's a professional job, I'd expect another at three o'clock. Can't see a damn thing can you?'

'No, nothing,' she answered.

They took the path to the left, and when they were out of sight behind a rock outcrop they sat and waited.

In the deep snow a hundred metres back, the earpiece under the white balaclava of one of the men following them clicked quietly three times. Three clicks meant 'RTB'. 'Return to base.' The men crawled backwards among the trees, sprinkling new snow to cover their tracks as they went, until they were out of line of sight with the target. They met in the car park some ten minutes later.

'Sorry boys, they made us. That fucking buzzard, just kept circling above me and Jack. Control said these people were good. They'd stopped, and were just waiting to see what would happen.'

'No problem, mate. We'll radio in, and keep close to them. I'm bloody frozen. Let's have a cup of coffee. Do you think they'll have a look, and find out where we were at?'

'They will. Who wants to drive?'

Back in the forest, the buzzard's call alerted David.

'They've gone. Come on.' He heaved her up from the large rock they had been sitting on. 'Let's investigate.'

They walked down to the main path and crossed it, climbing at right angles up the hill, to a position at three o'clock to where they had been.

'Over here, David,' she called

An area of snow had been disturbed. David carefully swept away the top surface to find the imprint of two bodies and two elbow marks where somebody had been supporting a pair of binoculars. Twigs and branches had been strewn around, once part of a small hide.

'There'll be another one like this, back down the main trail just below where the buzzard is now.'

As he spoke, there was a flash of white as the underbelly of the bird caught the reflected glare of the snow.

'So they left, because they knew that we were aware of them?' Christina looked back down the path.

'Yes, it seems so. They were only watching us, nothing else. But why, and more importantly who?'

They made their way down the slope to rejoin the main path, and climbed towards the top of the hill marked on the map as the Höhnberg. The track led to the east of the summit and then down to the next valley, where after another two hundred metres there was another path which dropped steeply to the south-west.

Christina checked the SatNav.

'We're very near. It must be here somewhere. Look down there, that old hut.'

The four-metre square hut was only just standing. The weight of its sagging roof had pushed one wooden wall out of true above the stone base, and the door was nearly all gone to rot. There was a plaque on a plinth by the door which Christina wiped clean of snow. It was from the German Denkmalschutz, their listed buildings department.

'It's the old well for the Lichtenburg castle,' she read.

'Christ! They had to carry the water a hell of a long way.' David pulled what was left of the door open.

The timber for the well winding gear was of oak, and in reasonable condition. Under it, two iron plates, locked together by a large padlock smeared with grease and wrapped in a plastic bag, covered the fine old stonework of the well opening.

'I'd guess that this well has a tunnel linking it to the Lichtenburg,' David said. 'A lot of old castles had hidden passageways linked to the wells, in case of siege and for escape. Could you do the honours with the lock, while I check that we're alone?'

David satisfied himself that they didn't have company, and went back inside to see a smiling Christina holding up the plastic bag with the padlock inside.

'Easy,' she said, smiling.

'You really are a smartarse.' He kissed her.

It took the two of them considerable effort to lift the doors, which weighed roughly forty kilos each. They put on their headband lamps and Christina peered into the depths of the two-metre wide shaft.

‘It’s deep; can’t see the bottom.’

David went outside and found a largish stone. He dropped it into the well and started counting seconds. ‘One…two… three…four…Christ…six…’ A far off booming sound signalled the stone entering the water at speed. It reverberated up the well walls like an underground train seconds before it emerges from the tunnel.

‘That’s bloody deep.’ He leant over the edge. ‘There seems to be something about fifteen metres down. Can you see that?’

Christina adjusted the focus on her headtorch to a narrow concentrated beam.

‘Yes, there’s something, it’s on the same side as the direction of the castle. We need to bring the rope.’

After re-locking the metal doors, they made their way back to the Lichtenburg, where there were now several vehicles in the car park, and the courtyard was busy with guests of the restaurant and walkers.

David used his monitor to sweep the car for trackers and found nothing.

They had known where to find them today, that couldn’t have been chance.

Christina drove them back to the hotel, pulling in several times on the way, to check if they were being followed. David was sure that whoever had been watching them, had known where they were, and that something they were carrying was transmitting their location.

When they had got back to the room, David told Christina about his worries.

‘Well, they can trace the SatNav signal, it’s all American satellites.’ She called from the bathroom.

‘They would’ve had to know that we’d bought it, and the serial number. It must be something else,’ he said, lying down on the bed.

‘Jimmy Nolan gave you a gun,’ she said, coming into the room.

'Shit!' He leapt from the bed, and got the Glock.

Christina swept her monitor over the automatic.

It's bugged,' she gasped.

'All this time. Shit!' He sank his head into his hands.

Ejecting the magazine, he took his multi-tool and undid the screws on the butt of the gun. As he slid off the side panel, he saw the tiny square chip and its even smaller circular battery, and extracted it with the tweezers.

'I don't think this is the Yanks. They were really pissed off with us both; they'd have pulled us in long ago.'

'Who then?' she asked.

'The Mossad aren't on best terms with us now either. They would've pulled us as well. It has to be your people or mine.

The guys watching us today were following classic SAS and 14 Intelligence procedure for covert surveillance. My people or yours, or both probably, traced the rental car in Frankfurt airport while we were in Sweden, found the gun in the car and bugged it.'

'So they know everywhere we've been,' she said, her head in her hands.

'That's about it, yes.'

'Yet they haven't done anything, only observed,' she said.

'It seems so. Why, I don't know.'

Later, they went down to the hotel restaurant for dinner. Only one other guest sat across the small dining-room from the table they were shown to, a man in his mid- forties with a well developed beer gut. He looked like a typical salesman, sporting the moustache that a lot of German men of that age favoured, bushy and wide.

By the side of his plate he had a computer print out, and was studying the figures as he ate. He looked up to greet them, giving Christina a once-over that stripped her three times, and had sex with her ten.

He continued to ogle throughout the meal, but waited until they were having coffee before he found the opportunity to speak to them. He stared at Christina until she was forced to smile at him, or pointedly ignore him. She did the former and immediately wished she had resorted to the latter.

'Hello. You are Americans, or?'

'South African, actually.' Christina glanced at David. She was about to look at her watch and suggest an early night.

'Oh. You are here for holidays, or?'

Christina remained polite.

'Yes, we're on holiday.'

'Did you visited my beautiful city Dresden up to yet?' He brushed his moustache with his forefinger, like a villain in an old silent movie.

'No not yet, maybe later. I hear that it's very nice.' She was now fingering her watch and kicking David under the table.

'I will go home tomorrow, after I will finish work. If you will came to Dresden I should like to showing you the city. Here is my cart.'

He came over and sat down uninvited, handing Christina his business card.

'Eberhard Renninger, Sales Manager, Kesslinger Brauerei. I sell beer, yes.'

'That's very interesting. I'm afraid we must…'

'Yes, tomorrow in the Rhön. You know the Rhön, or?' He smiled at Christina, completely ignoring David.

David was getting ready to get up when Christina gripped his hand very tightly.

'We've been in the Rhön, yes. Where are you going, tomorrow?'

'All about, and in Thüringen also. I become home late, very late,' he answered.

'I guess you need a comfortable car for all that travel,' she said.

'Yes, good German Mercedes E Klasse, fine auto, or?'

'Very nice, very comfortable. Sorry, but we're very tired, and have to sleep now. Have a good trip back to Dresden.' She shook his hand.

David shook his hand and murmured goodnight.

'Yes, sleep good, and if you will came to Dresden, I show you the city, or?'

Back in the bedroom, David picked up the tiny transmitter he had extracted from the Glock.

'Merc E class didn't he say? Dresden plates? Quick thinking, my dear. Back in a bit.'

David found the vehicle easily in the hotel car park, and rocked it from side to side. The alarm went off at once, and David hid behind the Range Rover which was parked three cars up.

Renninger came out of the hotel, frantically pressing the remote on his car key to silence the alarm.

David stepped out from the shadows.

'Hi,' said David.

'Did some person was near the car, or?'

'No, I've seen nobody, maybe you've left the window open a little bit?' David went closer to the car. Renninger opened the Driver's door, and opened and closed all four of the vehicles electric windows. As the back window nearest to David opened, he threw the transmitter into the foot-well under the driver's seat.

'Okay goodnight, again.' David walked back into the hotel. 'Prick, or?' He murmured, just loud enough for the uncomprehending Renninger to hear him.

Chapter 38

After David had retrieved the maps from behind the wardrobe, they checked out, deciding that before going back to the site at Völkershausen, they would drive to the small village of Neustädtles which was a kilometre to the north-west of Ostheim. A path from behind the church there eventually joined the track to the Lichtenburg well.

They bought some crisp bread, sliced meats and fruit and drink to last for three or four days, then drove to a hardware store for some spray paint cans.

In Neustädtles, they parked the car off the road, and packed their haversacks with all the equipment they would need, laying the sleeping bags across the top.

With a heavy coil of rope each, they looked like a two-man Himalayan expedition as they trudged through the deep snow.

The outline of the hut appeared in the trees off to the right, and they took the same path down to it as they had taken the day before, checking for any new footprints. Only the two old tracks that they had left were there, so when they arrived, Christina went in to take care of the lock, whilst David stayed outside checking that they were alone.

He helped her with the heavy metal doors, and when they were open, he inspected the state of the oak winding gear, pressing the large blade of his knife into it. The heart wood was sound and would be able to support their weight.

Taking one coil of rope, he wrapped it several times around the end nearest to the anomaly they had seen in the well wall. He then knotted it fast, gave it a few energetic tugs to check the strength of the wood, and satisfied everything was okay, attached the hauler pulley. The end of the rope dropped over the edge, where it snaked into the darkness below.

'I'm going down to have a look. If I find something, and you need to come down, send the gear first, then drop a loop. I can then lower you from below. I don't want those stitches popping, okay?' he said.

Pulling up some rope, he wound it once around the base of the well wall and donned the body harness and headtorch.
'This should be easy now, but please use the other arm for the main load, in case this bloody wood gives way.'
'What happens, if I drop you?' she smiled.
'Then we better say our goodbyes now. It's a hell of a long way to the bottom.'
He kissed her, and swung his legs over the side of the shaft, putting on his helmet and adjusting the torch as he did so.
She braced herself to take his weight, but with the rope wound around the wall, and the double pulley, it was a relatively easy load, as David disappeared over the edge and lowered himself on the harness.
As he descended, there was a smell of stagnant water and wet stone, so familiar from the abandoned mine shafts of Cornwall.
'Another couple of metres and I'm there…bit more. That's it. Yes, there's an inset door here. My God! There's a pipe carved on the wall next to it.'

The two-metre- high oak door in front of him had a simple wooden draw bar, which moved after some effort. Before him stretched an arched brick tunnel for as far as he could see in the narrow beam of the torch. It was two metres wide and a little over two metres in height.
He swung his legs in, giving himself a little slack on the rope, and edged into it using his limbs against the side walls for leverage. Once inside he sat up and removed the harness, tying it to the rope.
Leaning his head out, he called up to Christina.
'Okay, you can pull the harness up now. Can you drop a double loop of the rope down? I can fix it here.'
He knotted it to the draw bar.
'I'm just going to have a quick look where this goes and if it's still accessible. Five minutes.'
'Please take care David, and five minutes is five minutes, all

right?' Her voice echoed up and down the shaft.

'Yes I promise.'

The tunnel was, for the most part, surprisingly dry, but some moss growing along the right wall gave off a musty, earthy smell, that reminded him of looking for worms as a child, to fish for trout. He couldn't feel any warm air draught at all, and worried that this was another dead end. The shaft was definitely on an incline up towards the castle, and he wondered where the access to the main tunnel system was. The pipe marking on the outer door was surely Novak's, so there must be an entrance somewhere.

Two hundred metres later, and with the head clearance getting much lower, was a closed steel door to the left which was warm to the touch. The main tunnel continued on its upward path towards the castle, but he could see that after forty metres it was blocked by a rock fall, which must have left visible evidence on the surface,

On the wall beside the metal door was another crude carving of a pipe, below which was a small ledge with a greased paper packet on it. He picked it up and immediately felt the weight of something metallic. It was a key, which had been kept in reasonable condition by the wrapping.

David put the key in the lock but it wouldn't budge. He tried forcing it, and felt some slight give, so he turned it from left to right repeatedly. Suddenly, with a dull crunch, the lock gave, and the door swung open.

The blast of warm air was instant. Fine rock dust rose in the air current from a stone spiral staircase, that descended into the darkness below him. On a ledge at the top was another greased paper package, which was obviously a duplicate key for the other side.

He looked at his watch, deciding to go back for Christina before she tried to lower herself into the shaft, and opening the wound on her underarm.

'Christina, come down,' he called, when he got back to the entrance.

She lowered the two back packs and put the other coil of rope around her shoulders. Once he had them, he undid the rope and waited until he saw Christina's legs appear, slowly lowering her down until she was dangling in the harness in front of him.

'Hello,' she grinned.

He laughed and pulled her into the tunnel, feeling another surge of desire, as he felt her body against him. He kissed her tenderly.

'What was that for? I must be very attractive in this helmet and gear.'

'Yeh. It's the helmet. Never fails. Come on.'

He helped her on with her pack, and led on along the tunnel to the staircase. With the steel door open they could feel the hot air some way before they got there.

Christina traced the figure of the pipe on the rough stone with her fingertips.

'It's so strange, David. My grandfather was here. He carved this. He was actually here.' She shook her head in incredulity.

They took off their packs to carry them more easily, and David led on down the staircase. They had to stop several times to equalise the pressure in their ears and steady the giddiness caused by staring at their feet whilst circling the central pillar.

They estimated that they had descended over fifty metres before they came to the final step and, in the light of the head torches, a three metre high, three metre wide, unlined tunnel stretching out in front of them, dropping steeply into the distance. The air was dry, slightly scented by the salty potash rock.

Christina switched on the gas detector.

'Oxygen's a little lower than normal, but no other problems.' She set the sensor for audible alarm and clipped it on to her belt.

'How many gases does that thing cope with?' David focussed his headtorch beam and scanned the tunnel in front of them.

'Oxygen, Carbon Monoxide, Carbon dioxide, Hydrogen Sulphide and flammable. That's enough. Don't worry, I'll look after you.' She patted him affectionately on the back.

‘Come on, clever dick,’ he said, looking at the map, and the digital compass, which was unaffected by the potash rock. ‘This leads north-north-east and should, if it’s still passable, link up with the tunnel our friends the potholers were in. Hopefully well past the cave-in.’

Behind them, at the well, the rope was being unwound from the winding gear and thrown over the side. The pulley, sliding off its host, fell into the depths below with a deep, resonant splosh. The shaft returned to darkness, as the two metal covers were closed, and the padlock clicked as its male and female components embraced.

With a screech of chalk, a small Roman sword was drawn on one of the metal plates.

Chapter 39

They set off down the tunnel, their headtorches illuminating the void beyond in a crazy light show of dancing shadows. The bare rock sparkled with thousands of tiny star-lights, as the beams caught the salt crystals in their blue-white glare.

They passed a maze of tributary tunnels and chambers, but a cursory examination showed them to be either empty or dead ends. Those not shown on Novak's map they marked with a short burst of green paint from a spray can. Every two hundred metres in the main shaft they sprayed a red arrow, so that they would know where they had been, and in which direction they had been travelling.

After two kilometres, they were dropping steeply at a twenty-degree angle and were turning to the west. The rock face here was a lighter shade of ochre and harder to the touch, the air saltier on the back of the throat. The temperature was rising and the gas detector was registering 23°C and a dropping oxygen content.

Fifteen minutes later, they met a dead end, not a rock fall, just a dead end.

'Shit.' David stared at the blank wall.

Christina studied the map.

'According to this, it should link up to the Fladungen tunnel,' she said.

They moved around to illuminate the walls and the ceiling with their head torches. On the right hand wall, above a grill in the floor, was the sign of the pipe.

David knelt, and inspected what looked like a drain. 'It's too small, this can't be it.' He put his fingers through the metal bars and tried to lift. It gave slightly and moved a few centimetres, but it was much too heavy for its size.

'You're shifting a cover, David, look.'

She bent down to brush some of the rubble from around the drain, revealing a large piece of slate into which it had been fitted.

He pulled with all his strength, and suddenly the slab lifted to reveal a gently sloping shaft, wide enough for an average sized person to get down.

Christina slipped her pack off and took a coil of rope.

'My job to go first, I think. I'm thinner.' She tied the rope to her belt and handed the rest of the coil to David.

'Just in case there's a hell of a drop when I get to the other end.'

'Any more weight jokes, and there ***will*** be a hell of a drop at the other end. Take care. Give me two pulls when you're down, one for more rope, and three for pull me up. If I get two, I'll haul it up and send down the packs. I'll take a chance on plummeting to my death, unless you tell me otherwise.' He kissed her head as she slipped her body into the shaft. 'Be careful now.'

'I will, I will.' With that, she slid slowly down, until she was out of sight.

Thirty metres of rope had disappeared before he felt two yanks from below. He pulled up two metres, and tied the two packs and the other ropes onto it, letting them slide down a little. After a few seconds he felt the draw from below, like the tug of a trout as it takes the wet fly.

Fixing the end of the rope to his belt, so that he could get a helping heave from Christina if he got stuck, he dropped his legs into the shaft and wriggled his way down. It wasn't spacious, but he had enough room to move his arms up to protect his face, and to make sure he didn't lose his helmet.

He emerged onto a ledge which led into a small chamber, the size of a ten-person lift. Christina was below him, smiling and pointing to a cleft in the far wall.

'Through there's another tunnel, from the south-west. Must be the tunnel from Fladungen, beyond the roof fall.'

David clambered down, and realised, that from the chamber floor, it was impossible to see that the ledge led to a shaft above.

'Look there, David.' She pointed to the sign of the pipe on the wall.

Christina squeezed through the narrow gap and he passed all the equipment through. He struggled out, with some difficulty, much to Christina's amusement, and could feel the abrasion the rock was leaving on his stomach.

'It's all muscle,' he claimed, looking around the tunnel.

He was marking their location on the map when he heard something, and inclined his head to the left, straining to control the noise of his breathing.

A very distant, barely audible, but distinct sound of pneumatic drills against rock, echoed down the shaft.

'Who the hell's that?' She checked the safety catch on her automatic and David did the same.

Almost at once, the drills started up again. It was somewhere up to the north, but it was difficult to judge how far, because of the amplification effect of the tunnel system.

To the left, the unfaced shaft ran to Fladungen, where they had met the potholers. This was similar in size to the ones in the Merkers complex, and seemingly part of a major mine system. After a few metres, the tunnel was impassable where there had been a collapse of the roof.

David sprayed a cross to denote the blockage, a red arrow and the letters 'Flad' on the rock wall, and by the fissure in the rock, one pointing upwards with 'Ost', just below the carving of another pipe.

Turning right, they headed for the main Volkershausen to Jonastal tunnel which, according to the map, should be two kilometres to the north-east. They passed a large system off to their left arrowed 'Geblar' on a faded, hand painted sign. David marked it with the green spray.

The main tunnel was much wider than the others, a good ten metres across with rusted arc lights running the length of the ceiling. The light grey walls here were warm to the touch, with strata of brown and white rock running parallel at floor level. The atmosphere was bone-dry. At the junction was a sign pointing north marked 'Jonastal', and right to 'Sülzfeld'.

'Why isn't Vokershausen signed, David? There must be another access shaft there as well, where we saw the snow melt.'

'They obviously didn't know about it,' he said.

The beams of their torches played across something covered by tarpaulins, fifty metres or so in front of them. He adjusted his torch to a narrow beam, and immediately saw the Cyrillic script on them. They covered the area to a height of one metre and stretched for twenty. Christina took the corner of the first and carefully pulled it back, so as not to disturb the layer of rock dust lying thick on its surface.

A row of metallic casings three deep, the size of small equipment trunks, lay in a line which stretched on under the other tarpaulins, the universal symbol for radioactivity painted on the top of each. All were wired in parallel to a wall socket connected to a mains cable which ran along the ceiling. David put his hand on the bundle of wires and felt the warmth of electrical resistance within.

'Soviet demolition weapons.' Christina said, sliding back the cover on the nearest and revealing a small control panel. She went down the row, lifting the tarpaulins back as she went.

There were at least fifty of them. At five kilotons each, there was over two hundred and fifty kilotons of nuclear yield sitting there. All the batteries were charged and working, and the electric cable, as usual, was connected to the grid somewhere. All of them were on standby.'

Ahead in the blue beam of the lights, parked along the left-hand wall, were four, dark green Soviet military lorries and three personnel carriers. The lorries were covered in tarpaulins, the carriers open. All were Zil 131s, twin rear axle, six litre V8s, the workhorse of the Eastern Bloc. They were covered in rock dust, but in the warm dry air, were in reasonable condition.

A metallic groan and squeal echoed down the shaft as Christina opened the bonnet on the first lorry. They decided to see if they could start one up, he would try the troop carriers and she would look at the lorries.

David opened the door on the leading personnel carrier and pressed what appeared to be a starter button. Dead, as he had expected.

He found the bonnet release and had to pull with considerable force before the clunk of the spring signalled the catch had been freed. As soon as he lifted the cowling, he saw the empty battery stand and the cables hanging uselessly above it. He quickly checked the other two vehicles. Both were the same. As he dropped the bonnet, Christina was walking up from the lorries.

'No batteries in any.' She wiped her hands on her trousers.

'Same here. Could we use one of the standby batteries in the bombs?'

'Do you really want to try that?' She opened her eyes very wide in horror.

'They would do in the movies.' He faked a look of hurt.

'Well, my hero, if you'd like to try it, be sure you leave time for me to be twenty kilometres away…and in a bunker.' She put her fingers in her ears.

'I think I get your point. Let's get on. We should reach the Meiningen tunnel in six or seven kilometres. How is the oxygen level,' he asked.

'Getting lower, but still acceptable. It's 27°C down here. No other gases found.'

The intermittent sound of drilling was still very faint, but getting closer as they walked north. After ten minutes they noticed that the draught of warm air had all but ceased, and saw in front of them what they at first took for a roof fall. A barrier of some kind glinted in their head torches, a hundred metres ahead.

The beams were being reflected by two gargantuan metal airlock doors, which were closed shut across the tunnel. A thick rope hung from a pulley, and ran along the ceiling to the door mechanism. He looked at Christina questioningly.

'It'll work. As I said before, the Soviets and the East Germans always connected directly to the grid, so that it was impossible to trace.' She pulled the rope and the hydraulics hissed into life.

'You're such a...I love it.' He put his arm around her shoulders.

A rush of warm wind carried a slightly fruity, fishy odour, a bit like the smell of the concentrated orange juice that was spooned out at school after the war, mixed with the cod liver oil pills that were taken at the same time. The only thing David had loved in those days was the daily spoonful of malt after assembly.

'Oh fuck,' he yelled.

David grabbed Christina and spun her round grabbing at the back of her pack and shouting. 'G A!...G A!' He found her gas mask, and gave it to her to put on, simultaneously turning his back to her, so that she could get his pack open, in order to find his own mask as soon as possible.

Just past the airlock was a side chamber which had partially caved-in. As they swept their torches across it, they saw the hundreds of canisters marked in German, 'GA' or 'Tabun.' Developed before the war as an insecticide, it was deadly as a nerve agent.

The canisters were clean; too new to be WWII Wehrmacht. At the back of the chamber, crushed under tons of rock, many of them were leaking their deadly content onto the dusty floor.

'Did the GRU store this stuff down here too, near the border?' he asked, beckoning her to move on quickly.

'As far I know, there were stores of Tabun, Soman, VE,VG,VM and VX stored in secret dumps near the border,' she mumbled, her voice muffled within the face plate of the gas mask.

'No wonder everybody wants to get access to this stuff. Can you imagine?' He shook his head at the thought of it. 'Just makes me wonder what the hell's in the secret chamber?'

David pulled the rope to close the doors, and the airlock swung shut behind them, resulting in an immediate drop in the air flow. David pointed to the gas detector in Christina's hand and after consulting it, she signed him the diver's okay.

'Oxygen content's all right. It doesn't do nerve agents. We'd better keep the masks on, until we're out of this area.'

A large chamber opened to their right, and they could make out crates, packed one upon the other, in neat parallel rows. It was a massive storeroom, ninety metres square and five metres in height. In the near corner, a step-down transformer hummed and buzzed, and was obviously the source of power for the standby mode on the demolition weapons.

David found a row of switches encased in flexible plastic on the entry wall, turning them all on with a downward sweep of his hand. Multiple clicks and flickers of neon tubes bathed the chamber in light.

They both shielded their eyes, adjusting to the light after the long period of using only the beam from the headtorches. David started examining the designation on the crates, which were in both Cyrillic and German script.

'We didn't need to bring food or provisions with us. Look at this bloody lot. Canned meats, soups, stews, beans, dried fish, canned butter, flour, coffee, tea and water. There's even vodka and beer,' he said, excitedly.

'David, look at this.' She beckoned him to the back of the chamber.

There in neat rows, were thirty or so military vehicle batteries all plugged in to a charging unit. David shorted out the terminals on the first battery with his multi-tool and the sparks flew. Perfect.

Two long lines of dark green jerry cans, full of petrol, were sitting along the side wall, beside boxes of spares containing fan belts, sparkplugs, gaskets and filters. Next, there were picks, shovels, buckets, large rechargeable hand-held torches sitting in their charging sockets, and old style helmet-mounted torches also on charge. Hanging on hooks was a row of dark blue biological and chemical hazard suits, with a line of matching rubber boots neatly stacked underneath.

'Christina, I'm going to carry a battery down to the best of the vehicles, to see if I can get one started, then we can load whatever we think we'll need. Can you have a sort through and see what you can find?'

She rubbed her hands in pleasure.

'Don't come back too soon.'

'It's so nice to be wanted. Don't take too much.'

He uncoupled one of the batteries and groaned at the weight of it. 'This thing weighs a bloody ton.' He struggled to lift it to waist level.

Christina whistled to him. She had found a trolley. She set it upright, pushed it towards him, and carried on looking through the crates.

'Sometimes, Karranova.' He nipped one of her buttocks as he passed her with the trolley, loading a battery and two jerry cans of fuel before setting off back down the tunnel.

It was unlikely that there was a residue of atomised Tabun in his clothing, but he kept his gasmask on in case. Better safe than dead.

The third in line of the lorries looked to be in the best state, so he took the handle crank from its mounting on the side of the vehicle. After several minutes he was able to give the engine one or two turns to free it up a bit. He fitted the battery on its mounting and emptied the two jerry cans into the exterior fuel tank.

When he depressed the starter button half way, the dash light up. After letting it glow for twenty seconds, he then fully depressed the starter. The starter spindle whined and coughed like an emphysemic bear. Nothing.

'Bastard.'

Checking the fuel lines by the engine and then by the tank he found the problem. The cut-off tap was in the 'off ' position, so he turned it in line with the fuel line and turned the engine again.

Cough…cough…cough…cough…cough…cough…
ROAR.

'Yesssss.'

The engine spluttered for a few minutes, but was soon running reasonably smoothly. The exhaust, however, was typically

Soviet. Clouds of choking black smoke were emitted with every touch of the accelerator.

He turned on the headlights and, to his amazement, both dipped and full beam bulbs worked, although the beam on the driver's side went off at an improbable angle.

David was beginning to sweat profusely in the heat of the gasmask, and reasoned that enough time had elapsed for his clothing to be safe. He could always put it back on when he opened the airlock doors again. Wiping his face with his handkerchief, he shifted the lorry into gear, immediately stalling the engine as he engaged the clutch.

'Bugger.'

He started the engine again and experimented with the gearshift. This time he was sure that he had selected first, and lifted the clutch for the second attempt.

The lorry kangarooed for a few metres before he got the hang of it, but soon he was approaching the airlock. Stopping by the rope-pull, he donned the mask again before the doors opened.

Christina had placed a pile of articles and some jerry cans outside the storage chamber, and as he drew alongside, she appeared carrying two biochem suits and two pairs of boots.

'What shoe size, David?' She looked at the soles of the boots.

'9½ or 10. What's that in European? 42…43…44, something like that,' he answered, shrugging his shoulders.

'These are 44, okay?' She held them aloft.

'Haven't you got another colour?'

She gave him the middle finger and slung the boots on the pile.

'That's everything. I found a good East German medical field kit too, so we're equipped for some time,' she said, proudly.

They loaded the back of the lorry, and David was impressed that she had even remembered to find toilet paper. It was Soviet, and had the consistency and shine of kitchen greaseproof paper.

'One last thing to take.' She went back into the chamber and reappeared with two Kalashnikovs. 'There are two ammunition cases inside, if you would be so kind.'

They set off up the tunnel, keeping their masks on for some time to ensure that they were Tabun free. After fifteen minutes, they came upon the turning signed for Meiningen to the right, and David turned into it. Fifty metres in front of them, in the headlights, a rock fall completely blocked the shaft.

Christina got out to look, and came back on David's side, taking off her mask and massaging the creases in her temples left by the rubber retaining straps .

'Is it possible to stop the engine, or are you afraid it won't start again? I can hear something,' she said.

'I don't want to kill it so soon after having the headlights on. I'll back it around the corner fifty metres, that should be enough. What can you hear?'

'Don't know. Come and listen when you have parked.'

As he walked back from the lorry and turned the corner, he could immediately hear the drills. They were still a long way off, or so it seemed, but they were coming from the other side of this cave in.

'The Soviets didn't blow the Meiningen entrance when they built the wall, so Gehrling certainly knows where the original entrance was, and about the roof collapse,' she said, reaching up and taking his gasmask off.

'If Gehrling knows where it is, it's a certainty that Shoshanim knows, and the Americans, and everybody else. Gehrling's been under observation ever since his meeting with me in Greenwich. Why the hell don't they just take him, and anybody else with him, right now? If it's his lot, why are they letting them attempt to get access?'

They climbed back up into the lorry, and David turned left up a large side tunnel, which had several layers of black and light brown rock running diagonally along it. After thirty metres, this too was impassable, so they reversed to the main shaft, and drove towards Jonastal. Ten minutes later they came to another dead end where the roof had caved in. Massive boulders mixed with loose rock lay in a sloping mound in front of them.

The wheel lock on the Zil was good, but even so, David had

to make a seven-point turn, and without power steering he was grunting and groaning with the arm strength needed to turn the weight of the vehicle. He noticed the return of the tremor in his arm, and the pins and needles in the tips of his fingers, as he craned his neck to reverse.

Returning all the way back through the airlock gates, they put on their masks again as a precaution when they passed the store of Tabun en-route. They drove by the parked vehicles, the tarpaulin covered nuclear demolition weapons and the side tunnel to Fladungen and Ostheim where they had entered the main system, and carried on south for another ten minutes, heading towards Völkershausen.

Soon they came upon a metal sign for Sülzfeld to the left, and David turned the lorry into the side tunnel. After a kilometre they came across another row of dusty tarpaulins. He pulled up and Christina got out to investigate, going along the row lifting the covers as she went, occasionally bending over to inspect something at close quarters.

She jumped back up, into her seat. 'Twenty-three demolition weapons, all on charge and ready to go.'

Another kilometre and the tunnel was blocked. Just before the fall, was a side chamber off to the left, and Christina hopped down to take a look. David could see the beam of her headtorch swinging this way and that in the depths of the cavern, as he carefully reversed into it.

She clambered aboard and they retraced their route.

'Small store room. Nothing we could've used that we don't have already,' she said.

Turning north at the main tunnel, they took a sharp left back towards Fladungen, then right into the Geblar tunnel that they had marked with green paint earlier. The shaft stretched straight as a die, as far as the headlights could pick out. The rock face here was a lighter brown than before, but the air was damper, almost clammy.

The speedometer on the lorry was broken but, flat out, David estimated the speed to be about sixty kilometres an hour. They travelled for twenty minutes at that speed, stopping a few times to spray red arrows on the walls, and twice to spray green paint on two tunnels that tracked off to the right.

They arrived at the T junction of the Geblar to Jonastal shaft after a further fifteen minutes. To the left the roof had caved in, almost to the junction, and as they turned to the right the lorry bucked as it ran over piles of rubble that had been thrown into the main shaft by the explosive charges the Soviets and East Germans had set.

Travelling east-north-east for another twenty kilometres, they passed tens of small chambers and side tunnels and two main side galleries which branched off both sides of the main shaft. They stopped at both and sprayed them green before the tunnel took a turn to the east.

'We're near the Crawinkel entrance,' Christina said, the map open on her lap, 'Shoshanim said that it was blown by the East Germans.'

Four kilometres later, there was the staccato beat of blast debris hitting the underside of the lorry as it flew off the tyres. Then, in the headlights, came the dead end and the now familiar pile of rock and roof fall.

The shaft was wide enough for David to turn around, and they drove back towards Geblar, taking the first main shaft to the right and heading for the Ohrdruf to Jonastal system, spraying red arrows as they went.

In several side shafts and chambers they saw wooden crates which had been broken open. They stopped, and David read the contents lists on some of the discarded lids.

"MALEREI." Paintings.
Holländisch.1500-1900
Französisch. 1700-1800.
Italienisch. 1400-1800.'
Another had "MALEREI."
Russisch. 1600-1900
Tschechisch. 1700-1900

All the boxes were empty, the paintings had been taken, and David wondered which private collections they now graced.
'David, look at this.' She had a crate lid in her hands.

"GOLDFÜLLUNGEN."
"Treblinka. Dachau. Auschwitz-Birkenau. Sobibor. Bergen-Belsen. Dora. Buchenwald. Sachsenhausen."
'Gold fillings from the death camps. Look at that, David.' She pointed to the other broken crates stacked along the side wall of the chamber.
At least eighty plundered crates had the same marking, and David guessed that was just a small fraction of the total.
Eventually they drove on, and minutes later arrived at a T junction, where they turned east towards Jonastal.

What they saw next, half-an-hour later, took their breath away.

Chapter 40

The tunnel opened on to a vast cathedral sized cavern, two hundred metres in diameter and with a vaulted roof reinforced with steel plating. Square sided bricked and cemented shafts led off it at regular intervals.

Christina counted them.

'Twelve. Like a clock, one at every hour.'

A large sign above one upward sloping tunnel, announced "E bis 15e Geschoß." Ground floor to 15th floor. On the opposite wall was a similar sign with "16e Geschoß."

Dominating the whole chamber was a gigantic faded swastika flag, hanging from the ceiling twenty metres above, swinging very gently in the air currents of the system.

'We're on the sixteenth level down. Hell, it'll take us years to search this lot. That shaft leads to the other fifteen levels above us,' David said, dismayed.

One tunnel had a sign which read.

"Krankenhaus, Schlaffzimmer 25–740, Kino, Bibliothek, Schwimmbad, Turnhalle, Sauna."

The Hospital, Bedrooms, Cinema, Library, Swimming pool, Gymnasium and Sauna.

The next had, "Führerquartier." The Führer's quarters. Another, "Kirche, Besprechungsraumer." Church and Meeting rooms.

Two were two massive shafts, one marked, "Fabrik, Entwicklungscentrum." Factory, Research and Development centre, and the other "Waffenlager, Panzer und Fahrzeugparkplatz, Raketenlager, Brennstoffslager." Armoury, Tank and Vehicle park, Rocket store and Fuel depot. A smaller tunnel led to, "Verwaltung. Dr Kammler." The administration offices of the mysterious and illusive Dr Kammler.

'There's a whole city down here,' Christina said, looking around in awe, the headtorch inadequate in the colossal void of the hall.

'Let's take a look at the factory, and then the armoury,' David suggested.

Two hundred metres down the factory shaft, they came to another brick-reinforced cavern. It was at least three hundred metres long and a hundred metres wide, the roof strengthened with twelve-metre high steel uprights at regular intervals. Conveyor belts, presses, lathes, drilling machines, and large dip tanks were covered in a fine layer of dust. Beside them, emergency showers lined the side walls.

Heat treatment ovens stood in a line along the back wall. Their heavy steel doors were open, revealing racks full of machine parts. Many of the baskets under the milling machines were full to the brim with metal shavings and filings, and the smell of lubricant grease and oil was still heavy in the air

A queue of unfinished rocket engines sat on one of the conveyors, the top speed they would ever achieve being the one mile-an-hour of the belts. Other lines had half finished parts of tank turrets, artillery guns and rocket casings. Everything was where it was on the day that the war finally arrived in Jonastal, the factory had been frozen in time.

One day they had turned off the power and left, never to return.

It was the same in the Research and Development centre, a similar size to the factory, but divided into small laboratory cells and offices. They parked the lorry and walked into the main entrance, where everything was as if everybody had just gone home for the night.

Desks had papers and pens left on them. One chair had a jacket draped over the back, a raincoat and hat hung from a peg on a wall. Everything was covered in a film of rock dust which swirled at their feet as they walked through the complex of corridors, filling their nostrils and making visibility, in the light of the head torches, difficult.

At the end of one corridor was a lead lined wall and a gigantic steel vault door which was standing ajar. A large sign with a swastika over it announced. "Nur bestimmtem Personal zugänglich." Authorised personnel only.

They both heaved on the heavy door, opening it half way.

Beyond was another open steel door which led into a small lobby constructed completely of steel. Heavy duty cables led from it to a large electrical contact plate with what looked like a degaussing rod beside it. The area, seemingly, built up an intense electro-magnetic field, which had to be discharged with the rod. Why it should build up such a field was not clear.

Through this lobby, they entered a round observation gallery with forward slanting glass, which seemingly enabled people to view events in a thirty metre circular room below, similar to operating theatres in teaching hospitals. A large part of the window had been dismantled at some stage, probably to remove machinery from below. There had been an extensive control centre in the gallery, but all the equipment there had been demounted and taken away.

In the lower chamber was a six-metre diameter circular podium, loops of heavy duty cable running to and from it. Something big had been tethered here, but it too had been removed.

A wide, spiral copper staircase, green with corrosion, connected the room with the gallery. Above it, in the roof, was a solid copper panel five metres square which sat in a retaining slide. David cleared it of dust and detritus and pulled back the plate, using two handles on the end. He had to give it several violent tugs, before it finally gave, revealing a copper lined circular shaft, three metres wide, which rose as far as David could see.

'There's a cold draught, I can feel it on my cheeks,' said Christina, as she strained her neck to look up the tube. 'What was in here?'

'If that shaft goes to the surface, it must be over eight hundred metres long. Why would they need a shaft going to the surface and all these heavy duty cables and degaussing kit, and who took whatever the hell was on the podium?' said David.

A small piece of screwed up paper on the floor caught David's eye. It was underneath the control panel, and was covered by a fine film of dust. He stooped and picked it up, blowing it clean. Unravelling it, in the light of his headtorch, revealed some printing. The background was white with red diagonal stripes from bottom left to top right.

"FLEER'S." "Frank H. Fleer Corp. Philidelphia. Ingredients. Gum Base, Sugars, Corn Syrup, Natural and Artificial flavors. Established 1835."

'This is 1940s chewing gum. The Americans were down here,' he said, handing her the wrapper.

She studied the gum wrapper.

'The Meiningen archives didn't mention sixteen levels or anything in the Jonastal Project file. The Americans only spoke of a system on one level. Is it possible this got in here any other way? From guards of captured GIs, maybe?' she asked.

'It's possible, I suppose,' he said. 'Wait, there's something written on the back. "Artie. Tel. Denver 6968."

'They were down here!' she said, carefully picking her way down the spiral staircase to examine the podium, looking around for anything else, that might give them a clue as to what had once been there.

'David, look at this.' She was pointing at two small screws on the base platform.

'What's so special?' He looked at them, wondering what she meant.

'Try to pick them up.' She held her palm upwards, pointing at the base in invitation.

David knelt and took one between his thumb and forefinger. He was able to rotate the screw, but couldn't lift it from the metal base plate, as it was so highly magnetised.

'Now look at your watch.' She held hers out to him. Both watches had stopped.

'That's very interesting, and explains the degaussing rod. Any ideas?' He ran his hand over the top of his scalp, puzzled.

'No, nothing,' she shook her head.

They made their way back through the laboratories, to the lorry. As David was about to press the ignition button, the far off muffled roar of an explosion, somewhere in the system, broke the silence. The rumbling went on for at least thirty seconds as it bounced from shaft to shaft and level to level.

'Time to move, I think. I want to see if we can drive up to the other levels,' he said.

The vehicle belched copious amounts of black smoke into the tunnel behind them, as he started the engine.

'I'm worried by all the activity we can hear, David,' Christina said, putting her arm around his shoulders.

'They may well bring the roof down on themselves, and there must be one hell of a lot of rock to blast through, before they get anywhere. Unless they know something we don't,' he reassured.

They drove back into the vast hub chamber, and up the inclined shaft to the upper levels. Sixty metres up the tunnel it had been blown, the shaft blocked completely by piles of boulders and rubble. David pulled up, and got down to look at the walls. He had spotted some cabling along the rock face.

'There are still some charges in the face,' he shouted back to Christina.

This was WWII explosive, and probably after all these years, highly sensitive and volatile.

'Please be careful, David,' Christina said, nervously.

'Reverse the lorry back down the slope and wait. I'll take it easy,' he promised.

Gingerly he tugged at the nearest cable, and a stick of dynamite followed. He could clearly see the beads of nitroglycerine on the surface where the explosive had sweated over the decades. He pulled it out until he could read the printing on it.

In faded red was: "High Explosive. Dangerous." and in blue: "8oz Dynamite. Corps of Engineers. US Army."

He wanted to avoid the crippling headache that comes with skin contact with nitro, so he carefully pushed the charge back into its borehole without touching the sides of the stick.

A boot sticking out of the rubble, where the roof and walls had collapsed, caught his eye, and he bent down to pick it up. To his horror, it came away from the rock pile with the skeletal foot still in it, leaving twenty centimetres of the leg bones, the tibia and the fibula, sticking out of the rock like the remains of a chicken dinner. David clawed at the loose rocks around the bones and soon uncovered the other leg and part of the torso, still in uniform. One arm was twisted back at an acute angle to the body, the humerus clearly broken, the gloved hand gripping another dynamite charge.

'This guy must have been still laying charges when the whole bloody lot went up,' he spoke to himself, in shock.

Removing rocks until the upper body was visible, the faded tags and chevrons of a sergeant in the US 89th Infantry Division, Combat Engineers, emerged. The jacket pockets were empty, and there was no identity disc around the neck. He held his nose as the smell of rotted flesh, impregnated in the uniform cloth, made him gag.

'He must've emptied his pockets and taken off his ID before he started work. Why? Was he ordered to do that?'

There was a flash of colour inside the mouth of the left hand glove. David took out a small rigid packet, striped red. Fleer's chewing gum.

He guessed that there were several other bodies under the rubble. Had this been an accident or had it been a deliberate firing from the surface?

'David, what did you find?' her voice echoed along the shaft.

'Come and have a look.' As she joined him, he pointed to the body. 'Be careful, there's a very sweaty piece of dynamite in the right hand,' he cautioned.

Christina knelt and looked at the skeleton.

'Anything in the pockets?' she asked, turning her head away as she smelt the stench from the uniform.

'Only some Fleer's chewing gum that he seems to have hidden in his glove. Apart from that, nothing. He's not even wearing an ID tag.'

'Strange. This man hadn't finished placing the charges. He seems to have been killed deliberately. There are certainly more of the poor guys under there," she said, pointing at the rock pile.

'I'd guess so,' David nodded. 'It would've taken at least five of them to do the drilling and cabling.'

'So, if it was deliberate, they didn't want anyone to know what was down here, or what they took out from here.' She got up dusting her hands.

'I think it's to do with whatever was in the research and development centre, whatever was on the podium and caused the incredible magnetic field in there. I'm guessing they only had a limited time to remove stuff, before the Russians arrived,' David said, as they started to walk back to the lorry.

She hauled herself into the passenger seat and he started the engine. They were again engulfed in a plume of black exhaust.

'Jesus,' he spluttered.

'So, do you think that what was in the research centre's part of all this?' She studied the map and pointed to the exit marked "Panzer und Fahrzeugparkplatz" and "Waffenlager."

'I think that there was a hell of a lot of stuff down here that certain interested parties want kept very quiet,' he said, turning into the tunnel, which was wider than the others at around eight metres.

'Worth killing their own people for?' she asked

'Yes. My God! Look at this bloody lot.'

In the light of the main beam, lines of Panzers stretched as far as the eye could see, down the ruler straightness of the shaft. In side chambers were literally thousands of artillery shells and ammunition cases.

They must have travelled three kilometres before the line of tanks gave way to lines of sleek V2 rockets on their mobile launchers, stored in the main shaft and in many of the side systems. On their right, they came to the tunnel marked on the map as the shaft to Plaue. David turned in, and cut the engine.

'Could I have a look at the map, please.' he requested.

'Cut the lights, David!' she spoke with urgency.

David turned off the lorry headlamps.

'What is it?'

'Lights, behind us in the main tunnel.'

Chapter 41

She leapt down from her seat and felt her way back to the main shaft, running her hand along the rough tunnel wall, surprised at the heat of it. David joined her and they both strained their eyes in the total absence of light.

To the north-west, they could see the headlamps of a vehicle coming towards them in the system. The shaft was a straight run of fifteen kilometres, so it was difficult to judge distance, but they both reckoned it was a good way off.

'So. It's starting to get interesting. Did they blast their way in, or did they follow us down the well?' Christina asked, shielding the light from her headtorch and climbing into the back of the truck.

She returned with the Kalashnikovs and dragging a box of ammunition. She handed them down to David who put the guns under the passenger seat and the ammunition in the footwell.

They sat in the cab, studying the map in the light of the headtorches.

'My guess is that they fixed our position with the tracker in the Glock, so they must know about the Volkershausen entrance as well. It wouldn't have taken them long to remove the concrete slab there, with the right equipment. Or as you say, they came down the well. The question is, if they did, and they were after the nuclear weapons or the nerve agents, why are they still looking for us? This is about the secret chamber and what it contains. This is our people, I'm sure of it,' he said, as he put the truck into gear and pulled away.

She put her hand on his knee.

'We could get out now, and tell Shoshanim where the demolition bombs and the nerve agents are. As you say, our people already know, if they've followed us. My grandfather's body isn't worth getting killed for down here.'

He thought long, before answering.

'Do you really want to do that?' He put his hand over hers, as the truck lurched over some rock debris in the shaft.

‘No,’ she said, quietly.

‘Right then. This tunnel leads to Plaue, and should eventually be blocked. There ought to be a shaft off to the left, in three kilometres. If there isn’t, we’re buggered, we’ll be trapped in here. They’ll be following our tyre tracks in the rock dust,’ he said, pushing the accelerator pedal to the floor.

He drove on for five minutes, always keeping an eye on the wing mirrors for signs of lights behind them.

‘Something’s ahead, David. The tunnel’s blocked.’ He felt her grip on his knee tighten.

‘There’s the other shaft to the left. Bugger, it’s partially blocked by the fall.’ David pulled up and got down to have a look.

These were massive boulders, too large and heavy to move by hand, even with the two of them. Maddeningly, they had only partially covered the side shaft entrance, and David thought that it could be possible to try driving over the mound, the two wheels on the driver’s side staying on firm flat ground. But if they got stuck, they were in big trouble.

‘Is it possible?’ she said. ‘The roof looks really dangerous.’ She climbed over the mound and looked down the side shaft. ‘It’s clear down there.’

‘I don’t think we have a choice, unless we go on by foot. Shall we take the chance?’ He glanced nervously back down the way they had come, aware of the vehicle behind them.

‘Yes, let’s do it.’ She kissed his cheek, and clambered aboard.

David edged the vehicle forward as slowly as he could, given the eccentricities of the clutch, and mounted the first rock. There was a loud bang as the wheel cleared it and the underside of the side panel crashed down.

‘God. Not the fuel lines, please,’ he pleaded.

They lurched forward, and a part of the panel broke off with a groan of tormented metal. He struggled to hold on to the steering wheel, as it violently twisted from side to side. The nose of the truck was now in the side shaft, and there was only one large boulder left for the lorry to clear, when the cab filled with the acrid fumes of burning clutch facing.

Suddenly, the rear bucked upwards viciously, crashing with some force into the side of the tunnel, wedging them between the roof and the shaft wall. He depressed the clutch, and revving the engine to full power, released it as carefully as possible.

The teeth-grinding noise of metal against rock, with the latter winning hands down, echoed down the shaft. Something else was torn from the side, and then with a vicious lurch they were free. The roof collapsed with a thunderous roar, and his foot involuntarily lost touch with the clutch pedal, propelling them at some speed into the tunnel beyond. He kept going until the roar of falling rock behind them had finished.

He pulled up. 'You okay?'

'Whose idea was this?' she said, brushing her clothes down.

He got out to assess the damage to the vehicle, and was relieved to find that it was mainly superficial. Walking back sixty metres to look at the state of the shaft, it was obvious through the choking rock dust that it had been completely blocked by the fall. When he returned, Christina was checking under the truck.

'We've bought some time. The roof's down, they won't be able to follow us. Not here at least,' he said, clearing his throat of grit. 'Right, the map. Where the hell are we going?' he asked, as they both climbed back up into the cab.

'If we travel straight ahead, we'll cross three shafts and then come to the chamber. My grandfather's body's somewhere around there.' She put the map on top of the dashboard.

'We saw the other headlamps in the main Ilmenau shaft. Could they cut across in front of us?' David inquired.

'Yes, it's possible. The Ilmenau tunnel was blown up, so they could go back up the main shaft, or go down any we have to cross.' She widened the beam on her headtorch so that David could glance at the map whilst driving.

'I'm guessing that they only have a crude map of the workings, or the main shafts. If we keep to the side workings, I think we have the advantage, unless they pick up our tyre tracks,' he said.

'I'm tired and hungry, David. Do you think we could find a chamber in a side tunnel, eat something and sleep for a while?' she pleaded.
'Yes, you're right, we ought to keep out of sight for a bit.'
'My watch hasn't started again.' She shook it vigorously 'What about yours?'
'Kaput. I don't have a clue what time it is, but I could sleep,' he yawned.
'Please take these stitches out, they itch like hell now,' she begged, scratching her arm.
'No problem, I'll do it when we park up,' he said.
They found a small side shaft with a smaller tunnel off it, and a chamber with enough room to park the lorry out of sight, behind the entrance wall.
Christina checked the air reading in the chamber.
'We're really high on carbon gases now. It's the lorry exhaust. Oxygen level's quite good though.' She went out into the small tunnel. 'There's a strong air flow out here, David, and the oxygen level's near normal. Do you think someone's opened a new entrance?'
David joined her. 'Yes. It certainly feels stronger than anything else we've felt in the other shafts. Let's have something to eat and drink.'
Taking out some food and fruit juice from the their packs, they laid out their sleeping bags just outside the main chamber, where the air quality was better in the flow through the system. They kept silent for some minutes, listening to any noises coming along the main shaft, but could hear nothing. Christina fetched the Kalashnikovs and the night vision goggles, and they sat down to eat. Both were ravenous, so conversation all but ceased.
He looked at her underarm in the light of the headtorch, and after rubbing the wound with surgical spirit, carefully cut and extracted the stitches. There was a little bleeding, but all in all the wound looked healthy.
The noise of an engine echoed down the system and then

stopped. They both extinguished their lamps, straining to catch any noise. All David could hear was the thumping of his heart and the whistle of blood passing through his ears. A faint light appeared at the top of the side shaft, and then just as suddenly disappeared.

Click!

The truck cooling fan cut in with a rattle and whoosh, rising to a crescendo at maximum power. The light at the end of the shaft appeared again but fainter.

'Shit,' Christina said, somewhere beside him.

The fan cut out as David felt Christina pressing something into his lap. He felt the shape of the night vision goggles, and drew his finger along the side until he located the infrared switch. He donned them, tightening the rubber strap at the back of his head, and turned to a multicolour Christina, to give her the okay sign. The shafts were clearly defined in the infrared spectrum as the temperature of the rock face was above 28°C.

He looked up and down the small shaft and then walked quietly up to the next intersection, looking carefully left and right before going on to the next crossroads.

As he looked left, there was a burst of colour from the engine of a Zil lorry similar to the one they had taken, and probably from the same row of vehicles.

Turning off the infrared, he could see standing around it, two hundred metres from David's position, eight men, all with headtorches and Heckler and Koch submachine guns with laser and torch mountings. They were using hand signals to communicate and were listening with cocked heads to any signs of movement in the system.

One man was wearing headphones and operating a directional listening device. As he pointed it in his direction, David held his breath and waited until the man had swept the instrument past him, before moving.

The regiment. What the hell was going on here?

Backing up carefully, he retraced his steps to Christina. As he saw her, he put his forefinger up to his lips and then held up eight fingers.

She nodded and quietly cocked the Kalashnikov, but David put his hand on her arm and shook his head, holding out his other hand palm down, to signify they should wait. Putting his hands together at the side of his head, he pointed at her to sleep, and held up three fingers to signify a three-hour watch.

She took off her goggles, and lay on her sleeping bag whilst David took up position at the mouth of the chamber, a Kalashnikov cradled in his arms.

A little later, he heard the faint note of an engine. It seemed to be going away from them, as the sound soon became inaudible.

He found the task of staying awake in the total absence of light extremely difficult, as it was almost impossible to keep his eyes open when they weren't focussing on anything. Not wanting to waste the batteries on the night vision units, he resorted to what he estimated was ten minutes on and ten minutes off, which gave him a routine, and more importantly kept him awake. Once or twice he thought that he had heard movement, but saw nothing in the infrared.

The passage of time was harder to estimate than he had imagined. He reckoned that an hour had gone of his guard watch when he switched them on again.

Two goggled figures, carrying Heckler and Kochs, were walking down the tunnel towards him.

Chapter 42

The two men were fifty metres away, looking down a side shaft opposite. Both had high-tech vision goggles and small back packs, to which were attached water bottles and what looked like small flash bang grenades. One man was using a compass and making notes, the other had what David guessed to be an infrared torch.

He prayed that the lorry had cooled sufficiently not to need extra fan assistance, and that the smell of the exhaust had dissipated in the strong air current now moving through the system. Had the air flow been powerful enough to obliterate any tyre tracks that they had made in the thick rock dust?

The figure with the compass nodded and pointed down the side shaft, and they disappeared into it. David waited a few minutes, then walked up to the entrance. As he peered around the corner the two men were fifty metres in front, walking away from him and inspecting side chambers as they went. He decided to let Christina sleep on, as the shock of seeing the Regiment men had flooded his body with adrenalin.

An hour later, he was finding it increasingly difficult to fight the desire to close his eyes and succumb to the drug of Hypnos. He was beginning to hallucinate, in a half-dream, half-awake state.

When Christina woke, she put on her goggles and signed that he should sleep, and she would take the watch. He signed that two people had been very close to them, and indicated the shaft that they had entered.

As soon as he closed his eyes, he fell into a deep, dreamless slumber. He surfaced hours later, feeling refreshed apart from the taste in his mouth, which was dry and acrid. He turned on his night vision goggles and saw that Christina was swilling her face with water and brushing her teeth.

'Good morning,' she said, stroking his cheek. 'I think it's okay to talk. I haven't heard or seen anything.'

'How do you know it's morning?' he asked.

‘I don’t, it just seemed the right thing to say.’ She poked her tongue out.

He told her about the proximity of the lorry and the later close encounter, adding that he was one hundred per cent sure that these people were SAS.

‘What now, David? Do we use the truck?’

‘It’s too far to walk. We have to take it,’ he said. ‘They can’t have a detailed map of the system. We have. That’s our advantage.’

‘So, shall we go?’ She got up and brushed rock dust off her jeans.

‘Yes. I’ll just check in the main shaft and side tunnels. Can you fill the fuel tank?’

He had a good look around. Everything was quiet, so he switched off the goggles and replaced them with the headtorch.

When Christina had finished with the jerry can, he backed the lorry out, and they drove down to the next main shaft between the Ilmenau and Völkershausen tunnels. After twelve kilometres they came to a crossroads with a shaft in front of them, carrying on in the direction of the secret chamber.

‘I think we should turn right. Don’t know why, I just have a feeling,’ he said, worriedly.

‘Okay,’ she replied, picking up the AK from the floorwell.

They turned to the south-west, and carried on for twenty minutes until they arrived at the main Völkershausen to Jonastal tunnel, which was blocked to the south, near their supply chamber and the main airlock.

Wingless Messerschmidt 242s were parked on trailers along the wall as far as they could see to the north, their wings stacked beside them. Some of the trailers were attached to tow trucks and some were covered in grey tarpaulins.

‘Dear God,’ he exclaimed.‘This system holds an arsenal of stuff. If this line of aircraft stretches to Jonastal in the north, there must be several hundred of them.’ He turned the truck to the south, looking at the map as he turned. ‘We should be able to turn to the east in eight kilometres. That's if the collapse hasn't reached that far.'

They came to the shaft after fifteen minutes. It was a sharp corner, and David strained at the wheel to navigate the acute turn.

'David. Sorry, I need to stop.' She held her hands on her stomach.

David shook his head. 'Women. Wait two minutes and I'll try and find a side chamber for you.'

He pulled in to a small gallery with a large chamber off it. Christina climbed in to the back of the lorry to get a water bottle, and David turned off the engine and lights, and studied the map in the beam of the headtorch.

Just then something caught the sensors in his peripheral vision, a light somewhere, off in the main shaft. He switched off the torch and leapt down from the truck as Christina emerged from the chamber. He put his hand up to her head and turned hers off.

'Light in the shaft,' he whispered.

They stood in total darkness aware of an occasional flash of light somewhere along the tunnel. He took Christina's hand, and felt his way back to the truck, opening the passenger door as quietly as he could, whispering for her to get in. He groped around the front of the bonnet and climbed up through the driver's side door which he had left open.

'I'm going to drive like hell, hang on tight. Close the door when we get going.' With that, he pressed the ignition button. The engine turned over several times but didn't fire.

'Come on you bastard.' He pressed it again and the lorry belched black and fired up. He slammed it into gear and turned the lights on, flooring the accelerator through every gear change. The shaft was monotonously straight, and after two kilometres, he saw the lights of another vehicle behind them.

'They're behind us. Christina, can you keep us in the small shafts? I think we can lose them there.'

He took a turning off to the north, and after another kilometre she yelled, 'Right…left…keep straight on. In a kilometre there's a shaft which will lead us on to the chamber.'

A minute later David swung the truck right and had to slam on the brakes, as the shaft had collapsed at its entrance. He quickly reversed and they set off again.

'Right…here…then three or four kilometres and right again, that takes us in a semi-circle to the main west to east shaft. We cross that, and after a few kilometres there's a turn to take us down to the chamber,' she shouted, struggling to keep the map steady enough to follow it.

David nodded agreement, fighting with the wheel as they hit some rock debris at speed.

He carried on at a hefty pace through the maze of shafts, sometimes catching the back of the truck on the walls in a shower of dust and rock, as he took the bends too fast.

'I hope that you know where the hell we are,' he bellowed.

There was a crash as the rear of the truck lost traction yet again, and smashed into the offside wall, sending Christina crashing into the door.

'Turn right here, then fifteen kilometres straight ahead,' she grunted, rubbing her bruised shoulder.

As they turned the corner they almost ran over something lying across the shaft floor. David braked sharply. 'What the hell's that?'

'It's a body,' she said, leaping down from the truck. David lost sight of her as she bent down in front of the bonnet.

'David, come down here.'

'Is it your grandfather?' he asked.

'No, I think it's Gehrling. He's dead.' She rolled the man over.

In the glare of the headlights the figure was ghostly white, covered in a fine coating of rock dust. Gehrling's face was twisted in a grimace of pain. A tragic circus Pierrot. His skull was misshapen, and he had bled heavily from both ears, a sharp shard of rock still embedded in a deep wound in his left temple. An erratic trail of blood led back into the shaft in front of them, marking the German's final journey.

'These are blast wounds,' David observed.

'He has no torch or anything. He must've been in total darkness. What a horrible way to die.' She got up, shielding her eyes from the lights.

David heard the distant sound of an engine.

'We have to get out of here now, let's move him to the side. If he got down here, how many more of them did?'

They pulled Gehrling out of the way, and set off again. David kept glancing in the rear view mirror, he couldn't see anything behind them, but he knew that the guys following would be somewhere close by.

Fifteen kilometres later, Christina pointed to a shaft on their right.

'Right again, David, then I think it's a straight ten kilometre run to the chamber. We have to cross two main shafts on the way.'

When David crossed the first main tunnel he didn't lift his foot from the accelerator.

'You look for lights to the right, and I'll look left,' he said, half in jest.

'Nothing my side,' she answered, looking relieved.

'Yep, all clear here too. Let's hope it's the same all the way.'

Christina was thrown forward on to the dashboard as David slammed on the brakes.

Victoria Mason sat huddled against the shaft wall, cradling Faisal al Masri in her arms. Like Gehrling, they were both completely covered in white rock dust, and looked like an art nouveau alabaster figurine of lovers.

The Arab's neck was clearly broken and Victoria's lower jaw hung grotesquely, exposing shattered teeth and gum. Her hair was filthy and unkempt and she was rocking to and fro, her back hitting the wall behind her with some force. In her right hand she held an automatic pistol.

Beside him, Christina bent to pick up the AK47 in the foot-

well, her thumb flipping the safety catch to 'off '.
He climbed down.
'Hello Vicky,' he said, softly.
'Help him. Please help him,' she slurred, her jaw swinging sickeningly.
David felt a wave of pity and sadness for this girl, who he had seen growing up, and whose bed he had shared so short a time before.
'I can't help him Vicky. I can't. He's dead.'
'Help him.' She raised the gun, her hand shaking with emotion.
David heard Christina opening the lorry door, and cocking the Kalashnikov.
'He's dead Vicky, I can't help him,' David said, tears pricking his eyes 'I can't help him.'
She stroked the Arab's hair with her free hand, still pointing the automatic at David. Then he saw something deaden in her vivid green eyes. A sudden emptiness, a release, a migration of her soul, and he knew. He just knew.
She was a small girl again, playing rounders on the beach in St Ives, being read to sleep as he babysat. Her tales of early school, her first period, her first lover and her flirtations as a beautiful teenager.
She put the barrel in her mouth and immediately pulled the trigger, creating a bizarre tableau of the two white figures against a wash of deep red. The sound of the shot reverberated up and down the tunnel system like a lifeboat maroon in the night.
'Oh holy Christ!' He turned away wiping his face.
'We have to go David,' Christina said, quietly. 'I'm sorry.'

The next crossing was also clear, and they entered the shaft which would, according to Novak's map, lead them to the chamber. They travelled another six kilometres more slowly, still looking for the remains of Jo Novak, but without success.
They then came to a dead end. David cut the engine, and they got out to inspect the wall.

‘The chamber and my grandfather are here somewhere, David.’

Christina swept her headtorch along the side walls and the rock face in front of them.

‘Your grandfather wouldn’t have been able to mark this spot. Von den Bergen would have noticed. Look at this rock face to the right.’

He pointed to a ten metre wide, five metre high section, which was a slightly darker beige colour than the surrounding rock and grainier to the touch. David took his multi-tool and scraped at the surface.

‘This is a mud and rock mix, like a plaster. Clever.’

He climbed into the back of the lorry and reappeared with a pickaxe.

‘Will it make a lot of noise?’Christina asked.

‘No, I don’t think it will, until we hit the brick. Once we’ve shifted a few with the pick, it should be easy to move them by hand.’

He hit the wall, and there was a dull thud as the tool went deep. He levered the handle and created a fair sized hole in the rock face. He swung again and loosened the rocks in the bottom metre of the fill, which Christina started to remove by hand.

‘We’re through to brick here, David.’

He swung again at the base of the opening and they were able to remove enough rock to expose the rest of the brickwork.

‘Okay, this is where it gets noisy.’ He took a big back swing and brought the full force of the pick onto the wall.

A piercing, high-pitched whistle howled as a vacuum within the chamber was broken, and air rushed in. Christina hurriedly removed her jacket and stuffed it into the small hole to try to lessen the inflow.

‘Shit! They heard that in Moscow,’ she complained.

She moved the jacket, to allow more air to pass through without creating too much noise, and after some minutes the pressure had equalised. They both tore at the bricks with their hands to create a small opening.

Somewhere in the system behind them, they heard the sound of a heavy vehicle engine.

'Come on, we haven't got much time,' he urged.

David pushed more bricks out of the way to allow them access, whilst Christina got their packs and the AKs from the lorry.

They both squeezed into the chamber, Christina donned night vision goggles with infrared selected, and guarded the opening.

The room was roughly forty metres square, and in the middle, in the light of the headtorch, stood a large wooden crate mounted on a ten-metre diameter dais. Five metres high and four metres square, the Swastika and SS insignia still brightly painted on its sides, it dominated the room.

Beside it, was a low stone table, made from small boulders cemented together, a large marble slab as its top. On it was a canvas bag with a pull string at the neck. David loosened it, and inside were five, leather bound volumes, the covers still soft to the touch. Taking one out he saw the gold lettering embossed on the cover.

"SS Ahnenerbe. Forschungsgruppe. Dr.Hans Kammler. Nur fur Die Augen der oberste Führer der Schutzstaffel. Der Führer Adolf Hitler. BAND I."

"Dr.Kammler's Research group. Only for the eyes of the Führer Adolf Hitler. Volume I."

Volumes II, III, and IV had similar markings and Volume V was marked "Zusammenfassung." "Synopsis."

'Let's have a look in this crate,' he said, calling her over.

He used the pickaxe to prise away some of the wooden slats, Christina pulling them free until they had exposed one whole side. A gleaming egg shaped sphere of steel with heavy-duty electrical cables and copper windings circling its exterior, towered high above them, an evil Easter Island monolith. Twenty or thirty, equally spaced, copper contact lugs stood ten centimetres proud of the surface, making it look like an enormous old shipping mine.

All around its base, and connected by cables to the sphere, were twelve, one-metre square metal containers marked

Kondensator Z23. These were linked in turn to tanks with gas canisters on top of them. Further cables linked valves on these to a steel hinged box.

David lifted the lid, and inside was a clock mechanism. The dial had stopped at 23.42, 31st July 1945. Under the dial were six large cogs with small number windows. The display read six zeros.

'What in God's name's this?' David said. 'It looks like some kind of bomb. This must be the weapon Bormann refers to in the telegram. It was set to detonate at midnight on the first of August, and for some reason it stopped eighteen minutes before detonation.'

'Now I know why they want to keep this a secret,' Christina said, reading the book entitled "Synopsis" that she had picked up from the floor. 'It's called an "Antischwerkraft Nullpunktvakuum Waffen." It has a possible power of six billion tons of TNT. Six billion tons? That can't be possible.'

'An anti-gravity, zero-point vacuum weapon. What in hell's that? That's over a hundred times the yield of the Tsar Bomba, the biggest H-bomb ever detonated. Four hundred thousand times the yield of the Hiroshima bomb, it can't possibly be right. Hell, it would've destroyed most of Europe.' David looked at the book, over her shoulder.

Pages of mathematical formulae and calculations were far beyond either of them, but there was also a 1943 account of a test firing in Antarctica of a much smaller weapon which caused third-degree burns on prisoners up to one hundred kilometres away, and a 1944 test on the island of Rügen which ended in hundreds of deaths of technicians and scientists. The conclusion was that they couldn't control the yield of the weapon.

David looked at the other volumes.

'These look like technical construction manuals and calculations.'

As he opened the Synopsis, a blaze of light flared outside in the main tunnel, and the sound of megaphone feedback whistled mechanically.

A metallic voice, that David recognised as that of Peter French, boomed out in the confines of the tunnel.

'Lennox, I'm coming in. I'm not armed.'

'Who's this?' Christina had the Kalashnikov at her shoulder.

'A man called Peter French, from my old department. A colleague.'

'Is he friendly?' she asked.

'He's ruthless. Come back here, Christina. I'll talk to him at the entrance,' he said.

'Come on in Peter,' he shouted from the chamber. 'Hands out to your sides please.'

French appeared around the truck dressed in army fatigues, a bulky flashlamp in his hand.

'Hello Lennox, we knew you'd find this place, if anybody did.'

'You knew about the chamber then?' David asked.

'Yes, we'd been told by the Russians that it existed, somewhere down here,' French said, somewhat nervously.

'And the crate and books?' David enquired.

French looked puzzled and at the same time a flicker of fear crossed his face.

'What books do you mean, what crate? Do you mean papers?'

'No, I mean a crate and books. Climb into the chamber please, Peter.'

French looked at the AK47 that David was pointing at his chest.

'No problem,' he answered.

He stooped to climb in, and as he straightened up he saw Christina, and then the massive sphere.

'Ah. Pleased to meet you Miss Karranova, sorry about the circumstances.'

Christina nodded acknowledgement.

'Now, what books?' he said, shining his torch on the monolith in front of him. 'What the hell's that? Why do I get the feeling that you're not altogether pleased to see me…us? My minders aren't too pleased that you sent them all over Thuringia following a beer salesman,' he said, still staring at the sphere.

'I think you bastards trying to poison me, probably convinced me.'

'What in Christ's name gives you that idea?' French looked shaken and confused.

'Name of Jenny Carter ring any bells, Peter? When I say bells, I mean the whole fucking set at York Minster.'

'Yes, she works in some special department, under the direct control of Sir William Rush. How the hell do you know of her?'

'She worked as the receptionist in my local doctor's surgery. Used the name Rebecca Thomas and swapped my blood pressure pills for thallium. I nearly fucking died, Peter. If it hadn't been for Shoshanim and the Mossad, I would've done.'

Now French was looking really anxious. 'Shoshanim was in talks with Rush and the Russians this week. His people were assured that the ordnance down here would be taken care of,' he said, looking around the sphere.

'Did you know that the Israelis got hold of suitcase bombs from down here and exploded one or two in the Indian Ocean under the cover of the South Africans?'

French stood deep in thought, as though he was trying to piece all this information together and was coming up with more questions than answers. David knew how he felt.

The megaphone broke the silence. This time the voice did not have the public school accent of French, but the guttural twang of a Glaswegian.

'Mr French, sir. Are you all right, sir? Have you located the chamber and the papers, sir?'

'Yes Warren. Yes I'm okay. The chamber's open and we have the papers. Stand your boys down, and give me some time here please.'

'What's going on Peter?' David asked.

'I'm here to take you, and what I was told were papers relating to Hess, out of here. What are the books and what the hell's that

thing?' he said, pointing at the sphere.
'So we're getting out of here are we? That thing is…'

A massive blast lifted David off his feet and smashed him into the back wall of the chamber. A dark red veil of blood came down like a visor over his face and he slipped into unconsciousness.

Chapter 43

He didn't know how long he had been out. His mouth was full of dust, and he hawked and retched as he tried to spit it out. The light to his left was his head torch lying on the floor.

As he got to his feet, steadying himself against the wall to regain his senses, Christina groaned, sprawled across the stone table. Beyond her, French was half buried under a massive pile of rock and boulders, a trickle of blood coming in a crimson froth from his lips.

He knelt by Christina and felt her limbs for breaks. She groaned again, and opened her eyes, immediately gagging on the dust in her mouth. David found his backpack and the water bottle, holding it to her lips so that she could swill out the choking mass.

He let her have her fill, and then did the same for himself.

'Are you okay?' He held her to him.

'Yes. Yes, help me to get up. I'm just winded, I think. What about you? You're covered in blood,' she gasped.

'Just a small head wound. You know how they bleed, looks worse than it is.'

He helped her up and went to attend to French, who was moving his right arm, trying to get some purchase on the floor to move himself. David knelt and gave him water.

'Lennox, I'm sorry…that bastard Rush has shafted us. I didn't see it coming. My back's broken…can't feel my legs and I'm getting cold. You can't shift all this rock…so go and have a look at the tunnel. When you come back, I'll tell you… what I know.'

As David stuck his head out of the chamber, he saw the front of the flattened truck sticking out of the debris. The shaft had become completely blocked, and as he looked he heard another blast and the thunderous rumble of a roof fall further up the shaft.

'We're now well and truly fucked,' he groaned.

He went back into the chamber, where Christina was kneeling

next to French, giving him water. The man's breathing had become very laboured and his skin pallor grey. Christina looked up and raised her eyebrows in question.

David shook his head.

'The shaft's been completely blown and they've just blasted it again for good measure.' As he spoke there was another explosion from the shaft. 'These guys really don't want us to get out, do they?'

He knelt down beside her and the mortally injured French, who pulled David close.

'The Americans took…took something out…of the Jonastal system that was…still is top secret. A deep black project. They…and our government…were keen to keep whatever that was, secret. Dr Hans Kammler. Do you...know who he was?'

David nodded.

'He was taken to the States after the war…to run the project. He was the main administrator of the concentration camps… through most of the War. Oh Christ!' His face contorted with agony as a tremor ran through his body.

'So the last thing the Yanks wanted, with their Jewish lobby… was for the news to leak out, that one of the biggest…war criminals of all time, was alive and well…and living in Aspen. The plan was to lure the Mason girl, her lover al Masri and Gehrling down here…where we could eliminate them. We struck lucky…we got a Chechen warlord as well. They were trying to get in…by blowing open an old entrance in Meiningen. While they were…in the shaft…the regiment boys that were, supposedly, looking after me…blew the shaft on top of them. The plan was to seal...the shafts…forever. We dug our way in…at…Völkershausen, and were to blow it on our way out. The papers here were supposed to…pertain to Hess…and the British aristocracy. God, I'm so cold.'

David felt a sharp pang of remorse at the fate of Vicky Mason, the daughter of his best friend. His whole world had been turned over in such a short time. He thought how bizarre it was, that he and Griff had been eating her lamb dinner, and David had been making love to her, all in the peace of Marazion, just a few weeks ago. Now Griff was dead and David and Vicky Mason would share a grave, three thousand feet under the Thuringian forest.

He rubbed blood from his eyes.

'They're not still peddling that Royal family bullshit, are they, Peter? Did you know that Jimmy Nolan and I set up the assassination of Olof Palme?'

'Yes I did…it was linked in some way to what's …down here,' he groaned.

'Are you absolutely sure of that, Peter?'

'Don't waste time, Lennox. I'm dying. Of course I'm bloody sure, I looked at the files.' He winced in pain and coughed blood.

'Why did they kill him, for Christ's sake?'

'I wasn't supposed to…see the files…they were in Rush's wall safe. I got one…of my people to open it.'

'Why did you authorise that?' Christina asked as she swabbed the wound on David's head.

'Because...there was something…strange going on. I'd been approached…' A tremor ran through his upper body. 'Could I have…some water please?' Christina held a water bottle to his lips.'….approached by MI5…and another…department… within MI6...talk of elite groups within NATO and special services… and special branch…all linked to our department.'

He vomited blood and bile, and struggled to get his breath. 'On the file…a Roman sword on the cover. Report on Jonastal and Kammler. Palme knew… tunnels and Fjällman nuclear weapons was going…tell the Soviets…about possibility of secret entrances. Lennox, I can't see…can't see, can't breathe can't….'

His face grimaced hideously, and he gave a final death rattle, like bathwater on its final plunge to the drains below. French was dead.

Christina broke the silence.

'This is too fantastic. Palme and something to do with this

tunnel system. It's unbelievable.' She shook her head.

'This has to do with whatever was removed from that magnetised chamber, and what's in here,' said David. 'They wanted everybody eliminated who knew anything about the Jonastal system's secrets. I think we've both been suckered. Look at the list of deaths so far. Anyway, we're not going anywhere. That's why they have blown the shafts, everything's been sealed in for ever, including us, there's no way out.'

Christina wasn't listening to him. She was standing by the sphere. 'David it's making a noise.'

Chapter 44

Imatra, Finland.

Sir William Rush was sitting in a taxi on his way to the meeting in Imatra. He had flown in, to an almost snowbound Lappeenranta airport, by private jet from Helsinki. The meeting had been arranged by the Russians as the hotel was only five kilometres from the Russian border and the nearby town of Svetogorsk, and would be a discreet place for the three powers to meet. Several large paper mills dotted the area, and the hotel was used to seeing Americans, Brits and Russians.

The main road to Imatra ran ruler straight for miles, paralleling the railway line through kilometre after kilometre of forest to the northwest and the Russian border to the southeast.

Due back in London the next day, all the travel was beginning to exhaust him. Sixty, next January, he planned to finally retire, and spend the rest of his years with his family in Kent.

He took his mobile from his coat pocket to ring his wife, realising at once that Finland was two hours ahead of the UK. It was only 08.30 on the taxi's dashboard clock. He would ring her when she was up and about.

The car pulled up outside the Valtionhotelli, a Jugendstil castle with faux turrets, built at the turn of the twentieth century, overlooking the Imatrankoski rapids.

The river Vuokoski was dammed just above the hotel, but the rapids were shut off during the winter months, only turned on for a few hours a week during the summer for the tourists. They ran through a deep gorge just at the back of the castle where there were railings and viewing platforms on both sides, to see the race when in full flow.

At a congress centre, one hundred metres away, he would be meeting the Russian Sergei Kishishev and Henry Cummings, the American head of department.

Kishishev was a 'new' Russian, in his early forties, and well connected to the Kremlin. He wore tailored suits and hand made shoes and had investments in several private companies throughout the world. Petrakov, his old boss, was long gone to a stroke.

Gregor Petrakov had been old-school Russia, a bull of a man, with a wicked sense of humour, usually fuelled by several vodkas. Rush had only had one meeting with Kishishev and found him difficult to work out. He had a habit of frequently looking at his watch, and never showed any emotion or humour, preferring to dine on his own, avoiding small talk of any kind.

Henry Cummings was a Republican Hawk in his fifties, with none of the finesse and culture of his predecessor, Benjamin Tromans. He was loud and insensitive, a 'good ole Kentucky boy' in the worse sense of the term. He had risen through the ranks of the CIA and various deep black project departments, preferring leather jacket and jeans to the formality of the suit.

Cummings had never quite lost the mind set of the operative on the street in the world's many trouble spots. Rush reflected that many of these locations had not been trouble spots until the Americans had arrived, but that was another story.

He checked in, and was told that his colleagues were waiting for him in the Congress centre. He took the lift to his suite on the top floor and unpacked his overnight bag. Swilling his face in the bathroom, he realised how much he had aged over the last few years. He longed to be with his wife and daughter back home, in front of the open fire, with the Sunday papers.

A tunnel ran from the hotel basement to the Congress centre, but he decided to walk outside to get some fresh air. As he inserted the pass key, he could see Kishishev through the double glass doors, talking on his mobile phone. He nodded as Rush entered, offering his hand in greeting without missing a beat of his conversation, and with only a millisecond of eye contact.

'How ya doin', Sir William?' Cummings got up from a leather sofa to greet him, his hand extended.

'Hallo Henry, I'm fine, and you?'

'I'm doing just fine. Helluva journey out here ain't it?'

Rush nodded. 'Is there any coffee, Henry?'

'Just outside the room. Got some cakes too; they're real good.'

Rush passed on the cakes, but took a coffee, and went into the 'Koski' meeting room, which was heavy with the alcohol smell of whiteboard cleaner.

It was a facility for formal presentation with a rostrum and a control panel for all the AV equipment. Tables were arranged in six rows across its width, but a round one with three chairs had been set up in one corner.

The room looked out over the small park which bordered the rapids, and as he entered, the snow was starting to fall in the grey light of dawn, making him long even more for home.

He pressed the switch to close the blinds and put his briefcase on the circular table. Opening it, he took out a file marked Gladio, the logo of a Roman sword prominent on its cover, and sat and waited for the other two.

Finally Kishishev entered. 'Sorry, Sir William, something came up at home.'

'No problem, Sergei. How are you?'

'I'm fine thanks. Henry's just coming.'

As he spoke Cummings came in with a cup of coffee and took his seat at the table.

Rush thought again of home and retirement, and reflected on how the new breed of intelligence officer was not of his ilk. The age of truly international terrorism and militant Islam, was a far cry from the days of the cold war and the intrigues of post-colonial Africa.

'Let's get started gentlemen, it was agreed last time that I should chair this meeting. Is that all right?' Both men nodded agreement.

'So. I can tell you that the dealer Gehrling, the Mason girl, al Masri and Maskhadov and their people, after having failed to locate Lennox, tried to enter by the old Meiningen entrance, by drilling and dynamiting. Our Special Forces team blew the shaft above them.

Yesterday, Lennox and Karranova located the chamber and what we believed it contained, and we had French enter the chamber. I informed you at our last meeting that he'd got unauthorised access to the Gladio file after requests from other agencies. Those people have since been warned off from the highest level. Our team blew the shaft over a distance of two kilometres with French, Lennox and Karranova inside the chamber.

'So that's the problem finally solved, but do we know whether the manuals and the weapon were there?' Kishishev looked up.

'We had a wired button on the combat gear French was wearing, Sergei. We were able to confirm that French had found them before we blew the shaft. We didn't want the manuals to come out, or for anybody to read them. So now they're safe. There's now no way to get into the Jonastal system and certainly no way of finding, or getting into, the chamber.

Nolan passed on the name Fjällman to Lennox, and we, again correctly, calculated that Lennox would contact his friend in the Swedish Säpo, Lindén, and that another link in the chain would be taken care of, especially vis-à-vis the assassination of Palme. We hadn't reckoned it'd take Lennox so long to locate the chamber. The Mossad assassination of Mason delayed everything. When Lennox and Karranova had to ask for medical help, we calculated that they would seek help with the Israelis, and that their partnership would keep the Mossad from going it alone.'

'You nearly killed him before he got into the tunnels,' Kishishev complained.

'We didn't know how stubborn he was, Sergei.'

'Do the Israelis know of the peace moves by Hess and Himmler?' the Russian asked.

'No they don't. They're happy that the embarrassment of Von den Bergen has been taken care of, and that the suitcase weapons and nerve gases have been recovered and destroyed,' Rush assured.

'Churchill didn't believe Hess at the beginning of the war, and Roosevelt didn't believe Himmler at the end of the war. They didn't believe this weapon existed. What about this telegram Shoshanim spoke about?' Cummings mumbled, his mouth full of cake.

'We believe it was Mossad disinformation to see what we'd reveal, they must've heard of the existence of a hidden chamber from Lennox and Karranova. Let's face it, nothing happened in August 1945. If they did arm this weapon, it didn't work. Gentlemen all that we set out to accomplish, we have achieved.'

'What about the Germans?' Kishishev didn't look up from the table.

'They've been asking a lot of questions about Lennox and Karranova, both of whom they have now correctly identified from CCTV footage. The killings in Mellrichstadt, a burnt out car complete with bullet holes, and false passports, but our people within the German security service have muddied the waters sufficiently for us to deny any knowledge. They're not happy but…' Rush said, shrugging his shoulders.

'So, that's that then.' The American shrugged his shoulders and got up to peep through the blinds. 'It's snowing like shit out there. Will we be able to fly out from Lappeenranta tomorrow?'

'Any other business gentlemen?' Rush asked closing the file. The two men shook their heads

'So the case is closed.'

Chapter 45

David lifted the lid to the clock mechanism. The clock now read 23.52 and as he looked something whirred within. The last dial turned to 3 and a red light flashed on the console.

'The blast has started the bloody thing up. The clock's been released. We're going to get out of here now. Vertically,' he gasped

'How is it powered? There are no cables to it from outside the chamber,' Christina shouted as she ran around the crate.

As she spoke, the valves on the gas canisters opened, and the contents hissed into the tanks.

'The mixture of gases will create heat and convert it into a current. That'll pass into the steel Kondensators.

They are capacitors, they'll all discharge into the weapon simultaneously, then it's goodbye.'

The clock clicked to 23.54.

'Aren't we supposed to cut something,' she said.

'I'm no bomb disposal expert. Are you? Cut what? We need the disarm code.'

'Could be random, but wouldn't they use something they could all remember? Famous date, birthday, Fibonacci numbers. Simple one, two, three, four, five, six. Six, five, four. Who knows?' she said, picking up the 'synopsis' and rifling through the pages looking for any clue.

'Well we have to try so…' He started to turn the dials, straight ones, straight twos, straight threes and so on. The clock turned to 23.55. Then the Fibonacci sequence. One, one, two, three, five, eight and then reversed. Odd and even numbers forwards and backwards.

The red light continued flashing. 23.56.

He tried the only dates that he thought might be relevant, and that he could remember. The signing of the armistice in 1918 and the date that Britain declared war on Germany. One, one, one, one, one eight

'Bugger!' Zero, three, zero nine, three, nine.

There was an electrical buzz as switches within the weapon were activated. Metal objects within the chamber flew towards the sphere, making a clattering sound, like shrapnel hitting the outside of an armoured vehicle. Click. Whirr. 23.57.

'Hitler's birthday was the 20th April. It was the same as my ex wife's, we used to joke about it, but what bloody year? How old was Hitler when he died 53…54…55?

'Try them all. Try them all,' Christina shouted.

'Two, zero, zero, four, nine, zero…no…nine one…shit!…nine two…nine three...fuck it!'

The sphere emitted a gut wrenching vibration at sub sonic levels, which rose rapidly to an audible bass note. The Kalashnikov, that Christina had been holding, flew past David's head to attach itself to the outer metal skin. He felt as though unseen fists were pummelling his stomach, and he fought the desire to throw up.

Christina was holding her midriff and writhing in agony on the rock floor.

'Try the other way. Try eight nine,' she moaned.

David's left arm was now trapped against the weapon by his watch. He tried to pull it free, breaking the metal strap in the attempt.

23.58.

His vision was blurring with the vibration as he turned the last two dials. 'Eight, nine.'

Contact breakers snapped open with a flash of electric arc and a smell of ozone. The red flashing light went out and a green one glowed bright in its place. The capacitors earthed with a loud bang. The green light went out. Then silence.

David sank to the floor to check if Christina was all right.

'Well done you. 1889 it was,' he sighed. 'We're okay it's disarmed. Irrelevant really, there's no way out of here.'

She sat up still holding her midriff.

'I think there is, David, have a look here. When you helped me up, I noticed this.' She took him to the table. 'Look.'

David knelt down and saw the small pipe carved in the back edge of the top. He tried to move the table but it wasn't possible. He twisted, lifted, pushed and pulled but with no success.

'How big do you think the table is, David?' Christina was inspecting the walls of the chamber.

'One metre square, roughly. Why?' He looked up to see what she was doing.

'How big is the chamber?' She was feeling the walls.

'About forty by forty. He got up to look at the walls.

'How far along the edge is the pipe?'

'Twenty-five centimetres, about a quarter the length of the side.'

'So on the same scale, ten metres down the wall on the same side. Dig here, and pray, David.'

He took his multi-tool and scraped the surface of the wall. It was the same mud plaster mix as on the entrance to the chamber.

'I love you Karranova.' He grabbed her and gave her a kiss.

'We're not out yet. Hit it with the pick, please.' She leant outside the entrance, to get the pickaxe, and saw the devastation in the shaft for the first time. 'Well we certainly aren't going that way.'

David hit the rock face and he knew, from the feel of the blow, that this was a man-made wall. After several swings, it began to crumble and they were able to remove the rocks by hand, being careful not to cause a roof fall. They soon created a hole, through which they could see a small chamber on the other side. David swung the pickaxe again, and soon they had an opening big enough for them to crawl through, to the space beyond.

Taking everything they could carry, including the AKs, David put the five books in their canvas bag into his backpack, and they squeezed through the hole.

The alarm went on the gas detector.

'Oxygen content's very low here, David, very low.'
She rubbed the screen with her sleeve and showed him the display.

A narrow exit to this chamber led on to a passage, which went upwards at a steep angle. It didn't look like the other shafts, which had mostly been machined. Hand tools had hewn this tunnel. After ten minutes they came upon narrow-gauge rail tracks in the tunnel floor.

'This is an old mine working, like the one at Völkershausen. Let's hope the entrance is easier to open. I reckon we must be somewhere underneath the Meiningen to Suhl area. How's the oxygen doing?'

David realised that he was beginning to get breathless as they climbed the sharp incline of the shaft, and there was a stale taste to the air.

'Not good. Please can we stop to rest a bit, David?' Her breathing was becoming laboured.

They stopped for a few minutes to recover, and then like Everest veterans they plodded upwards, stopping to rest every twenty paces. At a fork in the shaft they saw the sign of the pipe on the left hand passage.

'Thank God for Jo Novak,' David gasped.

'The oxygen's better, but it's not good. I'm feeling bad, how about you?' Her breathing was rapid and shallow.

'Me too, I'm struggling. Come on, we can't let it beat us now. We've come through too much together to suffocate down here.' He took her hand, pulling her up the shaft.

'What about my grandfather?' she gasped.

'We really have to get out of here, Christina. Come on now.'

After twenty minutes, they were exhausted and panting. David felt as though his lungs just weren't big enough for the gulps of air he wanted to make, and he realised that he was beginning to feel euphoric.

'My vision's beginning to go, Christina.'

He looked around and she was doubled over with her head between her knees, trying to get some oxygen to her brain.

If they didn't move, they were going to die. If they moved, they were probably going to die anyway, he thought.

'No! Come on Lennox, it's all in the mind. Come on now,' he roared, his voice echoing along the shaft.
He grabbed her hand. 'Come on, Christina, no slacking.'He pulled her upright and saw the blank expression in her face and the blueness of her lips.
'We're going to make it, Karranova. We're going to make it. Come on now.'
'I feel so peaceful David…so happy…let me rest…please… I'm all right,' she mumbled.
'This is oxygen starvation, you know it is. Please come on,' he snapped, his voice breaking with frustration.
He dragged her behind him up the slope, his lungs heaving, tunnel vision now restricting his sight to a small area directly in front of him. Behind him, Christina started singing in Slovak, oblivious to the fact that she was repeating the same line over and over again. She got more raucous, and he couldn't stop giggling uncontrollably at every step-up in the volume. Putting his arm around her he started to sing along. They lurched drunkenly up the slope, stumbling and eventually falling together, laughing hysterically.
Something deep within his subconscious drove him to his feet, and on up the shaft, towing the now silent Christina along by the collar of her jacket.
He was hallucinating; moving aside to let traffic past, and swatting at swarms of hornets whilst stepping over writhing snakes that were striking at his ankles.
He wasn't sure how long it was before he came to a side shaft to the left marked with the sign of the pipe. Joseph Novak was sitting in the shaft in his striped prisoner's uniform, smiling and beckoning.
'This is your granddaughter, Joseph. Your daughter's daughter.' David pointed to Christina who was covered in snakes. He bent down and brushed them off, uncaring of the multiple bites to his hand and arms.
Novak knelt and stroked Christina's hair. 'Oh the poor child, she's so cold, so very cold.' He pointed to another sign of the

pipe by the entrance to a chamber to the right. 'This way to the light, this way.'

David stumbled into the chamber where Marilyn Monroe was smoothing down her white dress over an open grating.

'Here you are honey, you're real cute.' She handed David a key, and stood aside to reveal a small metal door in the wall. David tried to insert the key, but the lock kept moving.

Monroe took his arm and steadied it so that he could open the door, and a blast of cold, sweet air hit his face. He gulped lungful after lungful of life-saving oxygen.

As his head cleared and the hallucinations faded, David lifted Christina into the stream of air from the small metal door that he had, in reality, opened.

Her head lolled to one side. She was cold to the touch.

'Oh God. Please. No! Please, please, No.'

He felt her neck for a pulse and couldn't find one. Laying her down he started giving her mouth to mouth and cardiopulmonary resuscitation.

'Please Christina, please come on, come on, please.'

The tears were streaming down his face. As he pumped her chest they dropped on to her pale blue cheeks, rolling slowly down to her ears, almost as if she were crying in her sleep.

'Oh Christ, please…not now… please …please.'

He gave up after a half-an-hour, long after realising that she was gone. He would never hear her voice or her laugh again, nor feel her touch, or the warmth of her body against his. David sat sobbing on the floor of the chamber, cradling her lifeless body in his arms, stroking her hair, and kissing her cold forehead.

Behind him in the main shaft, propped against the rock wall, the bleached bones of Joseph Novak in his faded striped uniform, beckoned Christina with one outstretched arm. A still life Captain Ahab.

All gone. Gone to dust.

He let out a scream that reverberated along the shafts. He was primordial man in his cave, railing at an unforgiving and

incomprehensible universe.
He had never felt so alone in his life. Never.

Epilogue

The seventy-one year old pensioner in Gateshead was in tears, as he went back into the front room of his terraced home holding a small black ceramic casket in his arms.

'Whatever's the matter, Robert?' asked his wife from her wheelchair.

'It's me Dad's ashes, love. A man from the war graves commission just delivered them. He asked me if I was William Kenton's son, and said that they found them when a new supermarket was being built in Germany. He gave me this and left.'

A week later in the Slovak embassy in Berlin, an attaché read a letter he had just received, giving the position of a double grave in Thuringia and who was buried there. Joseph Ibrahim Novak and his granddaughter, Christina Jirina Karranova. The letter asked for the bodies to be returned to their family in Bratislava.

Ulrich Pummler was walking his dog near his farm on the outskirts of Suhl, when he heard a loud explosion from the forest on the hill above him. When he got to the site, which he knew was an old disused mine, he found a large area of subsidence and a fire burning with what looked like the remains of leather bound books, the flakes of burning paper rising in a mini-thermal above the flames, and falling to earth as they cooled, blending with the falling snow.

Sir William Rush took off his winter coat and left his briefcase in the hall of his home.

'Hello Darling. Good trip?' His wife asked, embracing him.

'Middle of bloody nowhere in Utah. Kept the Russians happy though,' he said kissing her.

'Come by the fire and have a drink,' she said, tidying the cushions. 'Oh. James rang from your office. One of your people was in a terrible car crash yesterday. Quiet road, no other car involved. Poor girl died. I wrote the name down here somewhere. Yes here it is…Jenny Carter.'

Sir William's hand was shaking badly as he instinctively picked up the telephone and held it to his ear.

It was dead.

Many of the personae and events in this book are based on fact. The links between them are not, but could be.

Richard von Weizsäcker: President of Germany 1984 –1994. Son of diplomat Ernst von Weizäcker. As a law student, Richard was a member of his father's defence team at the Nuremburg War Trials.

Walter Richard Rudolf Hess: April 26 1894 –August 17 1987. Deputy leader of the Nazi party. Flew alone to Scotland in May 1941. The reason for this is still clouded in mystery. Officially he committed suicide by hanging himself with an electrical cord in the summerhouse of Spandau Prison where he was a prisoner for over 40 years (He was referred to as Prisoner number 7.) His son Wolf always asserted that the British SAS murdered his father.

General Dr. Hans Friedrich Karl Franz Kammler. August 26 1901 -??: As a senior SS officer he designed facilities for the extermination camps, including gas chambers and crematoria. Was in charge of the demolition of the Warsaw Ghetto following the uprising in 1943. Head of ME 262 and V2 construction at Nordhausen and its attendant concentration camp at Dora-Mittelbau. Head of secret weapon development at Jonastal, where he allegedly worked with anti-gravity experiments. Disappeared in May 1945. Some suggest he flew to Barcelona in an American aircraft and from there went to the USA to recruit ex Nazis engineers and control all work on anti-gravity. All mention of this man has been erased from the Nuremburg War Trial records.

Reinhard Gehlen: April 3 –June 8 1979. A German Major-General during WWII and chief of intelligence on the Eastern

Front. After the war he was recruited by the Americans to set up a spy ring targeting the Soviet Union. He ran the West German intelligence service until 1968. He set up the Gehlen Organisation, over 4,000 agents of whom 350 were former Nazi intelligence officers. (See Gladio.) This organisation uncovered the existence of SMERSH the Soviet assassination department, and was a major player in the construction of a tunnel under Berlin to tap into East German and Soviet telecommunications lines. Apart from numerous German decorations, he was made a Knight of Malta.

Sven Olof Joachim Palme: January 30 – March 1 1986 (Shot at 23.21 on 28 February.) Prime Minister of Sweden 1969 – 1976. He was controversial because of his hatred of the apartheid regime in South Africa and his support of the PLO and the ANC. Shot in Central Stockholm; the assassin has never been identified.(See Christer Pettersson and Gladio.) He was to have had a meeting with the Soviets days after he was shot. His death has been the subject of many conspiracy theories. (See Allan Francovich.)

Bernt Wilmar Carlsson: 1938 – December 21 1988. Swedish UN commissioner for Namibia, and close political ally, confidante and protégé of Olof Palme. Died on Pan Am flight 103, which was blown up over Lockerbie 21 December 1988, en-route to UN headquarters in New York. Pan Am security officers declared that there had been irregularities with baggage swapping by SAA, and Carlsson's girl friend and sister couldn't find any trace or single shred of anything belonging to him at the property store in Lockerbie.(See Allan Francovich and Pan Am 103.) Pik Botha, South African Foreign Minister, the Defence Minister, the head of SA Intelligence and a delegation of twenty-two SA officials were booked on flight 103, but cancelled at the last minute and took an earlier flight.

Allan Francovich: 1941 – April 24 1997. American film

producer and director. Made several exposés about the CIA and secret 'Stay Behind Armies' in Europe. Francovich made several films about the activities of Gladio (See Gladio), and an assassination plot to kill Olof Palme, called Operation Tree. He made a film about Pan Am flight 103 called 'The Maltese Double Cross', throwing a completely different light on the official account of events. (See Bernt Carlsson.) He died of a heart attack at 56 whilst passing through the customs hall of Huston airport.

The Vela Incident: The Vela satellite was one of a pair put into orbit by the USA to detect nuclear test explosions. On 22 September 1979 it registered the double flash of an atmospheric nuclear explosion of two to three kilotons in the Indian Ocean, near islands belonging to South Africa. The Carter administration later dismissed this as a Vela malfunction. They said that the South Africans did not have any nuclear capability until two months after the incident. The week before the event, all SA naval facilities were in an unprecedented lock-down. There is much intelligence evidence to suggest that this was a joint Israeli/South African atomic test, code name Operation Phoenix.

Pan Am flight 103: Blown up over Lockerbie Scotland 21 December 1988.
Death toll 270. Conspiracy theory put forward by Allan Francovich in his film The Maltese double Cross. Among the passengers were :- Matthew Gannon. CIA deputy station chief in Beirut, Lebanon. Major Chuck McKee, Defense Intelligence Agency, Beirut. Ronald Lariviere CIA security officer US embassy, Beirut. Daniel O'Connor a CIA security officer Nicosia, Cyprus. Bernt Carlsson UN Ambassador to Namibia.

Gladio: (Symbol of the organisation a Roman sword:) A secret Stay Behind Army. First set up to fight as a resistance movement in the case of a Soviet invasion of Europe. There were training sessions in Hereford (SAS), Poole (SBS) and Fort Monckton (MI6) and huge arms caches and gold coins buried at numerous sites around mainland Europe. Later agents teamed up with right-wing organisations and carried out terror attacks to discredit Communists and left-wingers. (See Allan Francovich). Gladio agents infiltrated all levels of Government and security services, and were alleged to be an elite group within NATO and SHAPE and responsible for numerous political assassinations, (See Olof Palme) and behind military coups in Greece and the defeat of the Belgian and Italian communists in post-war elections. The CIA and MI6 have always refused to comment on the fact that they funded such activities, under the cloak of 'Security of the State'.

Jonastal: Jonastal is a valley in Thuringia between Crawinkel and Arnstadt in the former DDR. It was the location of a highly secret underground site for the Nazis, and was constructed by slave labour from the Buchenwald concentration camp under the command of SS. Obergruppenführer Hans Kammler. Officially, twenty-five tunnels were created and are now inaccessible. Many historians conjecture that the site is indeed far larger than admitted. The Bundeswehr now control the area and no entry is possible for civilians.

Several books have been written about futuristic weapons, planes and nuclear research undertaken there. The US Army was first to take the complex at the end of WWII, and classified everything as Top Secret. Kammler disappeared, never to be heard of again, although many think he was spirited to America along with many top scientists. This operation which included all the engineers involved with V2 construction at Dora (Werner von Braun and others), was run by Reinhard Gehlen and called 'Operation Paper-Clip'. The stealth bombers of the USAF are remarkably similar in shape and design to planes developed at Jonastal.

Lightning Source UK Ltd.
Milton Keynes UK
UKOW010140151011

180338UK00001B/1/P